Alexandra Raife has lived abroad in many countries and worked at a variety of jobs, including a six-year commission in the RAF and many years co-running a Highland hotel. She lives in Perthshire. All her previous novels, including *Drumveyn*, *Grianan*, *Belonging*, *Sun On Snow*, *The Wedding Gift*, *The Way Home* and *A Question of Trust* have been richly praised.

# PROMISES TO KEEP

Ian and Miranda were childhood friends in Glen Maraich, and student sweethearts who married while still at Edinburgh University. But those carefree days come to an end when Miranda becomes pregnant. Alexy is a demanding baby and the marriage collapses under the strain of sleepless nights and domestic responsibilities. Left to bring up her daughter alone, Miranda painstakingly establishes a viable life for them both, but is forced to uproot them when she receives an imperious summons from her father-in-law. She returns to the glen, and to Ian's neglected family home. With the new resolution she has learned, Miranda gradually brings warmth to the house — and thaws the hearts of its occupants.

Books by Alexandra Raife
Published by The House of Ulverscroft:

DRUMVEYN
GRIANAN
BELONGING
SUN ON SNOW
THE WEDDING GIFT
THE WAY HOME
A QUESTION OF TRUST

ALEXANDRA RAIFE

# PROMISES TO KEEP

*Complete and Unabridged*

CHARNWOOD
Leicester

First published in Great Britain in 2004 by
Hodder & Stoughton
London

First Charnwood Edition
published 2004
by arrangement with
Hodder & Stoughton
a division of Hodder Headline
London

British Library CIP Data

Raife, Alexandra
    Promises to keep.—Large print ed.—
Charnwood library series
    1. Mothers and daughters—Fiction
    2. Perthshire (Scotland)—Social life and customs
    —Fiction 3. Large type books
    I. Title
    823.9′14 [F]

    ISBN 1–84395–651–9

Published by
F. A. Thorpe (Publishing)
Anstey, Leicestershire

Set by Words & Graphics Ltd.
Anstey, Leicestershire
Printed and bound in Great Britain by
T. J. International Ltd., Padstow, Cornwall

This book is printed on acid-free paper

From the small balcony outside the upper bar Miranda watched the London shuttle coming in to land and, in spite of her need, and her relief at seeing it, found to her dismay the familiar pointless anger already beginning to burn. The anger of years. The anger which had become a habit so ingrained that by now she could hardly have defined its true origin. The anger, however, which this time she had been determined to keep under control.

For this time of all times there was no room for it. There were other, huge, frightening concerns to engage her today, concerns which it appalled her to realise were probably the direct and tragic consequence of those old quarrels. Today was not about Ian and herself.

Although a mean wind had whipped up, and most people meeting the flight had sensibly elected to wait in the warmth of the lower restaurant, she was not alone on the balcony. Nevertheless, as she watched the plane taxi in, she was sure Ian would have picked her out among the small huddle looking out over the parapet. He missed nothing. The thought brought an odd momentary comfort, then was overtaken by the resentment, generalised and baseless, that had long ago become automatic whenever she thought of him.

With an exclamation of frustration, which

could easily have turned into a sob of misery and dread at the prospect of the penetrating questions she knew she was about to face, she turned to go down. There was no point in staying out here any longer. The passengers would be out of sight as they entered the airport building.

Everyone else had made the same decision, giving little exclamations of relief as they found themselves in out of the wind. To Miranda, trailing after them to the baggage hall, it suddenly seemed extraordinary that she was meeting Ian at all, let alone in this place which in a few moments would be bustling with strangers intent on their own preoccupations, meeting and greeting, claiming luggage, picking up hire cars, hurrying for taxis.

Even in the years when contact had been fairly regular, though almost invariably, it seemed in retrospect, revolving around crises and problems, there had never been any question of picking Ian up at the airport. He had come to the flat, of course, but when some specific problem had had to be discussed they had found that meetings in neutral surroundings worked better — a hotel lounge, a restaurant, any setting which imposed a level of good behaviour, and kept a check on the hostility always so ready to erupt between them.

None of that mattered today, Miranda reminded herself again, as the passengers began to appear. Don't think about that. But at the sight of Ian among the straggling group, most with hair untidy and faces pinched and cross after their brief buffeting in the chilly wind, she found with a lurch of apprehension that none of the powerful feelings he could arouse in her were affected by the still-raw shock of what had happened.

He stood out distinctively, as for her he always did, from the crowd around him. In spite of the fact that he might have been the only one among them to have flown halfway round the world to get here, he looked, as ever, in control of events rather than at their mercy, already totally attuned to his new surroundings. Whether he dealt with jet-lag by sheer force of will, or whether it genuinely didn't affect him, Miranda was never sure, but she recognised his familiar look of being held back by the stolid pace of others, impatient to slice through the tedious minutiae of arrival and be first out of the stalls.

Or would she always see him as separate and different? Would Ian, for her, stand out in any company? Because he was so utterly familiar, or because, as had been the case in the past, her eye was infallibly drawn by his particular looks, his physical type, by the fateful chemistry of attraction which could operate even now. Today, among the faceless, colourless throng, she thought he looked amazing. His deep tan helped, of course, but his good looks seemed only to have become more firmly delineated as he matured, and the square frame which had made him look older than his years as a teenager was now ideally proportioned for a fit, vigorous man just entering his forties.

Then there was his smile. Coming towards

Miranda, for he had known where she would appear and had spotted her at once, that smile of greeting was still very like the irrepressible grin of the hard-living, hard-playing young man who had always known how to pack every second of the day with activity and pleasure. It could still rock her, and she was briefly flurried by helpless resentment to find herself responding to it now, today, when he had come in such circumstances.

But Ian's smile had vanished by the time he reached her. His eyes searched hers with anxiety, and the grip he took of her wrist, not her hand, had nothing to do with either of them.

'She's going to be all right,' Miranda told him, her voice as even as she could make it, in answer to that look.

# 1

They had still been students when they married.

Ian, some months older than Miranda, went up to Edinburgh ahead of her, to read Economics, because that was already his consuming interest. Though he played the field with enthusiasm in his first year, once she arrived on the scene, to read English because anything else looked too much like hard work, there was no one else for him. It had always been like that, for both of them. They had been part of each other's lives since earliest childhood, the original moment of meeting impossible by now to pin down.

When some new acquaintance, struck by their ease together and a quality of rock-solid permanence in their relationship unusual in the student world, asked, 'How long have you two known each other?' they would argue the point all over again.

'It was at my Christmas party when you didn't bring a present.' Miranda would generally get in first. 'That party when you got the other boys to pull you up in the old linen lift and the mothers went into orbit.'

'That's total rubbish.' Ian would contest this as much to wind her up as anything. 'It was at the Alltmore barbecue the summer before. Penny Gilmour was doing rides and you wouldn't get off the pony the whole afternoon and all the other little girls howled.'

'At that age I'd have been put on and taken off, no choice about it.'

'One of those creepy parties at Drumveyn then.'

'Couldn't have been, Archie wouldn't have been old enough to have parties by then . . . '

If whoever had asked the question had any sense, he or she would have left them to it by this time.

Ian, though sure it hadn't been when they'd first met, could clearly remember that Christmas party. His mother had never had suitable presents on hand for him to take, as everyone else's mother seemed to do, and he'd minded. Nor, on that particular occasion, had she got him there on time, and the party had started without him. Hating winter driving, she had put off leaving as long as possible in the vague hope that the weather would get worse and she could abandon the whole idea. Then, instead of staying at the party or even in town, she'd hurried home again, sending the gamekeeper down to fetch him far too early so that he'd missed the end as well.

But the truth was that he and Miranda would have been present at any number of similar gatherings. Their parents, though not close friends (did the Rosses have close friends?), had belonged to the same broad circle of affluent families in Muirend and its neighbouring glens and, since Ian and Miranda were both only children, their mothers had made sure they missed out on none of the social contacts available.

Neither the Rosses nor the Cunninghams had their roots in the hierarchy of local land-owning families. Ian's great-grandfather had owned a small sawmill on the outskirts of the town, which his son had developed into a flourishing timber business. It was he who had built the solid handsome house of Kilgarth, with a few moorland acres at its back and an enviable position facing south and west on the hilly byroad which wound along the flank of Glen Maraich. Ian's father, Gregory Ross, when he in turn inherited, had added considerably to the land, acquiring a small loch a couple of miles above the house and some excellent rough shooting.

For Miranda's family, prosperity had come from a tweed mill. Her grandfather, expanding as Ian's grandfather had done, had opened shops selling top-of-the-range country clothes in Dunkeld and Pitlochry, with his main branch in Perth, then, when Scottish skiing began to take off in the sixties, her father had launched a spin-off company for ski and après-ski wear, setting up his own ski school while he was about it.

No land for the Cunninghams; they opted instead for Cardoch House, a three-storied Edwardian mansion high above Muirend, built of red sandstone with big bay windows dressed with paler stone, and a garden descending in well-kept terraces to a dense shrubbery and high wall designed to keep the spreading town firmly at bay.

Whenever their first encounter had been, Ian and Miranda had presently found themselves at school together. Pamela Ross had originally chosen as the line of least resistance — the school Land Rover passed the house — to send Ian to the village school in Kirkton but, with his boisterous exuberance, his endless questions and capacity for inventiveness when left unoccupied, he had simply been too much for the system to contain, and she had soon been forced to accept the less convenient alternative of a small private school in Muirend.

'Expelled at five — not bad,' Ian used to boast, adding more wryly, 'and if my mother could have sent me to boarding-school there and then she would have.'

With that Miranda did agree. Her memories of Ian's mother were wholly negative — no noise had been allowed at Kilgarth, no running about the house, no hide-and-seek or exploring. She had always come away with an uncomfortable sense of having been found wanting — not something she was used to. And often there had been the mysterious warning, 'Remember, Ian's mother isn't very well, so you mustn't be a nuisance . . .'

Pamela Ross's natural lassitude and tendency to hypochondria had not been helped by marriage to a man of short temper, sarcastic tongue and firm views about his own comfort. She had been so drained by the effort of giving birth to Ian that friends watching her attempt to fold her solid, muscular baby into some shape which could be held, let alone cuddled, had marvelled that she could have produced such a child.

In fact, it was fortunate for Ian that his mother's preference for taking the easy route hadn't left him kicking his heels at the village school until she could decently send him away. The little pre-prep in Muirend was run by an energetic old lady with a lifetime's experience of private coaching behind her, and Ian, his energies channelled and his thirsty mind satisfied at last, had mopped up everything she could offer.

Miranda had arrived the following term, and from her first day she and Ian had been inseparable. Both high achievers, bright, confident and outgoing, they had been accepted without question by the other children as natural leaders. Even when, as soon as he was eight, Ian had been dispatched to his prep school on the east coast, their alliance had never wavered. Ian had found his feet in the new environment without loss of time, indifferent to the bitter winds off the North Sea which whined down the corridors and scourged the playing fields and made the autumn and winter terms misery for so many boys. He had done well in just about everything, especially shining at maths, had learned to play the bagpipes and had found himself in every junior team.

Miranda, after some lonely terms without him, had been sent to boarding-school in her turn, where she had not learned the bagpipes and had definitely not shone at maths, but like Ian had been in every team. But throughout the school years, other friendships notwithstanding, for

9

both the holidays had chiefly meant being together.

'Do you think we're wise to let them see so much of each other?' Georgina Cunningham would occasionally enquire of her husband as the years went by. The long legs and trim athletic body, the clear skin and shining hair of a nubile Miranda were enough to worry (if also gratify) any mother.

'How do you propose to keep them apart?' was Graeme's response. 'Anyway, think how you'd miss having Ian here.' The son she had so much wanted and failed to produce? But also, as he well knew, Georgina liked to give Ian a little of the spoiling and indulging she was sure he never got at home.

She would admit as much. 'Poor boy, you could hardly call Kilgarth the most cheerful of houses. I know for a fact, because he told me so, that sometimes he doesn't see his father for days on end. Not that Gregory is exactly cheerful himself. And those silly aunts are no better, stuck away in that cottage of theirs, feuding and complaining. Half the time I'm not sure Ian's even properly fed.'

'Doesn't look as though he does too badly to me,' Graeme would comment dryly. Ian's four-square build, filling out every year, his fitness and boundless energy, hardly suggested deprivation. But Graeme knew that, apart from buying clothes for herself and Miranda and keeping them both turned out to perfection (he'd have been a ruined man if he'd been in a different line of business, he would sometimes reflect), Georgina's main pleasure and skill lay in entertaining — producing superb food and having her comfortable and beautifully kept house enjoyed to the full by friends and family.

'All right, you can mock, but since Pamela died that house has become a morgue — oh dear, perhaps not the expression to use. But hardly anyone goes there now, and when they do they daren't speak above a whisper.'

Pamela had died when Ian was thirteen. Used to feeling ill in some degree for most of the time, or to imagining that she was ill, she had taken no steps when pernicious anaemia began to take hold. Gregory, equally used to blanking out a steady drip of moans about dizzy spells, exhaustion and other persistent but imprecise symptoms, and in any case only interested in his own affairs, had paid no attention either.

He had been seriously shocked when Pamela had quietly slipped away one night, her pallid face, as blank of expression as a soap carving, upturned on the pillow beside him, her pink self-adhering rollers framing it like the spikes of a mine. Once he had taken in the fact that she had really gone the first thing he had done, with clumsy shaking fingers, had been to unravel those vulgar cylinders, surprised into a small choking sound which had been closer to anger than pain to see the greying strands which clung to them. No other expression of grief had been wrung from him, but for Gregory, as for Ian, Pamela's silent departure would always after-wards stir uneasy feelings of failure and guilt.

It would be many years before Ian examined

these feelings honestly. His father never did; in his view, wallowing in emotion was a weakness. People who did so only had themselves to blame if they were miserable. He saw no point in dwelling on anything so tedious.

Ian, eventually, was able to admit to Miranda, in the days when anger between them was unimaginable, that a large part of his guilt stemmed from discovering that he enjoyed life at Kilgarth more without his mother.

'I kept finding it was a relief not to have to bother about all the minor niggles. Like keeping curtains half closed because the light hurt her eyes. Or having to shut doors behind you because of draughts, then being told off for not doing it quietly enough. Tiny things, that I'd be ashamed even to think of when I should have been missing her. But there were others. Meals got simpler, for one. No faddy diets and fussing — and no more tension between her and Dad. That was a big one.'

'Remember how you got into a panic in case your father asked the aunts to come back?' Miranda reminded him slyly, knowing this would divert his thoughts.

'God yes, nightmare idea. Aunt Binnie bursting into tears every time Dad barked at her, and wittering on about were my socks dry or would I like some nice cocoa. And Aunt Olivia crashing about and laying down the law left, right and centre.'

'But you can't seriously have believed your father would have let either of them over the doorstep?'

'Oh, I know, far too keen on his own preservation. But it did have me worried for a while.'

Miranda had never taken the idea seriously, even at the time. Gregory Ross had been only too happy, when he married, to turf out his infuriating sisters, housing them in what had been the chauffeur's cottage, situated in a dank hollow surrounded by trees and shrubberies, and conveniently out of sight and sound of the big house. It seemed highly unlikely, widower or not, that he would let them back in at any price. So it had proved, and to Ian's relief the aunts had stayed where they were, not without bitter strictures on Olivia's part about her brother's want of family feeling.

The housekeeping had been given into the rough and ready hands of Ruby Lawson, who until then had appeared daily to clean, but who now lived in, with a succession of local girls to help her. The standard of cooking (and the bills) had shot up, clean shirts had always been to hand, clothes could be left where they fell, the bathroom left awash, muddy boots kicked off and forgotten, and no complaints were ever heard. It had been hard for Ian to regret a more stringent regime.

As he grew up he'd been able to acknowledge, though this he didn't put into words for Miranda, that what had made him most ashamed had been his relief to be free of his mother as a person. Her dissatisfaction with everything around her, including him, had been a perpetual check on his own innate optimism.

He had felt that whatever he did she was disappointed in him, and it had been frustrating not to be able to grasp quite why.

There had never been much in the way of warmth or laughter at Kilgarth but, at least for a time after his mother's death, it had seemed to Ian that he and his father might draw closer.

'God, how I wanted that,' he confessed once, on a Sunday evening when he and Miranda were driving back to Edinburgh after a weekend at Cardoch House, where the evening before there had been a big party to celebrate Graeme's fiftieth birthday. They hadn't called at Kilgarth, or let Gregory know they were up, sure he wouldn't care either way, and the contrast between the generous hospitality of Miranda's home and the grudging bleakness of his own, normally taken in his stride, had got to him for once.

'But you used to fish and go out on the moor with him, didn't you?' Miranda tried for something positive to say but was hazy about the facts after so long.

'Well, for a while he didn't ask quite so many of his business chums up, that's true,' Ian conceded, 'and we did have the odd day together. But it was probably more a case of pandering to the conventions than wanting to be on his own with me. Not that he was worried about the conventions, but he'd see that other people might be.'

His mind went back, the disappointment he had felt still able to bite, to those chilly dawns and dusks in the cramped hide up at the flighting pond, the silent hours on the loch. Silent not so much because of the fishing but because father and son had ultimately failed to communicate. There had been a brief flurry of shared interest when Gregory had had some repairs done on the old boathouse, making the spartan picnic room more comfortable and shoring up the verandah, but once the work was finished the need to seek companionship had fizzled out.

'Let's face it, we bored each other to death.' Ian, usually pragmatic about facts that couldn't be altered, was unable to keep a grim note out of his voice.

'You'd never got to know each other when you were little, that was the trouble,' Miranda said, but knew it wasn't much of an offering.

'Yes, well, he didn't have to try for very long. Let's face it, once I'd told him I wasn't interested in his precious business, that was more or less it.'

He had been still in his teens when, with his usual straightforward approach not wanting false assumptions to take root, he had announced his complete lack of enthusiasm for the timber trade or anything connected with it. The gulf between his father and himself had widened with a speed and finality which had shaken him more deeply than he had ever admitted.

They had become adept at finding ways to avoid spending time together. Gregory had begun to stay in his flat above the office during the week and bring back friends, or more accurately business associates, at weekends to shoot or fish as before. Ian, acquiring his own wheels the moment he was old enough, had exercised his new independence to the full.

Mature for his age, outwardly he had managed to be objective about the deteriorating situation at home.

'We'd only scrap if we saw too much of each other,' he had said fairly, after the joking account of living under the same roof as his father but not having seen him for days which had upset Miranda's mother. It was true. Equable and laid-back as he generally was, he had his share of the hot Ross temper, and his father was the one person who could unfailingly spark it off.

It was that same temper which had kept his aunts in a state of more or less permanent warfare with the big house. They had fiercely (well, Olivia had been fierce, Binnie had sobbed) resented being put out of their home, as they saw it, and through the years since had only set foot in it to make those depredations which they regarded as their right.

Ian had continued, probably for longer than most boys of his age would have troubled to do without coercion, to pay occasional duty visits to the cottage, but in the end had decided the exercise was pointless. Binnie had gone on wanting to stuff him with cake as if he were still ten years old, and Olivia's raking glance and caustic comments, her need to attack his father no matter what subject they set out on, had invariably ended by making him feel uncomfortable, resentful and at fault.

'Maybe I was only looking for some mother

substitute anyway,' he said to Miranda, but the joke failed to mask the odd little ache the memory produced.

'In that pair?' Miranda hadn't failed him. 'Mothers? Can you imagine either of them ever — ?'

So, favoured as his life had been in material terms, emotionally it had been barren, and Miranda, though it was not something he'd been capable of evaluating at the time, had provided, apart from the pleasure of her company and the fun they had together, the vital missing elements of affection, communication and absolute, unquestioning acceptance of him as he was.

Throughout their teens the bond held, strengthened since both became shining lights in the schools ski racing scene. The best of tuition and equipment had always been there for Miranda, and by extension to Ian, and they had made full use of their opportunities. In fact Ian was up for selection at one point for the junior squad, but since he couldn't bring himself to give up his rugby he missed his chance.

Their success carried them into a wider and lively social scene, one which, with their reputations already established, they could continue to enjoy at university. Was it at this stage that their relationship altered? As with their first meeting, it was hard to decide just when they had fallen in love.

They were certainly seen as a couple, from the first day of Miranda's first term. With the Ski Club (in which, inevitably, they were office bearers, key racers and at the centre of every off-piste activity) as their social base, they were envied and resented by some perhaps, but pretty much accepted as belonging to that special breed who have everything in life handed to them on a plate.

Sometimes it would seem to Miranda, looking back on those heedless crest-of-the-wave days, that they had been victims of their own popularity and good looks. Ian had been easily the most attractive male around, and he was hers. She suspected that for him it had been the same. They were used to that being the case, and it would have been hard for either of them to give it up, and there was no doubt that the physical magnetism between them had been real and compelling.

That had hardly justified their getting married, though, or getting married when they did. She had still been in first year, everything university had to offer there for the taking. Yet, on little more than light-hearted impulse, or so it seemed looking back — not forgetting the joys of dazzling, magical sex — that was what they'd done. Had it been a colossal piece of showing off? Had they thought people would be impressed? Her parents hadn't been, nor a furious Gregory Ross, nor their respective tutors.

Their friends had said cheerfully, 'You must be out of your minds.'

But had the comment been entirely humorous? Or had humour evaporated later, when she had really blown it, and Alexy had arrived?

# 2

Even before they were married they had moved into a flat together, not so common a practice for students then as it would later become. The flat was in the Old Town, just off Charteris Wynd, three narrow flights up in a gaunt building of dark stone, with deep-set eyes of windows and steep-pitched roof. Once reached, the flat itself was surprisingly light, since a tiny, frail-looking balcony had been cobbled, presumably without planning permission, on to a gable window taken down to floor level, and inside a previous tenant had gone mad with glowing gold and burnt umber.

Miranda loved it, loved its blaze of colour after the dark stairs, loved its odd-shaped rooms and careless shabbiness, its sense of being a high, private retreat. She even loved the cramped and freezing bathroom because through its skylight you could watch the stars from the squat green bath. She was unconcerned by the cupboard-like nook which passed for a kitchen, with its double gas burner, its electric frying pan which was supposed to do duty as an oven, its chipped clay sink and dank wooden draining-board, its rickety cupboards whose buckled doors refused to slide. Kitchens were nothing to do with her. She still thought as a student where food was concerned — quick, easy, cheap.

She and Ian both had allowances which,

though generous, never seemed to go quite far enough. Neither was encouraged to exceed them, and in the circumstances sensible food wasn't a priority. They settled joyfully into their eyrie, conveniently near the university, and even more conveniently situated for their friends, and after the wedding threw a tremendous party there, Ian and his best man playing the pipes, and the crush so great it was impossible to move. Bride and groom fell into bed at dawn amid a welter of dirty glasses, empty bottles, a litter of jokey presents and, since the bin was crammed full, a good deal of the unsightly packaging in which the wedding feast had arrived. At noon some of the guests came thumping at the door and they all went to the pub.

Marriage, Miranda was to realise later, made almost no difference to the way they lived, an indication perhaps of how little they had been ready for it, or how little they had thought about the step they were taking. Yet after the wedding, so that afterwards it was easy to believe marriage had been the cause, many changes had come, and come swiftly. The shocks, she had labelled these events. To herself, for she and Ian didn't go in much for serious terms at that stage.

The first shock, though it was easy to forget it was the first, since for a while she refused to face her fears, was the suspicion that she was pregnant. This couldn't be happening, was her initial reaction. She and Ian hadn't discussed the possibility, beyond a casual agreement in passing that this was obviously a no-go area, with an exaggerated shudder at the mere idea.

Now Miranda did frantic sums, consulting her diary, in which she never wrote anything, and sitting on the edge of the bed with her packet of pills in her hand trying to make sense of the irregular pattern of tattered empty sockets and obdurately sealed ones. She knew she sometimes missed taking them. Her lifestyle of irregular hours, late nights and parties, last-minute decisions to go off for weekends with a frantic grabbing up of what they would need, led fatefully to errors. Usually she said nothing, skipped the spare pill, crossed her fingers, and when her period came round sailed on with no more than a momentary breath of relief. Repeated escapes had blunted both the anxiety and the thankfulness. Disasters of that sort happened to other people; she was always lucky.

Now she felt frighteningly at sea, unable to pin down any date with certainty. Though she never admitted it at the family planning clinic, because she thought it a bonus and didn't want it altered, the pill she was on had more than once caused her to miss a period, and this added to the scary feeling of the whole question being out of her control.

She put down the queasiness that had driven her to these calculations to a fish chowder which she had been more than dubious about the night before and — though afterwards this seemed incredible even to her — decided to ignore the whole thing. Her period would come next time round, whenever that was, and all would be well. Was it fear, or the in-built belief that nothing disastrous could ever touch her, that made her ignore the warnings? Why didn't she do a pregnancy test? Not so simple as it would become, but even then readily available. Had she acted out of naivety, cowardice or arrogance? A mixture of all three, Miranda would later decide grimly, for her airy confidence was to be much reduced and battered by the years.

Then the other shocks, which followed in such numbing succession in the first term of her second year, made it easy to forget the first, or at least do no more than shiver in passing apprehension when the thought obtruded at odd moments.

She and Ian went home for the weekend to Cardoch House. Miranda still thought of it as home, perhaps as clear a sign as any of her immaturity. The cheerful, messy flat seemed a mere term-time domain, and to live full-time in a city environment would not have occurred to her, or appealed to her.

Ian felt much the same. At Cardoch House there was always an affectionate welcome, good food, excellent wine and agreeable indulgence. Miranda could and did take home huge bags of washing, for Georgina was one of those women who always seemed able to find and keep an adequate supply of help. She paid well, certainly, and, in spite of Cardoch House being a steep pull up the hill, it was convenient for the town and no one had to live in.

Whatever the reason, uncomplaining and efficient service could always be relied on, or if protests were voiced they were never heard, and since Miranda saw nothing wrong in making use

22

of her parents' house in this way Ian wasn't going to argue.

But on this visit, instead of indulging them in their usual freedom to come and go as they pleased, Georgina caught Miranda for a moment after lunch on Saturday, Graeme being absent on Rotary business, and asked her to let Ian go alone to a meeting at the Ski Club hut. Early snow had brought the start of the season suddenly close, and work in hand on improvements to the hut facilities needed to be pushed along.

Although Miranda was in charge of the sub-committee convened to oversee the work, the request was so unusual and her mother's tone so firm that she agreed with no more than a token protest to let Ian take her place. She was invariably good-natured — she had never had any reason to be anything else — and a nagging pain in the small of her back, which she had been doing her best to ignore, made an afternoon by the drawing-room fire unexpectedly attractive, compared to a protracted inspection of plumbing and lighting in an unheated hut perched on a muddy slope with a bleak north wind moaning round it. The cheerful session in the bar of the nearby pub which would follow she would just have to forego for once. Perhaps, if the worst were true, should forego? She pushed the thought hastily away.

There was certainly no room in her mind for it when her mother embarked with some difficulty on what she had to say.

'Now that you're safely settled in your own

married life,' Georgina began, which Miranda, on reviewing the conversation, would think was putting it a bit high, 'your father and I feel it's time to make some changes. Well, we've been thinking them over for some time, but we didn't quite see how — we felt the moment wasn't — '

How much a child Miranda still was, blind to warning signs, oblivious of the problems and concerns of 'the grown-ups'. How much a child they had kept her, Georgina amended guiltily, to have spoken of none of this till now.

Graeme, it seemed, had been suffering for some time from cardiac problems, brought on by the unrelenting pace at which he worked, the level of stress at which he operated, and worries about having over-extended with a new shop. This part in itself was a shock. Miranda had always believed implicitly in her father's achievements. His absorption in the business had seemed entirely natural, part of him, part of the Cunningham tradition. To think of him as ill was impossible.

Ironically, her mother, having found it hard to bring herself to broach the subject at all, for to her Miranda was still her little girl to be protected and shielded, scarcely allowed the impact of this opening to sink in before going rapidly on. Since she and Graeme had been turning over their plans for some time, and had even begun to implement them, perhaps it was excusable to forget for a moment that Miranda was quite unprepared.

'We wanted to stay on here as long as we could for your sake. We felt we should provide you with

24

a stable home. Well, not just that, we wanted to, of course. But now that you're married and have a home of your own it's different, isn't it?'

A vision of the Charteris Wynd flat, which Georgina had never seen, rose before Miranda's eyes, the flat as they had left it yesterday evening, squalid, dredged with belongings, the bed bare because at the last minute she had stripped off sheet and duvet cover to add to the rest of the washing, the remains of their last meal sharing the table with a half-written essay and a heap of overdue library books.

'It seemed the right time to make the move,' Georgina was saying, the worried note in her voice tinged with defensiveness since Miranda had said nothing. 'It's ridiculous to run a house this size for two people, as I'm sure you'd agree.'

But it had been reasonable to run it for three people, Miranda thought, groping for anything to stave off alarming and unwanted revelations which seemed to be coming closer every second.

'It's always been a nightmare to look after, as you know,' Georgina hurried on.

Had it? Cardoch House had seemed to Miranda to run by itself. What concern of hers had been the enormous heating bills, the work it took to keep the heavy furniture in gleaming order, the grumbling about the kitchen being on one floor and the dining-room on another, the difficulty of finding anyone still prepared to sweep the tortuous chimneys, the slow disintegration of the lead flashings in the multiple valleys of the roof?

'And I've always hated living in Scotland, as

you know,' Georgina wound up, as though grasping thankfully at one aspect which at any rate was clear-cut and simple. She leaned forward to lift and delicately rearrange a half-burned log, using the long-handled and beautifully cleaned brass tongs to do so, then hung them back beside their beautifully cleaned companions.

Don't keep saying, 'as you know', Miranda protested silently, dumb with shock. I don't know. I don't know any of this. Hate Scotland? It seemed the ultimate treachery, a fact arbitrarily tossed in and to her inconceivable. Her mother had always made a big thing of her relief to be back in Gloucestershire when they had visited her sisters, but that had been a joke, surely? It must have been, because Miranda genuinely couldn't imagine anyone preferring England to Scotland.

'So really, it all seemed to fit,' Georgina was saying, her eyes still on the fire, her voice less calm and persuasive now. 'I know your father's reluctant to move, but if he stays here he won't be able to resist being involved with Cunningham's. He does see that really. He hasn't been at all well this summer, and he can't go on ignoring the warnings for ever.'

'But where are you going?' Miranda cried, instinctively rejecting the last part of this, which chimed too disturbingly with her own private fears. 'What are you going to do?'

'We thought of living near Aunt Nita. A perfect little house came up in just the right area. You probably remember it, that pretty cottage on the corner where the Sheepscombe road turns off. But the Cotswold winters can be very bleak, almost as bad as here, so we thought we'd opt for the sun instead and — '

'Where? Where are you going?' Miranda was exasperated to have cudgelled her brain to work out which cottage her mother was talking about and then find it had nothing to do with anything. But in her heart she knew that this momentary frustration was mere clutching at anything which would hold off the terrifying sensation of the foundations of life crumbling beneath her feet.

'Darling, you won't mind, will you?' Miranda's dismay had at last pierced Georgina's preoccupation with getting this difficult moment over. For putting the plan into words as something that would soon happen had given it a new reality, and the suspicion she had been trying to ignore for weeks, of having overridden Graeme's true wishes in the matter, had stirred uncomfortably. 'I know as long as you've got Ian your world is perfect,' she rushed on without waiting for an answer, 'and it's so easy to fly everywhere nowadays. We thought of Jersey, but apparently it's a bit like Eton, you have to put your name down before you're born or something, so in the end we decided on Provence.'

'Decided?' Miranda felt a dull sensation in her stomach close to sickness. It was a measure of how deeply her mother's news had shaken her that she didn't immediately relate it to her own possible condition.

It was indeed, all settled. Even Miranda, much as she longed to argue and plead, could see that it would be the purest selfishness to do so. She was a married woman, not the spoiled daughter of the house. It was salutory to realise that it had taken these events to make her see herself in that light.

What hurt her to remember later was that she never talked to her father, unable to put aside her own consternation and make the effort to appreciate how he must be feeling. There was no habit of communication between them, chiefly because they had seen so little of each other as she was growing up, but that was no excuse. For her father to live anywhere but Scotland, anywhere but in this supremely comfortable, absurdly ugly house, where he had been born and his father had been born; for her father to have wrested from him the whole purpose of his days, must have been a devastating double blow to face. And she had simply let him go, even priding herself on hiding her own feelings of loss and abandonment.

Home was now, literally, a couple of down-at-heel rooms in the warren of the Old Town, with icy draughts writhing in under the stair door, rumbling plumbing and chancy hot water, and a mildew map on the wall behind the bed. How could that be home? It was no more home than her cubie had been at school.

Ian, doing his best to comfort her about her father, and understanding something of how she felt over the sale of Cardoch House, guessed that she was suddenly seeing the flat with new eyes. For him, it was perfectly adequate. If he hadn't found it so he would have moved. And with money always in short supply, it made no sense to him to spend more on rent. But next year, when he was twenty-one, funds should increase considerably, so his suggestion was that they should rethink their options then if they saw the need.

Meanwhile, if Miranda was missing her parents, though as a Ross this was something he could only imagine with an effort, he was sure that Graeme would be more than happy to finance visits. Provence at Easter couldn't be bad. Ian, as ever, saw little to worry about.

'And we've always got Kilgarth to fall back on. There's a washing machine there too,' he would remind Miranda, never serious for long, and laugh at her when she pretended to be indignant.

# 3

The following Monday Miranda was summoned to speak to her tutor and warned that her work was falling far below the required standard and that something must be done about it. With her mind full of the changes threatening the entire structure of her life, which she had as yet barely had time to assimilate, she reacted to this information with a childish sense of outrage. She did as much work as anyone else, everyone was late with essays, no one got serious about work at the beginning of second year. She was defensive and resentful during the brief exchange, and her tutor saw there was little hope of constructive dialogue. He dismissed her to think things over, and almost as swiftly dismissed her from his mind.

In his view, she was a student who shouldn't be here, taking up a valuable place someone else might have had. Intelligent enough, indubitably, but she had never had to stretch her brain or apply herself. Now that this was asked of her, her only answer was to take offence. She had no idea what she would do with a degree, if she ever achieved one, and, as so many others regrettably did, seemed to regard tertiary education not as the start of adult life but as an extension of school, an easier option than earning her living. And now that she was married she had even less attention to spare for work. Half the time she looked barely awake, and certainly this morning had looked nothing like her former glowing self. She'd be pregnant next, silly girl. Well, that should concentrate her mind about what she wanted.

In fact, for the first time since her original fright, so many days ago now that she had been able to convince herself it really had been caused by the dubious chowder, nausea had overtaken Miranda this morning. She had just left the flat and started down the draughty stairs and she had clung, eyes closed, trembling, to the ice-cold rail fixed to the grubby wall, resisting with all her soul acceptance of what this meant.

There hadn't been time to think about it. She was late. She was always late these days. She had steadied herself, swallowed down with shivering repugnance the juices that filled her mouth, and hurried unsteadily on. She had to get through this interview, whatever it was about, and then she would think, she promised herself.

It was all part of her anger when she left her tutor's room, a jumbled, indignant anger, full of unfamiliar elements. She had been criticised in uncompromising terms, told her work was unsatisfactory and that she was behaving irresponsibly. It was an unpleasant sensation. Miranda was accustomed to cruising, keeping up with no struggle, performing so brilliantly in things sporting that scrambling through else-where had always been condoned. She was used to success and praise, to having no quarrel with anyone. It was easy to take such effortless popularity for granted, and though she had fallen into her fair share of trouble at school it had been part of the game, embellishing her reputation among her peers and arousing, as far as she knew, no particular animosity in the staff. Had some of them disliked her? The thought had never occurred to her. But this morning her tutor's voice had held an impatience which told her he saw her as an immature chit who shouldn't be allowed to waste his time.

Defiance swiftly took over. There was a lecture in ten minutes but, scarcely making a decision, Miranda knew she wouldn't attend it. Walking fast, paying no attention to where she was going, she let her anger grow into a billowing cloud of resentment. A waft of freshly roasted coffee made her realise how hungry she was — she must have been wrong about that earlier queasiness; she had just rushed straight out of bed without eating anything and that had made her giddy — and she turned down a steep flight of steps, and into a coffee bar she and Ian often frequented. A few people, by which she meant students, were already there, hunched over the ritual mugs of black coffee. One or two were smoking and the smell of the cigarettes was sharply offensive. Miranda nodded to the ones she knew, but in spite of a lifted hand of invitation didn't join them, sliding instead behind a table in the furthest, deepest corner, not even aware of how much she needed a dark burrow to hide in.

She demolished croissants ravenously, found they weren't substantial enough and added a couple of doughnuts. People came and went. She tried to remember what else she should be doing today but couldn't work it out. Then suddenly, a sweet light of simplicity replacing her muddled anger, she saw that it didn't matter.

So her work wasn't good enough? Fine. Why bother then? As with many people used to easy rewards, the unexpected check, instead of making her want to put matters right, produced the opposite effect of instant readiness to throw in the towel. Perhaps in her heart Miranda believed that even if she worked she couldn't do a great deal better, and didn't want to expose herself to that humiliation. Even in undemanding first year, when most people found they were able to get by without much strain, she had been startled by the vast difference between reading set books at school and letting her memory do the rest, and what 'English' had become here. An in-depth examination of the various routes by which a vowel sound had entered the language, discussions on whether a final 'e' was orthographic or organic, and the excruciating boredom of Middle English texts had come as an unwelcome shock.

Why was she beating her brains out about this stuff anyway? Because other options had looked less appealing? There had to be something to spend her time on which had a little more meaning to it.

In that alluring glimpse of freedom, realising that she could abandon the whole issue and no one would give a damn, Miranda also found she was able to face the other truth she had been evading. She couldn't go on shutting her eyes and hoping it would go away. She must find out for certain — though a deep-buried instinct knew the answer already — and she must tell Ian.

That moment was to return to her many times, not because it was the moment when she saw that she could abandon her university career without compunction, not even because it was the first time she allowed herself to accept the probability that she had conceived, but because she suddenly saw the relationship between herself and Ian with a new clarity.

Faced with the prospect of breaking this news to him, she realised a startling fact — they rarely talked. Really talked. It seemed hardly credible when she examined this, but it was true. They chattered and gabbled endlessly, and always had. They did everything they could together by choice, though they made no special effort to be on their own, perfectly happy as part of a crowd. They laughed at the same things and co-habited happily, never quarrelling. Love-making was wonderful; they were still hungry for each other and satisfied each other completely. This sure delight and fulfilment was for Miranda the basis on which the rest was built. But how often did they have a real conversation, except for the rare occasions when Ian spoke of his father? Perhaps part of the explanation was that they'd always known each other, and saw no more reason to discuss things than a brother and sister might. But they weren't brother and sister. They loved each other.

Love. Trembling almost as uncontrollably as

she had in that moment of sickness on the chilly stairs earlier, Miranda felt the word catch at her with a physical impact. What did it mean? What did she mean by it, murmuring the word dreamily as her satiated body relaxed into sleep in Ian's arms after they had made love? What did Ian mean by it, when he drowsily returned, 'Love you too'?

Suddenly she felt terribly frightened. Her mind turned, with a need for comfort which should have rung the alarm bells even more loudly, to her parents. They would be disappointed if she dropped out of her course, but no more than that. They would have been proud if she had graduated, as they were proud of all her achievements, but they wouldn't regard an academic qualification as important, particularly now that she was married.

And that surely was the point; she was married. Finding that she was pregnant, if she was, shouldn't terrify her in this way. There were no complications, no confessions to make, no defiant flouting of her family or Ian's to worry about. On the contrary, everyone would presumably be delighted. So what was her panicky resistance about? Dread of telling Ian, when they had so positively agreed that starting a family was not for them? Or the even greater dread, she had to admit at last, at the prospect of giving birth, of being a mother. She shrivelled with cowardice at the mere thought, then exasperation rushed back. Why even think of giving birth? No one had to do that nowadays if they didn't want to. She would have an abortion.

She could scarcely believe she had put herself through such hoops and not reached this conclusion at once. Ian would certainly agree, and the whole problem would vanish.

And I'll be back to *Gammer Gurton's Needle*, she mocked herself almost cheerfully, running up the steps to the street with her normal buoyancy back in place. Oh, my God, can I face it . . . ?

The first problem was to find an opportunity to talk to Ian. Miranda had never noticed till today how little time they spent on their own, nor how few of the moments when they were alone were appropriate for anything but their usual frivolous exchanges. During the week their days were fragmented by the demands of their different courses and though they generally managed to meet for lunch it was invariably in a group. Ian was taking his rugby seriously this term and spent a lot of time training. She herself was swimming a couple of evenings a week and had recently taken up fencing, which she was becoming very keen about. The Ski Club still absorbed a lot of their time. The pace had never been more strenuous.

Seeking a moment to broach a subject so adult and urgent that it often seemed to her it must concern two entirely different people, Miranda also realised for the first time how hard Ian worked. It was remarkable, in view of all the other things he managed to fit in, including some serious drinking, but it was a fact. He was fascinated by his subject, and when he worked was capable of an intense concentration in marked contrast to Miranda's own methods, which were piecemeal, self-indulgent and half-hearted. She liked music in the background, or even the television on, regardless of the programme. She yawned and lolled, flipped over pages with impatience, and treated herself to frequent placebos of food and drink. She welcomed interruptions, abandoning any pretence of work at the first breath of persuasion, cobbled together waffling essays on half-read texts, once producing a paper on *Diana of the Crossways* having read no more than the chapter headings, and was late with every assignment.

Ian couldn't see the point of leaving things till the last minute. In his view putting a job off meant more hassle than doing it four times over. Get it done and get it out of the way, was his policy, and though ironically this contributed to his hard-playing image, since it left him cheerfully laid-back about deadlines, in effect it was carrying him towards an excellent degree.

The week seemed to hurtle by, and no chance to talk presented itself. Afterwards, with the unforgiving opinion of herself which events were to force upon her, Miranda would wonder just how hard she had tried to create one. Surely Ian would have sacrificed an hour from his pressing commitments if she had made him realise the importance of what she had to say.

It was during this week that he learned he was to be on the bench for the game against Scotland A, and his joy over his selection took precedence over everything else — or Miranda was prepared to let it do so. In the event Ian wasn't called on, but he was there, part of the team, and after the match Miranda left him to the bonding and roaring and beer and, without repining, spent the evening at a twenty-first party.

On Sunday Ian, who had an extraordinary capacity for getting himself into action in spite of hangovers which would have crippled most people, was up at eight, and the flat was in chaos as they milled round getting ready for a day's skiing in Glenshee. A good build-up of snow above the two thousand foot level during the week had been consolidated by nights of hard frost, and an early club race had been hastily organised as a season opener. It was very much fun for the inner circle, not to be missed.

Then they were back to Monday. Almost by default, Miranda had continued going to lectures. If there was to be no baby, as of course there mustn't be, then there was no reason for not attending them. Or had she subconsciously known that to give up, to stay at home, would make a confrontation with Ian inevitable? For a confrontation she found herself increasingly certain it would turn into, with a corresponding uncertainty as to how he would view the situation.

From home, with a timing that made her feel more vulnerable than ever, came the news that the sale of Cardoch House had gone through with unlooked-for speed. To find a buyer for such a large house, at such a price, in literally a matter of days, had taken everyone by surprise. But the right person had appeared on cue, in search of a property which could be converted into what he called a 'country house' hotel, and the suitability of Cardoch House had been immediately obvious.

For Miranda there was an unpleasant feeling of slack suddenly being taken up. She realised that although she had known the house was on the market she had blindly assumed that Christmas would still be spent there. She was ashamed to feel so much at a loss at the prospect of being deprived of this much-loved and dependable treat. Memories swarmed, already sharp-etched with nostalgia, of the big warm rooms, beautifully decorated by her mother, of the tall tree in the curve of the stairs, the traditional round of entertaining, and the perennial problem of having the drawing-room fire blazing cheerfully before dinner on Christmas Eve, but sufficiently subdued for the temperature to be bearable for the reels which always followed.

And the presents, I suppose you want those too, Miranda told herself with contempt. These were childhood's images; she had to accept that she was reaching out to something which had gone for ever. Tears stung her eyes.

Would it be endurable to spend Christmas in Charteris Wynd, out of term, with most of their friends gone, town taking over from gown, in a city where they were temporarily displaced? How could she make this barren little flat look festive and inviting? How on earth could she produce Christmas food?

'Bad idea,' Ian assured her, when she told him about the buyer for Cardoch House and voiced some of these worries. 'Even staying at Kilgarth would be better than hanging on here. In fact, I think the old man's expecting to see something of us. I had a letter from him on Friday. I meant to say. He's asked me up to shoot this weekend. I'd quite like to go. What would you prefer to do? Come to Kilgarth too, or shall we stay in Muirend so that you can spend a bit of time with your parents, since things are moving so fast?'

'Yes, I think I'd rather we stayed with them,' Miranda agreed, 'if you're happy with that.'

'Of course I am. Perhaps your mother would like a hand with the packing,' Ian suggested with easy thoughtfulness, since he wouldn't be doing it.

'Yes, and maybe she'd like a hand from you,' Miranda retorted. Nice day on the moor for the men, boring chores at home for the females. But he was right; any time she could spend at home was precious now. And perhaps on the drive up or back she would be able to create an opening to talk at last.

But, as she should have known perfectly well by now, driving was something to which Ian liked to give his full attention, particularly on a wintry morning like this, when the mist, dense as they crossed the Forth bridge in a line of mudspattered vehicles, didn't lift until they were clear of the Tay valley.

They had abandoned the original plan of Ian spending the night at Cardoch House after the shoot, since, much as he and Miranda hated to sleep apart, he had thought Graeme and Georgina might appreciate a last evening alone with their daughter, before the perfection of the house which had been home to three generations of the family was lost for ever as the process of dismemberment began.

A well-meant idea, but one with disastrous consequences. In a rare mood of expansion after an excellent day at the pheasants, an almost faultless dinner produced by Ruby for the guns, and the wellbeing induced by for once overcoming his reluctance to decant his best port, Gregory Ross settled down, when everyone else had gone, to an enjoyable discussion with his son and heir about his plans for the company.

Since the necessity of making his father accept the facts, once and for all, couldn't be evaded, Ian, his heart sinking to realise that in spite of all the conflict it had caused in the past his father still obstinately refused to believe it, set himself to repeat what he had always done his best to make clear — that he had no intention, ever, of entering the family firm.

# 4

Ian didn't sleep at Kilgarth. He didn't walk out in a rage, fierce as the battle had become, for, always pragmatic, he didn't really think that one more night spent in his old bed would much affect the vast gulf in intention and outlook that lay between his father and himself. But Gregory, beside himself with rage and disappointment — and port never did him much good either — had gone the distance and forbidden him the house for evermore, adding a few more furious clauses that made Ian's square, strong face look suddenly a lot older than his twenty years.

Ian collected no more than a couple of items from his room in addition to his overnight bag, accepting with a resigned tightening of his lips that he was unlikely to see again the rods, guns and other possessions that he still kept at home, and left.

Knowing that Muirend would be battened down for the night, and unwilling to disturb the Cunningham household or to talk about what had happened yet, he drove down the glen as far as Sillerton, the home of the Hay family, and roused a chum who had a separate pad in a wing of the main house. Long inured to nocturnal invasions by friends who had just enough sense left not to drive on into town after a party, or who were confusing alcoholic intake with emotional despair, he sleepily let Ian in, had a

42

drink with him, talked obligingly about nothing for a while, and abandoned him to the sofa.

Ian left early, propping a note of thanks against the kettle, but didn't arrive at Cardoch House for lunch till later than he had been expected. He was never to speak to anyone about that morning, where he had gone, how he had spent the time or what his thoughts had been.

Once with the Cunninghams, recognising in spite of his own abstraction the cheerful tone masking a mood of farewell and last times, he put everything else aside, realising they were relying on him to help keep this mood in place. He was aware of a brittleness in Miranda's normal high spirits, and saw her father's hand tremble as he raised his glass in a quiet toast to Cardoch, and to the happiness it had held over the years. That was all, but Ian's throat was tight as they drove away, and he knew that telling Miranda what had happened at Kilgarth must wait its turn.

Odd, he thought, as he turned onto the A9 and gathered speed in the dreich light of another mirky afternoon, that for both of them, today, their childhood homes were vanishing. Why did that word, childhood, always have such a resonance, he wondered, seeking to lighten his mood. But poor old Miranda, she looked as though it had hit her hard. So little did, as a rule, that he felt an unaccustomed compassion fill him. She was much closer to her family than he was to his. She must feel a huge chunk of her familiar support system had been removed almost without warning. He'd scout around and find something to do at Christmas that she'd enjoy, spring it on her as a surprise at the last moment. Nothing too elaborate, though. His face set grimly again.

★  ★  ★

'But how long have you known?'

'I don't exactly *know* yet.'

The prevarication annoyed him unreasonably, a sign that all was far from well. 'Look, don't play about. When did you first suspect?'

'Oh, a few days ago.' Miranda didn't meet his eyes, and the airy tone and a small wriggle of her shoulders told him she was lying.

'Come on, Miranda,' he said shortly. 'It's not like you to fudge.' It was one of the things he liked most about her.

'Well, a week or two.' Miranda wasn't deliberately trying to mislead him. She was finding the total of days she had just calculated hard to credit and, flustered, was attempting to work it out again. She must have added in a week somewhere. When had they last stayed at Cardoch? Which Monday was it that her tutor had hauled her in?

'Miranda!' Ian had never spoken to her in such a tone of anger before. 'Don't you grasp that we actually need to know when it was? And why for God's sake didn't you tell me about it before? I can't believe you've been swanning around suspecting this and saying nothing, without even bothering to find out how I feel, or even checking to be sure that you actually are — '

His anger boiled up uncontrollably and he sprang to his feet to take the couple of paces to the window and the couple of paces back that were all the small room permitted. He felt trapped, his brain unready to take in the ramifications of this news, yet knowing it wasn't fair to take out his frustration on Miranda. Knowing, gropingly, for all this was so new and unforeseen, that there were other responses he should make. But that she hadn't *said* — or should he have known, had he been blind, too busy with his own affairs?

'I know I should have done something about it sooner,' Miranda was saying, apology in her voice now. 'Only at first I wasn't sure. I mean, it could have been anything, something I'd eaten, anything. And then, oh, I don't know, things kept happening and it was impossible to talk to you.'

'What things?' The level tone was somehow more ominous than his anger had been, and Miranda began to be aware of a horrible uneven pulsing of her blood which she had never experienced before.

'Oh, my tutor had me in, told me my grades were abysmal and I'd have to work harder.'

Ian was staring at her, dark brows down, and she could almost feel the moment when he decided that he would pursue that another time. He was right; it was a secondary issue. Now that she had finally told him what she suspected, she could fully understand his disbelief that she had said nothing till now.

'Then I didn't tell you because — ' What had happened next? It was hard to pin down anything specific, certainly anything that had seemed more important than this. 'You were playing rugby, there was the ski race, then this weekend we both had to . . . '

Her voice faltered as she faced his incredulous stare.

'Let me get this straight,' he said after a tiny pause. His voice didn't sound like his, flat and cold, almost clinical. 'You didn't tell me you thought you might be about to have our child because of a game of rugby and a club race? Is that what you're saying?'

He sat down beside her again, angled towards her on the armless double sofa covered in a cotton spread patterned with sunflowers. He was close because the sofa was small, not because he wanted to be near her, as she painfully realised. His shoulders were broad, cutting off the light, his head jutted forward so that he could look into her face. 'Is that what you're saying?' he repeated.

'It just seemed impossible,' Miranda said weakly, dismayed to find that he could be so daunting. 'You were always so busy.'

'I was always so busy.' He repeated the words without inflexion, as though tucking them away.

'Well, all right, we were both busy — '

Arguing such a point would get them nowhere, and he interrupted brusquely, 'What was the date of your last period?'

She stared at him miserably. 'I don't know.'

Ian put his head in his hands and, for a moment of stretching tension, silence filled the room. 'OK,' he said at last, very quietly. 'We'd better sort this out.'

'It does take two, you know,' she flashed at him, hating to feel so desperately in the wrong. 'It's not all down to me.'

She saw him take a grip on his anger. 'We decided not to start a family, yes?' he said levelly. His eyes held hers, and she was aware with a flicker of surprise of the degree of authority he had so effortlessly assumed. 'We decided on contraception, and we agreed on the method. You would go on the pill.'

She said nothing, her jaw mutinously set. But it was set because she felt not challenging but guilty, faced with this inexorable logic which put the blame exactly where it belonged.

'Yes?' Ian insisted.

'You should listen to yourself,' Miranda exclaimed in sudden fury, pushed into a corner and jumping up in her turn with an instinctive need to escape from it. 'I'm your wife! I'm telling you I'm probably going to have our baby. You're supposed to be thrilled or moved, or at least to feel *something*. Even if you've got it all straight in your own mind that the only answer is to get rid of it, shouldn't you at least go through the motions of understanding my feelings and finding out what I want? Perhaps I'm over the moon about it. Perhaps it's what I've secretly wanted all along. Perhaps my hormones have already got to work, and I'm delirious with delight at the prospect of being fulfilled as a woman.'

'Don't cheapen this,' Ian warned angrily, coming to his feet to face her, taking her arms in

47

a hard grip. 'Whatever you do, don't pretend. Do you think I couldn't tell from the way you broke it to me that you're angry and frightened? Over the moon about having a baby? You know it's the last thing in the world you want. At least let's be honest with each other. I'm twenty, you're nineteen. We're students. We were both a hundred per cent clear when we married that we had no intention of starting a family for years. Now look at me, Miranda, and listen to me. If you can truthfully tell me you want this child, then that's what we'll agree on. But I don't believe that's what you want, and I'm not prepared to have you blame me for what's happened.'

In spite of her defensiveness, she was moved by his honesty and his direct approach. With a pang of regret, she saw how differently he would have reacted if she had told him at once what she suspected. He might have been exasperated by her carelessness, but she knew his real anger was because she had concealed her suspicions, and because for someone like him, used to dealing with every problem promptly and swiftly, it was hard to believe that she could have let so much time slip through her fingers in so irresponsible a way.

At least now, having told him, she was not alone. She made a tiny movement towards him, resting her forehead against his chest. Ian didn't respond by putting his arms around her as she longed for him to do, but she could feel from the altered grip of his hands that he had accepted her mute appeal for comfort and a different level of discussion.

'I'm trying to fight with myself more than you, I think,' Miranda said, and to her relief caught a breath of laughter from him as at last he pulled her close.

'I think you are.' Then his voice changed, taking on a deep, raw note she had never heard in it before. 'You do realise, don't you, that what I mind most is your not telling me? You can't think how much that hurts.'

Fighting. Hurt. Guilt. New words indeed between two people whose relationship till now had skimmed the surface as lightly as a dinghy finding the best of the wind on a sunny day.

★ ★ ★

Fatally, incredibly, even after this exchange with its frank revelation of feelings, Miranda allowed a few more days to go by before she took any action.

She could never afterwards believe that she had yet again allowed events to take over. Perhaps there was a deceptive feeling, since Ian now knew, and had overcome his anger and been loving and supportive, that the problem had been dealt with, or at least made less urgent. Perhaps at some more obscure level instinct had been at work, warning her she was already too late, so that every day she delayed saved her from being forced to face the truth.

For she was too late. Maybe if she'd gone to another doctor she might have been given a different answer, but it didn't occur to her to go to anyone but old Doctor Fleming in Muirend, who had looked after the Cunninghams for years. In the manner of most of his generation, he strongly disapproved of terminating a pregnancy on any other than medical grounds. Miranda was young, healthy, and married. She could offer no dire psychological or economic reasons for not having a child, and she was in any case past the three-month point which was the latest at which he considered abortion should be carried out.

Dismayed though Miranda was, it didn't occur to her to seek a different answer elsewhere. Doctor Fleming was only telling her what in her heart she had guessed would be inevitable. She even wondered, driving back to Edinburgh, if for some deep-buried reason she had wished this outcome on herself; if some instinctive need had lain behind her carelessness and procrastination. Well, if so, she didn't know what it could be. For she didn't want this baby; didn't want it for herself or for what it would do to her life.

The prospect of no further studying, which a few weeks ago had seemed enticing, now looked more like missing out on something her peer group took for granted. There was an uneasy feeling too of having abandoned a challenge, and that didn't sit well with someone of her competitive nature.

There was, more starkly, the question of what she was going to do with herself. The baby's arrival was months away and she had never been good at idling. Well, she could spend more time at the gym, and she'd be able to ski every weekend, conditions permitting, even if Ian was involved with his precious rugby. It came as a jolt to realise that after a certain point she wouldn't be able to fall back on such activities to fill her time. It was a first cold breath of reality, and she winced to recognise how little, still, she had thought this through.

This was the jumble of conflicting fears and ideas which filled her mind during the drive home, and while she waited for Ian to come in.

She was unprepared for the visible shock the news gave him. The colour drained from his face and he stared at her for a silent moment with an expression which made the hair stir on her neck.

'Right,' he said then, turning away from her and going to see if there was any lager in the fridge. Finding none he went to check what was on offer in the cupboard of the thirties sideboard which had been half stripped down by a previous owner, who had abandoned the job when he uncovered two different kinds of wood. Ian found a bottle of Macallan there. With it poised over a glass he paused and lifted it towards Miranda in mute question, then with a brief tightening of his mouth as he remembered the new situation, he filled the single glass.

Miranda shook her head, as though the offer had not been withdrawn, equally unable to find words. Where was his anger now, when she truly deserved it?

'I know I should have gone on Monday and not waited,' she managed to say at last.

Ian looked at the amber liquid in his glass, swirled it gently, took a swallow, stooped to put the glass on the low table. 'No,' he said. 'Let's not pretend that that would have made all the difference. You should have gone weeks ago.'

She looked at him, ashamed and silenced.

'Look,' he said, after another pause, a pause during which Miranda thought how odd and uncomfortable it was to be talking like this, the width of the room between them, 'that's said now and need never be said again. We're in this together. It's happening. We've got plenty of time to sort ourselves out, make plans and get into a more positive frame of mind. Because that's important. Neither of us is overjoyed at present and we didn't plan it this way, but plenty of people have been where we are now and have made a go of it. And when it comes down to it, I can't imagine not actually wanting or loving our child, can you?'

Miranda knew he was doing his best to put behind him his frustrated anger at the way she had handled this, and she knew, respecting and admiring him for it, that he would have enough generosity and natural feeling to welcome this child when it came. What terrified her most in that moment was that she could by no means be certain of the same largeness of spirit in herself.

'Perhaps this won't be the most convenient of flats,' she commented, more from a desire to meet him halfway in positive thinking than to raise a problem.

'Ah.' Ian picked up the whisky bottle again. 'There hasn't been a good moment yet to tell you my news. It seems we suffer from the same problem,' he added, with a smile which held little amusement. 'But I think you should know that I've declined my father's offer of involvement in the business or a later partnership, and as a result have kissed goodbye to any handouts, inheritance or whatever he may previously have planned to give me.'

'Ian! That's awful!' Miranda meant any fight there had been rather than its consequences, whose relevance to their future she scarcely for the moment took in. 'Did that all blow up last weekend? But do you really mean it? I knew you weren't keen on the business but — '

He gave her a little quizzical look. 'I've always said I wouldn't be drawn into it. I could never work with my father.'

'I know you've said that, but — '

'But you didn't listen,' he finished calmly. 'And nor did he. Well, listen now, my love,' he went on, his tone suddenly changing, becoming almost savage. 'I want you to understand and take this in, not push it aside as just a few more idle words I couldn't possibly mean. I couldn't work with my father, not only because he's cantankerous and hopelessly set in his ways, or because I suspect him of, let us say, an ungenerous style of business dealing, but because it matters to me to make my own way, to start from who I am and what I can do, and build from there. I've never planned to do anything else. I know I've already taken a great deal from my father, in terms of education and countless other privileges, and since he's not withdrawing my allowance as long as I'm at college I intend to go on taking that too, particularly now. I can repay it later. I will repay it. But I've never intended to take any more than that, and the fact that we'll now have expenses we hadn't foreseen makes no difference. We shall be all right, the three of us. I shall see to it that we are.'

What impressed Miranda most, as she slowly took in the implications, was that never, in all the years she had known him, had Ian talked to her so forcefully, so passionately almost, about his deepest feelings. Everything for him had been a joke, or could be turned into a joke. She felt now, as she had when he had talked about accepting the fact of the baby, that in some way, when she wasn't looking, he had grown up and left her behind.

# 5

The tireless wailing of the baby could be ignored no longer. With a groan of despair for a problem which went far deeper than the immediate necessity of hauling herself out of the depths of the sofa, and for the sixth time since lunch going through to the gloomy bedroom, Miranda went to tend her daughter. The uncheckable spiral of child howling, child being picked up, child eventually quietening and being laid down in her cot, child howling, had her in its grip.

'Letting her learn that yelling produces results is the worst thing you can do,' Ian would tell her, patiently at first, then with growling exasperation as he watched this cycle harden into an unbreakable pattern.

'It's all very well for you, you're not here all the time,' Miranda would snap back.

How could he know how that remorseless piercing sound could wear you down? And how could you let a baby reach the state of misery — or rage — that Alexy was capable of working herself into, and do nothing? Miranda knew Ian was right in theory. She saw with the bitterest clarity the results of giving in, but she had the reality to deal with, day after day and night after night. She was too exhausted for theories; too exhausted for anything more than muddling through each hour as it came.

* ✻ ✻

The period before Alexy was born had been on the whole good. Very good, when Miranda looked back on it from the ensnarled present. First of all there had been the agreeable flurry of attention and good wishes when they had announced the news. To be made much of again, however temporarily, had briefly assuaged Miranda's guilt, and her consciousness of having failed to measure up.

Her parents, after the initial shock, had been delighted. They would have preferred it if Miranda and Ian had waited to start a family until they had a 'proper' home and a settled future, but these reservations they had kept to themselves. Georgina, in her first excitement, had even been ready to give up the former lavender farm in Provence, the purchase of which had already gone through, wanting to be on hand in case Miranda needed her and later to indulge in the delights of grannyhood. But Graeme's health had to be her first concern, and with wails of deprivation and the extraction of faithful promises to visit as soon and as often as possible, she had accepted that the plan couldn't be jettisoned at this stage.

Before their departure, Ian, saying nothing to Miranda, had gone alone to see them. The visit had been a business meeting, and accepted as such by Graeme. Though he had naturally hoped to see his daughter enjoying far greater financial security than she presently had, he was confident that Ian would see to it that her circumstances soon improved. Meanwhile, he thought Ian was right to complete his university education, and respected his determination to look after Miranda and the child as far as possible by his own efforts.

Ian had laid out the situation concisely. He had some investments of his own but, since he followed the market with close attention, he had been definite in his opinion that it would be folly to sell at present. His father-in-law, studying the portfolio with interest and impressed with what he found there, had concurred. He had been privately gratified that Ian was prepared to accept a loan from him — a loan which he had no doubt would be punctually repaid. He thought his son-in-law showed great good sense in steering clear of any similar arrangement with his father, for Gregory Ross was not held in high esteem by the local business community. Graeme would have preferred to have bought a house or flat for Miranda outright, particularly with a child on the way, but could only admire Ian's adamant rejection of any such offer.

Ian had written to tell his father about the baby, for though there had never been much affection squandered among the Rosses, famed not only for quarrelling but for their capacity to hold grudges, he still clung to a sense of family loyalty, and had felt Gregory had a right to know that a grandchild was on the way. He had received no reply, and had never told Miranda about either his letter or Gregory's silence.

Miranda herself had found it odd to be linked still to the familiar student circle, yet not of it. At first the distinction hadn't been too apparent. She had joined Ian and the others for lunch as before; they had continued to go with the same crowd to the same pubs and clubs, the same faces had appeared at the flat. On the surface little had changed, except that she had suddenly had loads of time on her hands, but her intimacy with the gossip and the jokes had gradually been eroded, and with a horrid blankness she had realised that far from being at the heart of the group — her accepted place — she was barely clinging to its fringe. In some insidious, unspoken, though never deliberate or unkind way, she had become, in the eyes of the group, Ian's wife, present because of him. No one consciously thought this, she was sure, but they were busy, cheerfully involved in their own concerns, and by becoming pregnant Miranda had moved on into some unknown, adult existence which had nothing to do with them. Student life was a world of its own, and Miranda was no longer part of it.

Fortunately, the end of term had been almost upon them.

'Why don't we get some skiing while you're still fit enough?' Ian had suggested. 'We needn't do anything too strenuous. What do you think?'

'Great idea,' Miranda had said enthusiastically. She had been dreading Christmas in the flat but had hardly felt she could say so. 'It won't be too late to book in somewhere, will it? Oh — can we afford it, though?' An apologetic afterthought; she had still found it hard at that stage to grasp that money wasn't available somewhere in the background.

'There are a couple of places going in the Aviemore cottage. We could grab those. That shouldn't break the bank.' Ian had spoken tersely. He minded more than he ever let her see his inability to provide for her the level of living she was used to, but for him too it had seemed imperative to be free of the confines of the flat for at least part of the holiday.

Miranda, about to ask why Aviemore, had caught the words back. Had Ian suspected that if they were with their own crowd in Glenshee she would mind not being able to hold her own in the scene where once she had shone?

'I'd love to go,' she had said instead, grateful to him. But never had the gap left by the loss of Cardoch House seemed so bleak and final.

The Aviemore interlude had not been a huge success. The early snow hadn't lasted, and two weeks of mild westerlies and steady rain had set in on the day they arrived. Too many people had been packed into the cottage, cooking facilities had been inadequate and the plumbing hadn't always been able to take the strain. Every room had been strewn with belongings, most of which had become permanently soaked as wet day had followed wet day in depressing succession.

In the second week three people had left in disgust, which had given the rest more elbow room, and Ian and Miranda, both reluctant to return to Charteris Wynd, though not exactly saying so, had decided to make the best of it, doing some damp walking, sampling the other activities on offer, and drifting with the rest from one pub or hotel bar to another in the evenings.

Miranda had reconciled herself in the end to being responsible about drinking, but had occasionally lapsed with a mutinous defiance which, though Ian had been sensible enough to ignore it, had shown that she was still far from ready to accept the changes having a child would bring.

She, even more than Ian, who could be happy anywhere as long as he had congenial company and plenty to do, had been glad, in spite of the atrocious weather, of the chance to be in the hills again. Though she had grown up in Muirend, the position of Cardoch House right at the top of the town had meant that the slow rise of moorland to the ridge dividing Glen Ellig from Glen Maraich began virtually at its back door. Miranda had always loved the accessibility and freedom of this landscape, and had also loved coming and going freely in the houses of friends tucked away in those beautiful glens.

In an area so sparsely populated, everyone had tended to be roped in for any childhood gathering, which had always meant a wide age range. So, while Philippa Galbraith at Affran and the Napiers at Drumveyn (a house to which visits had been a decidedly mixed pleasure, since a formidable grandmother had ruled the roost and repressiveness had prevailed) had been younger than her, Penny Gilmour at Alltmore had soon impressed them by disappearing into the grown-up world and getting a job abroad. Sally Buchanan, who had spent most of her holidays with her Aunt Janey at Grianan, had been closer to her own age. So had the Munros, and although they had lived in the south, with Allt Farr let for most of the time to shooting tenants, she had always looked forward to their visits to the glen.

She had looked forward even more to the appearances of James Mackenzie, who often stayed with his much older cousin in the bare bachelor house of Riach, which he would later inherit. He was one of the few people who had even temporarily displaced Ian in her affections, and once, for a whole weekend, she had been in love with him, after he had done his duty, gangling and unsmiling, by dancing a couple of reels with her at one of the Hays' enormous parties at Sillerton.

But it was Kilgarth she had known best and had loved, in spite of its chilly atmosphere, and she hankered far more often than Ian did for the sturdy square house in its open sunny position, with its wide views, and the moor climbing away at its back to the loch and the old boathouse which had been such a favourite haunt.

Back in Edinburgh in time for the Hogmanay street party, for which many friends had returned, they had readily let themselves be caught up in the celebratory mood. But once New Year was over, in the lull before term began, they had found themselves, pretty well for the first time, alone together in what was now their only home. Later, very much later, they were able to admit that for both of them this had been a dangerous low point. Miranda had wanted nothing more than to run for home, even if that no longer meant the reassuring comfort of Cardoch House. She had wanted her mother, had wanted to be spoiled, cossetted and told that all the terrors lying in wait for her would be chased away and need never trouble her again.

Ian, his natural ebullience temporarily extinguished by a new grimness, had had his own battles to fight, the chief of which was not to round on Miranda with angry reminders, when she complained about some minor discomfort, that she had only herself to blame. But they had worked through it, and had begun at last, before term swept Ian into new activity, to do some serious talking and serious planning.

Two weeks later Miranda had started work at a big sports shop on Princes Street; only on Fridays and Saturdays, when the ski department was at its busiest, but it had brought in some extra money and had taken her out of the flat, which had been a relief. She would be ashamed to think later that she had almost turned the chance down, since the hours would mean that she missed out on the weekend skiing scene, before remembering that not only was serious skiing out for the time being, but that she no longer enjoyed the luxury of being free to think so selfishly.

Perhaps because she had been earning something herself for the first time — and startled to find how strenuous the effort required for such a meagre return — she had also begun, though often naively and ineffectually, to pay more attention to housekeeping, and apply her mind seriously to economising.

Ian had sometimes found it hard to be enthusiastic about the results. Such anomalies as Miranda being thrilled to find a preparing-for-baby manual for 10p on a second-hand book-stall, then buying three elaborately worked Victorian nightdresses in an antiques shop had made it hard for him to hold on to his temper.

'But I thought you'd be pleased,' Miranda would protest. 'They're something we'd have to buy anyway, and they were second-hand.'

'Of course they're second-hand, or probably several other hands, if they're Victorian,' he would point out, containing his exasperation with an effort. 'And of course we need them, but not at thirty pounds a throw.'

But, angry as such extravagance had made him, he had been able to see how much it was asking to expect Miranda to overturn in so short a time the mind-set of a lifetime. It hadn't been hard to imagine Georgina falling on such finds with cries of delight. And if Georgina hadn't been in France there would have been, without any doubt, endless shopping expeditions, endless 'little' presents thrust into Miranda's hands, beside which three nightdresses would have been totally insignificant.

He had known from his own experience how the years of having everything one wanted, without ever seeing oneself as extravagant, made a sudden need for economy a matter of resolute scrutiny of every action and every impulse to buy. He had been on a steep learning curve himself, and had been well aware that the hardest part had been to stop going without a thought for quality at every turn. But — ninety pounds for garments that would lie in a drawer for a year at least and, if the baby was a boy, would never be used anyway. It hadn't always been easy to be tolerant when Miranda, whose intelligence he respected, had behaved so absurdly.

However, these and other differences of approach they had overcome and put behind them. Both had understood that their previous heedless happiness would not be enough to carry them through now. The remote, adult phrase, 'working at a marriage', had taken on a new significance, and they had been determined to do their best.

Ian had found a part-time bar job and Miranda had applied herself to hunting for a flat more suited to their needs. This time they intended to use her father's loan to buy, since Ian had no intention of paying out money on rent in their altered circumstances. Also, as the weeks had passed the steep stairs of Charteris Wynd had begun to present more of a challenge than she had been prepared to admit. Even so, she had been unable to reconcile herself to making an offer on any of the flats priced below the ceiling Ian had stipulated. Accommodation was getting harder and harder to find in Edinburgh, which, as Ian had pointed out, made it more imperative than ever to establish a toehold in the market, but it had made the search all the more frustrating and exhausting.

In the end it was Ian who had found the

answer. With his usual good luck he heard through a friend of a basement flat in the New Town about to come on the market. Miranda would have turned it down, because it wasn't near the university, because there would still be steps, though not nearly as many, and because the only bedroom was spookily dark, with a barred window facing across a narrow area to a dingy wall.

Ian had seen it differently. 'I know the steps are a drawback and I know you're the one who's going to have to cope with them, but it does have several advantages,' he had urged. 'The rooms are a decent size, there's that big entrance hall for the pram when we need it, the kitchen's fitted with everything you could possibly want and must be quite nice in summer with the back door opening from it. I think we could make something of it. We've never tried our hands at creating our own living space, just accepted what we ended up with. Now we have the chance to make a home.'

'I'm not sure I'm very good at home-making,' Miranda had reminded him dubiously. She had promised herself that this time she wouldn't dampen Ian's enthusiasm with unreasonable objections, but an image of spending her days in these sombre rooms, alone, at least until the baby arrived, and largely unoccupied, had made her shiver. Her domestic skills were still pretty basic, and the thought of trying to hone them in this dismal basement had not been alluring.

'You'll be fine.' Supremely adaptable himself, Ian had seen no reason why Miranda shouldn't rise to any demand. They might have moved on from their early uncritical adoration of each other, but for Ian, still, no other girl would ever come near her. Since she was one of those fortunate women whom pregnancy suited, he found her more attractive than ever. She had barely had a day of morning sickness, her appetite had remained excellent, and apart from a tendency to fall asleep immediately after dinner, or sometimes during it, and a nagging ache in the small of her back after a long day at the shop, she couldn't have been in more vibrant health.

They had made a successful bid for the Simla Street flat, moved in as soon as they could, and for a time it had seemed that in these new surroundings their happiness together was recharged. It was as if the changes they had not planned or wanted had been assimilated, and they had been set on a new course and would not look back. They had found, almost without realising it was happening, that they were looking forward to the arrival of the baby, and beginning to think of it as an actual person, though Miranda could sometimes feel guilty about how long it had taken her to arrive at this point.

During this positive period, she had found it easier than she had expected to be removed from the university orbit, accepting that that was no longer her life. She had been alone more than she was accustomed to be, but she had had plenty to do. Not that it had always been congenial, but as she had cleaned and painted and hung new curtains (ready-made), she had been relieved to find the oppressive atmosphere of the flat gradually relent, with lighter colours everywhere, the arrival of milder weather and, above all, familiarity. As spring had put in a tentative appearance Ian had been proved right. To have the kitchen door open directly onto the small yard outside was a definite bonus.

The flat was at the quiet end of Simla Street (a plus they hadn't fully taken into account until they moved in), well below the point where busy Fermore Road intersected it, and a flight of steps gave access from their peaceful cul de sac to a handy row of shops below. Because of this difference in height, their kitchen was at ground level and, beyond the courtyard wall anyway, there was nothing to impede an open view to the west.

Though Ian had been too involved in rugby this season to have time to train for any of the major skiing events, they had been up to Glenshee, and later to Aviemore as the race calendar moved there, on several Sundays, and if Miranda had minded doing duty as an official rather than covering herself in glory as a competitor, for most of the time she had managed to keep the fact to herself.

They had intended to go out at Easter to see the new house in Provence, then had realised that if they left the visit too late flying wouldn't be an option. Such ordinary considerations had sometimes hit them in slow time, and they had been angry with themselves when such reminders highlighted their lack of thought.

In the end Ian had taken a few days off before

term finished, though reluctant to do so, for he was taking his work seriously these days, and they had flown out. It had not turned out to be the best of visits.

A late spring here too had meant that cold weather had barely released its grip, and in spite of deliberately moving to somewhere where there would still be 'some kind of winter', as Graeme had put it, it had been obvious that Georgina for one had been seriously disenchanted by the way the mistral scoured the sere hillsides, and to find frost glittering in great patches on the walls of the house, warning where damp would be a problem later on. One prosaic irritation had almost driven her to give up the idea altogether — the shutters, the romantic shutters, so beautifully weathered to subtle faded colours, had rattled night and day under the vigorous hand of a wind which for their first weeks in residence had never seemed to relent. No one seemed able to solve the problem; indeed those summoned to do so had conveyed such blank astonishment at the request that Georgina had eventually given up in embarrassment.

Although she and Graeme had been adamant before buying that they had done their homework and were going into the project with their eyes open, it was clear that the intricacies of local bureaucracy, and the difficulties which reared their heads over every improvement they tried to make, had surprised and rattled them. Fortunately, the house had already been modernised to a reasonable level and was adequately heated. Now that spring was here everything would be perfect . . .

But on the flight home Miranda had been conscious of quite a new tug of responsibility. Her parents were still relatively young, but her father's health was far from good. Had it really been a sensible idea to move so far away? Once the baby had arrived it wouldn't be the simple matter she had once so breezily envisaged to go back and forth to see them.

Such worries had soon receded, however, as the extraordinary process of the new being inside her growing to the moment when it would be ready to leave her body, a moment it and not she would choose, took over her thoughts. Giving life to another human creature; suddenly it had been incredibly exciting.

Parents could warn, friends could warn, 'Your life will change for good,' but no words from anyone else, Miranda had at last been obliged to realise, could begin to convey the scope and completeness of the change.

# 6

They seemed to enter a desperate, cliché-ridden zone where the warning signs were perfectly clear, the remedies easy to see, but where circumstances were simply too powerful for them.

Or Alexy was too powerful for them. Alexia, to give her her proper name. Ian had wondered if some sort of pattern in Georgina, Miranda and Alexia would strike Miranda, but it didn't appear to, and he had agreed to the choice without comment. Almost at once it became Alexy anyway.

She had caused maximum hassle even before she was born, signalling her arrival with great insistence on three occasions, all inconvenient, until Miranda, mortified to be thought to be over-reacting, she who prided herself on never making a fuss about physical things, had almost left it too late. They had ended up stuck in the morning rush-hour traffic, Miranda well dilated, the pains coming with ominous closeness and regularity, and Ian wishing he hadn't dismissed the idea of going to ante-natal classes with such lofty disdain.

The birth itself, not as swift and easy as Miranda had felt she had a right to expect after this fraught journey, had been at once wiped out of her mind by the dramas and terrors that had followed. Alexy had turned blue, there had been questions about her heartbeat, her belly-button had been infected, the fontanelle had refused to close up and she had rejected Miranda's milk. She was very puny and, when she reacted unfavourably to every formula in turn, there had seemed a real chance that she would slip away after a brief life spent exclusively in anger and misery. However, she had finally accepted goat's milk, gained a minuscule amount of weight, her skull had behaved as it should, and a shattered Miranda had been able to take her home.

Nothing would ever come close to the debilitating terror of being left by Ian for the first time in the empty flat, listening to the frail cries swiftly gathering force, and knowing that nothing and no one lay between her and the responsibility for seeing that this fragile scrap of unhappy humanity stayed alive. Nothing had ever equalled, either, the anguished protective love she felt for it.

From that moment Miranda had seemed locked in a never-relenting battle. No other life existed. She grew used to feeling permanently harried and inadequate, no job ever finished, no job ever tackled because she felt inclined to do it, everything done under pressure, with a dozen other urgent tasks always waiting.

Recognising the self-perpetuating nature of the pattern, she would make an effort to break it. She would stop what she was doing, make coffee, sit down and attempt to establish priorities and work out some timetable which would not make her feel so haplessly bowled along. She would remind herself that she had one husband, one child and one small flat to look after. She was young, healthy and, in theory, active and energetic, though the days when she had felt either seemed a distant dream. She had no other demands on her time and, though still adjusting to new financial constraints, couldn't pretend she had any real financial worries.

But inevitably, before she could get any further, the first reedy sounds would make themselves heard from the bedroom, and tension would begin to build again as she resolved not to give in and respond, yet knew there was no alternative. She would find that Alexy needed changing, or had been sick or, quite simply, for no reason that Miranda could see, she wouldn't stop crying.

This was the core of the problem, this capacity to cry, night and day. It was hard to know where the tiny body found the strength. It meant that Miranda could never get enough sleep herself, and without sleep it became harder and harder to view anything rationally. Ian had said from the first that he would take his turn at getting up, and since Miranda wasn't breast feeding this had sounded feasible. But in the event not even Alexy's most indignant howls pierced his sleep and when, because he insisted that she should, Miranda woke him and he dutifully turned out, he stumbled round with such bleary-eyed clumsiness that she invariably ended up by going through and snatching the bottle from him.

'Look, I can do it,' he would protest. 'I want to do it. Just go back to sleep. I can manage.'

'How can I go to sleep with you crashing

about dropping everything you touch?'

'Ignore me. It'll get done.' It would, and she could rely on him to get it right, she knew, but her impatience was not so much for him as for the whole situation. She was no more capable of going back to bed and relaxing than he had been of hearing his daughter's cries in the first place. Even when Alexy was fed, if she accepted the feed without throwing it up again, after it she needed the endless walking and soothing which took such a toll of patience and vitality, before there was any hope of getting her off to sleep.

'Look, just leave it. I'm far better doing it myself.' It wasn't long before the fatal words were spoken.

'Well, don't say I didn't try to take my turn,' Ian warned, going back to bed, where in spite of his anger he was out to the world in five seconds.

Miranda wept, knowing he would never hear. Wept because the resentful little body in her arms would not be still, wept because as well as being a useless mother she was becoming a hateful person, snapping so ungratefully at Ian, who had only been doing his best.

She knew that not all husbands of his age would be as willing as he was to change nappies and sit patiently through the protracted business of coaxing Alexy to feed. Also he was scrupulous about ensuring that a supply of the essential goat's milk, which was not available nearby, was always in the fridge. He did his share of the shopping as he generally had the car, but the car too he was happy to do without if Miranda wanted it.

She rarely did. She had soon learned that taking Alexy anywhere was a nightmare. The slightest change of routine upset her. The nice idea of being one of those couples who shoved their obliging infant into a carrycot and took it everywhere with them, to get lost under the coats at parties, breast-fed in convenient corners and passed around to be cuddled and admired, seemed a remote fairy tale now. Even those most eager to hold her would hand Alexy back at speed when she choked up the usual little patch of frothing vomit on their shoulders.

Braving the signs that the doctor was losing patience with her, Miranda hauled Alexy back yet again in a desperate bid for help. The endless girning, the struggle to get her to eat, surely couldn't be normal. But no medical problem could be found and the over-worked paediatrician, who, unlike Doctor Fleming in Muirend, had not known Miranda all her life, was tempted to suggest after the third visit that perhaps there was some inherited tendency towards complaining.

Ian and Miranda, recognising the cycle they were caught in, did attempt to discuss ways in which they could break free of it. Ian even wondered if the doctor might not have a point, though if there were any question of a genetic disposition to be dissatisfied with life it came from the Ross side rather than the Cunningham. He was afraid, though, that the problem had a different source.

'You're having such a miserable time yourself,' he said. 'It can't be much fun being shut up here on your own all day, with Alexy playing up. Perhaps that communicates itself to her? I'm only guessing, I'm no psychologist, God knows, but perhaps if we could find some way to help you to . . . '

He didn't finish, abruptly aware of the thinness of the ice. Though Miranda managed to contain the defensive anger which filled her, anger she had enough sense to see was itself part of the cycle, he saw it in her face. She managed not to demand, 'So you're saying it's all my fault?' substituting instead, careful to make it a reason, not a complaint, 'I get so tired, that's all. I never seem to get enough sleep.'

'I know.' Ian put out a hand to smooth the dark hair which was not so silky nor so live to his hand as it used to feel. The bouncing health of her pregnancy had deserted her. She was too thin, pale from being indoors so much, and she had grown so tired of perpetually having to wash sweaters and blouses after they'd been on for no more than a couple of hours that she had fallen into the habit of wearing a few shabby favourites which dried easily and needed no ironing, and went about most of the time with a towel slung over her shoulder.

Did it have to be like this? Ian simply didn't know. He had the easier part, as he was well aware, and even though that was how things had to be, he lived with a persistent sense of guilt because he was able to walk away every morning, and had other concerns to occupy his mind. Not least of these was the ever-urgent matter of earning extra cash, though a generous aspect of the deal with Graeme had been that no interest or repayments were due as long as he was a student.

Ian did his best to be positive, longing, though this he didn't say, to enjoy Alexy as other couples seemed to enjoy their babies. He loved her, whole-heartedly and without question. Her very frailness drew from him an unreserved longing to protect and cherish her. Her crying disturbed him deeply, and though he stuck for longer than Miranda to the sensible rule of trying not always to pick her up on demand, when he did he cuddled and soothed her with tenderness and patience.

When he suggested finding a baby-sitter so that Miranda could get out sometimes during the day, to shop, have lunch with friends, go to the library, or merely be free and on her own for a while, these simple proposals would provoke a flurry of objections which Miranda knew were unreasonable but which she couldn't bite back.

The truth was, her self-confidence was by this time at zero. She was very far from the happy, enviable, heedlessly popular extrovert of the past, but she had no idea who she had become instead.

Though they tried not to let Alexy dominate their existence completely, their efforts to recapture their shared pleasure in life had little real chance. Baby-sitters usually found one visit to Simla Street enough; there were easier pickings to be had looking after sensible babies who shut up and went to sleep.

On the one occasion when Ian finally

persuaded Miranda to go out for dinner, the evening was so unsatisfactory that they were both appalled, though neither admitted it. Ian's first instinct had been to get together with the group as they always used to, thinking it would be good for Miranda to resume contact. However, since he would have done anything to make the evening a success, when she said she'd rather they were on their own he didn't argue, booking a table at a more expensive restaurant than they'd been able to afford for some time.

The food and wine were excellent, the surroundings agreeable, the band passable. They couldn't find a thing to say to each other.

From the moment Miranda had gone into the bedroom to dress, which always felt odd anyway on a light summer evening, she had felt she was acting a part. The room was chilly — or was she shivery with some obscure apprehension? — and her hands were clumsy as she got ready, the dress she had chosen feeling so unfamiliar that it might have belonged to someone else. Her hands were rough too, and she ruined the first pair of tights. She had almost forgotten how to put on make-up, and it was hard to believe as she tottered across the room in strappy high-heeled sandals that she had ever found them comfortable. For the first time she noticed how lifeless her hair looked, how pasty her skin.

Glancing at Ian in the mirror as he rapidly dressed, she wondered if he felt as reluctant as she did. But of course he didn't; he wasn't subject to post-natal depression, he hadn't passed weeks on end without sleeping for more than an hour at a time. He was focused and purposeful — and as good-looking as ever. But the response which the sight of him could always awake in her was threaded with a new, aching sense of loss. How long was it since they had made love, and when they last did had it meant as little to him as it had to her, her body refusing to take its remembered flight, her brain remaining aware of extraneous things, the way the pillow was bunched under her head, the threat of cramp in her instep, a cold whisper of draught on her thigh?

Perhaps tonight . . . ? But to her dismay the image produced not delicious anticipation but instant rejection, as though it could have nothing to do with them as they now were.

It wasn't a good way to begin an evening, and constraint lingered in spite of all their efforts. Or because both were making an effort. Only later, as they danced, swaying together wordless and relaxed, did something of their old physical delight in each other briefly return.

They sat wrapped close in the taxi going home, both desperately wanting to hold onto the mood, but desire and need shredded away when met by the baby-sitter's huffiness because they were late and Alexy's angry whimpering. As Ian saw the baby-sitter into the taxi, and Miranda contemplated a pile of dirty mugs and plates in the sink, their evening together seemed to have belonged to two strangers.

Though with the arrival of summer things became easier in practical terms, the simple fact of being able to put Alexy outside and sit out in the sun and warmth herself making a big difference to the days, Miranda knew that the rift was inexorably widening. Ian, still doing bar work in the evenings, picked up a supplementary job erecting marquees which, though lucrative, meant that he was often away for long hours and occasionally overnight. It was also strenuous work, and fit as he was he had no interest in anything much beyond getting his head down when he came home.

Things deteriorated even more when term started again. Ian had made the first fifteen, and it seemed to Miranda that rugby took over his life. She attributed to this the quarrels which flared ever more frequently between them, but their true cause was different.

It was not Alexy, either. She had by now let up on the ceaseless plaints and, though she still didn't sleep the night through, three or four hour stretches had become the norm. She was also eating better, though every meal continued to be an exhausting battle. These two factors made a huge difference, however, and Miranda, getting more sleep in her turn than she had had for months, was better able to cope with the difficult spells. She also found, hardly daring to believe they were real, that at last there were magical interludes of peace, when loving feelings not riven by guilt, and a new, unguessed-at sensuous pleasure flooded through her merely to hold an Alexy amenable and quiet. A single gummy smile at this stage could bring Miranda close to tears of happiness, so unimaginable had such a simple thing begun to seem.

Miranda herself was the problem. She had allowed herself to accept that to take Alexy anywhere, or to leave her with anyone, spelled disaster, and she no longer had the courage or initiative to break free of the trap she had created for herself.

Ian, his inherent ebullience and enthusiasm for life unchanged, found her rejection of every suggestion intended to help her more and more frustrating. The flat in Simla Street, never very comfortable or appealing since Alexy's arrival, was even less inviting when he was met with anger and resentment the moment he opened the door. Why exchange congenial company for this? Why not stay for the next round, go off for a pizza with the guys, put in a few extra hours of training? He couldn't persuade Miranda to come and join them. She was no longer tolerant of his rugby, his skiing, his friends or even his work, and he had long ago given up the attempt to study at home.

He did persuade her to go up to the slopes when the skiing season began, pointing out that other couples took their children along and it seemed to work. But, apart from the fact that Alexy objected vociferously to the cold, the wind, the snow and the hours in the car, Miranda found it hard to accept her own new role. Mothers and toddlers either huddled in the café, which smelled of bacon rolls and sickly hot chocolate, or skirmished with sledges and mini skis in the slushy snow near the carpark, doing little more than wipe noses and tug wet mittens onto mottled hands. Fathers skied, vanishing up to the higher lifts if they had any sense. What annoyed Miranda most was that the other mothers didn't seem to mind.

The evening scenario in the hotel wasn't much better. While most couples danced or relaxed in the bar, checking on their young when they thought fit, Miranda insisted that Alexy couldn't be left. Since Ian didn't agree she would end up going crossly to bed on her own. They would row when Ian came up, pointlessly since he'd been drinking, and they would row the next morning, Miranda wanting to go home, Ian reminding her that he was entered for a race. He would refuse to give in to her, and she would take off in a rage in the estate car which had replaced the MG — a change Ian had made without complaint — leaving him to find his own way home.

There was no doubt that Miranda allowed herself to become a victim at this period; indeed almost seemed to welcome it, though she laid the blame at Ian's door. *She* couldn't abandon her baby, *she* couldn't sit drinking for hours in the bar, *she* couldn't please herself. Etc.

They fought and fought, both too hot-tempered to halt the slide towards disaster. Miranda knew in her heart that Ian couldn't exist without company and laughter, stimulus and challenge. That made him the person she had loved. But still she blamed him with a bitterness she couldn't subdue. For deep below the surface, never properly examined or acknowledged, a different guilt gnawed at her.

Ian completed his course and got a first, which in the circumstances showed an impressive level of ability and application. The day the results arrived he was very quiet, staying around the flat for most of the time. Alexy was in bed and Miranda had begun to make supper when he said, in an odd, constrained voice which caught her attention at once, 'Leave that. I've organised the baby-sitter. She'll be here any minute. I'd like us to go out — anywhere will do. We have to talk.'

Afterwards, Miranda was surprised that she hadn't argued, or at least demanded to know what this was all about. But perhaps something had warned her; not precisely of what was to come, but that some significant moment was upon them. She had been aware of her heart beginning to bump a little oddly, her throat feeling dry.

Where had they gone to talk? She could never later recall. She remembered only Ian's serious face, his eyes holding hers, and the steady quietness of his voice which had warned her as much as anything he said that no argument on her part would be of any use.

When he said, 'You know it's over, don't you?' in that quiet tone, her blood seemed literally to chill. 'We'll never get back to what we had. We're not even trying to any more. We're not communicating, we're not sharing, and we make each other more miserable all the time. It's true, isn't it?' he persisted, still gently, when she gazed at him in appalled silence — appalled because she had seen, in a single flash of dismay, that this was going to happen.

'It seems to me, in the circumstances, that the

only sensible thing is to get a divorce.'

Stunned, filled with a wild alarm which she refused to let him see at the prospect of being without him, wanting to protest that there must be a hundred ways they could find to put things right, Miranda nodded. 'Yes, I suppose that would be best.'

'You know that I love Alexy, and will always be there for her. We can work things out properly in due course, when you've had time to think, but I'd always want to be in touch with her, know how she's . . . ' His voice was not so steady now, and it took him a moment to recover. 'And of course you know that I'll always look after you both, financially, I mean.'

It was hard for him to use the word. For Ian, the concept of looking after Miranda and Alexy had always meant something so very different.

Two months later, when Alexy was two and a half, with the divorce going forward and everything in place that he could manage at present for their future security, he left for Australia.

# 7

Single parent. Of all the labels Miranda had found attached to her in her adult life, feeling each time that events had somehow done the labelling before she was ready for it — wife, pregnant woman, mother, single parent — this last had the most impact upon her.

This time, however, she came out fighting. It was too late to do anything about all that had gone so devastatingly wrong, and she was still in shock over Ian's departure, though impressed in spite of herself by the resolute way he had handled everything, without recriminations but without wavering from his purpose. But this time she knew she must take hold of her life or go under for good. Looking back over the past two and a half years she saw them as a dark tunnel of muddle and inadequacy, strife and resentment. Not that making a decision to put this behind her meant that it happened overnight.

Since it was recent and raw in her mind, and since it had become a habit to focus her anger on his shortcomings, Miranda chose to see Ian's defection as a natural extension of his behaviour since Alexy's birth. He wanted to be free to do his own thing; it didn't suit him to have a wife and child dragging at his coat-tails. This view had become an article of faith with her, more deeply entrenched after every evening when a meal waited in the oven and was never eaten, after every phone call with cheerful pounding racket in the background to say he was somewhere quite different from where he'd said he'd be and would be late. Miranda needed that anger to fuel her new resolve. To succeed, to achieve something, she had no idea what as yet, would show Ian that she could manage as well without him as with him.

It had been a point he had made himself, when he had told her he intended to go. He had been forced to see, for a long time now, that his presence in the flat only provoked rows and caused more pain. For a long time he had felt that he had no function other than to provide, and this he intended to go on doing to the best of his ability.

Miranda chose to gloss over this part. In the blankness after he had gone, which left her feeling frighteningly out of touch with reality, to employ selective memory and blame Ian for everything that had gone wrong seemed the only way to survive. She hadn't wanted a child any more than he had, yet because she was a female she had had to bear the major burden of looking after it, while he had still been free to play his games and have his fun. She needed this anger to kick-start her life, and later there never seemed any reason — or time — to examine things more objectively.

The problem of what to do and how to cope could bring her awake at night shaking with fear. She had no training, no qualifications, a brain which barely functioned any more, and a fractious two-year-old for whom she was solely responsible and whose father hadn't been able to wait to put the width of the globe between them. Ian, presumably, imagined she would go on as she was, stuck in the circumscribed round she had grown used to, caring for Alexy, shopping, cooking, looking after the flat. A sense of fairness would stir when she remembered that he would get nothing from his father now, as in the normal course of events he had expected to do, then she would remind herself that it was his obligation to support his child. It wasn't up to her to worry about how he was going to manage it.

It was not for this reason that she intended to work. This wasn't about money, welcome though some slack would be. This was about self-worth, that almost forgotten concept. This was about breaking out of a dangerous mould before it was too late. There was also the incentive of knowing that she was not, as she functioned at present, a mother any child could be proud of. And since it looked as though she was going to be the only parent Alexy would have around as she grew up, this mattered.

Beyond all this Miranda was aware, more keenly than ever before, of the cold open spaces stretching around her. Ian's friends no longer came to the flat, and for a long time now they had been the only people who appeared there. In retrospect her own circle from university days scarcely seemed to have been friends at any but the most superficial level, brought together by circumstances and shared interests. Now they were scattered; in most cases she had no idea where.

Reviewing, as she had not done for a long time, the earlier friendships in Muirend and the glens, she was guiltily aware of how heedlessly she had left them behind. It was her own fault, she knew. She had been too absorbed in Ian — a dazzle of memory, like a shaft of light through cloud, gave her a glimpse of two carefree people far away in time, blissfully wrapped up in each other, a glimpse that made her catch her breath in pain — and in her own affairs and the demands of college life, to keep up the old contacts.

Some fragments of news she had heard through her mother, who was still in touch with many friends in Scotland. She had heard of Lisa Napier finally breaking free of oppressive Drumveyn and going off to London to do a secretarial course — and losing an astonishing amount of weight at the same time. She had heard of the unexpected death of Philippa's mother from heart failure, and of the sad state of affairs at Affran, where Lewis Galbraith was sinking rapidly into a life of gambling, drinking and debt. Sally Buchanan, her mother reported, had been having major rows with her aunt Janey, who had objected to her wild ways, and, in disgrace, was not for the present appearing much at Grianan.

There was more positive news as well. The Hays continued to flourish and multiply at Sillerton. Penny Gilmour had married someone called Andrew Forsyth, was back in her family home of Alltmore and already had two small sons. James Mackenzie had inherited Riach and

87

was now living there full-time.

Surely it wouldn't have been too hard to re-establish these links, had she really wanted to do so. But she knew it wasn't as simple as that. For one thing, who exactly was she nowadays? She knew that her personality, though she had never come close to admitting such a thing to Ian, even in their most serious attempts to put aside accusation and anger for a while and talk, had not stood up well to the demands made upon it. She knew she was immature and shallow, spoiled and selfish, and the knowledge filled her with uncertainty about her capacity to handle any relationship, however ordinary and casual.

Even more crippling than this was the deepest hidden guilt. Love Alexy as she might, protectively and passionately, she found it increasingly hard to like her. This seemed so awful to Miranda, so incredible, that it coloured her whole perception of herself. She couldn't imagine any other mother feeling that way.

But this wasn't about people liking her, she reminded herself grimly. This was about creating a stable and if possible contented home-base for Alexy, and bringing her up in the best way that could be achieved. Half-forgotten suggestions Ian had made, rejected at the time, came back to her, appearing full of sound sense now. With them returned the memory of his voice (a memory which could still rouse complex and disturbing emotions), warning that if she was depressed and negative about everything then there wasn't much chance of her child being happy.

Companionship for Alexy was another basic need. Miranda had realised for some time that it was becoming urgent — it had been yet one more source of disagreement with Ian — but she had been too caught up in her own resentment to do anything about it.

It was hard to know where to start. There was a strangely rootless feeling in knowing that every bit of her life could be unpicked and, if she chose, reassembled in a different form. Now that Ian had walked out — she began to use the phrase quite soon, stilling protests from some more honest self — there was nothing to keep her in Edinburgh, or in the flat. The trouble was, there was nothing to draw her anywhere else.

She thought of going to live near her parents, but she didn't particularly want to educate Alexy abroad. Also there was an element of compromise and second-best in ex-pat life which her mother had eventually admitted it was impossible to ignore. Doubtless her father found the same, though he would never say so, since they were living in this desirable place of exile for his sake. His health had improved, or so Georgina said in every letter and phone call, but Miranda couldn't help feeling this was owing to the pressure of work being lifted, and that the same result could have been achieved equally well nearer to home. She felt terribly cut off from them, never daring to attempt a flight with Alexy as an infant, and recoiling from the prospect with even greater alarm as she became a hyperactive and demanding toddler.

Georgina came occasionally for brief visits alone, tacked on to the longer stays with her family in the south which Miranda couldn't help feeling were the real pleasure of the trip. For Georgina was so scrupulous about not commenting on the fragmenting relationship between Ian and Miranda, so determined to hide her anxiety, that the barriers never came down, and each visit left Miranda feeling more isolated than ever. They also left her feeling defensive, for though Georgina poured out presents on Alexy and applied herself to every grandmotherly duty, she failed to achieve any real contact with the self-orientated child, and Miranda was far too ready to read implied criticism in her mother's disappointment. Fortunately she didn't guess that Georgina was actually repelled by Alexy's sharp-featured, pale face and cold eyes, finding it hard to believe that Ian and Miranda, so outgoing and positive, so blessed with striking looks, could have produced such an unappealing child.

There was no word from Kilgarth. Ian had kept his father informed of his plans, but received no reply to any communication, and he neither expected nor wanted any further help from him. Miranda felt she should try to keep some contact open for Alexy's sake, and continued to send cards at Christmas to Gregory and the two aunts, but soon gave up hope of any response. Gregory's disappointment in his son had bitten deep, and it was clear that he wanted to write off for good not only Ian but Ian's wife and child as well.

In spite of this, and a lack of any real ties in the area, Miranda often felt the tug of the familiar and beloved landscape. One part of her wanted to introduce Alexy to its beauty and give her all the things Miranda herself had enjoyed, the friendships, the ponies and boats, the country pursuits, the skiing. Yet a more independent instinct, late to develop but strengthening all the time, made her admit that such images were not only improbable fantasies but quite beyond what she could afford. That life had gone. This was about Alexy and herself. The life they would build together would, of necessity, be very different, but she would see to it that it was the best in her power to offer.

But in spite of good resolutions change was scary, and it was easy to let the weeks slip by in the safe routine she had become used to. Also to sway her would come one of those rare but miraculous moments when Alexy was happy, her attention caught perhaps by one of the games or puzzles Miranda did her best to engage her in. Watching the absorbed face, the neat-fingered hands, seeing the alert brain make some connection or leap to some answer, Miranda would feel that every second of the painful journey to reach this point had been worthwhile. When Alexy wrote or drew everything she did was small-scale and precise. Her spatial skills were amazing, it seemed to Miranda, though she did manage to remind herself that she had no yardstick to judge by.

In harmony like this, involved and interacting, Miranda would decide she was mad to think of looking for a job. There must be hundreds of mothers out there, obliged for one reason or another to work, who would give their eye teeth for the chance to be at home with their child like this, during the vital formative years. And she was all Alexy had. Wouldn't it be denying her something crucial which it was within her capacity to give, to hand her over to the care of strangers when there was no actual need to do so? But wasn't that the point? Wasn't she doing Alexy a worse turn by keeping her cooped up here with only one adult in her world? Couldn't that be even more damaging in the long run?

The question was effectively answered by a family holiday the Easter after Ian left.

Christmas and Hogmanay had been so desolate alone, the assault of memories in the lonely evenings after Alexy was asleep so unbearable, that Miranda fairly leapt at the invitation from one of her mother's sisters to spend a few days with the clan in a rented cottage near Coylumbridge. Having failed to persuade Miranda to come south to visit them, Aunt Nita, not unprompted by Georgina, had seen this as a chance to draw Miranda back into the family circle, and at the same time introduce Alexy to the mob of cousins and second cousins. It was exactly what Miranda had been needing, and as the grown-ups crowded round the kitchen table on the first evening, having finally got the junior element more or less under hatches, she realised that she had been desperately missing this kind of lively, relaxed and uncritical company. It was so good to slot

92

happily into her place in the hierarchy once more, accepted and made welcome, and to catch up eagerly on other people's news. That was perhaps the biggest pleasure of all, though it made her realise with shame how intensely focused on herself and Alexy she had let herself become.

The ingredients were all there for a marvellous holiday, and the way Aunt Nita cheerfully juggled the logistics of a constantly fluctuating household, as friends, family members, sundry dogs and other people's children came and went, brought back with vivid nostalgia the childhood visits to Gloucestershire, when Miranda, the only child, had flung herself so joyfully into the hurly-burly of the larger family group.

With the nursery slopes well covered and the lifts operating to the higher runs on all but a couple of days, with plenty of people on hand willing to take care of Alexy, if ever Miranda was to have the chance to enjoy lively adult company again, get some decent skiing and have some fun on her own account, here it was.

Alexy, however, super-sensitive to any threat to the established order, made sure the chance was all but wrecked. It was hard to believe afterwards that one child not yet three could have sabotaged it so effectively, but she did. She objected to everything. She refused to let anyone but Miranda touch her, wouldn't eat anything the other children were having, wouldn't go to sleep without her mother there, howled whenever a dog went near her and fought with silent vindictiveness to wrest away any toy any other child appeared to be enjoying. Above all she objected to being expected to venture into the horrible white expanses of 'outside'. Her wrath at this outrageous idea was so unbridled that for everyone's sake Miranda usually had to give in and let the rest go without them.

In wincing embarrassment she found the defects in her methods of handling Alexy laid bare one by one. Though she had thought she was aware of the dangers, she was forced to see how comprehensively she had failed to avoid the trap of over-compensating for Ian's absence. And in spite of recognising that it was vital to widen Alexy's horizons and hers, she had done nothing about it.

'Thank God,' she would exclaim fervently when an outbreak of howls turned out to be coming from someone else's child, and her cousins would laugh at her. But she had to accept the truth — on the whole the other children were co-operative and cheerful; they were expected to help according to age and capacity, and mostly they did; they took it in good part when they had to move over or squeeze up when newcomers arrived; but above all they were keen on things, and knew how to enjoy themselves.

Drawn once more into this almost forgotten milieu, more comforted by its affectionate, casual warmth than she would have imagined possible, Miranda couldn't escape seeing how dangerously she had subordinated her own life to Alexy's, and how unnaturally she had kept the two of them shut away.

Poor little Alexy. Miranda's heart ached to see her fighting and resisting at every turn. It was hard not to fight on her behalf, as protective love and defensiveness came surging up. How could Alexy be expected to adapt without a struggle when she found herself pitched headlong into this close-knit crowd of confident strangers? What chance had she ever had to develop social skills? Finding the cosy private world she inhabited with Miranda, where everything was done as she wanted it, suddenly replaced by these unfamiliar surroundings thronged by strangers who expected all kinds of unheard-of things from her, who could blame her for resorting to the weapons which had worked in the past?

Miranda felt she was endlessly apologising as the days went by fraught with battles, humiliation, compromise and bribes, peace only achieved when Alexy got what she wanted and had her mother to herself. It was a timely warning. As Miranda, her hand never free of a soggy J-cloth, wiped up yet another slew of food which Alexy had either swiped from the table or regurgitated from her square bawling mouth, she promised herself that as soon as they were home again she would take decisive steps.

For her own sake too, for the fun she was having when Alexy gave her the chance made her realise how far she had come from her old self. The long enjoyable evenings spent with congenial people, the feeling that her brain was waking from sluggish sleep, and above all the laughter, once so essential a part of life, brought home to her all she had been missing.

A well-intentioned letter from Aunt Nita after the holiday reinforced the message. Sympathetic and tactfully phrased as it was, it brought tears to Miranda's eyes. She had to face the truth. Not only was she becoming an unrecognisable person herself, but she was rearing a monster.

So she began the long slow haul; alone, at the beginning, as she had never been alone before. For beneficial as the renewed contact with the family had been, and lovely in many ways, it had been a bruising experience too, and pride, if nothing else, made her determined to climb out of the pit she had dug for herself, by her own resources if she could.

# 8

Although it was hard to adjust to the confines of the flat after the days in a wider landscape, and one whose beauty had brought back so many memories for Miranda, it was a relief to slip into the accepted routine again. Even so, it was clear that the first imperative was for Alexy to meet other children, though to find a nursery school or playgroup and expect to be able to take her along and leave her there was out of the question. On her showing during their holiday, there would be no second visit.

The alternative was to find a mothers' and toddlers' group, though the very name made Miranda wince, and steel herself for battle. There was no one to suggest to her that seeing it in this light made trouble inevitable. The group she found had been formed by a few people getting together on their own initiative, so no professional skills were on offer to help either her or Alexy. Its role was less to benefit the offspring than to provide a meeting place for the mothers, giving them a chance to peer through the bars of the cage with others in the same predicament (Miranda's phrase), complain about the men in their lives and brag about their progeny.

The hall they used was some distance from the flat and Miranda, finding the early sessions gruelling, would arrive home limp and exhausted, vowing she'd never go through that again. If there had been one person with whom she could have struck up a friendship it would have helped, but the mothers, though unanimously proclaiming themselves fed up with their domestic lot, never seemed to want to talk about anything else. Being with them, however, no matter how little she had in common with them, brought home to Miranda how fixed she was in her own groove of resentment and inertia. The truth was, she was no better than they were.

Harder than trying to fit in herself was persuading Alexy to integrate. For Alexy, recognising at a glance that, exactly as had been the case at Easter, in this new scene she wouldn't be the centre of attention, her mother no longer her exclusive property, drew on every weapon in her armoury. There were other children who threw tantrums or refused to join in or resorted to anti-social tactics such as biting and kicking, but they didn't do all of these things all of the time, Miranda would think in despair, knowing that the sympathy of the other mothers as they pretended not to watch cloaked shocked disapproval. She minded even more the supportive approach — 'Never mind, why don't we find her something to play with and leave her for a bit?' — when what they were really saying was, 'If that was a child of mine . . . '

Miranda stuck it out, though she hated it so much that she dreamed about it. Until Alexy was ready to be left with other people there was no chance of finding a job. In time, though Alexy was usually at the bottom of any fights, and continued to be treated warily by the other children, she did acquire a degree of social discipline. Finding that if she didn't toe the line she missed out on treats was too much for her in the end.

After a few months Miranda abandoned the toddlers' group, with undisguised relief on all sides, and on four mornings a week took Alexy to a nursery school only ten minutes' walk away, *and left her there.*

She had never felt so liberated, so physically unburdened, as in the moment when she crossed the road on Alexy's first day, went into the railed garden opposite and sat down, by herself, at half past nine in the morning. Not all her guilty awareness of how bad it was for Alexy to be with her so much, nor the concern of others, had made her realise till this moment of dizzy freedom how abnormal her life had been since Ian went.

Since before he went, for there had been all those unhappy months when he'd left her alone in the flat, more and more involved in his own affairs, this match so vital, this ski race the big one in the racing calendar . . . The familiar plaints, honed by the accustomed friction of her anger, poured readily back. But she pushed them away. This wasn't a moment to be wasted, this brief spell of time so free of demands that she could hardly take it in. Even now, she caught herself turning to check on Alexy. How long would it be before she stopped doing that?

What should she do with this astonishing freedom? She could shop without the litany of 'don't touch' and 'please put that back', the harassed weighing of how much was still on the list and how much more Alexy would stand, the inevitable being held to ransom. She could walk, at her own pace, without feeling obliged to arouse interest in anything she saw, without being assailed by whining so unrelenting that she barely heard it, without coaxing and cajoling, 'We'll go to the end of the path, shall we? Just as far as the ducks. You like the ducks . . . '

Most incredible of all, she could do nothing. She could sit here, as people did, idling in the thin morning sunshine. She could relax every sense, let time drip through her fingers. Perhaps after all that was what she had been missing more than anything. It hadn't been easy leaving Alexy, but she supposed she couldn't expect to get off too lightly. To be honest, she amended, there had been a stupendous scene and for a second she had almost given in, but the girl in charge had been firm.

'You must go. She'll yell as long as you stay. If there are problems I promise I'll let you know. We'll take care of her, don't worry. She'll be fine.'

What if there was an emergency? She couldn't be contacted sitting here.

But Miranda crushed panic down. To stay within reach of the phone whenever Alexy was at school would destroy the whole point of the exercise. She recalled the conversation when she had made her initial enquiry about registering Alexy. A soothing note had been applied to soften the brisk fluency of the information she was given. Reassurance for over-protective mothers, she had recognised. Mothers, in short, were the problem.

Undoubtedly true, she thought with a lift of light-heartedness, smiling as she tipped back her face to the sun, stretching out her legs, letting the sounds of traffic and the steps of people taking a short cut through the little garden fade from her consciousness.

But relaxing was something she was going to have to relearn. Almost at once she found herself wondering how Alexy was faring. She must feel bewildered and abandoned, in spite of all the care Miranda had taken to prepare her. The morning would seem like a lifetime. Remembering the concentrated resistance of her whole body as she'd fought against being handed over, Miranda was smitten by a pang of loving compassion. Oh, Alexy, are you going to go through your whole life fighting? Where do they come from, the desperation and the fury?

Ian's words came back. Though Miranda wasn't consciously aware of it, thoughts of him ran as a constant undercurrent in her mind. In a way they were her only company, her only form of sharing. As he had said, who she was and what she was would affect Alexy more than any other influence in her life.

And the truth was, right now, she was missing Alexy. So much for freedom. It felt not light and buoyant to be without her, but blank and empty. Probably all mothers felt this on the first day of school, but it sharply reminded Miranda that, though socialising Alexy might be the main objective, equally important, and long overdue, was establishing some independent identity of her own.

How she achieved it wasn't important. She could go out cleaning people's houses if it came to that. Perhaps you'd better start with your own, a sly voice suggested, and she grinned as she stood up. Well, that too. But the main thing was to find something. Ads, job centre. She would make a start at once. What better way to employ the morning?

★   ★   ★

She found her job, one which would carry her most adequately through the years, not by trekking to the job centre or trawling the ads, but by luck.

She had decided, as a sort of symbolic start to opening up her life, to improve the yard at the rear of the flat. Pleasant as it was as a sitting-out corner, adorned now with tubs of evergreens and two narrow beds of easy-to-grow flowers, the end wall cut off the view. Below it on the steep slope was a dank plot of overgrown laurels, which Miranda had assumed belonged to one of the flats. However, it seemed to have no access, and since in all the time she'd lived here she'd never seen anyone go near it, it seemed quite possible that by taking a couple of feet off the height of the wall she would upset no one.

However, she had discovered after Ian left that the flat was part of a listed building, within the New Town conservation area, owned by a proprietors' association. She had also learned she had to pay an annual factoring fee, covering routine repairs and charges, common to all occupiers, for services like rubbish removal and the cleaning of stairs and steps. It had never occurred to her to wonder before how this was taken care of. Searching through the densely printed pages of the lease for the right person to contact about lowering the wall, she had come across a name scribbled in the margin in Ian's writing, Danielle Kirkland. A name that was to change Miranda's life.

The telephone number also noted down by Ian turned out to be a private number, and that was the oddest chance of all, as Danielle no longer worked for the solicitors who had done the original conveyancing, but now ran her own agency for letting and servicing the flats.

Being a prompt and capable person, and gathering from Miranda's questions that she had a tenuous grasp of the terms of her lease, she offered to come round, have a look at the wall in question and give her opinion. She was in and out of houses in the area every day; it would be no trouble.

Danielle proved to be an incisive, no-nonsense woman in her forties, with very short hair and a lot of make-up, her waist thickening as a consequence of a passion for rich food and her posture suffering from a habit of sitting hunched at her desk typing furiously, eyes slitted against the smoke from her cigarette, with the phone clamped between jaw and shoulder.

She came clacking rapidly down the area steps, gave a peremptory double ring on the bell

103

and raked a searching glance over the condition of the hall paintwork when Miranda let her in.

'It's very good of you to come,' Miranda said as she welcomed her. 'Particularly as you weren't even the person I should have phoned.'

'Humph.' Danielle nodded an acknowledgement, but didn't waste any more time on that. 'Let's have a look at your wall, shall we?'

'This is my daughter, Alexy,' Miranda felt obliged to say, since Alexy had followed her to the door and was clinging to her leg with an iron grip. Seeing Danielle's eyes flick down and up again without a change of expression, Miranda cupped a quick hand round the head butting into her thigh, not aware how protective the gesture looked to Danielle's sharp eyes, nor how propitiating her smile.

'Right,' said Danielle.

With new clarity Miranda saw the clinging child, and felt her cheeks flush.

The question of the wall was summarily dispatched. 'Can't see any problem with that. Knocking the top off can only be an improvement. I'll draft a letter for you. Since I once worked for the factors I can wrap it up in the sort of language they like.' She whipped out a small black leather notebook which was soon to become familiar to Miranda and made a rapid entry.

'It really is good of you,' Miranda said again.

'Oh, well, I'm still in the same game, only shunted sideways, so to speak. I deal with these people all the time. I used to look after this very flat, as it happens, so I was quite pleased to have the chance of a nosy round.'

Miranda laughed, her spirits rising, recognising for the first time in far too long instant rapport with a stranger. She liked Danielle's aura of vigorous efficiency, leavened by a hint of sardonic humour, and she liked the flamboyance of the floating scarf in rich colours which she kept rewinding or tossing out of her way, and the heavy chunks of shapeless gold she wore round her thick wrists and short neck.

'Do the demands of back yard walls leave enough time for a drink?' Miranda enquired, not knowing she was going to suggest any such thing.

'Always time for a drink.'

The time they had fixed on had been 'after work' for Danielle, which meant about seven. Miranda had known there would be no hope of Alexy being in bed by then, but had hoped that if she promised a special treat for supper Alexy might at least let them deal with business without disruption. Control. As she found herself sending up a silent prayer for Alexy to be co-operative, it was as if Miranda truly recognised for the first time the degree of domination she had let her gain. She was appalled.

'Alexy, come along, we're going in,' she said abruptly. As she added to Danielle, 'I'm so glad you can stay,' she hoped her voice didn't betray her real need to hold on to this chance of company.

Danielle turned to look at her for a second, her glance sharpening, then followed her inside and slung her heavy bag into the corner of the sofa. 'Whisky,' she said.

Miranda wasn't sure if she had whisky. As a reaction to Ian's drinking, which she had chosen to see as part of their problems, and as an early and obvious economy when she was alone, she rarely drank now. But old habit meant that the drinks cupboard was still stocked, for whose benefit it would have been hard to say, and she was relieved to find a bottle of Macallan there — their old favourite. What if there had been no whisky? Did she really think Danielle would have stumped off in disgust and that would have been the end of that?

As it was they fell at once into the sort of rapid, inconsequential, enjoyable exchanges for which Miranda had been thirsting since Easter with the cousins had reminded her what fun they could be. It was like meeting someone from home after a long time in a foreign land. Unfortunately, however, it had to be carried on over and through one of Alexy's better performances.

Danielle was the sort of person who thought it reasonable to pursue an adult conversation regardless of the presence of a child, either believing that the child should accept being ignored, or that if one continued to ignore it it would be removed. Where to she neither knew nor cared. In fact she enquired presently, tired of watching Alexy pull Miranda's hair under the pretence of playing, and watching Miranda trying not to wince with pain, 'Can't you put her away somewhere?'

Since her tone suggested a dispassionate wish for information rather than overt hostility, Miranda found the bluntness acceptable. In fact, she decided with surprise, she found it definitely satisfying. There would be no pussyfooting round Alexy here.

'It doesn't really work,' she said honestly, trying to loosen Alexy's clutch on her hair and at the same time prevent her falling off the arm of the chair where she was rolling about, laughing mirthlessly to drown out the voice of this new arrival. For Alexy felt to the cold depths of her soul that here was an adversary it would be wise to rout without delay.

Danielle accepted this, though she raised her eyebrows, and Miranda felt that all her mistakes in handling Alexy, the ascendancy she had allowed her to acquire and her own guilt because of it, had been uncovered at a stroke. Their eyes met, and Danielle's asked, Why don't you let her fall off?

For one second Miranda, prying open the mean little hands, considered it. Not as an actual, brutal recourse for, apart from any more humane reason, the hell Alexy would raise when she hit the floor would put paid to any further hope of conversation, but as a reminder that alternatives to pleas and negotiation did exist.

'Meet me for lunch tomorrow,' Danielle said, suddenly bored. One of her best anecdotes about a client and a house disaster had been ruined.

'I'd love to, but I'm afraid I — ' Miranda glanced towards Alexy and moved her glass out of reach for the third time. But the wistfulness in her tone couldn't be mistaken.

'Then when?' Danielle demanded. 'There must be some moment of the day when you're free.' Of this horror.

'Morning?' Miranda hardly hoped it would do.

'I don't usually do coffee.' Out came the black book. 'Right. Eleven fifteen, the Florentine. Be there.' She made eye contact with Alexy as she came to her feet, and Alexy, startled by the message she received, stopped kicking her mother on the shins by accident on purpose.

Danielle was in charge of a number of properties in the New Town, and with demand ever growing was finding that the servicing, and in many cases the furnishing and equipping of the flats, was becoming too much to cope with single-handedly.

She brushed aside Miranda's objections about skills or experience. 'Forget all that. I need someone with brains who's prepared to work. Only part-time for now. It may build up. And I need someone who can put up with me — I'm a nightmare to work with.' But she took the trouble to add, and Miranda was grateful to her, 'Not that I think you'd let me trample all over you. You're not the type, whatever present appearances may suggest.'

It could not have been a more timely piece of encouragement, and Miranda, breathless at the unexpected opening up of this opportunity, was more than willing to forgive the way it was phrased.

# 9

Busy years. At first the restrictions of having to work only when Alexy could be looked after elsewhere were troublesome, but gradually these periods lengthened. Though it wasn't easy to find a child-minder who would agree to look after her more than once, Miranda did eventually track down someone who would take her for a couple of afternoons a week and who, in spite of frequent upheavals, could be persuaded to stick to the arrangement. Miranda supposed that, as with the girl at the nursery school, her battling daughter presented a challenge and she was thankful that anyone was prepared to see her in this light.

She enjoyed working with Danielle, though more effort and application were demanded of her than she had ever had to expend before. Her job involved the maintenance and equipping of the houses and flats, and showing them to clients. To her surprise she became genuinely interested in fitting them out in appropriate style, hunting down the exact lampshade, the right fabric to recover the dining-room chairs, or kitchen items that wouldn't look out of place, and she enjoyed the occasional challenge of furnishing one from scratch.

These glimpses of enticing places to live made her frequently think about moving from Simla Street, or at least from their present flat, for here she was ideally placed for the office, the little row of shops down the steps, Alexy's nursery school and the school to which Miranda planned to send her next. The child-minder lived an inconvenient haul away in Braid Hills, but otherwise she could hardly have had a better position.

So partly for the sake of that convenience, partly because she was too busy to face a move, but mainly because she found to her secret dismay that she wasn't brave enough to face one, she stayed where she was. She knew that sharing a room with Alexy was not ideal for either of them. It was a question which would have to be addressed soon, but whenever she thought of it she would find panic rising. Moving seemed to equate to abandoning a safe place where she knew she could cope and was left undisturbed. Any vision of a different setting, even another flat close by, threatened new demands and new encounters, and her self-esteem had taken such a beating over the years that she felt no confidence in her ability to meet them.

One reassuring thought was that if she did decide their present quarters were impossible, then Danielle was on hand to help and advise, push and organise. Danielle had sent a blast of dynamic energy through Miranda's circum-scribed life, refusing to let her centre it obsessively on Alexy. Dropping in at the flat whenever it suited her, insisting that Miranda come out to her cottage at Cramond at weekends (as great a contrast to the Georgian elegance of the New Town where she worked as she could find), she was stimulating company, and opened doors to other contacts and friendships. She also brought back laughter and fun, vital ingredients Miranda had hardly been aware were missing.

In one respect, however, Danielle was the worst person for her to be close to at this period. Danielle disliked and despised men, collectively and singly, and saw Ian's behaviour, as depicted by Miranda with well-rehearsed self-justification, in unrelieved shades of black. He had grabbed what he wanted and been happy with it as long as it was fun. When Alexy's arrival made things tough he ducked out. They were all the same. They wanted someone to do the mind-numbing chores, someone in bed (Danielle always rushed past this part with such vengeful disdain that Miranda began to wonder if she knew what she was talking about), then when anything more serious was asked of them they pushed off. Who needed them?

When Miranda reminded her that Ian had always been generous over money — for whatever he was doing in Australia was evidently lucrative — Danielle would scoff, 'What's money? Just stuff he finds in his pocket. Don't tell me it can give him much pain to provide for his own child? It's the least he can do, for God's sake.'

It was tempting to go along with this. Miranda needed to see Ian as the baddie, her own failings by now conveniently obscured by the resentment which had carried her through the months after he left. To disinter the truth now would take too much courage. And time. The job, Danielle, the flat, Alexy, fully occupied her. It was easy to go on from day to day.

This busy existence, which worked as long as she didn't examine it too closely, was severely jolted by Ian's return when Alexy was nearly five.

★  ★  ★

For the first time he wrote to Miranda directly, and for the first time she had an address for him. Seeing it on the page made her realise almost with shock that this vanished person, who had treated her so appallingly, had a continuing life of his own, a home, job, friends. Perhaps a wife. Miranda had not let herself think of this as a probability, and she folded the letter hastily, as though the address, which conveyed nothing to her beyond the fact that he was in Sydney, was as much as she could bear to take in for the moment.

There had been no contact between them. Everything, as Miranda had wished, had been done through the lawyers. Only the funds, greater even than their agreement stipulated, had appeared punctually in her account. There had been nothing to get in touch about, no crises over Alexy or changes in her circumstances of which Ian should be informed. Miranda had grown used to thinking of him as gone for good, existing only as the mental picture on which her hostility continued to centre, the image of a person to whom any difficulty, past or present,

112

however minor or unrelated, was traced back in her mind.

Now he wanted them to meet, wanted to see Alexy, and discuss Alexy's education. Hot wrath rose in Miranda, the jumbled emotions which the sight of his writing had produced coalescing in a trembling anger. How dare he think he had a say? How dare he expect to arbitrate about where Alexy went to school, when it was Miranda who was here, on the ground, dealing with the day-to-day mechanics involved, making it work, fitting her own life around Alexy's needs? What right did he have to come waltzing in now and imagine he could interfere?

She couldn't refuse to let him see Alexy. Access had been written into the legal arrangement, though as time passed Miranda had come to believe Ian would never be interested enough to insist on it. Not all Danielle's more combative views, dished out over a couple of bottles of wine and the dressed lobster she had collected on her way, in answer to Miranda's summons, could alter that.

Then anger would blaze up again. How could any man disappear from his child's life, making no effort to keep himself in her awareness except by the Christmas and birthday presents which unfailingly arrived, then expect her to be thrilled to see him when he turned up on a whim? Alexy rarely enquired about him. She asked from time to time why she didn't have a daddy, but it was simple enough to explain that he lived a long way away. Apart from such questions, prompted by being with other children, she wasn't concerned.

113

Alexy didn't deal in abstracts. Her attention was focused on the material and immediate; in short, on herself and what she could demand, wheedle and trick out of her mother and any other adult on her horizon. One day, inevitably, she would ask more.

Perhaps, if Ian intended the contact to be long-term, he was right to come now, while Alexy was young enough to accept his reappearance without question. But the prospect of seeing him again, of being caught up in the old anger, was too disturbing to let Miranda keep this reasonable point in mind.

Where would the meeting take place? She looked around the untidy kitchen in dismay. Not here, allowing the rage and frustration Ian could so swiftly arouse to invade her private space. Well, that decision at least was within her control. They would meet on neutral ground. With Alexy? No, impossible to talk if she were present. And when he did see Alexy, Miranda didn't want him to be with her here. He would have to come to collect her though. Collect Alexy, take her away? Where to, for how long? No, that couldn't happen.

Miranda felt totally unprepared for these questions, so familiar to most divorced couples. There had been no time to evolve some system that suited them, no time to prepare Alexy. And that of course would be down to her. No complications for Ian. He would simply turn up and expect his daughter to welcome him.

It was appalling to realise that someone else had a share in Alexy. Miranda had grown so used

114

to seeing responsibility for her as solely hers that she had almost forgotten there could be shared decisions about her. But Ian was paying for Alexy's education, she would remind herself, and point out to Danielle when they chewed over the issue, so perhaps he had a right to some input. But she couldn't make herself feel it was fair, and she was willing to let Danielle's indignation on her behalf keep her anger stoked up.

The truth was she had no way to meet Ian other than in anger. The version that had become set in stone over the years, of what he had done, of how he had behaved towards her, allowed no other starting point. Did she also, in some hidden honest part of her, know this was the only way she could hope to protect herself against what the sight of him would do to her?

Vain hope. At her first glimpse of him across the small restaurant a storm of feelings battered her. Physical reactions she had almost forgotten, bitter rancour of the kind that banishes reason, reckless readiness to face the challenge both of his presence and anything he could say to her, were mixed with a feeling of rightness and completeness at seeing him again which told her that all existence since he went away had been mere marking time.

It was this last, a sensation for which she had been quite unprepared, which made her clutch at anger as her only protection. She was dimly aware of someone moving towards her, of, without words — she wasn't aware of speaking anyway — the small formalities being dealt with, being welcomed, indicating that she was joining someone and had already located him, and then she was being escorted to the table. Or did she cross the room alone, had her jacket been taken as she came in or was it taken at the table? She remembered only the curious sensation as she walked towards Ian of her feet not quite making contact with the carpet, of her legs feeling at once pithless and strangely stiff.

Then there were Ian's eyes. It seemed, trying to piece the scene together afterwards, that she had stood gazing into them, held by them, for several seconds, aware of nothing else around her. But she couldn't have done, for no one seemed to have noticed anything odd, she was in her seat and another unheard but effective exchange must have taken place, for soon a glass of sherry appeared before her. Then she was staring at a great glazed menu on which black ripples danced and blurred. She was conscious of her hands gripping it, and of being unable to look up from its baffling patterns.

It was plucked away, and Ian's voice said, 'There's no hurry. We'll have a drink first.' Was he speaking to her or to another of these waiters who seemed to waft about with no substance?

'It's all right. We can take our time. I know this isn't easy.' That was certainly said to her, the tone quiet and comforting. And intimate. Miranda struggled with the need to object to that intimacy, to be outraged that such a note could sound in this stranger's voice, while the pure pleasure of hearing it smoothed the wild irrational billows of her anger.

116

Then, unforeseen, physical memories, treacherous and precise, overwhelmed her. He was too near, the space between them was too small, they were too enclosed in that strange intimacy of a restaurant table surrounded by strangers, the light was too soft, their corner too secluded. She could imagine that she felt his skin, and her own skin came alive; she was swept by a hundred sensations she had schooled herself to forget, and it was a colossal effort to beat them down, to concentrate on present reality, dredging up with difficulty the reason for this meeting.

As, haltingly at first, their voices unnatural, they began to talk, it appeared that Ian had come not only to discuss schools for Alexy, though at the outset declaring his readiness to let Miranda make the final choice, but also to make clear that he could and would finance whatever was decided upon. Knowing it would annoy her if he went into details of how he had prospered, through the type of lucky combination which so often came his way — the right place at the right time, meeting the right person, finding just the upswing in the property market he needed to start him on his way — he was nevertheless anxious for her to know that the funds were there. He was also ready, though knowing he must tread cautiously here and be seen to wish to contribute only to Alexy's welfare, to finance a move from the Simla Street flat if that was what Miranda wanted.

'That has nothing whatsoever to do with you,' she flared instantly when he broached this, and he recognised the well-remembered jut of her jaw. 'The flat is my home and Alexy's and whether we go or stay is my affair.'

'Of course I appreciate that. But perhaps it's my business in that I want to provide for Alexy, and where she lives is part of that,' Ian suggested carefully.

He had thought out what he would say ahead of time, knowing that thinking on his feet would be beyond him when face to face with Miranda once more. And how right he had been, he thought with an attempt at humour so laced with loss and nostalgia that it hurt more than it helped. She could stir him as no other woman had ever been able to do — that he had been prepared for. But that she should feel so much part of him, after all that had happened and the amount of time they had been separated, had shaken him in a way he had not been able to guard against. Watching her walk towards him with the light step he had always loved, seeing her tension, the tremor in her hands as she grasped the menu, the tightness of her mouth, a wave of need and regret had risen up and nearly choked him. It had been as hard for him as it was for her to focus on immediate practical demands.

Would it have been simpler after all to have met at the flat? But what memories and emotions would have wrung him in that remembered setting? And Alexy would have been there. Apprehension gripped him at the thought of seeing his daughter. Not a day went by without his thinking of her, hating to miss her childhood, yet he didn't exist for her, he would never enter her mind. He wasn't sure he was going to be able to deal with that.

Around the subject of Alexy's future, financial arrangements and every other topic that Ian introduced they circled warily, flashpoint never far away. In no time, hardly knowing how it had come about, the bitter arguments, accusations and blame were spilling out, and a sense of sick futility filled him to hear them.

Though he had scarcely formulated to himself what he wanted from this meeting, he saw now that ever since the moment he had decided to come his whole self had focused on it. To find that after half an hour he and Miranda were exactly where they had been when he left was a crushing blow. He had to accept that a second meeting would serve no purpose, and did his best to concentrate on Alexy.

To his dismay he found his contacts with her even less rewarding. He had not expected her to remember him, or to be able to strike up instant rapport. He knew she would need time to get used to him, and that he must keep his own feelings in check. In spite of himself, however, there had been the secret hope that some bond, some natural affection, would still exist, and he knew now that he had never really envisaged a complete absence of response. He had loved Alexy without reserve as a baby, and had not been able to suppress images of her jumping into his arms, his throat aching at the thought of a small warm body to hug close, her arms in a stranglehold round his neck.

The chill truth was that Alexy had no

intention of having anything to do with a stranger. When Ian arrived for the first time she was watching a cartoon and angrily resisted the interruption. As Miranda had been forced to accept, it would have been expecting too much of Alexy to ask her to go off with Ian at an initial meeting, and she had reluctantly agreed that the only solution was for him to get to know Alexy again in her own surroundings.

Alexy wouldn't let Miranda leave. Although she was used to being left with baby-sitters by now they had never been male. In fact, as Miranda was to realise when thinking over the disaster later, for Alexy there had never been much contact of any kind with men.

Not surprisingly, though she wouldn't let Miranda go, she wouldn't let her parents have any kind of conversation either. She barely glanced at the present Ian brought her, a trick she had learned caused pain and led to agreeable persuasion and attention, and not all Ian's rationalisation of this — she was barely five years old, she hadn't a clue who he was, what was a present and what did it matter whether she liked it or not? — could alter his profound sense of rebuff.

No subsequent visit improved matters, and he discovered to the full the baffling helplessness an adult can experience when a child blanks them out. Also there was something very disturbing about the cold glance with which his daughter raked him, with a calculation in her eye which made him wonder guiltily what damage he and Miranda had done her.

He had in fact, though he never said so, come back to Scotland to see whether there was any hope, if he were to live there again, of establishing some kind of divorced-father format for seeing Alexy, or even a workable parenting contact with Miranda. Further he hadn't dared to look, and even that much seemed incredibly naive in the face of the reality he found.

He had no place here, that much was evident. Yet if he went back to Australia the rift would only widen. But it was surely beyond repair already, and to remain in the vicinity of Miranda and his child, unable to establish any rapprochement with either, would hurt more than he could bear. Walking into that flat again had been the hardest thing he had ever done in his life.

He knew he hadn't given it long. To win Alexy's trust, to make her feel at home with him and to be accepted as part of her life, would require time and patience. These fraught visits crackling with the tension between Miranda and himself couldn't be expected to achieve much.

That was the nub. Even if it meant sacrificing his role as a father, he knew he couldn't lay himself open to Miranda's unrelenting hostility. She saw him in a light that had deeply shaken him. Not for one second in the intervening years did she appear to have relented towards him. No new perspective, no objective thinking, had softened her bitterness. He knew he had hoped that their long friendship, as well as the great happiness of their early time together, would have outweighed eventually the disastrous course things had taken once Alexy appeared, but this was so evidently not the case that he had to accept the inevitable.

Suddenly he couldn't wait to put the world between them again. He would fashion a life for himself which didn't revolve around thoughts of them. He would open doors he had kept firmly closed till now, no longer devoting every waking moment to making the money which had come to seem the only thing he could offer them. There were other things in life.

# 10

Miranda met Will through Danielle, as indeed she had met all her friends and acquaintances in the course of the last seven years. Danielle, growing bored with the Cramond cottage, had bought a tiny and eccentrically designed flat on the fringe of the Dean village. It seemed all corners and windows to Miranda and its outré style didn't appeal to her, but she could concede its attractions of height and light and cloud-scapes, and the charm of its plant-lined balcony.

Danielle threw a tremendous house-warming party for it, in which Miranda, of course, was involved from the moment of its inception. Everyone either of them had ever known seemed to turn up, and though Miranda did ruefully think in passing that with Cramond gone it would be harder than ever to drag Alexy into the fresh air, she had a wonderful time. So did Danielle, and the next morning her bossy vigour, so scornful of the weakness of others, had for once deserted her, and Miranda, coming round to help clear up, found her creeping about dabbing at the mess, a shattered — and snarling — wreck.

Which was why she and not Danielle was waiting to show Will the cottage when he came to view.

Will at first sight seemed rather colourless. Afterwards Miranda had to think to remember what he'd been wearing. Shades of fawn. Well-worn needlecord trousers, and slightly darker sweater over a check shirt and tweed tie; a car-coat of snuff-coloured loden cloth, far from new. Weekend clothes for an orderly man who lived in a city but was not a city person. She could imagine him clipping hedges or raking leaves in a small neat garden.

He was tall, his shoulders slightly stooped. His fair-coloured hair was soft and light-textured, and looked as though he had always had it cut in the same way and always would. He was very quiet, obediently looking at everything she showed him, but hesitant about questing into any area which could be regarded as private. At first Miranda found him unresponsive, and thought she was wasting her time and that he must have decided already that he wasn't going to buy. But gradually she began to realise that the quietness was receptive, and to sense the almost tangible kindness that was the basis of Will's nature.

She found herself relaxing, offering information about the cottage more spontaneously, revealing her own affection for it as though talking to someone she knew. She was also intrigued to note, examining the reaction as they went out together into the small garden, that she felt safe. Not safe from attack or actual danger, but safe as a person, safe to be herself. An odd feeling.

'This is a marvellously sheltered corner,' she said, as they stood in the angle created by the back of the cottage and the white-harled wall of the house next door, with its one window high up under the roof. 'The cottage, like all the rest, was of course built to look out over the firth, but since that's north this is where we always sit out. Though I admit there's not much of a view.'

Will turned to look at her, and though there was no measurable pause before he replied, she felt, then as always, that he had taken his time and knew exactly what he wanted to say. 'You come here a good deal.'

In those simple words, more a statement than a question, Miranda felt he had somehow divined the place this cottage had in her life, and her sadness to see it go.

'Yes,' she said, nodding her acknowledgement that he had understood. She glanced at the withered clematis sagging from its supports and remembered its strong green reaching fingers in summer, the profusion of its mauve-pink blooms. She looked at the flagged space where the barbecue used to stand. They had never been very successful with it, but had been willing victims of the popular belief that it produced something more appealing than the cooker could. She smiled; slow lunches, lazy hours. As lazy as Alexy would tolerate anyway.

'Yes, it's been a favourite weekend place for a long time now. Danielle — Ms Kirkland — has been very generous about letting us come here whenever we liked.'

Alexy had fought about going every time. She wanted nothing more than to stay where she was, lying on her stomach in front of the television and eating as many sweets and crisps as she could lay her hands on. Only if Miranda promised that she could do the same at the cottage would she consent, moaning all the way, to drag herself out to the car.

'You and your family?' Will asked.

'My daughter and I.'

'How old is your daughter?'

'Eleven. We live on our own,' Miranda found herself enlarging, though it was not something she thought about by now, or would normally have mentioned.

'I have two sons. A bit younger. I'm on my own too. In the same boat.'

Will added this with a brief twist of a smile, and Miranda knew he had not reflected that the implication might be unacceptable. She also knew, with a strange certainty, that this unawareness was not characteristic of him, even that the phrase wasn't one he would customarily use. He was making an effort, trying to hit the light note he thought required to refer to a situation that was new to him, and painful. Something else was clear to Miranda; coming to view the cottage was not something he had wanted to do. He had felt obliged to come. Because someone else had said so? Through circumstances? She found she would like to know.

Spring had barely arrived and, sheltered as the little garden might be, it was also bare and uninviting. The air coiling up from the river was cold and smelled more of silt and mud than of salt and the sea.

'Let's go in and have coffee,' Miranda said.

126

Will looked at her and smiled with his eyes, the fan of wrinkles at their corners deepening. His skin was pale, his narrow face deeply lined and the smile didn't reach his lips, but the impression he gave was of reserve rather than dourness, and he seemed a person calmly well-disposed towards all he encountered.

'If you're sure I'm not taking up too much of your time,' he said politely.

They drank their coffee sitting by the window, and Miranda's memories of that first conversation included fleeting gleams of sunlight on the old pine of the table, with its pale but ineradicable red ink stain at one corner, and the intense blue of the scillas in a minute semi-circular bed outside, edged with white stones. She remembered Will's long fingers laced around his mug, relacing into a different pattern as they began to burn. She remembered his quiet voice and his slow nod as she told him something, accepting, inviting more, and she remembered how easy it was to look into his face as she talked, as though they had swum with effortless strokes into some deep, calm pool of knowledge of each other.

(Later he was to say, referring to the strange simplicity of their meeting, 'I was close to tears.')

They washed and dried the coffee mugs, locked the house and went down to the beach. On its dark expanses a few people walked their dogs in the whip of the wind, hunched and brisk, cheeks purple and faces pinched.

'I used to haul Alexy down here whenever I could,' Miranda said. Already the small

127

framework of names was in place. Alexy and Danielle; Will Letham, his sons Adam and Tim. 'She hated it, to be honest, but I feel permanently guilty about how little air and exercise she gets. She's so different from me, I hardly know where to begin. At her age I wasn't interested in anything except games and riding and skiing. She never moves a muscle if she can help it.'

'It can be difficult, living in the city. I'm afraid I let school provide the necessary exercise — luckily both the boys are keen. I'm pretty much an indoor person myself, I must admit. I haven't been too fit lately either,' he added in his quiet voice after a fractional pause.

There was everything to learn about each other. Miranda felt at the same time an instinct to tread carefully, as though too many questions, or the wrong questions, might rub the delicate bloom off the moment, which could never come again, and a surprising need to discover any details that would make his image more complete, more clearly defined in her memory.

Roots. Hers in Highland Perthshire, his in the fatter farming lands of the wide vale of Strathmore. Both took pleasure in talking of them.

'I suppose what I regret most about living in Edinburgh is not being able to share the glen with Alexy, and all that world I used to love so much,' Miranda said, as at last they turned and began to walk back.

'Do you never go back?'

'Oh, occasionally. She finds the whole thing

128

pretty tedious, I'm afraid.'

It had often seemed to Miranda that Alexy was especially obstructive on these expeditions, receiving in sullen silence the idea that she should invite a friend to go with them, playing with some electronic game in the car and refusing to glance out of the window, her response to every suggestion a demand to know how soon they could go home. Miranda would find herself suppressing the very memories she had wanted to share, foregoing in silence visits to favourite haunts, looking at everything with the eyes of a critical tourist, and in the end wondering what on earth they were doing there. The Ross relatives had maintained their obdurate silence, so going to Kilgarth was out of the question. And without some hope of co-operation from Alexy it seemed pointless to try to get in touch with any of her own old friends.

As Miranda drove back to Simla Street after parting from Will, unable for a moment to place herself in the day — morning, afternoon, had she had lunch, what was she supposed to be doing next? — the most significant point to emerge from the throng of details she wanted to pin down and replay in order to enjoy them again, was the way in which she had said to Will things she never said nowadays to anyone. Had said them naturally and simply. Things that mattered to her. And she felt that many things she had not said had also been understood.

★　★　★

Though Miranda learned little of the story on this first day, Will had had a contented and successful career, teaching history first at Dundee High School, then as a junior master at Caterton Lodge, a prep school near Brechin, where he had eventually been made deputy head. With this sound record behind him he had been fortunate enough, when still in his early forties, to be offered a post at Moredun Academy in Edinburgh, and by accepting it he always believed he had invited disaster.

His wife Diana was, like Miranda, an anglicist, though it wasn't a term Miranda would have used. Her special subject had been Old Norse and she had read for her PhD at Uppsala. She was not cut out to be a schoolmaster's wife. At Caterton this had been a drawback but not a problem. They had lived in a cottage in the school grounds, and after a difficult term or so for Will it had been accepted that taking part in any school activity was torture for Diana, and she had been left in peace.

She had settled, apparently contentedly, into a lifestyle that was largely solitary. It had also remained faintly scholarly in that she would bury herself in her texts whenever the inclination seized her, abandoning domestic concerns to take care of themselves. From time to time she had made sallies into well-intentioned pursuits like keeping hens or producing vegetable dyes, experimenting with health fads or perfecting arcane skills like pouncing.

This, while not ideal, worked fairly well until the children arrived. Will had learned not to

130

mind the chaotic state of the house, keeping body and soul together by always having lunch at school, and dinner as well when he was on evening duty. With the advent of first Adam and then, a year later, Tim, things became more difficult. Diana's vagueness was growing in a way only Will was truly aware of, and for a long time he tried to conceal the knowledge even from himself.

It was easy to find excuses for her. He was too rigid and programmed, he couldn't expect her to share his ideas on punctuality and order, her personality was quite different. He had loved her for her gentle vagueness, her air of being unhampered by life's more niggardly demands. He had long been inured to her sporadic housekeeping, and was quite happy to iron his own shirts, take his suits to be cleaned and his shoes to be mended. Every so often he would have a blitz on the kitchen cupboards, followed by a shopping trip to stock up on more realistic items than those the latest food fad had left languishing (and often rotting and smelling) on the shelves.

But leaving a toddler and a newborn baby alone in the cottage with Diana, not sure that they would be fed and changed, or that she wouldn't drift off in pursuit of some whim of her own leaving the doors open and the fire without a guard, was another matter. A period of nagging anxiety began, of covering up for his wife and doing his best to protect the boys, while also giving them some degree of consistency in both love and discipline.

It said much for Will's strength of character, Miranda would think, when over time the painfully released fragments of this story could be pieced together, that he had not only contained the situation at home, but had managed to do so well in his job. Success in his career, however, with a dreadful irony, proved the fatal element, or at least that was how Will would later see it.

The Moredun Academy post came up just as he was beginning to believe a corner had been turned. The boys were now at school in Brechin, still too young for Caterton itself, and that had taken much of the pressure off Diana. She had also finally accepted that there could be medical grounds for her mood-swings and depression, had seen the doctor, agreed to counselling and was now on medication and much more stable.

Will was always to believe, to his shame, that he had wanted the Moredun Academy post so badly that he had convinced himself all would be well. He had talked himself into thinking Diana was more stable because this career move was so desirable. It had been pure selfishness to accept it.

He had, of course, talked the implications through with Diana, taking her to the school and bringing the boys to Edinburgh for a couple of nights so that she and they could decide whether they wanted to live there. What he had not known, and could not have guessed, was that a coveted house-master post would fall vacant within a year, and be offered to him, a virtual newcomer.

By that time Diana had adapted fairly well to the new environment. The boys, a tolerant and easygoing pair, had taken the move in their stride. Will did his best to impress upon Diana that if he accepted the housemaster job she would have her part to play and there would be no getting out of it. With the promotion had come a rather grand, if forbidding, tall terraced house nearby. This large dwelling, with its lingering aura of slow-paced dinners of too many rich courses, its heavy dark furniture, long sash windows, mean draughts and dubious wiring, had played, Will was convinced, a crucial part in what was to come. It was an unwieldy house to run, but since it wasn't allocated to them for their sole benefit it would have to be efficiently looked after, and there would be a good deal of entertaining to do.

'I can still hear myself,' he said to Miranda, finger and thumb pressed to the bridge of his nose, reading glasses pushed up into his hair, his voice thin with a tired guilt he could never shake off. 'Efficiently run. Entertaining. I actually used those words. Was I blinded by my own ambitions? I was the person who made the decision, I, the one person who should have known it was asking the impossible.'

He had been very busy, immersed in the demands of a job which he enjoyed but which had a great deal more to it than an ordinary teaching post. When Miranda pointed this out he said at once, 'I knew it would be like that, though, and it was precisely what I should have taken into account.'

Miranda suspected that what happened might have come about in any case, from other causes, or simply as a result of the tragic flaw in Diana's make-up. But conscious of her own ignorance of the subject, and also understanding that no amount of rationalisation would help Will, who had to work through this for himself and in his own time, she said nothing.

Diana had become more and more erratic and unreliable, dressing weirdly, forgetting appointments, failing to collect the boys from school, bringing home strange assortments of food, and once serving a stone-cold *coq au vin* to a visiting cardinal, who, Will had thought with protective indignation at the time, could have exhibited more human sympathy and understanding, and less concern for his already ample stomach.

The end when it came struck a sensational note which made it all the harder for Will to bear. In the middle of an ordinary weekday morning, with the boys at school and nothing happening that he could ever pinpoint to trigger such a bizarre action, Diana, dressed only in a ragged nightdress, left the house and, reaching the busy road into the town centre before anyone stopped her, stepped out into the flow of traffic. Nothing hit her, though a crash was only avoided by the swift reactions of two competent drivers. A passer-by pulled Diana back onto the pavement, a concerned knot of people gathered around her, the traffic moved on.

Apart from covering her up and the difficulty of finding out who this shivering, silent and blank-eyed woman was and where she lived, there seemed no serious problem. But Diana had for some time only been pretending to take her medication, and this morning had mixed what she had kept back with all the pills she could find in the house and swallowed the lot. The damage was already too serious for her to survive.

# 11

The publicity surrounding Diana's death, and
the angle the papers had seized upon — that she
had been neglected or in some way maltreated,
and that there was a sexual connotation because
she hadn't been properly dressed — had rocked
gentle Will to such an extent that for a time he
could barely cope with ordinary living.

'I couldn't hold down the job, of course. I
realise now they should have told me sooner that
I wasn't fit to do it. I suppose they wanted to
give me every chance. I didn't even see it
coming. I thought I was better, but I must have
been gradually going to pieces and wasn't even
aware of it. I hate to think now of how I must
— Anyway, I was in hospital for a while.' His
voice was jerky, tight, warning that he didn't
want Miranda to comment. He had not talked of
this to anyone. 'A sort of breakdown, they said.
Everyone was incredibly kind and helpful. The
school bent over backwards to make things as
easy as they could. My parents — they live near
Kelso — had the boys for a while. My father's
retired now, of course. He used to work for *The
Scotsman*. My mother had a fall a few years ago
and has been pretty well housebound since, so it
wasn't easy for them to cope. But they did what
they could.'

His tone was affectionate but wry too, as
though the problems of that time could still drag

at him with the knowledge of his failure to cope, and the weight of gratitude for all he had been obliged to accept.

'The boys were amazing. They looked after me when it should have been the other way round.' Will's face was turned away and Miranda knew he didn't want her to see his expression. 'A lot of arrangements were made on my behalf that I didn't even know about. Caterton Lodge, the school at Brechin, agreed to take the boys earlier than planned. Tim isn't even eight. It was a sensible move, because it was a familiar environment for them, and it saved finding some interim solution, but it was strange, finding that the step had already been taken and they'd gone. Such a major step. Once they go to boarding-school you have to accept that the pattern's set for good. School, university, jobs. Only part of their lives will ever be spent at home again, with you. Oh, don't misunderstand me,' Will added, suddenly aware of the regret in his voice, 'I was only too thankful they'd been taken care of so well. But it was a bit strange to find everything was in place.'

Miranda, imagining how she would feel if Alexy were removed from her in such a way, without her knowledge or agreement, could readily relate to the emptiness of such a moment, and the emptiness of the days that followed.

They were leaning towards each other across a small table in a Rose Street coffee bar, oblivious to the noise and movement around them. It was not the first time they had met like this. It

137

was Miranda's lunch hour and she had warned the two assistants who now did most of the office work (one of whom, Hazel, very usefully doubled as a minder for Alexy in the holidays or after school) that she might be back late. She so rarely was, often not bothering about lunch at all, that they had been full of friendly approval, urging her to take as long as she liked.

'So you're looking for a house for when the boys are home?' she asked Will, turning to a safe practical aspect. 'You mean to stay in the Edinburgh area?'

'I'll have to find some kind of post, perhaps fill in with supply teaching while I'm looking. I have to be where the jobs are.'

'There's no chance of your going back to your previous one?'

Will looked at her and hesitated. 'I'm not really sure how well I am,' he said quietly after a moment. 'I'm still on the sick list, officially. I couldn't look at a job like that at present, with so many varied demands and such a degree of involvement. But I shall teach again, of course. I shall find something.'

In the brisker tone she heard the deep-seated fear that he would never be able to return to his profession, or perform adequately within it if he did.

'I need to find somewhere to live which will suit the boys, but it really ought to be more central than the Cramond cottage. Also the price would stretch me, to be honest. I'd always planned to buy one day. It can be a dangerous trap, living in accommodation that goes with the job. My father's adamant that he'll help with school fees, which is a great help, but even so I shouldn't stretch the budget too far. In fact, I shouldn't have let you waste your time showing me the house, and I ought to let Miss Kirkland know without delay that I'm not interested. Sadly.'

His eyes smiled at her, and Miranda laughed.

'I'm glad you did look at it,' she assured him.

In the event, Will didn't buy a house. He stayed in his rented accommodation in Colinton, built as a granny flat and very cramped when the boys were home, until the autumn, when he and Miranda combined their households two flights up in Simla Street, in the first-floor flat.

★　★　★

It seemed huge compared to the basement, with two bedrooms, a dining-room which they turned into a third, large drawing-room, study, and big kitchen looking out over the same familiar view. Its price terrified Will but not Miranda, used as she was to dealing daily with Edinburgh rentals at the top of the market.

She was a partner in the letting agency now, the refurbishing and hands-on care of the properties her special area. Danielle, a ferocious worker with few interests outside her job, still fielded the twenty-four-hour emergency call service, admitting to enjoying the hassle and dramas.

'I'm crisis-dependent, don't believe I'm functioning unless I've got a problem to deal with.' Sure enough, she would be at her most buoyant after a Christmas spent hounding plumbers and electricians, or airport trips to meet planes that were hours late or diverted, bearing clients from Saudi Arabia, Japan or Buenos Aires.

Miranda, for her part, had developed skills of her own in grooming the opulent apartments for which they paid so steeply. There was a real buzz in knowing she had got it right, integrating the latest kitchen innovations or bathroom trends into the traditional style of the elegant terraces, co-ordinating colours and fabrics while supplying as discreetly as possible the essential technology, and chasing down every tiny detail.

Walking home one day in a mood of mellow euphoria, after lunching with a delighted client who had also proved excellent company, she suddenly remembered for some reason the casual housekeeping of Charteris Wynd. Smiling, but with a little stab of pain, she wondered if perhaps Georgina's standards had rubbed off after all?

Georgina was now living in Gloucestershire, as Miranda had always guessed she would given the chance. Graeme had died three years ago, slipping away one morning as he sat on the terrace under the shade of the great vine, the *Financial Times* unopened before him. The simplicity of his departure more than compensated, in the view of both his wife and daughter, for the bureaucratic tangles they had to unravel to bring him home. He had provided well for them both, but for Miranda the influx of capital

140

had been more unsettling than reassuring. There had no longer been any need to stay in the basement flat; she had her own excellent salary; Ian took care of every expense for Alexy. It was bizarre to cling to this limited and unsatisfactory accommodation.

Everyone had put this to her. Her mother, obliged to stay in a hotel when visiting and finding it a soulless arrangement; Danielle, who had never reached more than a wary truce with Alexy and thought the way Miranda still had her in her room both weird and incredible; and Ian, though he was more tactful, when he visited Alexy.

For in spite of his deep sense of rejection after his first return, he hadn't found himself able to keep to his resolve of making a complete break. He had done his best to fill his life, and not only with work. Though business interests still came first, an absorbing one at this time being the setting up of a new charter airline, he had acquired a beach bungalow on an island in the Great Barrier Reef where he enjoyed scuba diving and deep sea fishing. At least tussles with the great black marlin occupied the mind. But no matter how strenuously he filled his life, the tug was still there, part of him, and he had started to come back on a regular basis, doggedly persisting with his visits so that, no matter what Alexy thought of him, he was part of her life. That was all he wanted, to keep the link intact. When she was older she could make her own decisions about keeping in touch.

These visits weren't easy. Though both parents

141

tried to find out how Alexy felt about them, they didn't get very far. She was grudging about every plan mooted, not appearing to care whether Ian came or not.

'You don't have to do anything you don't want to,' Miranda would urge, seeing the scowling face and the arms tightly wrapped round her chest as Alexy waited for her father to collect her. 'Just say what you'd like.' Alexy would hunch a shoulder, her face mutinous. If Miranda persisted she would turn on the television and become intent on whatever appeared on the screen. Returning from outings all she would say was, 'I got lots of presents,' or crow about Ian providing some extravagant treat which she knew would annoy her mother.

She was no more communicative to Ian, though she was prepared to enthuse about the presents, not wanting the supply to dry up. The most he extracted if he probed for a response about anything else was, 'It's OK, I suppose.' He found these occasions gruelling, both emotionally and in terms of getting through the time. He saw himself in the classic role of trying to please, hoping in a few hours to establish the closeness which needed days and years of everyday life in which to develop — chaotic breakfasts, bedtime stories, tears in the night, and seeing in different moods the small face he knew only as watchful and calculating. He wanted to see Alexy laughing, or absorbed in something that fascinated her, anything but locked in this unrelenting reserve. And he wanted to see pleasure in her face at the sight of him.

142

He would fly back to Sydney tortured by the gulf between all he was missing and the reality of the stumbling, effortful hours spent with a child who was a stranger.

The less justification there was for remaining in the flat, still sharing her bedroom with Alexy, the more Miranda felt an irrational need to stay. She couldn't explain it even to herself. Resisting the words unhealthy and unnatural, she nevertheless found them constantly in her mind. But what actual objection could there be? The room was huge, Alexy was deprived of nothing that other children had, in fact her belongings took up three-quarters of the space. If friends came home with her after school she could be with them there as if it were her exclusive territory. But Miranda noticed that if one was too outspoken in her amazement — 'You have to share a room with your *mother*? Yuk, gross!' — she wouldn't be seen again. Then, knowing she was glossing over the issue, she would remind herself that none of these friends lasted long anyway. Alexy was essentially a loner.

When, as she sometimes did, Miranda made herself dig deeper through the layers of excuses and half-truths to her true reason for clinging to this long-outgrown arrangement, she realised that she was putting off making a change through fear, the primitive dread of finding herself alone in a room at night without another living presence near. It would mean finally accepting that she was a person alone.

She knew that having acknowledged this she should be able to deal with it. It was unreasonable and absurd and she was ashamed of it. But she couldn't bring herself to talk about it, even to Danielle. Or especially not to Danielle, who considered living alone the ideal state, and whose rooted dislike of Alexy would have made her astringently outspoken on such a point.

It was concern over the long-term effect on Alexy that finally induced Miranda to try to establish how she felt about it.

'Alexy, I've been wondering, are you beginning to get a bit tired of sharing a room?' she found a chance to ask, her voice more tentative than she had meant it to be. 'Now that you're getting older, I mean.'

Alexy instantly caught that tentative note, and her head came up. With the nicely calculated scorn of someone twice her age, she looked round her deliberately. 'Why, do you want me to sleep in the kitchen?'

'Darling, no, of course not. I meant that it may be time to think of moving, finding somewhere bigger.'

Silence. Alexy pulled a cushion against her chest and clasped it to her.

'Wouldn't you rather have a room of your own?' Miranda could hear herself already sounding cajoling.

Alexy, however, had no intention of revealing how she felt, about this or anything else. She stared at the blank television screen, as though longing for the moment of release from this boring topic, and remained mute. She had perfected the trick of letting her eyes go out of

144

focus, and all Miranda's efforts to elicit some response were met by this irritating blankness. Only when she heard exasperation rising in her mother's voice did Alexy ask, 'You mean we're going to live with Daddy again?'

Winded, Miranda stared at her. Where had this idea come from? Was it something Alexy privately dreamed of? Had her friends said something? Or had Ian talked of it? Surely not; that would be outrageous, unforgivable.

Alexy's eyes swivelled to her mother's face, and a look of satisfaction briefly gleamed in them.

★　★　★

The easiest course had been to stay. Miranda, assuring herself of this, would try to push back into whatever dark corner they'd come from doubts about her subconscious motives for doing so. Did the flat represent for her, still, something she wasn't prepared to relinquish? But what possible lingering feelings could she have for it, the scene of so much quarrelling and despair, so much bitter frustration during the years when Alexy was small, when she had been trapped here, alone, cut off from everything, while Ian . . .

The unavoidable encounters when he was over were not pleasant. They circled each other warily, ready to read accusation or criticism into the simplest comment. Only once, when Alexy was seriously ill with bronchitis and Ian flew back without hesitation the moment Miranda

145

contacted him, was their hostility forgotten, no longer important in the shadow of this shared anxiety.

But, grateful as she had been to him for coming so quickly, and for his support through the crisis — how luxurious it had felt, though she never said so, to be free for a while of the unrelenting burden of sole responsibility — Miranda reverted to antagonism as soon as it was safely over. It was almost as though, without the familiar anger to underpin her thoughts, she wouldn't have known how to live any more.

After she and Will met, their ease together and pleasure in each other never in doubt from the first day, this undercurrent of anger did finally begin to weaken. Though when they started to look for somewhere to live, it was ironic that they should find what they wanted not only in Simla Street but in the same house, when a larger flat, ideal for their needs, became vacant with timing that seemed almost too good to be true.

For Miranda the main criterion was to stay within walking distance of Alexy's school, and ideally of the agency as well. Will had thought a garden where the boys could kick a ball around would be good, but as they were always so adaptable he felt he couldn't make it a requirement. As to the rest, he was easy. Obviously the primary need was for space, for neither he nor Miranda imagined that merging the two families was going to be simple, and obviously the less everyone was on top of each other the better.

Alexy, inevitably, was the chief worry but, in

146

spite of distressing scenes when the subject of living with Will was broached, this time Miranda knew she couldn't be allowed to have her own way. In fact, Miranda was aware that by making available to her, whether she wanted it or not, this broader family scene, she was probably giving her the best thing in her power to offer. Not that anything would persuade Alexy of it. Miranda winced at the prospect of the battles to come.

# 12

When Miranda thought of her life with Will one word always came to mind, a word she wouldn't have used aloud to anyone, her private word of gratitude and love. Assuagement. That was how it felt, an assuagement of loneliness and self-doubt, of single-handed battling, decision making and responsibility. There was a sensation of time slowing, of being able to stand back and look at things with less urgency at last, a feeling of elbow-room, of pressures lifting — and of warm, secure happiness.

There were major adjustments to be made, of course. For Miranda there was the feeling of emerging from a familiar burrow where, in practical if not in emotional terms, no demands would be made which she couldn't meet. There was, too, a sensation of coming into the light, blinking and hesitating, which made her see how out of touch she had allowed herself to become with other people's reality.

The new flat seemed amazingly spacious and, after a bedroom where the light always had to be on, her new room was a delight, if at first a trifle bare since it wasn't strewn with Alexy's belongings. Only when Adam and Tim's possessions were in place in the room they were to share did Miranda realise how much, by comparison, she and Ian had lavished on Alexy.

Will owned little apart from his books. He had

a minimal wardrobe of comfortable, well-worn clothes, always put off till the last moment the chore of shopping, and when he could avoid it no longer bought clothes as like his old ones as he could find. He wasn't a man for gadgets and technology either, and would happily have done without a car if he had had only himself to consider. He was impervious to heat and cold, and couldn't have said what colour the carpet was or what pictures were on the walls. Miranda, whose daily business it was to exercise herself about such things, found his obliviousness rather soothing.

The only thing she missed about the basement flat, very much at first though she didn't say so, was the door to the yard and her regular intake of sun and air. The difference in living two floors up was something she hadn't quite taken into account, and though the great sash windows ran up easily and she could always sit on a sill to read in the sun, the sense of being shut off from out-of-doors persisted.

Adam and Tim, as Will had guessed they would, adapted cheerfully to their new circumstances. If they minded not having a garden they kept the fact to themselves. They were at home in the city and soon found interests and occupations for themselves in a way Alexy never seemed able to do. Will made them members of a nearby sports club and they spent a lot of time in the gym, at the nets or playing football according to season. They had bicycles, which Miranda had been doubtful about, but Will trusted their good sense and, beyond requiring them to ask before leaving an agreed area, let them go.

Miranda, beginning to adjust to sharing decisions and already trusting Will's judgement, realised with dismay how unenterprising and inward-looking she had let Alexy's life become.

'I used to try to do things with her,' she said guiltily to Will, 'but then as she got older she seemed to despise every suggestion I made, and when Alexy sets her face against something there's no point in persisting. I suppose in the end it was easier to concentrate on my own affairs and simply let her do what she wanted, which was be on her own.'

'Yes, but being left to cope alone with one child is very different from having two,' Will reminded her. 'The boys have always had each other to do things with.' They were also as different from disdainful, resistant Alexy as it was possible to be.

Miranda in her turn didn't make the observation that Adam and Tim's independence must to a great extent be a result of their mother's erratic care. Accustomed to doing everything for Alexy, she had been astonished by how aware they were of the practicalities of running a house. They would hang up wet towels, empty the dishwasher, add items that were running out to the shopping list, put their washing in the laundry basket and if necessary forage for their own food. Though this efficiency may have been prompted by self-interest, the fact remained that they didn't regard their welfare as devolving automatically on the nearest adult.

It made Miranda realise how, by her over-anxious care, not forgetting a cowardly wish to avoid conflict, she had more or less incapacitated Alexy, who was three years older than Adam.

Alexy, predictably, was the source of most of the difficulties and disruption as the little group of five began to take shape as a new entity. Miranda, ashamed of how her offspring was behaving, but even more ashamed to have the poor job she herself had made of bringing her up so blatantly exposed, was quick to flare into exasperation. It was Will who would plead Alexy's cause, though not in front of her. While she was there he confined himself to taking the heat out of the immediate situation if he could.

'This is the hardest thing she's ever had to face,' he would remind Miranda. 'She's had you to herself for virtually her whole life. She may pretend to be self-sufficient, but we're wrenching her out of an unusually close one-to-one relationship, and giving her no choice about it.'

Though he never referred directly to Miranda having shared her room with Alexy for so many years, suspecting that her own need for this proximity had in fact been the decisive factor, he thought it more than time for such an unhealthy arrangement to end. 'Don't forget,' he said instead, 'that for her these changes are very raw and new. We must give her time.'

'But you've all had to move too.'

'True, but the break-up we had to face is well behind us now. We've had time to adjust.'

'Alexy's so horrible to the boys,' Miranda said

guiltily. 'None of this is their fault.'

'I think we should let the three of them work it out for themselves,' Will advised. 'I can't see much that Alexy can say or do upsetting my pair. It'll be water off a duck's back as far as they're concerned. They won't let her go too far. Come on, you can't exactly imagine them lying awake at night worrying about it, can you?'

This Miranda, smiling, had to concede.

'I'm not sure what I've done to turn Alexy into such a dreadful person, though,' she said ruefully. 'I know I've got a temper, and Ian could lose his pretty dramatically on occasion too, but Alexy has a capacity all her own for cold hostility and a sort of — I don't know — inner resentment which never lets her enjoy anything. It's something I find hard to understand, yet somewhere along the line I must have been the cause.'

'You don't really believe that?' Will asked.

She shrugged. 'There's only been me. I don't think I can dodge the consequences.'

'What about her genetic make-up? Going back further than either you or her father?'

Miranda's eyes widened. 'Goodness.'

'Well?' Will smiled, watching her. Sometimes she seemed very young to him. He admired and valued her capacity to get things done, her glowing health, her straightforward way of tackling problems, so different from Diana's self-absorbed vagueness, but at moments like this, when she turned to him for reassurance, he thought he loved her even more.

'Gregory!' Miranda exclaimed. 'Ian's father,

152

and the most horrendously bad-tempered person you could ever meet. His sisters are nearly as bad, come to think of it. One of them is, anyway. And Ian's mother, who died when he was still at school, was a pretty dismal character too. You know, Will,' Miranda frowned in concentration, and Will could see he'd given her plenty to think about, 'it really might be part of the answer. I've always believed Alexy was so difficult because she resented me for driving Ian away, and blamed me for living as we did, only child, single parent, all of it. I never thought of family traits, perhaps because we never saw much of the Rosses. I just felt I wasn't providing a proper life for her, but couldn't see what to do about it.'

'Oh, sweet, you did your best,' Will protested, putting an arm round her. 'No one can do more. However you'd lived — and not all that many options are available to a single parent, remember — nothing could have altered Alexy's basic character. We can only do what's to hand, and you've held down a pretty demanding job as well as bringing up a child. A child who's highly intelligent, moreover. I suppose you realise that?'

'I know she does well at school,' Miranda admitted, instantly ready to be consoled by this. Then she laughed at herself. 'Oh yes, very clever, calm the mother down by praising the child. But, to be fair, if Alexy is bright then it's down to Ian, not me.'

'Don't sell yourself short,' Will said, giving her a hug. 'What parent in the world can say, hand on heart, 'I've done a brilliant job'? Perhaps we'd better wait a few years before we do any judging.

Who knows what those three are going to throw at us?'

'What indeed,' Miranda agreed with feeling. With Alexy on the brink of her teens the scope seemed limitless.

But, against all probability, Will's quiet and even-handed authority had its effect. Whether it was an instinctive response to the father figure till now absent from her life, or whether the refusal of the two boys to let her faze them or interfere with their lives in any way stumped Alexy, Miranda wasn't sure but, as they settled into the new pattern of living, Alexy's antagonism was much less in evidence. She still maintained her watchful reserve, and no one could have called her ideal company, but at last Miranda could feel love for her unmixed with anxious defensiveness. More optimistic about the future than she could have believed possible, she was deeply grateful to Will for what he had achieved.

The biggest adjustment for Miranda herself was sharing her life with a man again. Sharing a home, a room, a bed, her body, with Will. Though the calm certainty of their need for each other had always included sex, there had been little opportunity to enjoy it in the months after they met. Not only had it been out of the question in her own flat with Alexy always on hand, but Miranda hadn't felt very relaxed about it when she had gone to Will's flat in Colinton either. Alexy wasn't used to her being out in the evenings. Although she had grudgingly accepted that Miranda couldn't always be there when she

154

came home from school, and had eventually stopped giving Hazel a hard time, she had bitterly resisted the idea of having to go to bed while her mother was still out. Though Miranda had sometimes insisted on going on principle, seeing through Will's eyes how thoroughly she had allowed Alexy to get the upper hand, the storms when she left hadn't produced a mood very conducive to love-making.

Perhaps too she had been ready to have a slow pace imposed. On the brink of a new life, with her sustainable and familiar one cracking apart, her mind had inevitably turned back to the years with Ian. Even now, after all the fighting and the bitterness, after the long separation and the exchanges as between strangers when he came to see Alexy, treacherous responses could still wake when memories caught her unawares. Nothing had ever matched the physical impact he had had on her, and images of him, laughing, teasing, full of exuberant energy, sweeping her along with him, could still shake her by their vividness.

Will stirred none of these extreme reactions, and she was glad of it. She wasn't sure she would have been able to cope with them at this stage. There had been so few men in her life since Ian had left, either on a personal level or, rather oddly as she saw now, in day-to-day contacts. Other parents she met, the staff at the office, the friends she'd made through Danielle, were almost exclusively female. Would the picture have been the same, she wondered, if she'd run into someone different when making her move back into the work-place?

In a loving relationship once more, she realised how unquestioning she had allowed a blanket intolerance of men to become. It had suited her to lump them all under the same heading — selfish, irresponsible and arrogant, paying lip service to equality because the times demanded it, but light years away from genuinely subscribing to it.

Will was as far from this stereotype as it was possible to be. His whole self was focused on caring for his new household and making it work, hardly believing in the good fortune which had brought him Miranda. Her looks, her fit young body, the courage and determination with which she had carved out a career for herself, could still make her seem someone totally beyond his reach, and he would wake at night thinking it had all been a dream, dazed with relief to find her there beside him. He could never have put into words his longing to keep her safe, to make her feel secure in his love and care for her and to loosen, very gently, the stranglehold of mutual need which he saw as harmful both to her and to Alexy.

In all, it was a deeply happy and positive time for Will. His parents were delighted that he had someone new in his life after the tragedies of the past, though not quite able to resist asking when he and Miranda hoped to marry. And Will's sister Carol, not as a rule greatly involved in family affairs, not only wrote to Will and Miranda but came in person to wish them well.

Will, who had his own sense of humour, said

156

nothing to warn Miranda, who was thunder-struck when a talkative, flamboyant extrovert came swanning in, dressed in a style that made her blink. With very high heels, very tight skirt, professional make-up and a great deal of splendid bosom on view, she was as unlikely a sister for Will as could well be imagined. Apart from the good deal of bosom, there was a good deal of bright rippling hair, plus billowing waves of expensive scent and sexy vitality.

'They hadn't told you about me, had they?' she challenged Miranda, clearly amused, when Will had gone to make coffee after lunch.

'Of course I knew Will had a sister,' Miranda protested with give-away haste. 'He told me you ran your own business in Glasgow and were very successful.'

'Yeah, I bet,' Carol said, the amusement deepening. 'I run a dating agency. Mum and Dad, poor dears, equate it to being a madam, and Will's not much better. You can see why I'm a bit detached from the family scene. I'm there, though, if you need me, so don't forget it, and I'm delighted you and Will have got together.'

For both Miranda and Will it was an enjoyable visit, and it was good to know that both families gave their backing. For Georgina too made no secret of her pleasure that Miranda was no longer alone, and she had taken at once to Adam and Tim, hardly daring to believe they could be as laid-back and amenable as they seemed, after the years of tip-toeing round Alexy and holding her tongue about what she saw as Miranda's glaring errors in bringing her up.

This was a good time for Miranda, and for Will too, full of hope and happiness, though Will was never quite able to recover his pleasure and satisfaction in his work. At first he did supply teaching which, though no one could call it an easy option and it was often both frustrating and exhausting, did have the advantage of limited involvement. School politics and in-fighting which created a teaching environment he found deeply alien could at least be left behind when his stint was done. However strange it felt not to be engaged in every aspect of school life, it wasn't possible, or required, to take problems home with him.

Before long, however, hoping to find it more rewarding, he took a full-time post at Calton College of Further Education and here he encountered attitudes, from both staff and pupils, so far from everything he believed education to be about that before long he felt threatened all over again by the stress and self-doubt which had ended by putting him in hospital. Constantly tired, he began to suffer from headaches and occasionally from blurred vision, though he accounted for both by telling himself he'd been reading too much and sitting up too late. He had his eyes checked, got new glasses, put a stronger bulb in the reading lamp on his desk.

And he made an effort to rationalise his failure to relate to his new students.

'It makes me realise how privileged I've been,' he confessed to Miranda. 'Having the system behind one, providing an ambience where knowledge can be imparted without a running fight, was a luxury I didn't even recognise at the time.' And even then I couldn't hold down the job, the cold voice of fear reminded him.

'It's a big step,' Miranda comforted. 'And these mature students, who've made the effort to return to education, must need you more than the boys did.'

'That's the trouble,' Will said restlessly. 'They do, but I'm simply not on their wavelength. I talk a different language. They stare at me with a sort of weary disgust, if they bother to turn up at all. They never ask a question, because they know I couldn't answer it in terms that would mean anything to them.'

'Perhaps there'll be that one student whose life you'll alter for ever,' Miranda suggested.

He smiled at her, knowing she was doing her best to cheer him up, but also knowing how far he was from conveying to her his gnawing anxiety about his failure to adjust.

The deepest source of his self-doubt, however, and this of all things he couldn't say to her, was the decision not to marry. Miranda had been so definite about it that letting her have her way had seemed the only course open to him. He suspected Danielle's influence, though that he wisely kept to himself. But he wanted to marry, wanted the certainty and commitment, the long view, wanted to know that he and Miranda and the children were now one unit, going forward together.

He had felt his first serious pangs of jealousy over Ian when Miranda had refused to change her mind. He knew that for him there was none of the passion she had felt for this first love, who had been part of her life from her earliest days. He had consoled himself by thinking that if the heights of passion weren't there, then neither were the depths of anger and bitterness, and he'd tried to convince himself that he was content to settle for that. Now uncertainty rode him. Did Miranda not see their commitment to each other as long-lasting? Had she compromised because of Alexy?

His earlier worries about not being able to offer enough in the relationship, and make what he saw as his due contribution to their joint home, assailed him again. Miranda had provided the bulk of the finance for the flat, Miranda continued to hold down a demanding job and run her enlarged household with impressive ease, while he . . .

As he slept less well, tormented at night by doubts of his own abilities, ill at ease by day in the philistine atmosphere of the college, he began to be obsessed by the strength of the hold Alexy still had over her mother, which he saw as extending to him, through Miranda, and to Adam and Tim through him. The idea that Miranda was resisting marriage because of her took deeper root.

Off balance as he was at this time, though not yet aware of what was happening to him, Will began to lose the ground he had gained with Alexy, and she, sensing with the hyperacute antennae of the profoundly self-centred a shift in his attitude towards her, instantly drew back.

To Miranda's dismay, the trust and communication which had begun to develop between them was swiftly eroded. It had meant so much to her to see Alexy drop her guard even a little, allowing others to glimpse the good qualities Miranda so passionately believed she possessed. How good that had been, and how hopeful for the future it had made her.

# 13

It felt so strange to be taking the well-known road to Kilgarth again, after all this time.

Miranda had known that by coming she would be putting herself at the mercy of a whole range of emotions, but even so found she wasn't prepared for their potency. First and most obviously, the sight of Glen Maraich itself filled her with delight, nostalgia and a piercing sense of loss. It was nearly the end of May, and the great copper beeches bordering the drive to Sillerton were magnificent in the delicate pinky-fawn of spring foliage. Slowing to admire them, Miranda recalled hearing from Georgina that the Hays were finding it increasingly difficult to keep their huge and cumbersome house going. With none of the younger generation willing to take it on, there were even rumours that they might sell. Miranda pushed the thought away, wanting, today, everything in this landscape of childhood to be as she remembered it.

Down here on the low ground, fields were vivid with new grass, and though the daffodils had long been over in Edinburgh a few were still to be seen in the gardens of the sparsely scattered houses. As she turned into the narrow side road and began to climb, her first glimpse of the hills ahead almost startled her. The eye definitely adjusted to a different scale if one stayed away too long. She felt tingling excitement rise to be back at last.

Equally powerful were the memories that jostled, streaming back so rapidly that she could hardly pin them down. Driving through Muirend, the figures of the past had been so clear — her mother, elegant and brisk, slim and active, smiling and loving; her father, more muted and restrained, distanced from her, it was easy now to recognise, by lifelong worries over the decline of a business which had in reality always flourished; and herself, a happy, secure, confident and privileged child, tripping dutifully down the hill each day to the sanitised security of her posh private school. What a little horror she must have been.

Not far to go now. She was already within walking distance of the loch and the boathouse, where in summer they had spent so much of their time. Those peaceful hours of fishing, the endlessly drawn-out summer gloaming (not forgetting the midges), the swimming, the picnics, the days when rain drove them inside and they lit the old iron stove and played poker for hours, packed round the big wooden table that always smelled of fish. A lifetime away. Yet the people who had shared that place were still here, many of them, busy with their own changed lives.

How could she have allowed herself to lose touch with them so completely? With a panicked feeling that these final moments were slipping by too fast, that she must hold on to them, she wasn't ready, she groped to piece together bits of news relayed to her over the years by Georgina.

Archie Napier, she knew, had divorced his first wife Cecil and married again, and gloomy Drumveyn had been transformed, it seemed, by his new young wife. And children? Hadn't there been word of a child or children? There had been other changes in Glen Ellig. Janey Buchanan had died, and Sally now owned Grianan, though no one seemed sure what she intended to do with it. Here, the Munros were back at Allt Farr, and at neighbouring Riach James Mackenzie, whose wife had been killed in a bizarre accident, of which there seemed to be several versions, had been left with small twin daughters to bring up.

But there was no time to sift or assemble these fragments, for as she crested a rise there ahead stood the square, solid house of Kilgarth, staring out across the glen, its face to the sun.

Suddenly Miranda found her hands were trembling so violently that she could scarcely hold the wheel. Shaken, she pulled onto a level patch of turf where tourist cars often paused to enjoy the sight of the hills stretching away mile upon mile to the west. But it was not the crowding memories nor the spectacular view which had produced this physical reaction, and she knew it. It was the presence, real and close, of Ian.

From the moment she had turned off the A9, slipping away into the hills, the image of him had been there behind all the other thoughts — Ian with his fit, compact body, his dark good looks and teasing eyes, his laughter, his vibrant energy which could lift the mood of a room the moment

164

he walked into it. Ian as he had been, before the fighting began. Before Alexy.

Closing her eyes, Miranda gave in at last to that insistent image; let herself hear his voice, let her fingertips remember the feel of his skin. With a response so emphatic that the intervening years seemed wiped away, her own skin was at once aware and alive. It seemed incredible, and unbearably sad, that he, the young, vital Ian who had loved her so much, was not there at Kilgarth, waiting for her; that he would never exist again.

She tilted back her head in an attempt to stem the tears. But they welled up just the same, escaping her tightly squeezed lids, rolling down her cheeks, and she knew she was weeping for lost youth as much as for Ian — that evanescent, irreclaimable time, with its glow and enthusiasm, its vivid passions and heedless optimism.

Then with a fierce effort she got the tears under control. To give way to them, to break down and sob, as she longed to do, was no way to prepare herself for the encounter ahead. For she was on her way to visit Ian's father, Gregory, the unforgiving tyrant himself, and mature thirty-something woman as she might be, she couldn't for a moment fool herself into imagining that she would find him any less daunting now than memory painted him. He might be more daunting, in fact, for he had had fifteen years in which to brood over his anger and disappointment. Knowing the Ross temperament, Miranda was not naive enough to

165

hope that the effect would have been mellowing or salutary.

However, he had summoned her; that was worth bearing in mind. Or, more precisely, he had summoned Alexy. After years of obdurate silence, with not a word from any member of the family (and Miranda knew, from her contacts with Ian over Alexy's affairs, that for him too severance had been complete), this curt message had arrived.

Miranda had always seen it as her duty, though sometimes she hadn't been quite sure why, to keep her father-in-law informed of Alexy's progress. She supposed she had had some woolly idea of not depriving her daughter of her rightful connection with her father's family, though Alexy herself showed no more interest in the Rosses than she did in her maternal grandmother, whose visits she endured with uncooperative sullenness.

Nevertheless, any major events affecting her, which naturally had included Miranda making a new home with Will, had been duly reported, though Miranda had long ago given up expecting any response. In the three years since then there had been little to communicate and Miranda had included what facts there were with her annual Christmas card. She had always pictured Gregory cursing furiously when he opened the envelopes, if he ever got that far, and pitching the cards straight onto the fire.

What had made him demand to see Alexy now? As a first move towards a reconciliation with Ian? Or had he already been in touch with

166

Ian? (Why that pang of — what, feeling sidelined, being left out? How odd.) Or was Gregory's health failing? Was he becoming aware of his age? She tried to work it out. Mid-seventies? So what did that make the aunts? She had a feeling they were younger than Gregory, though as a child they had all seemed a million to her, much older than her own parents. Were they even still alive, she wondered as she pulled out onto the road again. And still living in that dank little cottage? What on earth did they find to do there? She had never considered the question before.

In another second she was passing the cottage. It stood lower than Kilgarth itself, and Miranda saw how closely mature trees and evergreens crowded round it. Had it always been so enclosed and she hadn't noticed? More to the point, why was she clutching at such trivia? To displace her dread of what was coming?

She hadn't told Gregory she would be alone, but she had had no intention of exposing Alexy to some bitter attack, or alternatively to some calculated play for affection, without first sounding out the ground. She hadn't asked Will to come as moral support, nor — something quite new — had she told him where she was going. There was no reason for him to be disturbed by unnecessary doubts or questions if, in the event, this meeting with Gregory was to have no impact on their lives. She had left the house this morning at her usual time; she would be out, as usual, all day. There was nothing there to worry him.

By now Will's health was a constant source of anxiety. Miranda would always be convinced that he had gone back into full-time teaching far too soon, in an environment where his gentle and scholarly approach had been undervalued if not actually scorned. He had come close to a second breakdown before she had been able to convince him that, no matter how important it was to him to feel he was an equal contributor in the household, the Calton College job was not the answer.

There had been a strained period when he had doggedly gone after job after job, no matter how unsuitable, each rejection making him look more weary and dragged down. Eventually Miranda had persuaded him to talk the painful issue through, and he had admitted that by this stage the very thought of facing a class appalled him. The idea that pupils should come to him, so obvious once it was put forward that she was angry with herself for not thinking of it before, had been Miranda's. Will had good contacts in the academic world, and quite soon a steady trickle of students had appeared at the flat. On a one-to-one basis Will was able to give, as it was his nature to do, every ounce of himself, and with tangible results to show for it the debilitating sense of inadequacy ceased to torture him, to Miranda's immense relief.

His health, however, had not correspondingly improved. He was easily tired, the least stress causing a swift adrenalin rise, and more than once he had confessed to a blurring of vision. A year after he and Miranda had started living together he had been diagnosed as diabetic which, though it had meant adapting to a new and rigid regime, had at least meant that the symptoms had been recognised and could be dealt with.

Miranda had been thankful, when the diagnosis was made, that Will had already been working at home and she wouldn't have to worry about his driving. His natural preference for solitude and quiet meant that being in the house all day was no hardship for him. Still concerned, however, that Miranda was carrying more than her share of the domestic load, he had decided to learn to cook and, to his surprise, found he very much enjoyed it.

'I'm a potterer by nature,' he would say, when Miranda, admiring the latest culinary triumph, complained that he made her feel lazy. 'And I'm still getting the best of the bargain. What greater luxury than knowing every morning that I don't have to stir outside the door? I wouldn't swap places with anyone.'

He was, no surprise, extremely conscientious about his diet, his injections and regular averaging tests to make sure correct blood sugar levels were maintained. He attended a day centre for monitoring, and learned all he could about the disease, keeping to himself fears raised by an occasional loss of sensation in his legs and feet due to an impaired blood supply, and by the indistinct vision which more frequently troubled him. He knew that damage to the retina, or the possibility of the retina detaching, was a real threat, and that he was in the age group where blindness was not uncommon. This was his hidden dread, and he lived with it daily.

Miranda had come to realise that caring for Will, and concealing her own fears from him, had developed something in her character which she had scarcely known existed. At first in their relationship she had seen him as the protector, rescuing her from the trap of circumstances she had been unable to change for herself. There had been relief in relinquishing sole charge of Alexy, and in being able to articulate at last her deep-rooted sense of failure over how she had handled her upbringing. But, over time, she had come to accept that she was in reality the stronger partner and that, in view of Will's deteriorating health, the balance would never swing back. She had also found that, responding with loving compassion to Will's need, she didn't mind this. She wanted to look after him.

How different this was from her struggles to do her best for Alexy, which were also based on love. Everything she tried to offer her daughter seemed somehow to go against the grain. Looking after Will gave her a happiness and satisfaction she had never known before, his love the foundation on which her new life rested.

Even Danielle had conceded that the arrangement had worked out better than she'd expected. 'I hate to hear myself say that any woman is better off pandering to some male ego than living alone, but yes, you did the right thing. Not that I ever had you down as the domestic type,' she hadn't been able to resist adding with a curl of her lip, watching Miranda allocate the last

170

item of a huge mound of ironing to its pile.

Miranda, folding the ironing board, had smiled at her peaceably. 'I've been lucky. It could have been a nightmare. But the boys are so easy to live with I sometimes think they've been the key to the whole thing. Though they scrap from time to time, of course, they run their lives with amazing efficiency. And they're really fond of Will, which is what matters most.'

'But not so fond of Alexy?' Danielle had released a little bark of laughter. 'How's that side of things?'

'Don't prod the sore spot with quite such relish!' Miranda had begged. 'The boys can't stand her, as you very well know, and who can blame them? I'm only thankful they're prepared to take time off occasionally from their own pursuits to put her in her place. She certainly needs it.'

All the same, it had been good to have Danielle's approval, Miranda decided, as she turned in at the gate of Kilgarth. The drive curved round a big lawn to a pillared porch, and out again by a second gate. She just had time to wonder if she had deliberately invoked thoughts of Will to brace her, then she was at the door. The double oak leaves, which always used to be folded back during the day to let light into the hall through the glazed inner door, were closed and blank. She pushed against them, but the bar was evidently down. She pressed the bell firmly, but there was no way of telling if it was ringing.

She felt rebuffed, and also angry. She was here by appointment. She suspected a deliberate message in the barred doors, and imagined Gregory already relishing having scored a point. Well, she certainly wasn't going round to knock meekly at the kitchen door. There were other options.

As she went along the front of the house towards the garden door she was saddened by what she saw. In her memory, though not the most cheerful house of her acquaintance, Kilgarth had always been well kept, its general impression one of substantial prosperity. Its open position, its big windows and well-proportioned rooms with their large mirrors and pale chintzes, had always made it seem light and sunny. Now it seemed shut in on itself, shabby and uncared-for. The lawn and the strip of grass between drive and house needed cutting. The japonica bushes which had been trained against the wall sagged heavily down, tangled with leggy mahonia. Turning the corner, Miranda saw that the formal garden, whose borders she remembered bright and neatly tended, had been grassed over.

It was strange, and brought a slight unease, to see the downstairs windows shuttered or with their curtains drawn carelessly across. Who was looking after the place? Ruby must have retired long ago. Yet in a house like this there was always some other Ruby. Conscious of an unexpected reluctance to look further, or discover the answers to these questions, Miranda put out a hand to try the garden door. Though she had never known it locked, she wouldn't have been surprised to find it so today.

It was open. She stepped into the corridor which led to the main hall. Then two things checked her.

The first was the realisation that, since here there was no bell, she should knock. She was no longer a familiar of the house, coming in without ceremony to look for Ian (though always hoping to dodge his father), welcome in Ruby's kitchen, her presence accepted by anyone she chanced to meet. Now she was not merely a stranger, but in a sense the enemy, the divorced wife of Kilgarth's estranged heir. But the mother of the granddaughter of the house, she reminded herself, with an ironic smile for the convolutions. And invited.

The second thing to make her pause was the smell, alien and wrong. It hung dense on the chilly air, the smell of neglect, of age, of unused, uncleaned rooms. A smell of human life reduced to basics.

That was fanciful and exaggerated, Miranda knew, unable to suppress a shiver of distaste. But however unappealingly this place had altered, she had an obligation to fulfil here; an obligation to her daughter. The reminder recalled her to practical reality. Reaching back, she rapped sharply on the door, cocking her head to listen for any response. There had always been dogs at Kilgarth, and she half expected an explosion of barking to follow the intrusive, echoing sound.

But still silence hung, resistant, and Miranda found herself swallowing with nerves as apprehension and tension gripped her, and the fusty air fingered past her towards the sweeter, and

173

measurably warmer, air of the garden. Pushing the door shut with a thud, she went on towards the hall, suspended in the strange interweaving of past and present, everything she saw familiar yet subtly changed, but conscious above all of the deadness of the air, the impression of a house deserted.

# 14

Still no sound as Miranda reached the hall and looked up the curving stair which was its most graceful feature. With a mixture of shock and yet of somehow having known it would be so, she observed that its carpet of gold fleurs-de-lis on deep blue was worn through on every step.

There was no point in checking the big rooms at the front of the house; they were clearly not in use. The house felt so untenanted, her ringing and knocking having made no impression on its brooding silence, that she even wondered for a moment if Gregory had thought better of the meeting and gone out, bringing her here then abandoning her as some malicious trick. But he had expected her to bring Alexy, whom he presumably wanted to see.

Since he obviously couldn't be in the library, where the curtains were drawn, he was most likely, unless he were ill, and his letter had made no reference to illness, to be in his business room. Rather than gather her courage to invade this sanctum, Miranda decided to try to flush out someone else. He couldn't be living here alone.

Pushing open the heavy door which led to the rear wing a mean draught met her, and when she went into the kitchen she saw that the outer door was open. A middle-aged woman was coming in, an empty but squalid plastic scrap-pail in one

175

hand and an ash bucket in the other. From the latter the fine white residue rose around her in a soft cloud and settled on her hair and clothes.

'Oh my, you gave me a start,' she said at the sight of Miranda, but in a perfectly calm voice, suggesting a level of phlegmatism hard to ruffle, as she disposed of the unwashed pail under the sink. 'Mrs Ross, is it?' She looked at Miranda with frank curiosity. 'I was just out back at ma banties. I was meaning to get the front door open first thing, knowing you were coming, but I never got that length. Don't ask me where the time goes to. You got in all right, anyway, that's the main thing.'

It evidently didn't occur to her to enquire how, and Miranda saw no reason to explain.

'Good morning. Yes, I'm Mrs Ross. Is Mr Ross here?'

'Is he here?' This, apparently, did wake faint surprise. 'Aye, he's here. He's not stirred across the threshold this past year. Now, will I make the pair of you some tea? No, coffee it had best be, perhaps, with a wee plate of biscuits. Or will I bring it in to you after a whilie . . . ?' As she pondered aloud on the fitness of these options Miranda felt herself relax, amused.

Something in the broad features and heavy movements of the figure now rattling the ash bucket down beside the Rayburn made her ask, 'Are you by any chance related to Ruby Lawson, who used to be housekeeper here?'

'I am. I'm her niece, Pattie. I'm the housekeeper noo.' It was said with great complacency, accompanied by an almost frisky

176

wriggle of the stout hips. 'And she'd turn in her grave, too, to know it, the auld — ' This time she laughed outright, then recollected herself. 'You'll no' remember me, though. She wouldna' let me near the place when I was a lassie. Said I was a slut.' This was said with some wonder, as she toed off her muddy gumboots, leaving them lying where they fell. 'A slut, me, that's rich. Some nerve she had.'

She took the enormous kettle, which Miranda was certain was the one she remembered, and went to the sink to fill it.

'Look,' Miranda suggested, noting the amount of water she was running into it, 'why don't you take me to Mr Ross now, and bring in the coffee or whatever he asks for when it's ready?'

'Asks for? That one?' snorted Pattie with fine contempt. 'He can ask away, I'll dae what I see fit.' Evidently her earlier ruminations had had nothing to do with meeting the wishes of her employer.

'Are the main rooms not used now?' Miranda asked, as Pattie led the way along the passage towards the back of the house. She asked chiefly to stave off the apprehension which had come coiling back. She couldn't recall being in the business room, Gregory's sacrosanct lair, more than once or twice in her life, but she knew from what Ian had told her that any unpleasant confrontations had always taken place there.

'Who's to go into them?' Pattie enquired simply, and Miranda winced at the bleakness of this.

He *is* ill, was her reaction at the sight of

177

Gregory, concern overriding all other considerations. His chair was pulled close to a sullen fire,
he had an old tweed Inverness cape round his
knees, and his hands were folded over the knob
of a stick. In the dim light of a lamp with a
too-heavy (and dust-clogged) shade, Miranda
saw that his skin looked yellow, his face sunken
as if he'd forgotten to put in his teeth, and that
his hands, corded with veins, looked almost
transparent, their bone structure visible through
the brown-blotched, shiny skin.

Something else struck her almost as forcibly:
there was no dog at his feet. It made him seem
diminished, depleted, no longer himself. As she
went forward to greet him, she saw quick anger
in his face, yet he made a stiff movement to rise
with a mumbled greeting, impelled by an
ingrained formality which not all his bad temper
and antagonism could eradicate.

To save him getting up, which was obviously
an effort, Miranda took the chair opposite his
without waiting to be invited, part of her mind
registering its unwelcoming hardness and smell
of ancient dust.

'I'll leave you to it then,' said Pattie, cheerfully
oblivious of the currents of emotion surging and
colliding across the burn-scored hearthrug.

'See to the fire first, woman,' Gregory said
impatiently, and the harsh order brought vividly
back the man Miranda had known, the remote
authoritarian figure, all-powerful ruler of his
business empire, household autocrat. At the
same time she could hear in his voice that this
man was old, disillusioned and tired.

'Where is she?' he demanded, as soon as the door shut behind Pattie, whose attentions had made no appreciable difference to the fire. 'Have you left her outside? Why? It's my granddaughter I want to see, not you.'

A poor start, and the entire encounter could hardly have been described as agreeable, but in the end Miranda found it easier to keep her temper than she'd expected. This lonely, bitter man was too pathetic for anger. It was easy to see through his rudeness and attempts to be dictatorial to the underlying need which had driven him to make this overture. It soon became clear that he hadn't approached Ian first, but wished to make contact with Alexy direct. In fact, he made it very plain that he meant to go on refusing to see Ian to the end of his days. This saddened Miranda, but for the moment she concentrated on what she had come to say.

She made it equally plain, in terms Gregory could not afterwards pretend to have misunderstood, that she had no intention of allowing Alexy to be used as a pawn in some devious game. If her grandfather genuinely wished to see her then that was his right, but Alexy's happiness and peace of mind came first. (Though Miranda couldn't avoid an ironic mental lift of the brows to use such terms in connection with her chronically discontented daughter.) She didn't mince her words, and her incisiveness brought the glimmer of a smile to the old man's hooded eyes.

'I think I take your point, young woman,' he told her, with something of his old authority. 'My

179

wits have not entirely forsaken me, though my confounded legs sometimes have trouble bearing me up.'

'It's important that we understand each other,' Miranda said more gently. 'If all a meeting achieved were more family quarrels then it wouldn't be worth it. Though I should warn you,' she added, with a fleeting smile in her turn, 'that your granddaughter is not the most amenable of characters. In the first place she may refuse to come here at all, and if she does — and I shall let her decide for herself — you may not find her the malleable young thing you are perhaps expecting.'

'A Ross, is she?' Gregory perked up visibly at this caution. 'Well, I can hardly expect a rapturous reunion. Let's say it's time a start was made.'

On that Miranda felt they could agree, and over some disgustingly weak coffee which, though served in a pot, was certainly instant, and fancy biscuits of a kind presumably favoured by Pattie, since Gregory irritably waved the plate away, she turned to other topics.

They were not well received. Her conventional enquiry after Gregory's sisters, Olivia and Binnie, was met by a cold stare and the caustic demand, 'How should they be? Perfectly well as far as I know. Idle pair, never lift a finger between them. God knows what they do all day in that damned cottage. I could get an income from the place if only they'd take themselves off somewhere. Too much to hope for, I suppose.'

Miranda cut across his peevish mutterings by

180

asking about his own health.

'Never felt better,' he replied sarcastically, adding half to himself, 'for God's *sake*.' Then, sensing that he was about to lose his audience after this piece of rudeness, he embarked on a long rambling complaint about how badly the company was doing, how no one else could be trusted to run it, how infuriating it was not to be able to get out on the hill, and how useless someone called Derek, apparently the gamekeeper, was. Though Ian's name wasn't mentioned, this was patently as much a tirade against his son as against the hated depredations of the years, and self-engrossed and hostile as he was, Miranda couldn't help feeling compassion that he had come to this.

She left the gloomy room at last with a sense almost of anticlimax, having braced herself to meet a challenge which had not turned out to be as gruelling as she'd feared. She wondered what Will would think of what had been agreed, but the thought had no impact. This issue was quite separate from her life with Will. She would talk to him about it, of course, but she knew already that his views wouldn't affect the outcome. There was a momentary sense of being alone again as she acknowledged this, a feeling almost forgotten, but, in this one matter, that was how it must be.

As she let herself out of the house its shabbiness caught at her again. Would it depress Alexy to see Kilgarth for the first time in its present state? And how would she, so self-orientated and contumacious, react to the

181

arrogant old man? On the other hand, would it bring something to Kilgarth, and to Gregory, to have the only member of the new generation return?

Ian, like Miranda, had not married again though, like her, he was in a relationship. But so far there were no children, and Miranda, ready to find an excuse for anger in every thought of him, had her own interpretation for this: having seen one wife turned into a complaining harridan by a squalling baby, he had no wish to find himself in a similar situation again. Thinking of Ian, the memories which had assailed her as she drove up returned. How it would hurt him to see his home now.

Without conscious decision, she went to open the back of the car. She had thrown in jacket and boots before leaving, almost a reflex action to knowing she would be in the glen. Had she also known all along where she would go?

The hill gate was new, metal, wider, swinging at a touch. Well, that was one change for the better, she conceded, remembering her struggles to haul back the sagging wooden one for Ian to drive the old Land Rover through. As she set off up the track she let them come, the names, the faces, the voices, the laughter. She let the self of those days return and, for the first time in far too long, let Ian return without the distortion of resentment and accusations.

He was beside her as she walked, yet simultaneously she missed him with an aching vividness she would normally do anything to evade. She knew he represented something in her life that she would never find again, and in rare honest moments like this she was ready to admit that she had let it go too lightly.

With the same odd feeling of being utterly at home yet a tentative intruder which she had experienced in the house, she took the track at a steady pace. It seemed narrower than her memory of it, boulders shouldering close, its peaty ruts gouged deeper. As she walked, exhilaration began to grip her. How she had missed this openness, this freedom, and having keen, clean air in her lungs.

Topping the final rise, she saw the loch at last, a gleaming level in the long swells of bent and heather, silver under a cloudy sky. Was it smaller than she remembered or had the reeds been allowed to encroach? The boathouse looked tiny too, a dot in the great open sweep of ground, made lonelier by the haunting cries of curlews. Weathered, wind-battered, it mutely awaited her arrival, and Miranda, picking her way by the short cut as the track looped round, sphagnum moss oozing round her feet at every step, began to feel almost reluctant to invade its privacy and stir to life the ghosts who waited in that forlorn little building.

As she came closer, she saw that the verandah rail was sagging away at one end where the rain-soaked planks had rotted through, though the absurd little fretwork porch of the side door had somehow held on in spite of the gales that could howl up here. Even more surprisingly, the old boat, its blue paint little more than a faint blur on its broad sides, still lay in the covered stone dock at the end of the building. Or perhaps not surprisingly; perhaps that was exactly what she should have expected in this general climate of indifference and neglect.

The door was locked, the windows boarded up. Miranda didn't attempt to find a chink to peer through, but leaned on a firm section of verandah rail and let the mood of the place draw her in. The early sun had vanished, swallowed up by cloud, but the delicate tones of grey and silver had a beauty all their own. Looking north, the outlines of the hills seemed to float in mist, turning the well-known glen into a mysterious and enchanted place. Then her eyes were drawn by the dizzy maze swallows and swifts were weaving over the water. This fluid, ceaseless pattern, the flight of any one bird impossible to follow, gradually worked its spell upon her, as steady snowfall induces sleep. Her mind opened, became receptive, and a strange calm overtook her.

Oddly enough, the first memory to swim up didn't relate to the distant past which had been in her mind as she came across the moor, but belonged to the year before she met Will. It would seem to Miranda, thinking about it afterwards, almost that it had been waiting for some moment such as this, when it could be honestly confronted. As though it had been locked away complete, and now refused to be buried any longer.

It concerned the time when Alexy had been so ill, when it had seemed more than once that she wouldn't pull through. Ian had flown back the

184

moment he was told; that was simple fact. He had been concerned and ready to help in any way he could. That too, had been accepted. But what Miranda had never told anyone, had never truly let herself own, had been the quality and completeness of the support he had offered her. Exhausted after sleepless nights and days, dragged at by fear, she had felt recharged by the powerful current of his love for Alexy, startled by a level of caring she had never guessed him capable of, and deeply grateful for his presence.

But she had never told him how she felt. Her thanks had been formal, bald, inadequate, her gratitude impossible to express as normality returned, reminding her how things stood between them. She had not even been able, constrained by the misunderstandings and quarrels of the past, to soften the blow when Alexy had rejected him as soon as she was sufficiently recovered to know what was happening, adamantly refusing to let him come to the flat when she was home again.

Had there been — Miranda winced as she made herself ask the question at last — a certain base relief to see Alexy resist him, and reassurance for herself in knowing he wasn't going to usurp her place? That was awful, if it were true. Her only excuse could have been her dismay at everything she had worked so hard to achieve being threatened — and having to re-examine long-entrenched views of Ian which might not stand up to inspection, she amended wryly now.

But surely here, in this place they had both

loved so much, with only the luminous misty light around her, half mesmerised by the arrowing of the birds over the barely rippled water, she could at last confront the true feelings of that time. Or go further, and admit her stark sense of loss when Ian had written, once he was back in Sydney, to say that he no longer intended to maintain contact with Alexy.

Suddenly, urgently, she wanted to write to him, to tell him the things he should have been told at the time. The memory of his face, openly revealing his love and anxiety as he sat hour after hour by Alexy's side, the only sound her harsh, struggling breathing, was so vivid that for a moment writing really seemed possible. But at once Miranda's resolve sank down again. So much pain, so much conflict, to risk stirring up again. Anyway, Ian had his own life with Heidi now. (Heidi! What sort of woman had a name like that, Miranda let herself demand unreasonably.) He had made his decision, and probably he was right. Alexy would never relent. Her capacity for vengefulness was frightening.

Miranda stood for a few moments more, hollow disillusionment replacing her earlier pleasure to be here. Well, at least she had faced a few truths. But had she hoped for something more by coming here? Had she hoped that by some occult means Ian would receive and understand her message of gratitude and apology?

You are such a fool, she told herself, unlocking her chilled limbs to step stiffly down onto the sodden turf. Reaching the top of the rise she looked back. The boathouse was no more than a simple shack, abandoned to dereliction and decay, the featureless miles of moor a tedious slog she had to put behind her to return to the present; a present which now, she remembered with a shiver, included unforeseen new possibilities.

# 15

Will's death came with terrible suddenness. In the first shock it seemed there had been no warning at all. His heart had simply stopped. One morning Miranda had slipped out of bed at six as she often did to profit from the early quietness, had written some letters, got everything ready for breakfast, gone to take Will his tea and found him dead.

Later, in the sleepless, grieving hours, alone in the wide bed, she would question and question whether he had already been dead when she woke; had been lying dead beside her in the night. It was a nightmarish thought. She would have known, surely she would have been aware, she would tell herself over and over again in horror. Even more distressingly, she was gradually forced to recognise that there had been signs and warnings, and she had been blind to them.

Will had been increasingly dogged by a tiredness never directly related to any activity, to a late night, or to extra pressures. They had grown so used to this over time that they barely registered it any more. He had admitted occasionally that his eyes gave him trouble, but always immediately reasoned it away by saying he had been doing too much reading and should get out more, take more exercise, do things with the boys, so Miranda had never let herself see it

188

as signalling other, graver causes.

There had been too his growing forgetfulness, though this he had always refuted, irritated when anyone referred to it, however lightly. That in itself had been a change that should have alerted her, Miranda told herself in anguish, going over these things obsessively till her head throbbed and her eyes could cry no more.

But he had gone, quiet, unassuming Will, and though she might have appeared to others to have been the driving force in their partnership, Miranda was aware of an appalling emptiness with his support and protection lost to her. He had protected her chiefly, she knew, from the worst side of herself. He had given her a new equilibrium, building a confidence not in what she could achieve but in who she was, and for a long time after his death she felt she would never be able to claw it back again.

There was loving help on every hand, but nothing could lessen the numb sense of isolation, of having to start again, alone, on an exhausting climb. Georgina came north to look after the day-to-day needs of the household. Danielle, filled with irrational anger at not having been able to deflect this tragedy from Miranda, and also to know she was the last person to understand what Miranda must be feeling, dealt with arrangements for the cremation and a small gathering after it, and organised accommodation for those who needed to stay.

Will's parents, as much in need of comfort as Miranda herself, and deeply distressed for their grandsons, had at first thought they must somehow make the effort to get to Edinburgh. But at Danielle's suggestion it was decided to hold the service in Kelso which, apart from saving them the difficulties of the journey, meant that for a day or two at least they could have Adam and Tim with them.

Almost more help than anyone in those first stunned days was Will's sister, Carol, though she was not a person capable of showing her grief in conventional ways, and bluntly said as much to Miranda.

'Of course I care, I know that and he'd know that, but I'm no good at this sort of thing, mourning, funerals, the whole performance. It's not my scene. But one thing I can and will do, I can take on the parents. Now and for the future. I know I've been chiefly notable for my absence till now — couldn't take all those well-meaning attempts to overcome alarm and distaste, and find things that could be safely talked about — but time moves on, and they need more care now. That's my job.'

'I can't tell you what a relief that is,' Miranda said gratefully. 'I've been so worried about them but I'd scarcely begun to think how I could help them.'

'Don't think about it. You'll have your hands more than full with Alexy and the boys — ' Carol's firm voice suddenly sounded less certain. 'My God, that's rather an assumption, isn't it? Though I'm afraid it's one we've all been making. There's no reason on earth why you should take on Tim and Adam. Since you and Will weren't married, they're not your stepsons.'

190

It was the fear the boys themselves were trying to deal with as they waited, wretched and uncertain, to learn their future. Until Carol voiced the doubt, Miranda hadn't even realised they would need reassurance.

'But we're a family!' she protested, horrified. 'Of course I regard the boys as mine. I wouldn't dream of letting them go — as long as they want to stay, of course.'

As she added the rider, in sudden uncertainty of her own, she saw how vital it was to have this question settled without delay, for everyone's sake.

Having made sure for the moment that the boys knew they would be coming back to Simla Street as a matter of course, Miranda made it her essential priority, once her mother had returned to Gloucestershire and, as it were, the first day of the new sad reality had come, to gather the boys and Alexy for a round-the-table talk.

'I think you're old enough now,' she began quietly, 'for us to discuss our situation together, each saying how we feel, and looking ahead a little. But before anything else,' she went on, her voice less easy to control as she looked at the boys, their faces too tight, too determined not to show their anxiety, 'I want you, Adam and Tim, to know with absolute certainty that I see you as much my children, my family, as I do Alexy. There's no difference, in any way.'

Their faces relaxed a little but their eyes remained fixed on hers, and after a tiny pause Adam asked, speaking almost roughly in his extreme shyness on this point, 'But you weren't married to Dad, were you?' It had been the corrosive doubt behind all the shock and turmoil of his father's death, the doubt that had sent Tim and him spinning into some awful void. He knew of no one else whose situation matched theirs, and that alone was terrifying.

Now that Miranda had seen that going on as before was not necessarily the obvious course in everyone else's eyes, she could understand the need for it to be established beyond all doubt, and was prepared to go on repeating her assurance as long as it was required.

'No, we chose not to marry,' she said steadily, looking down at her linked hands on the table for a moment, rocked by a fresh awareness of what had happened, then putting that aside and looking into Adam's anxious but slightly defiant eyes, which warned that he didn't want to be fobbed off with any adult half-truths.

'Marriage is one kind of promise to love each other and live together. A public promise, if you like, a promise made in church for people to whom religious vows are important. Other people prefer to make private promises, but they're just as important and binding. Your father and I were as committed to each other as if we had had a wedding in a church or register office, and we included you two, and Alexy, in our commitment to each other. Your father would want you to be with me now. I'm sure of it. Don't you yourselves feel that he would?'

Tim, much less mature than Adam though only a year younger, and with much of Will's quietness and humility, gazed at her with serious eyes, but unexpectedly it was he who answered. 'I think he would,' he said, his voice thin with eagerness and still underlying anxiety. 'I don't think he'd know where else we could go.'

'That's not the point,' Adam cut in with the quick superiority of the elder brother. 'But would it be . . . I mean, is it normal?'

What would the boys at school say.

'Families grow and alter in different ways,' Miranda pointed out. 'Second marriages, divorce, illness, single parents or parents who have simply decided they want to be together. I expect among your own friends you know of all kinds of permutations — step-parents, half-brothers and half-sisters, adopted children.'

'It's not the same though, is it?' Alexy put in sharply. She had slouched in grudgingly after several calls, not quite ready to refuse to appear, since she wanted to know what was going on, but showing resentment in every line, in the way she scraped out her chair and flopped sulkily into it, in the way she was sitting now, half turned away, legs splayed, spelling out her boredom in yawns and scowls. 'I mean, you're not related to us, are you? Mum's my biological mother, but she's not yours. She's nothing to do with you.'

For two painful heartbeats there was silence in the warm, faintly humming kitchen. Miranda felt an actual coldness in her blood at the calculated cruelty of this speech, and a wrenching, physical shame for having produced the person who could utter it. She longed wildly for Will, and

193

flinched at one of those crushing moments of realisation that he had gone, which seemed each time harder to bear, like fresh blows landing on an injured place. For a second she was unable to make her lips and tongue work to shape words to answer.

'Yes, I mean, that's it, isn't it?' Adam said, not looking at Alexy, and Miranda saw how his jaw was ridged, and how the sprinkling of freckles across his nose stood out against the new greenish pallor of his face.

'That's only one part of it.' Miranda made a huge effort, and was relieved to find her voice surprisingly calm. 'You're old enough to know that there can be love, and need, and sharing, and caring for each other, which have nothing to do with a blood relationship. And I'm sure you also know that relations can quarrel and hate each other and do terrible things to each other.' And if anyone asked me who, of the three people here at this table with me now, I actually like, I should have no difficulty in answering. 'Alexy, if that's all you can contribute, I suggest you hold your tongue.'

'Oh, yes!' Alexy said, drawing in her legs and swinging round to sit hunched forward across the table, with what looked like a glitter of triumph in her pale eyes. 'Let's be grown-up people, let's talk things through. So it's listen to anything the boys have to say but as soon as I open my mouth it's, 'Shut up, Alexy'.'

Miranda had regretted her words the moment she had spoken. No matter how vicious, no matter how it had angered her, she should have

194

dealt with Alexy's input in the same manner as she had dealt with the boys'. Collecting herself to respond adequately, she registered, something which could always shake her, how coldly Alexy had spoken. She never resorted to overt insolence, but made her point almost tonelessly, which gave her words, spoken with such contemptuous control, a power that was strangely adult. Now she was also visibly satisfied by her mother's discomfiture.

'Yes, you're right, we're here to try and establish how everyone feels and what each person wants,' Miranda managed to say evenly. 'But only within the broad framework that, unless Adam and Tim prefer some other arrangement such as going to live with their grandparents, then this is still their home, with me. That isn't a question for debate.'

'We couldn't live with Grannie and Grandpa though, could we?' Adam asked before Alexy could speak. 'They couldn't look after us. And there isn't really room.'

'Changes can always be made,' Miranda said gently. 'There could be extra help, even a different house. You mustn't think that couldn't happen if it's what you really want. They asked me to tell you that.'

She let them digest this but could see their doubts, and knew herself that, though George Letham had staunchly made the offer, such a plan would be fraught with difficulties, and could hardly be a long-term arrangement in any case.

Alexy, with a 'see what I mean' shrug, had

withdrawn into silence again. She had been smouldering with inner rage ever since it had become apparent that the thing she had seen as obvious, that all links with the Letham family would now be broken and life would revert to what it had been before her mother met Will, hadn't so much as entered Miranda's head. Although at sixteen Alexy regarded herself as an adult, and indulged in practices and tastes which would have considerably startled her mother, she was young enough to accept that parents still decided the larger issues. Well, even if she had to put up with having these cretins around for the time being, it wouldn't be for ever. She would be out of here. For now, they were away at school most of the time, and had learned to keep out of her way when they weren't.

She was totally unprepared for what her mother was about to propose.

'There is another possibility,' Miranda was saying to Adam and Tim. 'But you must take all the time you need to think it over, and be sure you understand that there's no pressure from anyone to make you choose one course rather than another. The thing is — and this is what I should prefer myself — I could adopt you.'

The look of instant blazing eagerness and relief in both the boys' faces told her more clearly than any words how deep their sense of insecurity had been.

But both heads jerked round, and Miranda felt her own heart give a startled jump, as Alexy's chair crashed back and she leapt to her feet in incandescent fury.

196

*  *  *

Pausing only to tell the boys not to worry, this wasn't going to affect the outcome, Miranda went after Alexy.

She was angry with herself for handling the matter so clumsily. Of course she should have talked to Alexy first, prepared the ground, given her the chance to air her views and made her feel they had been taken into account, not callously over-ridden. Numb with shock over Will's death, her principal aim to reassure and comfort the boys who were so clearly frightened and adrift, she had seen only that the existing family unit should be preserved.

In spite of recognising the urgency of having this talk, for everyone's sake, as she had said, she had barely considered Alexy's place in the equation, and had she done so would have thought her the person least affected by what had happened.

Now Alexy's almost forgotten resentment of Will, whose advent had broken apart the cosy enclosed world shared with her mother, in which everything had been done according to her whim, came spilling out, increased a hundred-fold by the discovery that his death was not to mean the removal of her much-resented rivals for her mother's attention. For Alexy had seen, the moment that her mother, white and shaking, had come into her room on that first morning to tell her what had happened, this obvious and simple result, and she had been delighted.

'I should have told you first. I'm sorry,'

Miranda said steadily. 'I shouldn't have let you hear it like this.'

'But you're still going to do it, aren't you?'

'Alexy, the boys are part of Will. I see them as my family. That will never change. I want to look after them. You're my daughter, and though I couldn't ever feel about anyone else as I feel about you,' (the frightening question of what precisely she did feel was pushed hurriedly aside), 'I do love the boys too.'

'I loathe them.'

'Oh, Alexy, what is there to loathe? What have they ever done to make you hate them?'

Alexy twisted restlessly, her mouth ugly with contempt. 'They're such creeps. They keep their room tidy.'

Miranda hid an involuntary smile at the bathos of the accusation at such a moment, yet in its way it said a good deal. The boys, though they had to be chased up on occasion, were in general amenable and saw the point of order, as their father had done. It had always made Alexy furious. She saw their helpfulness as currying favour, wimpish and unreal. Her own room, where she and Miranda now were, was a pit of squalor. She objected to her mother going into it at any time, and Miranda, trying to meet this need for privacy, never felt she achieved even a passable level of hygiene in there.

She hated being in it at this moment, as she tried to draw the conversation onto a more constructive level. She disliked the minimal lighting, the threatening posters crowding the walls and the faint disturbing smell, a mixture of trainers, scented candles, cheap cosmetics and the clothes kicked into corners which had missed her hasty trawls.

'Alexy, couldn't we try to talk more?' Miranda asked on a sudden impulse of longing. It was too easy, always busy, to slip into accepted patterns and forget to make an effort.

'About what?' Alexy's tone was ironic, almost amused.

'Well, about how we feel about things. Our views, our ideas. What you want to do with your life.'

Alexy looked at her. 'You don't know anything, do you?' Again she used the flat, weary tone which could be so baffling and final.

Miranda held onto her temper. 'You're sixteen now,' she said. 'Perhaps we could try to understand each other better. I hadn't quite realised, you know, how much you minded the boys being here.'

'No, you hadn't, had you?' Alexy glanced at her watch.

Miranda was glad that in the subfusc light the blush which rose in her face couldn't be seen. But suddenly she didn't feel so guilty any more. The boys did need her most at present; Alexy had behaved with unforgivable selfishness.

'Well, if you ever do want to talk, I'm there.' The brisker tone didn't suit Alexy at all.

'Whatever,' she said, then, as her mother reached the door, the intention to wound clear in every syllable, 'if it gets too shitty I can always go and live with my father.'

# 16

My father. As Miranda swung round she registered the choice of words. Not the 'Daddy' of babyhood, which was so remote that Alexy must by now have forgotten ever using it; not the 'Dad' of her peers, casual, everyday, familiar; but 'my father', statement-making, a deliberate provocation.

Even as this flashed through Miranda's mind, she knew she was yet again displacing with a peripheral thought the central one she hardly dared to face, loaded as it was with challenge.

About to exclaim, 'But Alexy, you know that's not even an option!' she managed at the last second to snatch back the instinctive protest. Instead, getting her shock under control, she asked, 'Is that something you've been thinking about?' turning back into the room, reluctant as she felt to tackle such an important issue in its unsavoury gloom.

Had Alexy been in touch with Ian? Had this been discussed between them? With a sensation of the ground shifting under her feet, Miranda found the end of the bed and sat down again.

'I could, any time I wanted to.' Alexy was casual now. 'It'd be cool, living in Australia.'

Miranda groped for some safe opening which wouldn't rush them into headlong collision, though it was difficult to think calmly. A strange sensation had been dogging her during recent days, mostly as she woke from jumbled and distorted dreams to the fresh awareness of her loss. In the dreams Ian had died too, vanishing from her life as completely as Will had vanished. This had been strange and disturbing, and she had found it hard to escape a deep sense of disloyalty towards Will for having her grief for him invaded by such a powerful sensation of a different loss.

The image had been beyond her control, however, and had made her feel more than ever alone. One aspect had nagged at her, surfacing at odd moments and disconcerting her each time — the fact that Will's death was not something of which Ian needed to be told. Accustomed as she had been to communicating to him any major event in Alexy's life, it had been hard to get used to the idea, after Alexy's illness and Ian's decision to break all ties, that this was no longer necessary. But to find herself thinking, as she so often did with a jolt of guilt, 'I haven't told Ian about Will,' was surely weird. Then each time she thought this, the emptiness she now faced would almost overwhelm her.

'Have you been thinking about this seriously?' she asked again, making a determined effort to shake off her sense of disorientation by concentrating on Alexy and what she was really saying.

'Why not? I can go if I like.'

'I'm not sure that you can.' Miranda was careful to keep her tone reasonable. 'Has your father suggested it? Have you discussed it with him?'

'I might have known you'd get heavy about it,' Alexy said disgustedly, pushing her fine hair up into a spiky mass on top of her head then letting it flop forwards to cover her face. Not a promising sign.

'I think I'd need to know whether your father has been in contact with you about such a plan,' Miranda said. 'Since it would involve him rather.'

'Do you always have to be sarcastic?'

Levity never worked with Alexy, as Miranda should have known. 'I don't mean to be. But come on, Alexy, you must see that I have to know whether this is something that's been talked about as a possibility. It's perfectly all right if it has. There's nothing to say you can't be in touch with your — '

'In touch! That's pretty good coming from you. You saw to it that we wouldn't be, didn't you?'

'I did? What on earth do you mean?'

'You hate him. You were always rowing. Every time he came to take me out you had a go at him. And that last time, when I was ill, it was because of you he said he wasn't coming back. You've no right to ruin everything for me just because you can't stand him. And now I'm stuck with those two horrible little creeps, all because of you — '

The long habit of the years, dating back to before Alexy even left the womb, the habit of wanting to compensate for everything Miranda felt she'd denied her daughter by her own mistakes, was suddenly swept aside.

202

She came to her feet in straightforward, healthy wrath. 'Alexy, I've never heard anything so outrageous! Your father and I bent over backwards to make sure you could go on seeing him, whatever our feelings about each other were. He did his best to keep in touch and get to know you as you were growing up, but you were quite appalling to him. You took everything you could get and never gave an ounce of affection or warmth in return. No, don't you dare interrupt me!' as Alexy opened her mouth to argue. 'You're going to listen for once. When you were ill he flew back at once, putting his business affairs, everything, on hold. You may not remember, but he sat by your bed for hours. He did everything he could for you, and you rejected him — totally. You were quite old enough to know what you were doing too. He decided then to give up coming to see you, because there wasn't any point any more, but he's never abandoned his responsibility for you, not for a second. He's seen to it you have everything you could possibly want, and you should be grateful to him.'

Alexy looked thoroughly startled at this torrent of words, the shrugging dismissiveness she normally fell back on deserting her for once. Her mother had never spoken to her like this before, in passionate anger. Alexy had often toyed with the idea of going to live with her father, liking to imagine how much her mother would mind, fantasising about being lovingly welcomed to a luxurious new life, her notion of which was based on Australian soaps. It had

203

never been more than a fantasy. She hadn't been in touch with her father, and had only thrown the idea at her mother hoping to hurt her.

★ ★ ★

It took Miranda some time to calm down after her outburst. She knew it had shifted her relationship with Alexy onto a different plane and though, since Alexy was sixteen, this was probably inevitable anyway, she hardly felt capable for the moment of assessing the implications. She felt milled and battered by the events of the evening, exhausted by the emotions and needs and fears which seemed to fill the flat. But she had no regrets.

She thought of phoning Danielle, who would applaud her resistance to Alexy and who would certainly be ready to come over and tell her so if asked. But Miranda wasn't sure she had the energy for Danielle, hardly ready to live up to her exacting standards of female solidarity tonight. For truly, truly, what she wanted, grief returning, was a male voice giving comfort, male arms around her, male strength to tap into, and these she couldn't have.

It wasn't until the next morning, when the boys were gathering their belongings to go back to school and Alexy still hadn't emerged from her room, that it occurred to Miranda to wonder whether Gregory had had anything to do with the Australian idea. Subterfuge, a hidden agenda with unforeseen fallout, were very much his scene. Yet surely the last thing he would want

204

would be to engineer a reunion between his son and granddaughter. The opposite was more likely to be true.

She must make clear to Alexy, however, that if contact with her father was what she wanted, then on her side there was no problem, and she couldn't imagine Ian, no matter how hurt and angry he had been, refusing such an approach. For one second a vision of life without Alexy began to take shape. She pushed it hastily away.

Driving home after leaving the boys — they were at Glenalmond now, their grandfather's old school, and in their usual straightforward way appeared to be contented there — it was thoughts of Gregory which kept returning. She acknowledged at last that these thoughts had been nudging for some time and she had been evading them.

Alexy had been to Kilgarth more than once by this time, and though, theoretically, re-establishing contact had to be a good thing, Miranda had been left each time with an obscure sense of unease.

She admitted now that its basis lay in the fact that Gregory Ross and his granddaughter were so markedly alike. Though Miranda had imagined she was prepared for this, she had not anticipated the impact it would make on her to see them together, to recognise their identical intention to be on their best behaviour, behind which lay watchfulness, calculation and self-seeking.

Gregory had chosen to play the part of the enfeebled and lonely old man, deserted by those

205

he loved, deprived of all that made life worth living, patiently sitting out his final days. Alexy on the other hand was the eager granddaughter, unable to understand why she had never been allowed to visit him before, answering questions about school and friends (a highly limited and shifting group) with a sweet loquaciousness that had made her mother gape.

When that bored Gregory on this first visit, as it very soon did, he had sent them outside, 'So that you can at last show her something of the place,' he had said pointedly to Miranda, laying the blame for Alexy having never seen it before squarely on her mother's shoulders.

The only refreshing note had been struck by Pattie.

'What's he up to now, the old weasel, that's what I ask myself,' she said darkly, when Miranda took the tea tray back to the kitchen, more to escape the dark power-games of the study than out of a feeling of duty. 'Granddaughter, is it? There's been no talk of granddaughters before this.'

Miranda, amused by the faint overtone of *Lear*, had rebelled against returning to the business room, and had gone instead to wander round the garden, where unchecked summer growth, if you didn't get too close, had a beauty of its own, and had tried to reason away her discomfort. It had been unnerving to observe, watching them as they talked, the striking similarity between Alexy and her grandfather, not merely in colouring and general appearance but in cast of character, and to see their own unspoken but instant recognition of this. Although it had once been agreeable to think not all the blame for Alexy's shortcomings of character could be laid at her door, and that family traits would persist whatever she did or failed to do, now that she was face to face with the reality it was not encouraging to think what else might emerge over time.

She had been reminded of something Ian had said, when Alexy had been ill and they had been waiting together at the hospital. It was apropos a comment that Alexy had not inherited her looks or colouring from her parents.

'I suddenly realise who she's like,' Ian had remarked, looking at the beaky face and light hair, lank and stringy on the pillow. 'Poor little toad, she's the image of Aunt Binnie. I'd never seen it before. Well, I wouldn't have wished that on her . . . '

It had seemed to Miranda, as she wandered on down the lawn, to lean on the dyke beside the old summerhouse, now fallen into a sad state, and look up the glen towards the hills beyond the village of Kirkton, that life had not dealt Alexy a fair hand. In material respects, perhaps, she was fortunate, and certainly in her excellent brain, and her ability to absorb facts with minimal effort. But the capacity for happiness, warmth and natural affection seemed to have been left out of her makeup altogether, and that was a fearful legacy for any child.

On the way back to Edinburgh after that first visit to Kilgarth, Alexy had had little to say. She had looked pleased with herself, however, which

207

was never reassuring. Once she had asked, 'Is my father good at what he does?' and Miranda, taken aback, had hardly known where to begin to answer.

'He's been very successful, as far as I know. He works tremendously hard. He always used to, anyway.'

'What exactly does he do?'

'Property development mainly, I think, but he has other interests. He's a bit of a wheeler-dealer — '

'A villain, you mean?'

'A *villain*? Alexy, of course not. No, I only meant he can't resist a deal. If he sees an opportunity or a gap in the market he goes for it, and he had a sort of natural flair for knowing when to buy or sell.'

She had paused, wondering why she felt an instinct to justify what Ian did, or who he was. Wondering even more where these questions were coming from. Alexy had never asked such things before. In fact it was a long time since she had talked about her father at all; her indifference about him had always seemed complete.

Gregory. It was Gregory who had been asking. Instantly feeling his motives must be suspect, Miranda cast about for possible grounds for such interest. Was he coming round to a need for contact, a wish to put his house in order? Did he feel time was running out? Was he merely curious, or seeking some new excuse for anger and contempt, hoping to hear of failure so that he could gloat over it?

What Miranda would never realise was that the foundation for Ian's success lay in part in the driving energy of a man who never quite finds what he's looking for, or feels quite complete. The other major factor, which Gregory would never grasp, was his reputation for unshakeable integrity. As a young man he had been given glimpses of how his father operated and he hadn't liked what he saw. Though he never spoke of it, to deal with total probity was a personal goal of his, and the name he gained for it in Sydney's hard-hitting business world meant a lot to him.

Much as Miranda had disliked the atmosphere of their visit, there had been nothing in it to which she could reasonably object. She felt she had a duty to keep Alexy in touch with Ian's family if that was on offer, and when Gregory wrote to suggest a second visit she had known she had no reason to refuse.

★　★　★

Gradually, as the shock and initial pain of Will's death receded, they settled, she and Alexy and the boys, into a workable pattern of living. At first Miranda, quite apart from missing Will desperately for herself, and still sometimes unable to accept that he had slipped away so quietly without warning her, very much missed his being always at home. It had been so reassuring to know he was there. None of them had ever had to come back to an empty house.

Now it was hard to adjust to being back in the

209

working single-parent mode. Though in many ways it was easier to have three teenagers to look after than one small child, and when the boys were home she was grateful to them a dozen times a day for their independence and good sense, adolescence brought its own problems. Predictably, Alexy put her through nearly every hoop in the book, bunking off school, wearing appalling clothes, gravitating towards some really scary friends, and even being caught shoplifting in spite of the extravagant way she spent her large allowance on anything that caught her eye. She was also extremely uncooperative about every aspect of life at home, never relaxing her antagonism towards the boys.

She put Miranda through every hoop but one. She didn't touch drugs. Miranda knew that every mother wants to believe her offspring when they assure her they aren't involved, but in this respect she did feel secure. Alexy scorned the entire drug culture, unable to comprehend the stupidity of anyone who let themselves be sucked into it. She saw the damage done as pointless and mindless. She had experimented to see what it was about, as she freely revealed, and had been unimpressed. One of the reasons Miranda believed her was because she understood that Alexy would not want for a second to be at the mercy of any external influence. She was the sort of person who lived by her wits and would hate any diminution of control.

Though in this one area Miranda felt confident, there was nothing else in their relationship to be complacent about. She knew

210

that by her serious error after Will's death in not talking to Alexy about her plans for the boys and soliciting her support, she had gone back to the beginning.

There seemed no way to reach through to understanding or even a semblance of normal affection. More and more Miranda found herself valuing the company of Adam and Tim, looking forward to their returns home from school, dreading taking them back. She liked doing things for them and planning things they would enjoy. She liked their humour and good nature, and the boost of high spirits which so altered the mood of the flat. In fact, most of the time she was utterly thankful that Will had bequeathed them to her. They were her link with him, but they were also a pleasure in themselves, and she considered herself lucky to have them.

They offered her too, shyly, mostly without words, the comfort of sharing her grief. It was not just that they mourned Will themselves. They seemed able to go beyond that and to grasp at least something of what Miranda must be feeling. Such perception and sensitivity were beyond Alexy, indeed would be actively despised by her.

This time of recovery, demanding and busy, with at least a degree of balance achieved between such diverse needs and personalities, and by and large maintained, began to stretch forward in Miranda's mind into a settled and bearable future, at least until the next major change came, when Alexy would leave school.

It didn't last that long.

# 17

For her eighteenth birthday Gregory Ross's gift to Alexy was to change his will, giving her the house of Kilgarth when she was twenty-five, and leaving her the estate and everything else he owned when he died. With his sense of self-preservation still in good working order, he didn't tell his sisters, shut away out of sight down the shrubbery path, of his intentions.

His gift, as might have been foreseen, came with conditions. Alexy was to make Kilgarth her home until it became hers and, even more preposterously since none of this had been discussed with her, Miranda was to live there as well for the same period.

That was Miranda's first reaction. It was a preposterous plan, its aim manipulative and devious, its impact on their lives wholly unacceptable. Resistance rose in her as she reread the letter from Gregory's lawyer breaking the news of this legacy. Then common sense reasserted itself. It could never happen; it was probably nothing more than an attempt to make trouble, and even if Gregory actually meant what he said Alexy would never agree. She would resist being coerced in this way, she disliked Kilgarth and everything about it, in particular its remote setting, and though she never talked to Miranda about her visits to her grandfather, she certainly didn't give the impression of having developed any fondness for him.

Yet she had been to see him more frequently than Miranda had expected. And there was that disturbing likeness between them. In fact, Miranda was obliged to admit, it was impossible to know what terms they were on by this time, as for the past year Alexy had visited Kilgarth alone. On her seventeenth birthday Ian had increased her allowance, also putting a large lump sum into her account, and she had bought a car. Ian had presumably intended this, and Miranda, though annoyed with him for doing it without reference to her, had had no alternative but to accept the new independence it had given Alexy.

Had Gregory discussed the scheme with her? Had Alexy known this was coming? The suspicion that she probably had deepened Miranda's resistance. Knowing her daughter, she kept her voice neutral as she told her what was in the letter. It was Alexy, as she took in what Miranda was saying, who for once couldn't control her feelings. Her usual blank impassivity when someone looked for a reaction from her failed her. She came to her feet, pale face flaming with sudden colour, eyes wide with intense excitement — and another emotion which repelled her mother, triumph, pure, selfish triumph.

'Yes!' She punched the air, her face jubilant. 'Yes!' She picked up her plate, still with toast on it, and, as though needing to release emotions she couldn't express in any normal way, cracked it sharply on the edge of the table and pitched the piece across the room.

'Alexy!' The sound, the violence of the gesture shocked Miranda. She felt, as she so often felt with Alexy, that they had moved into realms where she didn't know the rules or understand the basic reactions. 'That was hardly necessary. Did you know about this?'

'I thought he might do it,' Alexy said, still with that look of intense satisfaction, sounding as though she hardly knew her mother had spoken. 'I thought the horrible old creature might. But not so soon.'

'Alexy!' Miranda protested again, hearing the helplessness of her parrot cry, as little heeded as if she actually were hung in a cage in the corner. She made an effort to order her thoughts, but each opening that occurred to her was negative. 'Of course you couldn't think of . . . ' 'Obviously the whole idea is impossible . . . '

It was no use starting there. She floundered as anger gripped her. How dared that selfish old man act so high-handedly, no doubt to further some dubious plan of his own. *She* was responsible for Alexy, *she* decided where they lived. Suddenly the whole fabric of their lives, which she had created and held together through the long hard-working years, felt fragile and makeshift.

'All this must be carefully discussed,' she made herself say calmly. 'A proposal like this has far-reaching implications and shouldn't be taken lightly.' It was the best she could do, but even so she could hear a repressive tone taking over in spite of her. 'Though I can't really

214

imagine that you'd want to — '

Alexy focused on her now, her eyes still bright with triumph. 'I know you can't. You never can. But do you seriously think I won't want to accept this, from my own grandfather? Oh, please, get real. A decent house to live in, after these ghastly poky flats, and a house that will be *mine*! And a proper life, not stuck here alone with a mother who goes out to work. The sort of life other people have, not endlessly cooped up here with nothing to do, never going anywhere, never enjoying anything . . . '

A vision of Alexy, unchanging through the years of her childhood and adolescence, sprawled in the corner of the sofa, a cushion clutched to her stomach, her chin on her chest, eyes glued to the television screen and refusing so much as to turn her head when spoken to, swept into Miranda's mind. Helpless despair at the gulf between them filled her. Was this how Alexy had seen it? Had she hated so much the life Miranda had made for them? But even in her pain, Miranda knew that to pursue these questions would achieve nothing. She put them aside. Wounds to be dealt with later.

'Alexy, are you seriously telling me you would consider living at Kilgarth? You always say you loathe the glen and complain there's nothing to do there.'

Alexy gave her a long stare. 'I'm not a child,' was all she said, and Miranda had the impression that she had rejected half a dozen other things she could have said as a waste of breath, certain not to be understood.

215

'There would be a lot to think about,' Miranda began, though scarcely capable of marshalling the ramifications yet herself. 'There are other people besides yourself involved and — '

'Who? Nobody's involved. You're not going to try and deprive me of this as well as everything else, are you?' Alexy demanded, her eyes narrowing in a way that carried both warning and challenge. 'Just like you've always deprived me of everything else.'

Silenced, breathless, Miranda stared at her. Was this really what Alexy thought? It was as though every disagreement they had ever had, every difference of attitude and character, had met in stunning collision. Whatever else she might have achieved in her entire existence, which she admitted was little enough, Miranda knew she had failed with this child of hers, failed in the only thing that mattered.

★ ★ ★

With their whole way of living suddenly in question, with a thousand doubts churning in her head, Miranda found her most immediate problem was her fierce resistance to her own life being wrested from her control. It was totally unacceptable that Gregory should dare to make her presence at Kilgarth a proviso, and that without her views being consulted she was faced with the prospect of abandoning the business she and Danielle had built up, of parting with Danielle herself, whose support, if sometimes abrasive, had been solid and unquestioning

216

through every crisis, and of being plucked from her home with its associations with Will, its familiar comfort and convenience. What right did Gregory Ross have to impose such conditions on other people? And there were the boys, though fortunately they weren't due home for a couple of weeks, so their position in this was not something that had to be considered in the first flurry of shock.

But no matter how Miranda resisted the idea, no matter what arguments she assembled against it — the potential damage to Alexy's character being even more worrying than the disruption of all their lives — she felt, with a chill sense of the inevitable rolling unstoppably towards her, that it was going to happen. The guilt which had underpinned her relationship with Alexy, from the day she knew she had conceived her, made the outcome certain.

She had no right to prevent her daughter from receiving an inheritance from her father's family. And, more chillingly, Miranda knew that if she refused to agree to Gregory's condition, and he withdrew his gift because she would not comply, there would be no forgiveness from Alexy.

Sometimes, in the restless hours of darkness, she would think, why not? Why not simply let it come to that? Accept that the plan is fraught with evil intentions, and in the long term will do Alexy more harm than good. But if Alexy insists on her rights? Then stay clear of the whole issue. Alexy's eighteen, technically an adult. If she goes, she goes. There's no hope of reaching closeness or understanding anyway; let it go.

217

Then every instinct of maternal protectiveness would instantly rebel.

Miranda was disconcerted to find how often Ian was in her mind, as these thoughts battled and revolved. Imagining his anger if he knew what his father had done, or the manner in which he had done it, was oddly comforting. For giving Kilgarth outright to Alexy was still, even after all this time, as likely to be a blow directed at Ian as any loving gesture towards Ian's daughter. Would Ian too see it as potentially harmful to Alexy to accept a legacy with such strings attached? He himself had walked away when Gregory had attempted to impose similar conditions on him. Would he think it better for her to be denied this easy option, no matter what she thought she wanted? In Ian's case the condition, of entering his father's business, had involved only himself. Here, other lives would be affected.

The conclusion Miranda came to, having examined the situation through Ian's eyes, was that there were two things she must do without delay. The second depended on the first, and the first was to go and see Gregory.

★　★　★

She guessed from his manner that he had expected her, even, in a perverse and faintly distasteful way, that he was stimulated by the prospect of a confrontation with her. There were little patches of colour in his sallow cheeks, and a glitter in his watchful eyes as Miranda crossed

218

the room which made her skin crawl for a second. He was pleased, she was convinced, to have stirred up trouble, yet so confident of the hand he held that he had no doubt of ultimately getting his way.

She didn't waste time on anything but the briefest of greetings. She had let herself in and had come straight to the business room, so there was no waiting for Pattie to take herself off, no fussing over coffee.

'As you'll gather,' she began crisply, 'we have received the letter from your lawyer. It was startling, as you no doubt intended, but apart from that there are one or two points I should like to clarify.'

'I should have thought the situation was clear enough,' Gregory retorted, turning away in pretended disgust that that was all she had to say, but still watching her out of the tail of his eye with a malevolent gleam she didn't miss.

'No, that *I* wish to clarify,' Miranda repeated, and was pleased to see the malice replaced by a sudden watchfulness.

'You're about to thank me first, I suppose,' Gregory put in, recognising a danger of losing control of this exchange, not something he had expected or welcomed. 'It's not every day that an eighteen-year-old receives such a gift.'

'Perhaps because the general view might be that such a gift isn't necessarily beneficial for an eighteen-year-old.'

'What are you saying?' Gregory rapped, after a tiny crackling pause.

Miranda deliberately changed her angle of

219

attack. 'Am I to understand Kilgarth will only be Alexy's if I come to live here and make it our home?'

'That was clearly stipulated.' But his tone was not so patronising now. Something in Miranda's manner warned him that he would not override her as easily as he had foreseen. He had never taken much notice of her, beyond seeing her as partly responsible for Ian's defection, and he had never had a high opinion of her brains or character, regarding her as spoiled, superficial and immature. Now he was abruptly conscious of meeting a strength he hadn't anticipated, and he knew he must tread more warily than he had supposed.

'And if I don't find that acceptable?'

'The consequence could hardly have been made clearer,' Gregory answered shortly, registering with new alertness that she was not wrapping this up with reasons or explanations. He rather liked that.

'You would withdraw the gift?'

'I think it unlikely that any mother would deny a child her right to such a valuable piece of property.'

The sneer he allowed to creep back into his voice, to bolster his own aggression as much as to crush Miranda, was an error of judgement.

'I should be perfectly prepared to do so,' she told him calmly.

The pause this time stretched, long enough for Miranda to become aware of the dragging tick of the clock and the light tap of a straggling branch against the window, closed against the spring day.

'What is it you want?' Gregory demanded at last, his jaw jutting, his hands clenched on his stick so that the bones started out.

Miranda felt a release of tension deep inside her. 'Why is my living here a condition?' she asked.

'Humph.' Gregory darted a calculating look at her, then unexpectedly broke into a brief creaking laugh. 'To run my damned house for me, what do you think?'

'That's exactly what I thought,' Miranda agreed. 'But I have commitments of my own, you know.'

'That agency you run. There's nothing to that. Give it up. You'd have no expenses here. Everything would be taken care of, that was thoroughly gone into.'

'Well, it may surprise you to know,' Miranda remarked, annoyed for a second at the easy dismissal of her job, then deciding since he didn't know the first thing about it anyway it couldn't matter, 'that money is not the sole issue or motive for everyone.'

'Don't take that tone with me.' Gregory slapped her down at once, but though his tone was sharp she detected a thread of amusement there too.

'Gregory, look.' Though it had surprised her she responded to it by leaning towards him with a gesture of abandoning preliminaries, and he, astute old warrior, recognised that they had come to the crux of the matter, the point that had brought her here. 'As you know, there are

221

Will's boys to think of.'

'They're not yours.'

What a pretty pair you and Alexy make, Miranda thought, but didn't allow herself to be deflected.

'They are my sons. I have adopted them. They're as important to me as Alexy is, and I have an identical responsibility for them. A greater one, in fact, since they are younger.'

'You'd want to bring them here?'

Miranda watched him, saying nothing.

Outfaced, he muttered, 'Damned nuisance, but I suppose there's room, if they keep out of the way.'

In some obscure corner.

Miranda held on to the temper which could still let her down in spite of her best intentions. 'I don't think you quite understand. This is not an arbitrary decision to be thrust upon them, as you attempted to thrust it on me. I would talk to them, find out what they wanted, and act upon it. That's how I believe people should behave towards each other.'

Gregory was watching her closely, as angry as she was, but in no doubt now as to her strength of purpose. He knew there was more to come.

'There is one more aspect I think important,' Miranda said.

'Go on.'

'I should like to know how Ian feels about this.'

'Damn you!' His stick struck the floor resoundingly, and he made a clumsy, scrabbling movement to rise, instinctive but oddly helpless,

222

as though he scarcely knew what he was doing. 'This has nothing to do with him, nothing!'

Miranda had moved quickly to take his arm and help him back into his chair, but as soon as she saw that he was no longer attempting to get to his feet she stepped back, watching him with a set face. It had hurt more than she had expected to speak Ian's name here in this room, as though the ghosts of the past had crowded for a moment too achingly close.

'He has a right to know,' she said, her voice not quite steady. 'My coming here depends on what the boys want as much as on Alexy. And if we come then this becomes their home too, fully and legally. But before anything is decided, Ian must be told.'

# 18

Miranda wrote to Ian, unable to muster the courage to broach the subject by telephone. Huge doubts assailed her. He had made so clear his intention to withdraw from all contact with Alexy. He had his own life, perhaps by now remarried and with a new family. Other than financially, there had been no link for a long time. Why did she feel she must communicate with him at all about this? Was she merely trying to offload some of the responsibility for the decision?

More obscurely, and even reprehensibly if it were so, did she feel that Gregory's action would hurt Ian, and for her would appease in some way the deep-running current of anger which thoughts of him could always bring to the surface? But no, this had nothing to do with old conflicts. This, she was honestly persuaded, had to do with his rights as a father.

But once the letter had gone and the wait for a reply began, Miranda, vacillating between disbelief that she had written at all, thereby opening the doors to familiar frustration, and anxious impatience for an answer, knew that in the simplest terms she needed support. Such a decision, affecting Alexy's whole life, should be shared between them. She had had to write.

Ian didn't write in return. He came. And that, for one moment before the fluster of conflicting emotions he always aroused could engulf her, brought pure relief. It was agreed that he should come to the flat. Trying to gather her wits to suggest a place to meet, when he phoned to say which flight he would be on, Miranda had dismissed with sudden impatience the idea of some restaurant or hotel lounge. That expedient seemed unnecessary now, outdated, belonging to the fiery past when it had been essential to meet on neutral ground to keep the fighting in check. Also the flat she now lived in had not been their battle area. It was Will's territory, and his gentle presence seemed to return, steadying her, when she imagined Ian in it.

Here they would be able to talk undisturbed, the boys away and Alexy at school, in the throes of A levels. Surprisingly, and to Miranda impressively, she had not allowed the bait of Kilgarth to rock for a second her concentration on her own immediate concerns. No matter what riches were in prospect, these exams mattered to her. Dependent on good results was a place at Durham to read engineering, and that place she intended to have.

She had always worked adequately, the drop-out tendency Miranda had feared for someone so generally disaffected never an option for her. She had a drive and single-mindedness very like her father's, and she didn't intend to allow her mother's resistance on the subject of Kilgarth, infuriating as it was, to distract her from going for the results she needed. It made for a highly unpleasant atmosphere at home, but that wasn't something that had ever worried her, and if her mother didn't like it then she knew what she could do.

Practical though it was to suggest that Ian came to Simla Street, Miranda found the reality, as the moment approached, extremely disturbing. Would she ever be able to meet him calmly, as an ordinary, separate person, once linked to her life but now hardly connected to it, she wondered with something like despair, as she felt her pulse begin to race and her muscles tense at the mere sight of him.

With him in it, searching her face with his direct look, his shoulders as square, his back as straight, his movements as athletic and co-ordinated as ever, the familiar sitting-room became a different place. They might just as well have met in some impersonal hotel setting for all the comfort and reassurance she derived from being in her own surroundings. Ian seemed to take them over by sheer force of character. Where was Will's quiet presence now?

This isn't about me, she reminded herself firmly, or about Ian in relation to me. He's here as Alexy's father, and I need him in that role, and that role only.

His views were clear. Gregory was enjoying playing puppeteer, and if Alexy had any sense she would refuse to allow him to pull the strings.

'Have you pointed out to her that even if she turns down his present offer she'll end up with everything when he dies anyway?'

'But we can't be sure of that,' Miranda said. 'Knowing your father, there's no guarantee that he'd do anything so normal.'

'What do you imagine he'd do with the place otherwise?' Ian demanded, and the positive tone, in spite of the fact that he was asking a question, reminded her all too sharply whose son he was.

'He's quite capable of pulling some leave-it-all-to-the-cat-home stunt,' she argued.

'My father? He's a Ross, remember. This is Ross land we're talking about, Ross money and Ross property. He won't leave any of it outside the family, as you very well know, and who else is there to inherit?'

'What about his sisters? They're both younger than he is, aren't they?'

'They are, but he can't stand either of them, if you remember. They all fell out years ago, and I can't imagine much has changed there.'

'But the years pass. If Alexy refuses to go along with his plan he might do that out of spite.'

Ian grinned, a brief white flash in a face that even in the Australian winter never lost its tan.

'He wouldn't think that would annoy me quite enough, and annoying me is probably the main objective.'

'I'd wondered that. Do you mind at all, now, about losing Kilgarth?'

He hesitated for a second before replying. 'When I think of it as a place, as distinct from the family home, I do feel the odd twinge of nostalgia, to be honest. Calf country, I suppose. It will always be a landscape that will mean something to me. But when the personalities get into the picture, the atmosphere of the house, all that side of it, then no, I regret nothing. I certainly don't grudge it going to Alexy, if that's

227

what you're wondering.'

'But you think it would do Alexy more harm than good to agree to the deal your father's offering now?'

'Deal's always the word with him, isn't it? Yes, I think Alexy should hold on to her independence. Not get sucked in. She's only eighteen, I'd like to think of her making her own life without this sort of pressure being applied. What are her plans and ambitions, if any?'

Miranda felt a moment's thankfulness that there was a positive answer there at least, and told him as much as she knew. 'She keeps things pretty close to her chest, as you may imagine, but she works. Well, she tends to do the minimum, but when she does apply herself she mops it up. She gives the impression that the output of effort is calculated to a hair's breadth, but I don't think she'll have any difficulty getting the place she wants.'

'Well, I shall see her through university of course. That's always been the intention. Afterwards it sounds as though she'll be more than capable of looking after herself.'

'I don't think she can be expected to see the point about being her own person, though. She would only see us, me, as trying to cheat her out of something which is her due, being freely offered.'

'It doesn't come free though, does it? Nothing from my father ever does. It means you turning your own life upside down, and it would affect Will's boys as well.'

Miranda didn't notice how narrowly he was

watching her, as though he hoped for something from her which he had small hope of hearing.

'None of that would worry Alexy,' she said with sudden weariness. She had remained standing as they talked, too restless and too conscious of his presence to relax, and now she turned and folded her hands on the cool edge of the marble mantelshelf and laid her forehead on her knuckles, closing her eyes for a moment. 'I'm afraid the years haven't improved her character,' she told him. 'And no,' turning as though to forestall criticism, 'I haven't been able to do much about it.'

How could she begin to put into words Alexy's terrifying coldness, her absolute concentration on herself? He should know it anyway; he should have been here to face it, to help her to deal with it and not let it become the rooted thing it was. Familiar anger began to twist, as though almost glad to have found once more its accustomed focus.

Ian watched her for a moment more, as though still waiting for something, then said, 'You're going to accept Gregory's terms, aren't you?'

'I don't know yet. There are so many — '

'You are going to agree because you'll never deny Alexy anything,' he cut in. 'You'd never forgive yourself if you thought that because of you she had missed out on something she should have had. That's the truth of the matter, isn't it? You're afraid to say no to her. You always have been. You feel guilty.'

Taking this as an accusation, Miranda missed

the bleak understanding in his tone. 'Guilty?' she flared up at once. 'Why should I feel guilty? What more could I possibly have done for her? It's easy for you to talk about making her wait to inherit, though knowing your father there's no certainty that she ever would. You're not the one who'll have to face her — '

'I'm quite happy to talk to her when she comes home. In fact, perhaps this is something that should be decided by the three of us. Alexy is quite old enough to — '

'How do you know what she's old enough for? And it's not just facing her this afternoon, it's coping with her when you've gone, living with her when she thinks I'm the cause of her missing out on one more thing, just as she's missed out on having a proper home, a father, everything everyone else has, because of me. That's how she sees it, when it was you who walked out and — '

'Don't.' Ian was on his feet now too, at her shoulder, and overpowered by his bulk and nearness she instinctively moved away. 'Don't go down that road. For God's sake, haven't we gone over all that, time and time again? There's no point in throwing all the old accusations at each other. But if that's how you feel I don't understand why you wrote to me. Why drag me here to go through the farce of discussing this when you knew all along what you would do?'

'She's your daughter as well, remember, and this is to do with your father. Why should I have to decide? You can't expect to dodge all the difficult things.'

'Don't!' he said again, more violently. 'I won't

be dragged into all that. How is it that nothing can be discussed between us without these same old worn-out incriminations coming up again? I've done my best, God knows, to — '

'Yes, you've sent money. What effort did that cost you? It's too simple. I don't expect you even noticed it going out of your account.'

Ian turned away and took a couple of rapid paces towards the window, staring out till he got his anger under control. Then he drew a deep breath and turned back to her, though without coming close.

'Miranda, I know it was easy. I know you've had all the crises and hands-on difficulties to deal with. But there was nothing else I could offer.'

Perhaps if she hadn't felt so cornered, both by events and her own corroding guilt over Alexy, Miranda might have pulled back and admitted the truth of what he said. She might have been receptive to a rare note of pleading in his voice. He had done all it was open to him to do. If that came down to money then so be it; she had been glad enough to have the financial burden of Alexy taken off her hands. But she couldn't say so. Oppressed by the course before her, acknowledging at last that by contacting Ian she had somehow hoped he would be able to save her from her own actions, dreading the prospect of living within Gregory's orbit and under Gregory's influence, she failed to muster the honesty needed.

Instead she summoned the old resentments to her aid. Ian had always escaped his

231

responsibilities, from the days when he would walk out of the flat whenever Alexy howled, to go off to drink or work out, play rugby or go skiing, with precisely the same freedom as he had enjoyed before they were married. Nothing had changed. This decision was down to her, just as every other decision over Alexy had always been down to her. There was no escape.

★ ★ ★

Not all the long hours of the flight were enough to get his anger and disappointment under control. Ian felt drained by the seething images which refused to leave him in peace. No efforts to turn his mind forward to home, to the concerns which had been engrossing him before Miranda's letter arrived, even his latest mining project, were of any use. He was torn again by the feelings the sight of Miranda unfailingly aroused, and by the frustration she could fire up in him without the slightest effort. He had hoped so much that after this interval of time they could have met without antagonism, had hoped that in this matter of Alexy's future they could have found a basis for agreement. It was so obvious to him that becoming embroiled with Gregory was a dangerous ploy, and he had been sure Miranda would feel the same. Well, she did, for Christ's sake, but she was so eager to have another scrap with him that she was giving in to the evil old plotter just the same.

Almost groaning aloud in his defeated anger, he remembered again Alexy's stony eyes. He had waited to talk to her when she came back from school, but she had refused to discuss anything with him.

'What's it got to do with you?' she had asked, and the expressionless tone, flatly asking for information, had disconcerted him. Few people could achieve that lack of challenge in such a question, or lack of overt rudeness, yet succeed in being so rude that he had longed to shake some natural response out of her.

He had longed even more to go up to Kilgarth and confront Gregory, warning him not to damage Alexy's life as he tried to damage everyone else's. But he had pictured Gregory's thin victorious smile, heard his scornful voice. 'Damage, when I propose to give her my house and everything I own? I fail to see your grounds for objecting. Jealousy perhaps . . . ?'

What a fool he had been to come. He had made the decision years ago to stay away, and he had been right. He felt tainted by anger and quarrelling, with that helpless feeling of being meshed in a limed thicket that his father could so effortlessly create. Well, it was the last time. He would stay away now.

★  ★  ★

With a strange sensation that none of her actions had anything to do with her, Miranda took the next step and the next and the one after that.

The one reassuring element, and afterwards she felt she should have trusted them to provide it, was the response of Adam and Tim. They

233

were unreservedly delighted at the prospect of living at Kilgarth.

'But you seemed happy here, in Edinburgh,' she protested, rather taken aback by their enthusiasm.

'It was OK. We didn't mind,' Adam said quickly.

'But it's not as good as the country, is it?' Tim added reasonably.

She recalled that their early years had been spent in the Angus countryside and that they had been happy there. How amazing they were, these boys of Will's, saying so little, but always ready to accept what came their way. A surge of love and admiration for them rose in her; they could have made her life so difficult, and they had been so staunch and uncomplicated. She wanted to hug them, but knew they'd hate it.

Then a truer instinct took over. She wanted to hug them and she did. They looked a bit surprised but definitely pleased. She began to laugh then found she was closer to crying.

'Don't worry, everything'll be fine,' they urged, hating to see her upset.

'The only thing is,' Adam began, finding his voice hard to control, but anxious to seize this moment of unusual emotion.

It sounded as though an objection of some sort was coming and Miranda hastily pulled herself together to meet it. 'Yes, what, Adam? You must honestly say whatever you feel. That's very important.'

'Well, just, you know, that you're taking us too. I mean, it could have been just Alexy.'

'Never,' Miranda said fiercely, resisting the impulse to hug him again. Once would certainly be enough for one afternoon. 'Never. That couldn't ever happen. You're my sons, my family, and you have every bit as much right as Alexy to choose or decide. If you had hated the thought of Kilgarth we wouldn't have gone there, any of us.'

'Yeah?' They looked at her wonderingly.

Yes. It would have been the only consideration more powerful than her deep-rooted fear of, by her own inadequacies, robbing Alexy of anything that was her right. The knowledge was as comforting to her as it was to Adam and Tim.

Danielle was appalled, and angry.

'Quite apart from deserting the partnership you'll be sacrificing all you've achieved on a personal level. I can't believe you're even thinking of going.'

'I don't feel I have a choice.'

'But you're making the choice. No one else is. Let Alexy go on her own. Oh, God, I suppose that's out of the question. This mother-love business, it's nothing but a hideous compound of self-abnegation, craven seeking for approval and affection, cowardice, dishonesty . . .'

She had stormed out of the office, unable to contain her rage, and Miranda had had to go round to her flat that evening and beg admittance before she would relent sufficiently to talk. She wouldn't discuss Miranda's motives, however, unable to trust herself if she did, and it brought home to Miranda how the whole question of Alexy had always been a limiting factor in their friendship.

'You know how much I'll miss you,' she was able to offer, a bottle and a half of Sauvignon later. Indeed she could hardly bear to think of Danielle's brusque good sense being removed from her life, along with the laughter, the companionship, the satisfying feeling of shared achievement. 'Don't abandon me completely, however much you disapprove.'

'You know where to find me,' Danielle retorted, and with that Miranda had to be content.

Will's parents were cautiously approving. 'Adam and Tim will love it, of course. But won't it be a bit far for you to come?'

'Only an extra hour and a half. We'll come just as often, I promise. You won't see any less of the boys.'

'Handy for Glenalmond, living up there,' George Letham remarked and Miranda smiled at him gratefully.

Carol was less enthusiastic when Miranda phoned her. 'Only do it if it's what *you* want,' she warned. 'Never mind what that crosspatch daughter of yours thinks — though I can see you fluffing up your feathers at the description. You've established a workable way of life, all credit to you, and in your place I wouldn't give it up unless I was very sure the alternative was going to be better. No one can put that sort of gun at your head unless you let them.'

Georgina's reaction was more encouraging, initially anyway. 'Oh, darling, how you'll love being in the glen!' she exclaimed warmly. 'I know

236

you've missed all that. And Kilgarth is such a lovely house, or it could be. But living with Gregory — ' her voice became less certain. 'Goodness,' as she thought about it, 'are you sure you can face that? And really, Alexy is so spoiled already — I don't mean that *you've* spoiled her, of course,' backtracking too late, 'it's horrendously difficult bringing up a child on your own, everyone knows that, but I mean she does like her own way, doesn't she?'

Echoes of Aunt Nita and the complaints of the Marchwood cousins during tense family holidays.

Miranda, ruffled by this exchange, did her best to cling to the positive part of it, the prospect of being back in the landscape she loved. Though how changed would she find it, and what life would she be able to make for herself there in these new circumstances?

# 19

Miranda made many serious attempts, both before and after arriving at her decision, to discuss the subject with Alexy on every level she could think of. The point on which she was inflexible, however, as she made clear from the outset, was the position of the boys.

'They can't come. It's going to be my house, and I can decide,' Alexy had flatly stated, and Miranda had looked at her for a long considering moment.

'Alexy, you can forget that approach for a start. Kilgarth isn't yours yet. It will be your house if your grandfather's conditions are met, but only if he honours his promise. No, don't interrupt, you have to understand this clearly. There's nothing to say he won't change his mind, and you'd do well to remember that. However, if you go to Kilgarth, and I go to Kilgarth, then the boys go too. We're a family and we stay together and that's that.'

'If I don't agree you couldn't do anything.'

'Other than remaining here in Edinburgh, you mean, and continuing to live as we do now?'

'You wouldn't do it. You'd never stick to it.'

Again Miranda contemplated her in silence, employing Alexy's own tactic, with a look of calm decision that was more than sufficient answer. What Alexy couldn't know was her mother's ache of disillusionment to realise that no thought of how she would feel at giving up her own life and home had entered Alexy's mind.

'So, with that point settled, could you tell me why you feel it's a good idea to accept this offer?' Miranda asked after a moment, trying to keep the question as free of loading as she could.

Alexy scowled, looking suspicious. 'I'm being given a house. Surely you can understand that. It belongs to the family and I'm the only person who can inherit it.'

'But have you truly thought through the reality of living there? It's a house in surroundings you hate, where you always say you're bored to death and can never find anything to do.' Then, catching a gleam of what looked like complacency, she exclaimed, 'Oh, no! Alexy, you're not by any chance thinking that when the house is yours you'll be able to sell it? You're not imagining anything so absurd?'

'Why is it absurd?' Alexy demanded, looking ruffled for once.

'Because there's no chance on earth that Gregory would leave any loophole which allowed that to happen. He will have made certain that Kilgarth house and Kilgarth estate remain one unit and, as long as a single Ross is left alive, that it will remain in the family. Was that your real reason for wanting to move, for if it was I don't think it's a good basis for being happy there.'

But what place could offer happiness to this discontented girl? The question dragged at Miranda with a familiar hopelessness.

All such attempts to talk, all attempts to paint

239

an accurate picture of what life would be like in a house still ruled by Gregory, all reminders of the remoteness of its situation and the fact that they barely knew anyone nearby except two elderly great-aunts whom they could hardly expect to be welcoming, were met with instant protests that Miranda was only trying to prevent Alexy from having and doing what she wanted.

From the way she refused to meet her mother's eye as she made this accusation, Miranda concluded that Alexy found it the simplest and most effective way to dismiss reason and warnings. Alexy was too intelligent not to see the sense of what Miranda was saying, but her mind was obviously made up.

In the end, as Ian had known, there was no real choice. How often Miranda's thought turned to him in those difficult weeks, full of resentment that he had given her so little support, vanishing again almost as soon as he arrived, and arguing with him in her head as each day took her nearer to the inevitable. But beneath the indignation there was something else, something that would catch at her in moments of apprehension and loneliness — an obscure sense of loss.

Mostly she pushed it away, denying that it was even there. When she was feeling deeply dispirited, however, she would let herself acknowledge that when she had known she would see Ian again, after such a gap of years, she had hoped — here the thoughts would jar and check. What had she hoped exactly? For contact without anger. That seemed the closest she could get to defining the tug of need and regret. To be able to admit her pleasure at seeing him, without at once clouding it with antagonism and blame. She would remember the expression on his face as he realised that Alexy's hostility was still real and deep, and that nothing he could say or do would persuade her even to talk to him. He had done his best to hide that look of disbelieving hurt, but he had not quite succeeded, and the memory haunted Miranda.

One of the hardest things to deal with, in the busy days while everything was being finalised, was the withdrawal of Danielle's backing. She wouldn't relent.

'You're simply hurling yourself back into the subservient female role,' she would insist scathingly, whenever Miranda tried to reopen the dialogue. 'You're kowtowing to some man because he's waving a bit of cash in your direction. You're letting him turn you into his *housekeeper*, for God's sake. I can't believe you're doing it. Because you're a female you're supposed to be happy and fulfilled shifting dust about and heating up dead creatures for some male who's too lazy and arrogant to look after himself.'

'I spend a lot of my time as it is doing things like changing lampshades and putting up curtains and counting cups and saucers,' Miranda pointed out. 'That's about as domestic and mundane as you can get.' The idea of Gregory dusting raised a smile even as she saw how fruitless it was to pursue the argument.

'But for yourself, of your own choice,' Danielle

241

angrily persisted. 'Don't you realise that you let us all down when you regress like this? I know you think you're obliged to do it for that wretched daughter of yours, but basically you're jumping when a man says jump.'

Miranda, holding onto her temper, was suddenly aware of several things. For Danielle this was a feminist issue, and the divide between their levels of concern in such matters, normally glossed over for the sake of peace, now yawned unmistakably. Then Danielle had allowed her opinion of Alexy, grudgingly suppressed for years in order to maintain a working relationship with Miranda, to be revealed without concealment in that one word, 'wretched'.

Miranda also saw, something she had never thought about before, that the friendship which was central to her own life was one friendship among many to Danielle. It had revolved principally around work, and if that link were broken then very little would be left. It had been based, and this was the vital point, on Danielle's willingness to tolerate the demands Alexy imposed on Miranda's life, and to work round them.

As though for the first time, Miranda saw how Alexy, and her own anxiety about never loving Alexy enough, never being able to give Alexy enough, had shaped every aspect of her life. And now she had decided, driven once more by that same obsession, to live in circumstances which filled her with greater dread and distaste every time she thought of them.

* * *

What have I done? The question would assail her a dozen times the first evening at Kilgarth. In spite of conscientious efforts to think through every aspect of the move, her attempts to prepare the ground for Alexy and the boys, and her talks with Gregory, the lawyers, even with Pattie in the kitchen and Derek Cramb the handyman-keeper, now that it was happening there was a despairing feeling of having leapt with her eyes closed, ready for nothing.

A touch of light relief had come, as usual, from Adam and Tim. They had listened patiently, though obviously longing to be elsewhere, to her involved speeches about what she saw as potential difficulties, then had grinned at her and said, 'Don't *worry*, Mum.'

(Awkwardly, tentatively, they had asked how she would feel about their calling her Mum when the adoption process was complete. Thrilled, scarlet with pleasure, she had wanted to rush into excited embraces. They had eyed her with trepidation, slightly drawing back their heads. Adam had said, 'It'd be easier,' and Tim had added, not managing to be quite so casual, 'At school and everything. You know.' And that had been it. The memory could still amuse and warm her.)

* * *

She was hardly aware of driving through Muirend. It was just an ordinary little country town, tackier than she remembered it, busy with summer traffic, meaning nothing to her today. Afterwards she couldn't remember sparing a glance for the glen either, in spite of having more and more often turned, as the day of departure approached, to the thought of its beauty as one reliable delight in the whole uncertain plan.

A van was bringing their personal possessions. Seventy-five per cent of its load seemed to belong to Alexy. It felt strange to Miranda to have left behind the objects which had been part of her life with Ian, then part of her life with Will. More than once as she drove she was caught out by the panicky thought that she had forgotten something important, and she had to crush it down with the fierce reminder that these things had gone for good.

Summer afternoon though it was, the day was sunless and the wind cool from the north-east. The house of Kilgarth, in spite of the double doors to the porch being folded back, faced them with a look of blank reserve. For Miranda there was a moment of wild doubt, as though it were desperately important to get this right, as to whether they should ring or simply go in. She rang; they were strangers still.

Afterwards she remembered the scene, the whole first evening, as though they had arrived in the dark, but it was only that the house was so blankly unwelcoming, with its unlived-in smell and heavy air.

As Miranda went along the corridor to Gregory's room, leaving Pattie to look after Alexy and the boys for the moment, such

244

queasiness churned in her stomach that she thought she would have to make a rush for the downstairs loo. She paused and laid her forehead against the glass of the corridor window, leaning awkwardly across the deep sill created by the thick stone wall, closing her eyes as she waited for her nausea to subside. When she opened her eyes she saw that the astragal of the window was grimy, its paint cracked and lifting, a couple of dead flies gummed by a dusty spider's web to the edge of the hole where the sash cord ran.

The enormity of what lay ahead of her oppressed her; even more the realisation that there was no one in the world to whom she could voice her doubt and dread.

'So you're here,' Gregory grunted when she went in. 'Where's that daughter of yours? Manners not good enough to come and say hello?'

Alexy had refused to go and see her grandfather until she'd seen her room, no doubt fearing that the boys might steal a march on her. Adam and Tim, very subdued, were ready to do whatever they were told. Miranda made a mental note to reassure them at the first opportunity.

'She'll come in very soon.' Miranda felt the moment should be marked by some gesture of gratitude, some statement of good intent, but, wary of Gregory's readiness to turn anything he saw as weakness to his own advantage, it was hard to find suitable words.

To her surprise he forestalled her. 'Well, so you're here,' he said, leaning forward to give the fire a violent stab. 'It was good of you to come.'

Miranda only just caught the words and for a moment thought she had misunderstood. Or was he being sarcastic?

Gregory shot a quick glance at her, and this time she didn't miss the sardonic gleam in the watery old eyes. 'Surprised you, did I, saying that? Yes, well, it hasn't been the best of ways to live.'

He left it at that. Did he mean he only welcomed her as hopefully a more competent housekeeper than Pattie? (Danielle. The wound dealt by the swift unravelling of their friendship would take a long time to heal.) Or did he mean more, recognising that clinging to bitterness and loneliness is a poor way to pass one's life?

★　★　★

Other memories of that evening always remained muddled. Most revolved round some kind of problem or deficiency, and it was hard to resist starting a list then and there of things to fix, mend or buy.

The first crisis, not surprisingly, was created by Alexy. Gregory had told Pattie she was to have Ian's old room. Probably his thinking, if he gave it much thought, was that she was here to take Ian's place and therefore this was the obvious arrangement. Although nothing belonging to Ian was there now — Miranda had for the second time been assailed by physical reluctance when she found herself at the door, filled with fear of memories and change alike — the room itself was unaltered. There were the same worn

246

brown carpet (Gregory didn't waste money on pampering a boy), the same dingy curtains which didn't quite meet, the scarred mock-Jacobean furniture, the cumbersome wooden-armed chair Ian had had in his study at school, the window seat which was nothing more than his school trunk with a tattered chintz cover.

Alexy was appalled. 'It's a servant's room,' she said flatly.

It was the first thing Miranda would have put on her list. Not the room. Alexy's words. Where did such a phrase come from? Was this the attitude with which she proposed to embark on her life as the heir apparent? But it was not the moment to go into it.

'It was your father's room,' Miranda pointed out.

'I don't care whose room it was, it's horrible. Why can't I have a decent one?'

'I'm sure you can, only why not sleep here tonight, since Pattie has got it ready for you, and we'll decide on something else tomorrow.'

'I'm not sleeping in here, it's like a morgue. And feel this bed. It's awful.'

(I think I have. Past and present fused in a moment's disabling confusion.)

'Alexy, it's just for one night. It's not very polite to your grandfather to change his arrangements the moment we arrive . . .'

Alexy walked past her, heading for the front of the house. Miranda held herself still, waiting for her anger to ebb. There would be other, more serious issues, she was sure, for which it would be wise to reserve her fire. The boys hung at the door of the room they'd been given, hating as always the way Alexy made waves, and Adam, more as he grew older, hating the effect it had on Miranda.

'Are you two all right?' she asked them, managing a smile. 'How do you feel about sharing? I know you're used to it, but there really is plenty of room here.'

'We're fine,' said Tim. 'Look, you can see right up the glen from our window, it's brilliant. And we've got this huge cupboard, you can walk right in.'

Miranda looked at Adam.

'It'll be OK,' he said, not meaning the room.

Pattie became very boot-faced when Alexy, having chosen for herself a big room overlooking the drive which in all probability hadn't been used since Pamela Ross died, started turning the house upside-down demanding heaters and hot-water bottles.

Miranda knew that here was a matter that couldn't be shelved. Easygoing as Pattie was, she could not be expected to welcome such an influx as this. She was accustomed to a life of, on the whole, peaceful indolence. It had not been too taxing to look after one housebound old man and ignore the house itself. Though Pattie tackled everything in such a hand-to-mouth way that any job took twice as long as it should have, there was still plenty of time left for sprawling in her comfy chair by the Rayburn, drinking endless cups of tea and stuffing in whatever goodies she chose to buy on the household account. Gregory's complaints and bad temper washed over her unheeded, in fact she rather admired his more acid outbursts, taking them as an indication that he was feeling 'better in himself' rather than worse.

Now change was obviously coming, and vague ideas of working in Tesco's, recently opened in Muirend, or perhaps doing the rooms at the Cluny Arms in Kirkton, had been struggling round her brain. And if that little madam carried on like this every day of her life, Pattie thought with unaccustomed vehemence as she filled the kettle yet again, then the sooner she, Pattie, was out of here the better.

Though the standard of Pattie's work was another question which would have to be addressed, Miranda knew it would be highly inconvenient to lose her. She well remembered the difference between the ease of finding help for Cardoch House and the problems here, where there were few jobs for the men, few neighbours, no public transport and no nearby shops. A house like Kilgarth needed more than one pair of hands. Once well-kept, it had fallen upon sad times, and Miranda quailed at the prospect of re-establishing even an ordinary level of comfort if Pattie's help were withdrawn.

As Pattie came lumbering across the wide landing above the hall, two unreliable-looking hot-water bottles limp in her hands, she caught Alexy's comments on the state of the drawers and the lack of sockets. The latter complaint passed over Pattie's head; the first wounded her. Nothing had been said about this room being used, as she roundly pointed out.

'How's a body expected to clean a house this size from top to bottom, with no call for half the rooms from one year's end to the next?'

'You could at least do something about the mice,' Alexy retorted. 'Look at this lot,' indicating chewed fragments of drawer linings and dark droppings.

Miranda saw the indignant flush deepen on Pattie's heavy cheeks and, angry herself, stepped in quickly.

'Alexy, a room was prepared for you and you chose not to have it. Now you're on your own. I mean it,' she added sharply, as Alexy swung round on her. 'You're behaving appallingly. Pattie's brought the hot-water bottles you asked for so I suggest you thank her and let her get back to all she has to do.'

Though she had reacted partly from a wish to protect Pattie, as she spoke she found anger take over. They were here because of Alexy. 'Do as you're told,' she ordered crisply, and caught Alexy's look of surprise, instantly covered by indifference.

'God, what a place,' Alexy muttered, then with exaggerated punctiliousness, 'Thank you so much for the lovely hot-water bottles.'

'I'll see to your tea,' said Pattie, and waddled creakily away.

Miranda felt a momentary hope that perhaps they would avoid open warfare, then it died as Alexy pushed a bottle into the bed and found in the first place that there were no sheets, and in the second, with a yelp of pain, that the bottle had burst.

When, after the turmoil of unpacking, finding what they needed for the night, discovering that the hot water was no more than lukewarm and, on the part of the boys at least, of making a brief delighted exploration outside, they at last sat down to dinner, Pattie informed them that Gregory was having his in the library. Rebuffed for a second, Miranda hastily pulled herself together.

This, surely, had to be a good plan. One of the images that had filled her with dread was of the five of them ranged round the dining-room table, all exchanges stifled by Gregory's ill-tempered presence, resentment and boredom thick in the air. This way they were in their familiar group, not necessarily in accord, but used to that. Although Alexy's antagonism towards the boys had been rekindled by Miranda's insistence that they were family members with equal rights, Adam and Tim had long ago developed strategies to take the heat out of her resentment, and Miranda decided she could live with the arrangement for now.

She wasn't sure she could live with Pattie's cooking, however. Grey-green soup, over-salted; boiled potatoes peeled with a heavy hand, which disintegrated when touched; runner beans the colour of the soup; pork which curled like Aladdin's slippers from a dark sea which was either gravy browning or Oxo, and lumpy apple sauce of a tartness to bring tears to the eyes.

Or were her eyes ready for tears? No, that was

not how it was going to be. The thing was done; they were here, and whatever else the days brought they were clearly not going to be unoccupied.

# 20

Miranda took the sloping path between the rhododendrons with a sharper sense of the past being close than even sleeping in the big house had given her. In the two years since Gregory had first summoned her to see him, on none of her visits bringing Alexy had she ever come this way. It used to be an attractive walk with neat verges, the bushes a tidily clipped wall, covered in huge blooms in a glorious variety of colours in early summer. Now they were leggy, uncared for, narrowing and overarching the path. Though it was August, the air was dank, sharp with the smell of rotting vegetation. Water lay in the ruts of the path, whose gravel had long ago disappeared under mud. Miranda wrinkled her nose, repelled by the whiff of decay and neglect, tempted to turn and go back.

After all, there was no need to see the aunts today. Indeed, Gregory would be enraged to know she proposed to do so. He had made it plain that there was no contact between Kilgarth and the cottage where the chauffeur used to live, out of sight in its hollow to the east of the house. Although Miranda thought his attitude absurd and was determined to have nothing to do with any such feuding, or to let Alexy and the boys become involved in it, this was her first day at Kilgarth. A visit could wait. She had told no one where she was going; no one would know if she changed her mind.

But that would be cowardly, and today was supposed to be about positive thinking.

It was a day which had begun before three, when she had woken in jolting panic to realisation of what she'd done. How could she have stripped away so ruthlessly all she owned or was or had achieved? She had longed in those appalled moments to be back in the flat, waking to a day when nothing but familiar commitments lay ahead, crises and challenges too maybe, but nothing she wasn't confident of being able to handle.

Here a day of unknown demands faced her in a house that was not only strange to her by this time, but hostile. How had she thought she would spend her time, living here? What did women do who were home all day? She hadn't been at home since Alexy was a grizzling, fretful baby, and the hours had been filled with the endless and exhausting round of chores involved in looking after her.

And what would Alexy do in such a place, today or any other day? She would go mad with boredom before lunch. What would the boys do? They were strangers here, scarcely even welcome, knowing no one. How could they be expected to occupy themselves? What had she imagined any of them would do? It was a nightmare and one she had created.

Unable to get to sleep again, as dawn slowly came and panic subsided, she had gradually hauled her mind round to a less negative view. No matter how empty in personal terms this new life looked, she could hardly imagine she would be short of things to do. However prosaic, however fraught with the need for tact and caution, there were a dozen basic needs which had to be addressed. First of all, she must get Tim, Adam and Alexy comfortably settled in their rooms. Then she must work out the best plan for living in the rest of the house, and air and clean and make welcoming the rooms they would use. Above all she must establish a working relationship with Pattie. That should do for starters.

It had been odd to realise that mapping out the next few hours was all she needed to do. She was no longer half of a partnership, with the responsibilities to another person which that had for so long entailed.

Rather liking this idea, she had decided there was no point in wasting any more time in bed; she'd never get back to sleep now. Going to pull back her curtains (God, how they smelled), and looking out onto the dewy, shaggy garden, where early sunlight sent the shadows of sheltering firs fingering far across the lawn, she had realised that the only sound to be heard was birdsong.

More tired than she had perhaps known after the effort of organising a move about which she had felt at heart so doubtful, and having managed very little sleep, this beauty had moved her with unexpected power, and the tears she had resisted last night at dinner had been impossible to check. Not precisely attributable to regrets or apprehension, they seemed more a natural release of feelings too vague and large to cope with, and she had felt better for having shed them.

What was done was done. They were here. Now it was up to her, for everyone's sake, to make the best of this fresh start. And suddenly it had been exciting. Life had taken a new turn, and whatever problems lay in wait she was back in this marvellous part of the world again. What was she complaining about?

As she'd dressed, pulling on a cotton sweater and a denim skirt 'the red of a weathered New England barn', as the sales pitch had put it, she had taken another step forward. She had had a quick vision of her city self, the dark clothes, the high heels, the briefcase, face pinched against traffic fumes, pinched because she was late, hurrying, under pressure, her mind turning over some problem. Had she really enjoyed what she did? She'd always thought she had — luckily, since it had been her livelihood for sixteen years — but now, from one moment to the next, she found she was utterly thankful never to have to do any of it again.

Dizzy at this discovery, which seemed suspiciously neat and convenient, she had examined it more closely as she ran downstairs in the silent house. She had liked equipping the flats, buying, selecting, achieving a particular look she'd aimed at. She had liked meeting clients, and had relished the upsurge of the market with Edinburgh's future as the seat of Scottish parliament assured. She had felt at the centre of things, in touch. Now, disconcertingly, she had found she was seeing it in a different

256

light. Never again would she have to watch some face fall at the sight of a room she had thought particularly successful. Never again would she have to waste her time waiting in chilly flats for someone who had decided not to pursue the deal but hadn't bothered to tell her. Never again would she have to trawl crowded, overheated shops to buy such uninspiring objects as pedal bins and loo-roll holders for other people. How could she have imagined that she enjoyed it? With it swept away she really didn't know.

As she'd opened the inner hall door, and lifted the heavy bar securing the outer ones, it had been good to think that now they could stand open to sun and light, all day, any day, as she chose. Pausing on the wide stone step, she had looked down the lawn to the unpruned bushes which now obliterated the wall and hid the fields falling to the river. But she could see across to the main glen road; nothing moved there. Behind it the hills climbed away to the west, bell heather on their lower flanks still flaunting vivid colour in the morning sunshine.

How lucky to have arrived here in the summer. Why had that obvious fact not struck her till now? She felt as though she had spent far too many years with her head down a burrow. Why had she stayed in Edinburgh? She had only gone there to get a degree, for God's sake, and hadn't even achieved that. Well, she had stayed because she wanted good schools for Alexy, of course.

She had pushed the thought away, not wanting the moment of pleasure marred. Then she had caught it back. It could be turned around. They were here because of Alexy, and whatever loneliness or discomfort or inconvenience life at Kilgarth might bring, nothing could detract from the delight of its setting.

How unaware of the seasons she had let herself become. A morning like this, promising a beautiful day, had meant little more than trying to decide how hot it would be later, and what to put on at seven to see her through the next eleven or twelve busy hours.

August. In earlier days this would have been the most social time of the year at Kilgarth, with the house full of shooting guests — and every other house in the glen full of shooting guests. Probably they still were. The thought was actually surprising, as though that lifestyle must have become part of the past for everyone else as it had for her. She had turned to look northwards up the glen, placing the remembered houses.

Nearest, up the small road on which Kilgarth stood, was Dalquhat, owned by boring old Colonel Arbuthnott; and hadn't Philippa Galbraith (what was her married name?) had a cottage somewhere along here too? Across the glen was Baldarroch, the Thornes' hideous Victorian pile, where Michael was apparently living a strange, reclusive life with a new partner. Past Kirkton came Alltmore, where the two Forsyth boys were about Alexy's age, then Riach, concerning which the most startling news of all had filtered through — that James Mackenzie and Joanna Munro (or Drummond as she'd

258

become) had married, or were about to be married. Right at the top of the glen, Allt Farr, she'd heard from her mother, was being rebuilt after its dramatic fire, and Max Munro was engaged.

These families had been among her friends, and contact could undoubtedly be made again. It was important that the boys be absorbed into this new scene. Memories crowded back. They'd had such fun. Was anything of the sort still on offer for the next generation? Not for Alexy, presumably. Miranda couldn't imagine her tolerating for a second the activities she herself used to enjoy. But in a few weeks Alexy would be off to Durham, so really worries about how she was going to like it here were pointless. University would become the main focus of her life. Would she make friends there, friends she would be willing to bring home? If school was anything to go by it seemed unlikely, but the choice was Alexy's.

She would be virtually leaving home. Another fact that hadn't been fully absorbed yet. I shall be glad, Miranda had realised, startled guilt at the conviction mixed with a new pleasure to admit it. It would be a huge relief, in fact.

Feeling increasingly light-hearted, she had taken the top drive and wandered on along the road. No vehicle had passed her. The only sound, apart from the voice of the river below, had been a tractor early at work on Dalquhat. Was Martin Arbuthnott as pompous as ever? How nice it had been to think it wouldn't matter a damn if he was.

She had suddenly felt eager to make the first moves, get in touch again, more eager to face the world, in fact, than she could have imagined possible a few hours before. Fortified by this new optimism, she had come back to the house to be swamped by drama, wrath, contention and confusion.

The two boys, with the best of intentions, had started making breakfast for themselves, surprised by the absence of microwave, grill or toaster, but ploughing on manfully, and proposing to eat the results at the kitchen table. Pattie had been incensed on both counts, but 'hadn't liked to say', that most irritating of excuses. So, instead of telling them that the dining-room table was already laid (after a fashion), she had gone instead into a martyred flouncing routine, though its message had been cheerfully lost on them.

Alexy, having found the water still barely warm, had pinched the kettle from the Rayburn to wash her hair just as Gregory had rung for his breakfast, which luckily he had upstairs. Pattie had refilled the huge, solid-bottomed kettle to the brim and, such organisational skills as she had scattered by these upsets, had been able to think of nothing better to do than stand and stare at it as she waited for it to boil.

Breakfast over, Alexy had spent the morning equipping her room, pillaging indiscriminately from the rest of the house and raging whenever she was foiled. In the best tradition of country-house bedrooms there was one socket in her room, an inch from the floor beside the fireplace. Miranda refrained from saying that she should count herself lucky it was thirteen amp.

Into this outlet Alexy had every intention of plugging television, computer, printer, CD player, Lady-shave, VCR, radio, hairdryer, heated brush, convector heater and a couple of lamps.

'Why don't we put the bigger things within reach and you can plug them in as you want them,' Miranda had suggested, in the bright mother's voice which betrays precise knowledge of how the suggestion will be received.

Alexy had lifted her lip. 'I'll use adaptors.'

'Alexy, you'll burn the place down! You can't build a wobbling edifice of adaptors and expect the wiring to stand up to it.' Come on, you're proposing to take a technical degree. Work it out for yourself.

'Then somebody will have to come and put in a whole lot of extra sockets, today.'

'That isn't the sort of decision we can make,' Miranda had protested. 'It's our first day in the house, after all. You can see what your grandfather says, but the wiring may not be up to it even if he agrees. Goodness knows when it was last renewed. It's the sort of thing you have to accept in old houses.'

'The sort of thing you accept.' That clinical, toneless rudeness Alexy could summon so effortlessly.

'Why don't I ask Derek? He's the handyman. He might have an extension lead so you could use the socket on the landing as well. That would help for the time being.'

Alexy had stared contemptuously, then turned her back.

Ten minutes later Miranda had found her in the corridor leading to the garden door, where in the fashion of an earlier day the telephone had been sited, crossly balancing a Yellow Pages on the inadequate shelf.

'No.' Miranda had said definitely, putting out a hand to stop Alexy lifting the receiver.

'I'm not going to mess about with one socket, whatever you say,' Alexy had hissed furiously. 'And all the other rooms are the same.'

'Of course they are.'

'So I'm going to do something about it.'

'No, you're not.'

'I'll pay, if that's what's worrying you.'

'You know it isn't.'

Alexy had given her an exceedingly evil look. 'I don't think you can stop me.'

'I think I can.' Afterwards Miranda was to wonder whether it had been the optimism stirred by the morning beauty of the glen which had helped her to a new cool resolution as she'd stared Alexy down. 'There's no question of your making any alteration to the house without permission. Later, when the time's right, we may be able to make improvements — no question that they're needed. But for now, as newcomers, we accept the house as it is. You brought us here, Alexy, and I'm not prepared to have you fighting and complaining about everything that doesn't suit you.'

'I suppose you're going to throw that in my

face whenever anything goes wrong,' Alexy had retorted bitterly. 'I brought you here, so I'm to blame.'

'As often as it occurs to me, yes, I shall.' Miranda had agreed, and the steadiness of her voice as much as the strength of her opposition had startled Alexy a good deal more than she had let her mother see.

Derek Cramb who, Miranda had decided, knew as much about wiring as she did, had been summoned and, after prolonged tea-drinking and chit-chat of a valueless nature, had produced an ancient extension lead, with a white socket covered in oily finger prints at one end and a plug held together by insulating tape at the other.

Alexy had for once held her tongue.

Adam and Tim, with stranded kit of their own, had abandoned it philosophically to whatever answers might be found, and had sensibly disappeared on their bikes.

Gregory, his morning routine upset and disliking intensely the new rumours of war which penetrated even to his protected bunker, had made his indignation felt, and on the whole Miranda had not thought it the best time to open a debate on rewiring the entire house.

And now, to add to the dramas of day one, she was about to call on the redoubtable aunts, whom she hadn't met for twenty years: Olivia, who must, like Gregory, be in her seventies, and Belinda, known as Binnie, the youngest of the family.

As with the rhododendron path, Miranda

263

hadn't remembered the cottage being so shut in and dark. A pair of yews, originally planted to make an arch over the gate, and kept clipped sufficiently to allow entrance, had otherwise spread unchecked. Holly and laurel crowded the small garden. The grass had been cut with a Flymo, but its yellow tinge told that mowing had been left too long. Over both garden and cottage fully grown conifers towered, shutting off the light.

Not welcoming. Miranda felt nervousness return, along with a sensation of being watched with disfavour, as she struggled briefly with the gate and went up the short path. Deep-set windows peered out of damp-dark stone walls; the green paint of the door was peeling, its brass knocker dull with verdigris and streaked with bird droppings. When Miranda lifted it, it fell with a hollow sound, as though the door was damp or rotten or both.

After a tense moment she heard the sound of heavy feet. There was a pause while a key rasped; she half expected to hear a rattle of chains. The door was dragged open across stone flags. (Why didn't they tighten the top hinge?) Olivia Ross filled the doorway, a large woman in a tartan skirt and sagging beige jumper, her strong jaw jutting, her face unsmiling.

'Hello, you probably don't remember me. Miranda, Ian's wife. At least, I used to be married to Ian. We've come to live at Kilgarth, Alexy and I.' Miranda found herself gabbling nervously, and baulked at the thought of explaining Adam and Tim. 'We arrived last night.

264

I expect you'd heard we were coming. I thought it would be nice to . . . I mean, I just thought I'd come and say hello.'

'Humph,' said Olivia.

# 21

'You'd better come in.'

For a moment, trying not to shiver in the still air and the cold shadow cast by the yews, Miranda had thought Olivia was not going to suggest it.

'Thank you,' she said faintly, and winced as the door screeched again across the flags behind her.

'Left,' Olivia commanded, putting her stout shoulder to the door, which seemed unwilling to fit into its frame once more.

Miranda turned into a small sitting-room of such gloom and discomfort that she wished more than ever that she hadn't come. A fire was laid but not lit in a grate whose high, hideously grained wooden surround was quite out of proportion to the tiny space for the fire. On either side of the fireplace were two islands; occupied territories Miranda would come to think a more accurate description. The centre of each was a chair, one large, expansive, cushioned and worn, the only good lamp in the room beside it, a copy of *Henry Esmond* face down on its hollowed seat; the other prim, high-backed, so narrow that its arms impeded the elbows of the occupant, who if she wished to knit or sew or drink tea was forced to perch at an angle.

The occupant of this island, of course, was Aunt Binnie, and round her spread a choppy sea

266

of spectacle cases, skeins of wool, biros, memos to herself which she could never later puzzle out, a Victorian needle-book trailing threads, crumpled tissues in spite of the handkerchief which permanently bulged in her sleeve, clippings from the church magazine, library books she rarely finished because she never knew what to choose, and tubes of indigestion pills, peppermints and catarrh pastilles, their wrappers raggedly unwinding.

'Miranda dear,' she exclaimed, making a move to get up in welcome, catching ineffectually at various items which were dislodged as she did so, then, as if fearing this had been too effusive, looking guiltily at her sister, who loomed behind Miranda with a most unpromising expression on her strongboned face.

'Hello, Aunt Binnie.' Miranda stepped forward hastily. 'Please don't get up.' As she rescued a pair of embroidery scissors and a packet of Smarties — Binnie snatched the latter from her and stuffed it out of sight — she was aware of a single arresting fact. As Ian had once said, Alexy did look exactly like this pale, beaky-faced woman, and the glimpse of her daughter as she would be in fifty years' time was disorientating. Though Alexy would never, Miranda had time to reflect with a pinch of pain, wear the look of anxious kindness which Binnie gave her, as she resettled her belongings with one eye on Olivia, as though needing to be sure she wasn't in trouble.

The reminder of Ian, who had hovered somewhere on the edge of her consciousness all day, was also unsettling, and Miranda knew she must face up to the thoughts and memories without more delay, and if possible move on from them.

Olivia, tramping across the room with an emphatic tread that made the wobbly little table by Binnie's chair threaten to shed its load altogether, made a commanding gesture towards a third chair, humble, armless, drably covered, a line of dust visible round the back of its seat. It was set back from the fire in the middle of the room, a low table, holding a *Times* that had taken a severe mauling and a couple of hand-me-down copies of *Country Life*, intervening between it and any hope of warmth. It was lower than the other chairs, and as Miranda obediently sat down a broken castor made it lurch dangerously. As Olivia and Binnie surveyed her across the gap, she decided that if this added up to a deliberate tactic then it was remarkably effective.

Behind her a long-case clock, a big sideboard and two cumbersome glass-fronted bookcases crowded, too overpowering for the low-ceilinged room, items which had presumably started life at Kilgarth. A variegated ivy, out of control, filled a third of the small window, gripping the wallpaper at the side with strong brown fingers. The whole room had a crammed, stuffy, unhealthy feel to it, but even more unmistakable was its atmosphere of mingled challenge and unease.

'Well?' demanded Olivia.

It was so outrageous an opening that Miranda inwardly gasped, but it made her want to laugh

268

too. 'I've just come to call, as I said,' she replied, keeping her voice as natural as she could.

'Yes, of course,' Binnie began, clearly not ready to obey the call to battle, but Olivia fixed her with a warning glare and she fell silent, rootling nervously for her Setlers to give her reassurance.

'Does my brother know you're here?' Olivia demanded.

'No, he doesn't.'

'Hah!' A rasping sound that held unmistakable triumph.

'But I shall tell him that I've called.'

The tension tightened a notch.

'Will you indeed.' Olivia's voice was flat with disbelief, and also managed a hint of contempt which brought quick colour into Miranda's cheeks.

'We've come here to live,' she said steadily. 'Whatever quarrel you and Gregory have is nothing to do with me, or with Alexy. I should like to come and see you sometimes,' (well, true in theory, even if for the moment she could hardly wait to get away) 'and Alexy too.' (Into the realms of the unimaginable this time, but it had seemed possible as she came down the path.) 'Of course if you hate the idea we won't intrude on you, though I think that would be a bit sad. I know I don't belong to the family any more, but Alexy is still your great-niece.'

'He's inveigled you here to look after him. You realise that, don't you?' Olivia said sharply, ignoring this piece of sentimentality. 'He's getting past it, and he knows it. Pattie sinks deeper into sloth with every day that passes and he can't be bothered to sort her out.'

Gregory's plans for Alexy's inheritance could not be mentioned, though seeing the gleam in Olivia's small eyes, creased to watchful slits above the slabby weathered cheeks, Miranda suspected that she had already worked them out.

She did exactly as Olivia had done, and deflected the attack. 'My two sons are here as well, Adam and Tim Letham. Kilgarth is now their home. You know Will died three years ago.' Such major items of news had appeared on the left-hand side of Christmas cards. There was no need for the aunts to know that she and Will had never been married. Invoking his name was strange; he seemed remote here, without substance.

'We were very sorry,' Binnie began, her kindly face with the soft sagging skin perturbed.

'So how old are these boys?' Olivia interrupted, with an antagonism that spoke of fears of noise and hooliganism and footballs kicked into the garden.

'Don't worry, they won't break your cucumber frames,' Miranda assured her, reading this with ease. 'They are fifteen and fourteen, and reasonably civilised.' Unlike Alexy; familiar uncomfortable rider. A glint in Olivia's eye told her that her deliberate choice of the dated expression had found its mark.

Abruptly she had had enough of undercurrents and malice. Time to wrap this up. Clearly no hospitality was about to be offered. She had done all she came for and couldn't wait to be out in the sun and warmth again.

'Well look, you know I'm at Kilgarth now, so if there's ever anything I can do for you, shopping or whatever, do please — '

'Oh, that would be very — ' Aunt Binnie began, rustling her nest in her eagerness.

'That won't be necessary,' Olivia forestalled her. 'We manage perfectly well.'

'Of course. I'm sure you do.' Miranda came to her feet with a social smile. 'It's been so nice to see you both again . . . '

Released, she ran up the rhododendron path as fleetly as if her young self really had returned to Kilgarth, though having to stop and get her breath back at the gate into the garden slightly marred the illusion. What a pair. They were like some dreadful old married couple, permanently at odds with each other, but without the justification for staying together of having made a vow to do so. Why on earth did Binnie allow herself to be trampled over like that? What a fearsome, arrogant, humourless bully Olivia was. Or perhaps Binnie was so used to being treated in this way that she didn't notice it any more, even clung to it like some grubby old security blanket. Had she ever decided anything for herself in her life? And that cheerless little cottage. Did they hole up there all day long, bickering and quarrelling, without ever taking the trouble, or perhaps not knowing how, to make themselves comfortable?

She went along the shrubbery path and out onto the drive and there, as though she had come upon it unawares, Kilgarth as it used to be waited for her, the sun on its face. She caught her breath and stood still, as though afraid an incautious movement would make the image shift and fade before her eyes, to be replaced by the shabby reality of the present, where not only a bitter, disagreeable old man lurked in wait, but where her equally disagreeable daughter was busy digging herself in to her own satisfaction.

Not unlike the aunts, it occurred to Miranda, each with her safe patch of ground. What was that spot in the bullring called, to which the bull retreats over and over again in pain and baffled fury? His *querencia*, his chosen spot. Would Alexy need such a place always? And how unfair it was to call her disagreeable, when Miranda knew that she herself, by her own shortcomings, had turned her daughter into the person she was.

But even this thought couldn't for the moment banish the past. Seeing the house dozing there in the summer afternoon quietness, other images jostled. She could hear the voices, see the faces. She could almost feel her own boundless energy again, the lightness of her step. She had been so fit in those days; how she had loved competing and pushing herself — and how she had loved excelling. She saw Ian's face, clearly this time, alive, laughing, teasing, and glimpses of faraway days were suddenly there for her to take out and look at like a pile of photographs. She saw his grin as he ripped off his goggles after a race, his eyes gleaming out of the shape they had printed against the snow-dusted, wind-darkened skin; saw his concentrated expression as he settled himself to address his ball on the first tee; saw the agony of effort in his face as he went for a try, expending every ounce of physical and mental determination. She saw him coming towards her, eyes alight, hand out, kilt swinging, as one of the reels they always danced together was called.

The happiness of those crowded days filled her again, standing in the sunlight looking at the home Ian had so resolutely left. He had had guts to do it, and no one else could be as aware as he of the dangers of bringing Alexy here under his father's scheming terms. It was rare to think of Ian without defiance and hostility immediately replacing every well-disposed thought, but today the younger Ian she had loved had been very close, memories surfacing at every turn, and suddenly Miranda wanted to acknowledge them, honestly and fairly.

For a time they had been completely happy, their lives revolving round each other. How long was it since she had admitted that? The spell still holding, she allowed pictures long banished to take shape. Standing here it was easy to remember such details as roaring up the drive in Ian's beloved first car, hearing steps crunch the gravel, and fragmented calls and arguments as a big crowd of them packed the Land Rover to go up to the loch, to make a fire and cook the catch, lingering in that high open place till the light was red over the water and the glories of sunset unfolded before them. How shivery and bumpy and endless the drive down the track had seemed afterwards, legs goose-pimply, feet freezing in sandals. Her place had always been the middle of the front seat squashed against Ian, hitching up her right buttock as he released the handbrake, knees scrunched sideways to keep clear of the gears till he was in third. How good his solid warmth had felt, how delicious the prospect of the hours to come. For after noisily driving away to take her home, they would leave the car and come back over the wall, to creep by a roundabout route up to his room. And nothing since had ever been so rapt and happy and complete as their lovemaking.

In the room Alexy had been offered yesterday and had so contemptuously rejected.

The past could not survive that reminder, and Miranda felt a strange bleakness, in spite of the sun's warmth, as the vivid images slipped away. Would they become less and less distinct, with less power to move her, as the new reality overlaid them? She shook herself, turning to the front door, deliberately finding a practical focus for her thoughts.

The matter of Alexy's room was urgent, for that was where her life, by her own choice, had centred ever since they had moved to the new flat with Will and the boys. A new thought occurred to Miranda. Was this a chance to wean Alexy from her habit of cutting herself off from the family group? But at once common sense rejected the idea. What did she imagine Alexy doing in the morning-room, which Miranda had selected as their base, since the thought of removing the dust sheets from the drawing-room and stirring its dead reaches to life, or of invading the library, Gregory's alternative sanctuary, had seemed equally unappealing. Alexy's interests had moved a long way from anything ordinary television channels offered. She was addicted to an electronic world which Miranda knew little about. She needed to be locked into sound and to the world of the screen which shut everything else out. She liked her own videos, her own music, and though she read quite a lot she confined herself to the sort of technical material which Miranda couldn't think of as reading at all.

She must also talk to Pattie, Miranda remembered, unconsciously displacing a problem which had no answer with one more capable of solution. Also there was the question of Gregory. Would he loathe his privacy being invaded, or would he be offended if no one came near him? Would he prefer to see only Alexy? Frowning, oppressed once more by the conviction that she hadn't done enough thinking before coming here, Miranda went in.

Since there had been no tea on offer at the cottage she went to the kitchen. Did Pattie go up to her room in the afternoons or did she nap by the Rayburn? Hearing voices as she went along the passage, Miranda realised that Pattie did neither. She entertained.

Miranda hesitated for a second, recognising the second voice as that of the dour Derek Cramb. But she hadn't let the fearsome Olivia flatten her, Miranda reminded herself. She could face these two.

It was a peaceful scene, the chairs with their never-plumped, napless velvet cushions pulled close to the cooker, in spite of the temperature outside. A hefty green enamel teapot stood on the Rayburn. To hand at the end of the long table were milk carton, sugar bowl, *The People's Friend* and a *TV Times*, plus a slab of dark and expensive Walker's fruit cake.

The two faces turned as Miranda came in, blankly resentful, automatic defensiveness at being 'caught' mingling with a determination to block any suggestion that they should get up and do some work.

'Any tea in the pot?' Miranda asked, and winced as she heard her unintentional lady-of-the-house tone.

'Aye, should be,' Pattie said after a fractional pause, as her sluggish brain worked out that if she suggested Miranda having tea in the wee sitting-room she was so set on using, then she, Pattie, would be the one who'd end up taking it in to her.

'Good.' Miranda found a mug, flinched momentarily at the sight of its stained interior but decided this was no time for niceties. 'I'm glad you're both here as I've been wanting to talk to you.'

They stiffened. It was against all the rules to talk to them while they were having their break. That was work. That was infringing their rights. They watched in offended silence as Miranda drew a chair out from the table and turned it towards them.

'I take it you both want to go on working here?' she asked affably, and as she concentrated on cutting a slice of cake for herself she could

276

feel the electric quality which the silence took on. 'I mean, even though things have changed rather?'

'Who's said we're to go?' the burly Derek demanded, pulling himself together first, his face very red. Pattie gaped, wordless, her complacency shaken.

'Oh, no one.' Miranda pressed a fragment of cherry and a couple of crumbs together with her fingertips and put them into her mouth. 'I just wanted to make sure you were happy to have us all around. It will change things somewhat, especially for you, Pattie.'

'Aye, it will that,' Pattie agreed, now wary and even conciliatory. 'I've enough to do as it is. I canna be always running about after that young — after yon lassie. And cooking dinner and breakfast and all, with the laird at me for his trays and will I fetch him this and that and the next thing, and will I poke the fire for him, though what he's wanting with a fire in the middle of summer beats me.' Miranda resisted the impulse to draw her chair back from the fiery glow before them. 'And ringing that dratted bell when he's nothing better to do with himself. Half the time I ken he does it just for badness, then cursing me up and down when I'm a minute or two late, and me with the washing to see to, and the cleaning and ma banties and . . .'

Having lost the thread of her argument Pattie put three extra spoonfuls of sugar into her mug to console herself, and drank the resulting sludge with loud hard-done-by gulpings.

'I know,' Miranda soothed. 'But what I'd

thought was this. You and I can share out the jobs for the time being. The children will help, of course — ' two of them will, anyway ' — and then we can decide whether or not we're going to need extra help. In a few weeks Alexy will be at college and the boys back at school, so there won't be nearly as much to do.'

She could have wished both faces had not so unmistakably shown their pleasure at this news.

'I canna' have those lads stravaiging about disturbing the moor, though,' Derek put in, taking upon himself, in this more promising climate, the authority and belligerence of a proper keeper, since there was no one there to say he wasn't.

'Oh, I think they'd be keen to help you,' Miranda said, and saw in his eyes that this would be even less welcome. Derek wasn't at all sure that even townies like this lot could fail to notice that he had barely been near the moor this past year.

'Only if you want them to, of course,' Miranda added sweetly, certain by this time that there was nothing to worry about from these two. Though their jobs might not be as cushy from now on as they had grown to expect, still they were jobs. Derek's came with a cottage, where he ran a useful sideline carving crude crooks from rams' horns for the less discerning end of the tourist market, while Pattie had a warm and downy nest in the house, which she had long ago arranged to her satisfaction and which she would be loth to abandon.

Miranda went back along the corridor fanning

278

its cool air round her face with relief. She had planned to be tactful and even rather propitiatory with Pattie, not sure how she would cope without her, but the firmer approach, adopted on the spur of the moment, had worked surprisingly well. Though she didn't think she was ready for any more battles today, all the same.

Where were the boys? Had they enjoyed whatever they had been doing? Then she smiled, realising that her mind had turned to them as a source of certain pleasure. When had that habit begun to form? But form it had, and it never failed her.

# 22

'Hi. Is this a good time or an appalling one?'

Miranda, coming through the hall carrying a great stack of folded curtains, her back arched by both their weight and her keen desire to keep her nose away from the knock-out blend of long-ago wood fires, peat, cigar smoke, food, dust and neglect which they gave off, craned her head to look round them. The pile began to slide sideways and she was glad of the quick hand which came out to steady it.

'Here, shall I take a couple from the top?'

Across some rather nastily streaked beige lining Miranda found herself looking into a plump, pretty, smiling face a few inches lower than her own, surrounded by a bobbing mass of curly brown hair. The first details she took in, apart from the friendliness of the eyes, was the soft texture of the skin and the delicate pink of the round cheeks.

'Sorry to barge in. I did ring but no one appeared. Where do you want these?'

'Oh, dump them down anywhere. God, aren't they revolting?' Miranda gasped, thankfully divesting herself of the solid bulk of the curtains onto the wooden chest that had always held, and still held, tennis rackets and croquet set.

'Dining-room,' said her visitor, sniffing cautiously. 'That can't be anything but Brown Windsor. I'm Muff Carmichael, by the way, from

Balgowan. Across the glen, just above Sillerton, where the — '

'Oh, yes, I know it. We used to go there often when the Sargents lived in it. Lovely house.'

'Um, well, these days it may not be quite as smart as it was then, I'm afraid.' Muff grinned, not sounding too worried about it.

'Nor is this place,' Miranda said, glancing round the big hall where, as in every other room in the house, years of careless cleaning seemed to have left its contents looking dulled, muted and depressed. 'Sorry, I'm Miranda Ross. How do you do? Oh, perhaps not recommended,' she added, as she held out her hand and then saw what colour it was.

Muff, however, shook it warmly, undeterred. 'I know, I'd heard you were here. Usual grapevine.'

'How nice of you to call,' Miranda said, and meant it, drawn to this beaming girl with her easy friendliness. 'Can you stay and have tea?'

'I'd love to, but I've got a carload of kids outside. When don't I have a carload of kids?' she asked in a mournful aside. 'That's the trouble, I've gone past quite often, since school started again anyway, but it's never been a good time to stop. It isn't a good time today either, I'm just putting my nose in really, but I knew if I didn't do something about it we could go on like that for ever. Which reminds me, I'd better make sure nothing too grisly is happening.' She trotted off towards the door, a dumpy figure in a floral cotton skirt that dipped to her ankles and made her look even wider than she was. 'I know I could have phoned,' she went on over her shoulder, 'but it's never the same as meeting, is it? Too formal, too 'I'm doing this because I know I should'. And even if you think you'll get on, when you meet the person in the flesh you can be fearfully disappointed. Hang on a sec.'

She disappeared and Miranda could hear her issuing threats and commands. Amused, she went after her to the door. A Jeep Cherokee was parked askew outside the drawing-room windows and what looked like a dozen juvenile and canine heads were bobbing about in it, though on looking more closely she saw some were immobilised by being strapped in.

'Heavens. How many are yours?' Miranda asked, as her visitor came back.

'Only two. Well, two of this lot. I say, it's just occurred to me, why don't you come back with us now? If you could stand the racket. Though I start dropping bodies off quite soon. Why not come and have tea, and I'll run you home later? Or are the curtains urgent?'

'Since they haven't been disturbed for about a quarter of a century I can't imagine another hour or so will make much difference,' Miranda replied, feeling a half-forgotten interest, almost exuberance, stir.

'Come on, then.'

Gregory, Alexy, the garden, the house and the work required to make it habitable again, where every day a new job joined the queue of those already demanding her attention, a queue which appeared to stretch away into infinity, suddenly looked delightfully unimportant.

'Do you know, I think I will. Thanks.'

'Good. OK as you are? Nothing you have to do?'

'Nothing.' A heady moment. Normally Miranda would have gone in to tell Pattie she was disappearing, maybe to have a word about dinner, at the very least to pick up her bag. But perhaps because this unknown girl (Muff?) had come walking in so simply, perhaps because she herself was at last accepting that the busy life in Edinburgh was truly behind her, she responded to the invitation with a spontaneity she couldn't remember feeling for years.

'Nobody to lock up, tie down, pen or otherwise confine?' Muff asked.

'Not a thing.'

'How lucky you are,' Muff remarked with heartfelt envy as they went across to the jeep.

'I can't wait to make the acquaintance of your household,' Miranda told her, her spirits soaring.

Muff laughed as she opened the passenger door and started to unbuckle a car-seat holding a slumbering baby.

'Hey, don't move him — her. I'll go in the back.'

'Are you sure? There's not a lot of room, and it seems rather inhospitable, having shanghaied you.'

'Of course I don't mind.'

'OK. Jimsie, can you squeeze in beside Morag? Smith, lie down, there's no need for you to get involved.' This to a portly black labrador who was trampling over various unconsidered children in his efforts to reach Miranda. 'Thanks, Jimsie, that's great.' Muff cast a rapid, practised glance over the disposal of her load, and deciding enough people were sitting down, went round to the driver's door.

Could Muff really reach the pedals, Miranda wondered, amused again, in spite of that fat cushion visible over the back of the seat. She could not have explained to anyone the simple thrill it was to be driven away like this, without so much as shutting the door, crammed in with the silent, staring children, while a grey-muzzled labrador tried to make her acquaintance on a far too intimate level, and the plump cheerful stranger at the wheel swung her big vehicle with breezy confidence down the tight bends. For a few moments Miranda felt she didn't know where she was going and didn't care, then, making a mild effort to be a little more sensible, summoned from memory a picture of the attractive, rambling house of Balgowan.

It had originally been one of the Sillerton farms, but the Sargents, friends of her father's, had bought it in the early sixties — had the Hays even then been feeling a financial pinch? — and throughout Miranda's childhood and teens it had been a familiar place.

When all the passengers had been dropped off at various track-ends or cottages, and only the Carmichaels were left — Fleur, who had started at Kirkton Primary this term, and the sleeping baby, Henrietta — it was strange to wind once more up the well-remembered drive after so long and in such different circumstances. The white-washed farmhouse, with roofs at three heights as various bits had been taken in from adjacent buildings, with roses climbing to the rones, and a conservatory she didn't recall added at the western corner, looked badly in need of a coat of paint, but it also looked immediately and undeniably friendly, with its door and windows open, a silt of toys on lawn and terrace, and the borders beneath the windows massed with flowers. She had forgotten that great view to the south, and the depth of the river gorge below. But she felt an instant ease here, as though any changes had been assimilated in that single glance, the present character of the house blending readily with childhood memories.

Two boys, three or four years older than Fleur, raced out to greet them, followed by a gangling puppy.

'Thomas and Jack, but don't worry about all the names. They go back to school in a few days, thank God, so you won't see them again for a while.'

The boys offered a dutiful minimal greeting and scudded off, pursued by Fleur, wailing.

'They get so bored with her. She is a bit of a whinger, I have to admit. She'll soon be back. Come on, let's grab tea while we've got the chance. With any luck Henry will leave us in peace for a bit longer.' Muff dumped the car-seat on the kitchen table with a careless bump Miranda would have thought enough to wake any child, but since Henrietta didn't so much as murmur she presumed she was inured to such treatment.

There never was peace at Balgowan, as Miranda was to discover, then and on subsequent visits, but there was a casual warmth, an atmosphere of hospitality and refusal to be hurried which she found very agreeable.

'Muff?' she enquired, as her hostess made space on the messy garden table for two mugs of tea and a blue and white biscuit barrel stuffed with the fanciest and most cholesterol-laden biscuits available in Muirend. 'Where does that come from?'

'Myfanwy, can you believe. What a nightmare it's been.'

'Surely nobody reads enough to make bicycle jokes these days?'

'You just did,' Muff pointed out indignantly. 'So what was your subject?'

'You've guessed.'

'Mine too. Where?' And they were off, on the first of a hundred hundred conversations, invariably conducted over and in spite of the demands of the Carmichael children, of all the extra children who were dumped at Balgowan with regularity, and of a multitude of birds and animals which Miranda never attempted to keep track of. Helping Muff was a leggy Danish girl, with grey eyes and cropped light hair, who closed her o's in a precise way rarely heard from native speakers, and whose intellectual reading tastes terrified Muff, who never got beyond page two of the most frivolous novel before she fell asleep. Her name was Feodora, but in Scotland she preferred Freddie. As Henrietta was usually called Henry, Miranda felt confusion threaten.

Over all the comings and goings Muff presided calmly, dispensing cuddles, commands,

286

biscuits and an efficient de-ticking service with a smiling serenity which Miranda guessed would survive most trials.

Only one aspect of the visit jarred. They made a tour of the house, so that Miranda could see how it looked now. (She liked it, but thought Mrs Sargent would have been horrified at lively amateur murals, a tent pitched for some reason on the drawing-room carpet rather than on the lawn, a plastic slide fixed to the front stairs, and a spew of clothes and toys spilling out of every bedroom, through which Muff led the way, talking all the time, with complete indifference.) Then Muff glanced at her watch and said regretfully, 'Now, without wishing to seem in the least unwelcoming, we ought to decide if I'm to take you home before Colin gets back or afterwards. I know he'd love to meet you, and I'd love you to stay, but it might be a bit late before we got you home. Unless you'd like to stay to dinner, of course? That would be best of all. Only the thing is, Colin likes me to be here when he comes in, and I always do my best to be, though the time can vary because he often gets stuck with a client.'

Miranda had already learned that Colin was a solicitor in Muirend. A vision of Danielle's face if she had been presented with such an artless choice rose before her. She too, from habit, at once resented the idea that any man should expect such an indulgence, and get away with it, whether it suited his wife or not.

'No, really, I should be getting back,' she said. She found she had no wish to meet Colin. 'I'm sorry to give you the trouble of taking me. I should have followed you over in my own car.' Such an obvious course had not crossed her mind in the euphoria of the moment.

'It's no trouble. Of course it's not. I only wish you'd stay longer.'

'I ought to do something about dinner, I suppose. Though once Alexy and the boys are away things will be more relaxed.'

'We'll make plans then. Goodness, I can't tell you how glad I am I've met you. Well, if you're sure . . . ?'

The pressure of Colin's needs encroaching on the relaxed mood could be felt, while none of the demands and interruptions Muff had dealt with in the last couple of hours had fazed her in the least. As they drove back Miranda sensed that Muff was conscious of the time all the way. When they reached Kilgarth she barely paused for goodbyes, but whirled on down the loop of the drive with a hasty wave.

Thank goodness I'm not answerable to any man like that, Miranda thought as she went up the steps. Even Gregory's complaints seemed more acceptable.

★　★　★

She was finding, in fact, much to her surprise, that as the days passed her feelings towards Gregory were changing. She had dreaded most, of all the things that had seemed undesirable about living here, the contact with a man so bad-tempered, deliberately unpleasant and overtly

288

hostile. When they had arrived and she had seen that he intended to keep to himself, preserving as far as possible an unchanged lifestyle, it had been a relief. But gradually, feeling more at home in the house once known under such different circumstances, she had seen that that was not necessarily the best arrangement. It couldn't be good to let two separate camps develop, each uncomfortably aware of the other, each ready to resent the other. One aspect of this was that it would relegate Adam and Tim to the status of barely tolerated extras, the opposite of what she had wanted for them.

There was also the question of exactly how ill Gregory was. Why did he get up so late and spend the day huddled in a chair, in his office or the library, doing little more than doze, grumble at Pattie, or work himself into a tantrum over something he had read in his *Times*? He was sufficiently mobile to have a bath, dress, get himself downstairs and take himself upstairs again after the Nine o'Clock News. It had been hard to find a way to ask why there was so little action in between.

The chance came when Gregory stumbled getting up from his chair and fell, bruising his shoulder and cutting his forehead though not doing any serious damage.

'He's more angry than anything,' reported Dr Fleming (son of the Dr Fleming whose firm old-fashioned views on abortion had long ago so affected Miranda's life, in a sense being responsible for Alexy's existence, and by extension for Ian's departure), as she led him

289

into the sitting-room. 'But unfortunately he's getting so stiff with all this inactivity that such falls are likely to occur again, particularly on the stairs.'

'But why does he spend his days doing nothing?' Miranda asked. 'He never goes out of the house or takes any interest in what's happening to the estate. He used to be so involved. I've never understood exactly what's wrong with him.'

'You're to be here on a permanent basis?' Charlie Fleming enquired. He was older than Miranda, but vaguely remembered her from Cardoch House days.

'Yes, we live here now. I have two boys as well as Ian's daughter Alexy.'

Charlie Fleming frowned. 'There's no serious medical condition,' he said. 'High blood pressure, which he refuses to do anything about. Rheumatism, which is particularly troublesome in his knees. But basically he's lost interest in living. He can't motivate himself any more. He's so fixed in this habit of never stirring from the fireside that his chief problem is that his joints are seizing up. At the stage he's reached any movement becomes so painful that the thought of doing even the gentlest loosening-up exercise is daunting. What he needs is a course of massage therapy, producing a gradual build-up of movement, but since he has no inclination to do anything more than he's doing it's impossible to persuade him to embark on it. He's given up hope, and that can be a trend hard to reverse.'

Given up hope. What was it Gregory had

hoped for? That his son would relent? Or had the decision to make Alexy his heir been not so much a vengeful blow aimed at Ian as a reaching out for something? For the first time Miranda felt genuine pity for the bitter old man. However much he had called his present loneliness upon himself it was a sad way for anyone to live.

When they first arrived Alexy had dropped in occasionally, for a few moments at a time, to see her grandfather. But she had soon grown bored with that. Miranda suspected she felt her position here to be already so secure that there was no need to make herself agreeable. Her affability had lasted long enough to persuade Gregory to have extra power points put into her room (Miranda's intervention, and her offer to foot the bill, had added more in the boys' room, kitchen and sitting-room) but once that was organised to her satisfaction Alexy either shut herself away in her room or took off in her car, destination unspecified. She often went down to Edinburgh, Miranda knew, though when they had lived there she had appeared to have few friends with whom she would want to keep in touch.

Miranda, therefore, on a day when the house was empty, Pattie taken down early to Muirend for her day off, made lunch for Gregory and took it, with her own, to his frowsty business room.

'What's this?' he demanded belligerently, when she set the table in front of him for two and drew up a second chair.

'There's no one but us here today,' she said airily. 'It seemed silly to eat in separate corners.'

291

'Damned impertinence,' he huffed, but that was all, an acquiescence which made Miranda ashamed not to have taken the initiative long before this. She didn't particularly enjoy the tense atmosphere, or the mostly silent lunch they shared, but she persisted in the plan, and gradually they found things to talk about, and familiarity created a degree of ease between them.

But when Miranda asked if the boys could go up to the loch and fish, or do some rough shooting or perhaps walk up some grouse with Derek, Gregory shot her an angry glance. 'Trying to get a toehold, are they? Trying to take the place over?'

Miranda looked at him in astonishment. She thought of the raw deal Adam and Tim had had in this house, never made welcome, always the focus of aggression from Alexy, fitting in as best they could and hiding whatever sense of rootlessness they felt. They had lost both their parents, their home, a way of life where they had been content, and they had done their best not to add to her, Miranda's, problems. Anger boiled up.

'That is a totally base suggestion!' she flared. 'You may see things in that light but I can assure you they don't. Perhaps if you had had the courtesy to make an effort to get to know them you'd see what I mean. They're adapting without complaint to a completely new life, and I think they deserve to be given the best it can offer. And your wretched moor needs shooting anyway, since you've abandoned interest in it

292

along with everything else.'

'So,' said Gregory, watching her with a more lively expression than had appeared on his thin face for a long time. 'Touched a nerve there, did I? So you're prepared to fight for these boys, I see. Well, what do I care what they do, so long as they keep themselves out of my sight? Tell them they can do what they like within reason. And if Derek gets awkward let me know.'

Miranda, getting her temper under control, reflected that releasing it had produced as satisfactory a result as when she had done so with Alexy. The Rosses appeared to like being challenged.

'Got rods and so on, have they?' Gregory called as she was going out.

'I can provide whatever they'll need.'

'Don't be a bloody fool, woman, place is crammed with stuff no one will ever touch again.'

It had been a huge step forward.

# 23

It made such a difference to have Muff to talk to. Though the friendship with Danielle had been good, and had meant an enormous amount all through the years of struggling to reshape her life and bring up Alexy alone, there had always been a challenging edge to it, a need to meet Danielle's exacting standards. Also, looking back, it was possible to see that, whether she had been aware of it or not, Miranda had felt most of the time that she should be apologising for Alexy. Certainly Alexy and Danielle had pulled her in different directions, and often it had needed a considerable effort to reconcile their demands. Danielle's readiness to write her off, hardheaded as ever, when Miranda ended their working partnership had been a shock, and it still hurt.

With Muff there was a different kind of friendship. There was warmth, tolerance, laughter, sympathy and support, though rarely her undivided attention.

'You are so heroic to tackle that crew of cross old things!' Muff would exclaim in admiration, as she rapidly stripped the lower half of a kicking Henrietta, or kneed away the importunate Smith as she added warm water to the biscuit in his bowl, when Miranda had passed on some outrageous barb of Gregory's, or related with amused resignation the latest spat between the aunts.

For Miranda, in spite of her initial reception at the cottage, had decided, for Binnie's sake if nothing else, that she must persist in her efforts to establish ordinary day-to-day contact. The lives of the two elderly women seemed almost as shut in and restricted as their brother's, and not only did Olivia's relentless unkindness and Binnie's usual meek acceptance of it seem unnatural, but their actual living conditions were unwholesome enough to merit a health warning.

It seemed extraordinary that, apart from going away to school, they should have passed their whole lives at Kilgarth. Neither of them had ever had a relationship outside the family nor, as far as Miranda could gather, had ever thought of earning her own living, or been required to do so. Gregory, if he referred to them at all, would always end up muttering, 'damned useless pair', or, 'no better than pieces of lumber'.

Miranda learned more in time, though in Olivia's case the thaw was reluctant and slow, and it wasn't easy to piece the story together. Olivia had been in her teens during the war, and her dream had been either to become a Boat's Crew Wren or, if rowing about Kilgarth loch was not found to be sufficient experience for this coveted role, to drive an ambulance, preferably somewhere hot so that she could wear khaki drill. She had grown up with these visions, sure the war would wait for her. Gregory and his friends, heroic dazzling creatures, had all been involved, and she had known in her heart that when her turn came she too would shine,

295

proving herself brave and competent, tough and resourceful.

Then suddenly the war had been over. In her dismay she had had the sense to realise that it would hardly do to repine openly, but she had never forgotten the blank feeling of being unneeded, unwanted, the focus of her existence removed at a stroke.

She hadn't known what else to do. In spite of the social changes, and changes in attitude to women working, brought by the war, it had still been acceptable for a girl of her background to stay at home and aspire to nothing more, if she liked and her family could afford it, than to ride, shoot, fish and play golf, 'coming out' at whatever level her parents thought fit. Most girls by this stage had wanted something more challenging, especially those who had been in the Services, but Olivia, though undeniably heavy-handed at such daughter-of-the-house duties as doing the flowers or washing the Meissen, and too blunt and gauche to be much support to her mother socially, had shone at more robust country pursuits, and life at Kilgarth had suited her. Almost by default she had gone on living there. With, of course, somewhere ahead, the expectation of marriage.

'You filled in the time till it happened,' she said once with a shrug to Miranda. 'It was what came next, house to run, children to bring up. Normal life.'

Large, slow-moving Olivia, with her deep powerful voice and big turned-out feet, her tweed jackets and baggy-seated skirts, her taste for the nineteenth-century novel and her disdain for the culture and fashions of her generation, hadn't noticed for a while that no male ever so much as looked at her. When she had noticed she minded terribly. Seeing herself as others saw her for the first time in her life, she had taken a reckless step. She had decided to be a nurse. Female career choices had remained fairly conventional, in spite of the war, and since she hadn't wanted to teach or be someone's secretary it had been the obvious course.

She had never talked afterwards of those brief weeks at Guy's, not even to Binnie. Floundering, clumsy and disliked, mocked, driven and perpetually found fault with, hating not only hospital life but the city environment, she had had what had amounted to a nervous breakdown. She had been dispatched by her impatient mother, in time-honoured fashion, to an ancient nanny in Dorset — what the nanny, who had probably believed she'd got clear away, thought of the infliction is not recorded — and there had recovered some equilibrium.

More critical and intolerant than ever, she had returned to Kilgarth, where she had resumed grooming the dogs, picking up for local shoots, meddling with growing confidence and bossiness in glen affairs, having her thick coarse hair permed every three months in Muirend and being unkind to Binnie.

Binnie, meanwhile, had dreamed sadly of lost love. Even more impressed by her brother's fellow Air Force officers than Olivia had been, she had succumbed to a secret passion for a slight, fair, punctiliously polite flying officer called Sholto McDermott. But when the war ended he had vanished and Binnie, appalled at the consequences of Olivia's venture into the great world and only too aware of her own inadequacies — her failures at school, her pallid looks, her lack of talent — had known, when the brief stilted letters in response to her eager outpourings ceased to arrive, that her only recourse, too, was to bury herself in the safe tedium of home.

She had padded dozens of coat-hangers and covered them in ruched silk. She had made a great many sachets (a word she liked), embroidered, quilted, lace-edged and heart-shaped — her ingenuity was endless — and she had sketched and painted in watercolours, even designing some saccharine greeting cards which Olivia had bullied a Muirend stationer into attempting to sell. She had briefly kept budgerigars, till one day, overcome by sadness at the thought, which had never occurred to her before, of what it must be like to spend one's life confined to a space so tiny (she had struggled to work out how tiny, the word cubic eluding her), she had released the current favourite, only to come across the farm cat with the pretty corpse in his mouth ten minutes later.

When Gregory, who for many years after the war had shown no inclination for any such extravagant behaviour, had unexpectedly married, perhaps prompted by his father's death and the fact that Kilgarth was now his, panic had nearly sent Binnie into a breakdown of her own.

Scraps of news, each plunging her into new misery, had from time to time reached her about Sholto. He was living in Budleigh Salterton, had married someone called Meryl, had two sons. Would she and Olivia have to leave Kilgarth? But where could they go? What would they do? Who would want them? After this flurry of terror Gregory's decision to shunt his sisters into the chauffeur's cottage had been accepted with secret relief by them both, though they, or Olivia at least, had rallied sufficiently once the move had been made to be vocally indignant about it. But in truth anything had been better than being asked to fend for themselves, and they'd known it. Each had her small slice of capital. Each had learned to fill her days.

Just as Miranda, when events uprooted her from Edinburgh, could hardly believe she had let so many years slip by there, so Binnie and Olivia, if something occurred to remind them of the passage of time, were astonished to have been in the cottage for so long. But mostly they didn't think about it. It was better that way.

The real quarrel with Gregory had come when he quarrelled with Ian, Binnie upset and begging him to relent, Olivia scornful because he'd failed to make Ian toe the line. After this the rift had never healed. Only Binnie had truly wanted it to and what influence had she ever had over her bellicose siblings?

So here they were, living in a shadowland of their own making, and filled, on Olivia's part anyway, with rancour and contempt for all they didn't understand.

Miranda thought it very bad for them, in particular disturbed to see someone of Binnie's sweetness and natural gregariousness caught in such a web. The other thing which concerned her was the spartan level of living they had come to take for granted. Ordinary standards of comfort and warmth were disdained, whether from habit or a sense of superiority (wartime thinking still?) in *doing without*. Or perhaps there was a need to economise? It seemed all too probable that their financial affairs had never been reviewed since their father died, and Miranda shuddered to think what return they were getting on their original capital. She assumed, hoped, that they paid no rent, and she knew Derek kept them supplied with logs. She also knew they had a sizeable vegetable patch where Olivia was often to be seen in muddy wellingtons, guddling about with some uncouth and ancient implement. But, though Miranda had never been interested in gardening — all she was attempting at the big house was basic tidying and rescue work — she couldn't believe that this dank spot, hemmed in by trees, could be very productive.

'Do the aunts ever go out, do you know?' she asked Muff one afternoon, as they struggled to suspend several pounds of stewed rowan berries in a bulging pillowcase, already an attractive pinky-orange shade from similar previous service, over a pail to strain. (Which might work provided no creature drank it, knocked it over, or fell in and drowned in it, Miranda privately amended.)

'They turn up at meetings about the church roof, well, Olivia does anyway, and she's keen on Conservative stuff. Phones you up if you're late voting, apparently, and bullies you into going along. She was so rude to someone one year that they voted Labour in a rage. So the story goes, anyway. We weren't here then.'

'That must take up a lot of her time,' Miranda commented with mild irony.

Muff grinned. 'Umm, what else?' She mused, tugging tighter a knot she would certainly have to cut in the morning. 'She did a lot of agitating about the new bypass at Bridge of Riach, but I don't think even she thought she could stop it happening. And she gets hyperactive at Games time, or so I'm told. Has rows with the committee, objects to the drinks tent, tries to block new ideas, harasses people for donations. (Fleur, you're going to get horribly sticky if you do that, and you'll hate the taste anyway. There, now look at you.) That's about it. Apart from shopping in Muirend once a week.'

'But don't they ever see anyone?' Miranda asked, following her as she carried a squirming Fleur at arm's length to the sink. 'They must have some friends?'

'Everyone's pretty well given up on them, I think. They hate callers, refuse all invitations and half the time don't even answer the phone, so I suppose it's understandable.'

'And Gregory?'

'Ah, well, you must admit, Gregory is in a category all his own.' Muff looked over her shoulder with eyebrows raised expressively. 'He

301

appears to have carried on open warfare with so many people for so long that everyone's terrified to have anything to do with him.'

'So Kilgarth, as a unit, is pretty unpopular?'

'Well, it has been. It's sure to change now, though, isn't it?' Muff always wanted to be kind. 'Your boys are good ambassadors, for one thing.'

'It's the boys I'm thinking of.' It wasn't reassuring to realise that in the future, when it belonged to Alexy, Kilgarth was likely to be as inhospitable and unappealing as it had ever been. 'When I phoned one or two people to see if they could get some beating, there was — well, not a coolness, everyone was perfectly friendly and said all the right things about how nice it was that I was back and so on — but there was a sort of lack of follow-up. Joanna Munro, Mackenzie, I mean, said, 'How lovely, you must come up and see us.' Though I'm sure she meant it at the time, I haven't heard from her again. Then I tried Archie Napier's new wife, well, new to me, and she sounded terribly friendly and was helpful about the beating, and when the boys went over she looked after them beautifully, but I had the feeling that she didn't think of Kilgarth or Rosses in general as part of the Drumveyn scene.'

'Oh, Pauly's an absolute honey, one of the nicest people you could ever meet. But yes, I suppose everyone has grown used to thinking of Kilgarth as holding aloof. So many advances seem to have been snubbed over the years. But now you're here I'm sure you'll be drawn in. You know lots of people from when you used to live in Muirend, and Adam and Tim don't exactly drag their feet, do they?'

Miranda laughed, agreeing. The way in which the boys had taken to life in Glen Maraich had been one of the most rewarding things she had ever known. If only Alexy had a fraction of their enthusiasm and energy. Oddly, they often reminded her more of Ian than of their father.

She thought of Ian a lot at present, reminded of him a dozen times a day. She would find herself talking to him in her head, as though sure everything at Kilgarth would interest him. She had longed to report the outcome of the wiring battle, her success in getting the old summer-house, which had been a special place of theirs, safely shored up, and a major breakthrough when she and Binnie had picked plums and made jam, though at the cottage not the house, and on a stove so antiquated that it was a valuable antique. She wanted him to hear about the way Derek had gradually warmed to the boys' enthusiasm for anything he could teach them, and how he seemed to be taking more interest in his job as a result. She had wanted to tell him, with an ache of nostalgia, how she'd felt on the day she'd gone up to the loch with Adam and Tim, and they had put the old boat, now repaired, into the water again, and a new generation, though not precisely of Rosses, had fished and cooked the catch in the old place. And who but Ian would have enjoyed the detail that the trout, undisturbed for years, had been obliged to eat each other to keep numbers down, with the happy outcome that they were delectably pink and firm-fleshed. Nothing so sweet as a cannibal trout; she could hear him saying it.

Most of all she needed to share with him her ever-present pain at Alexy's refusal to relent. About anything. Miranda knew she had hoped that when Alexy got what she had appeared to want, and knew her inheritance was secure, she would become more amenable, and even show some satisfaction if not actual pleasure. But, watching her as she undeviatingly pursued her own ends, everything about her warning that she would bristle at a word, fending off all contact, Miranda knew her hopes had been hopelessly naive. Did she, still, after eighteen years, not know anything about her daughter?

Then the despair over Alexy, Alexy the unreachable, would inevitably slide into resentment of Ian. It was a habit too ingrained to be easily abandoned. If he hadn't left her to deal with everything alone, if he'd been there to discipline Alexy and stop her sliding into this self-engrossed contempt for everything around her, if he . . .

Miranda knew she laid herself open to the wounds Alexy so carelessly dealt. She had never learned to protect herself; perhaps mothers never could. She still hoped, still tried to offer help and support which Alexy not only disdained but which filled her with resentment. Her departure for university was a case in point. Because Alexy had refused to go to boarding-school this was a huge hurdle for Miranda. She could, in exasperated moments, look forward to it keenly, then it would hit her that this really was for good, childhood was over, Alexy would never live at home again, and anguish would rush up. There would be no more chances; she had failed.

Doggedly, deaf to the warnings of experience, she did her best to participate. She tried to discuss Alexy's accommodation, what she'd need to equip it, her clothes, even her books though, as a subject, engineering, civil or otherwise, was as remote to Miranda as astrophysics.

Alexy received these efforts with a weary contempt which plainly said that she had not the slightest hope of her mother understanding anything, ever, and said tersely, 'It's all organised.'

'But surely, there must be something you need? What about your clothes, for instance?'

'Dress up for lectures? This is now, remember.'

'No, I meant — Heavens, even we didn't — ' How easily Alexy could wrong-foot her. 'But it would be fun to have new things.'

Alexy looked past her, as though what she could see out of the window was a great deal more interesting than this exchange, and waited.

Did I really use the word fun to her? Miranda groaned inwardly. 'Something for your room, then?'

'No, thanks.'

'But this accommodation you've arranged, you haven't told me anything about it. Is there an approved list? Are you sure you're not supposed to live in hall during first year? I'd at least like to see where you're living.'

Alexy's air of waiting for her mother to get this

rubbish off her chest if she had to sharpened into watchfulness. 'It's nothing to do with you,' she said, with that capacity, perfected over the years, for making an insolent statement without overt rudeness in her voice which Miranda still found it impossible to deal with.

'It certainly is — ' she began hotly.

'I hope you're not going to say, 'I am your mother, after all',' Alexy remarked, and watched with satisfaction as Miranda struggled to crush down her anger. 'It doesn't have anything to do with you,' she went on with sudden vengeful swiftness, 'because my dear absent father is paying the fees, and because I have an allowance and I'm eighteen. It's my life.'

Unable to hide how much this hurt her, Miranda caught the lift of the thin lip with which Alexy read her distress before turning away, subject closed.

Miranda held back tears till Alexy had gone. Almost the hardest thing to bear, she made herself acknowledge, was that Alexy would have arranged everything with perfect efficiency. She would have done nothing unwise, and would not be putting herself at risk of the slightest discomfort, let alone danger. When the day came she would pack her car and take herself off. She didn't need help, supervision or protection; she didn't need anyone.

# 24

It was very strange after Alexy had gone. Adam and Tim, who, though perfectly capable of looking after themselves when required, had been quite happy to let Miranda immerse herself in lists and kit-marking and anything else she was prepared to do for them, had gone back to school a few days earlier.

The house, silent once more, seemed suddenly larger and, in spite of the care Miranda had already lavished on it, its rooms in some peculiar way reverted to their former look of barren reserve. The ceilings seemed higher, the floor spaces wider, though when she caught herself thinking this Miranda was able to laugh at her own absurdity, even if the laughter was a touch uncertain.

Since Alexy was born they had never been apart. That seemed appalling suddenly, quite wrong. How could she have allowed it? There had never been the usual overnight stays with school friends, or visits alone to the cousins in Gloucestershire. Alexy had turned down her mouth unmistakably at all such proposals. In the early years in the basement flat there had been no room to have a friend to stay, had she ever showed any sign of wanting such a thing; nothing to break up the too intense closeness.

Remembering how long they had shared a room could disturb Miranda when she thought

307

of it now. How could she have let that go on for so long? No wonder Danielle had been tart on the subject. No wonder there had been no other friendships or relationships for herself, and few casual social contacts. It all looked so bizarre in retrospect. Thank goodness Will had come into her life, with his gentle sanity and kindness, and the family scene had changed and broadened.

Miranda was ashamed to find how hard it was to adjust to Alexy's absence. Since coming to Kilgarth there had been no more than minimal contact between them, yet without being conscious of it there had always been somewhere in her mind an awareness of Alexy's presence, hostile, critical, disruptive even, but always from long habit the first thing to be considered. Now there was a dreadful emptiness, an aching need to have her back, to be able to try again, do things differently. Yet also, at first mixed with fresh guilt that she could feel this way, there was an amazing, breathless sensation of freedom.

It was a compound of emotions she found difficult to handle, and for several days after Alexy's departure she didn't visit the aunts, spent less time than usual with Gregory, and avoided even Muff.

She needed time to work through this, and face up to things about herself which it seemed there had never been time till now to analyse honestly. She walked a good deal. In the weeks since they had come to Kilgarth it had dawned on her, another slight shock, that nowadays she rarely took exercise in any form. What had happened to the fit girl who couldn't bear not to be active? She had turned into an indoor city woman approaching forty, that was what had happened to her.

The first walks had been short, snatched breaks from the busy days, but it had been a delight to retrace remembered paths and tracks, even if she did nothing more ambitious than drop down the steep fields to the river in the crisp mornings of early autumn before the house stirred to life (getting hot and breathless on the haul back), or wander up the road for ten minutes before bedtime, with the September dusk imperceptibly creeping forward each evening.

These had been the times when her mind turned most readily to Ian, and she found the same now, when she had the opportunity to go further afield, as the last of the Dalquhat barley was cut and the first tentative autumn colours began to merge with summer green, soft yellow tinging the larches, the bracken turning, the great beeches at Sillerton beginning to brown and bronze.

And at last, after sixteen years, through the new uncomfortable knowledge of herself which Alexy's absence forced her to face, she was able to reach a more honest understanding of all that had gone wrong between herself and Ian. He hadn't been to blame. They had both been too young to handle the change Alexy had made in their lives. That Alexy had been born at all was due to her, Miranda's, carelessness and nothing else. Sometimes it seemed that, having at last admitted this, the next natural step was to tell

Ian, and there would be a check, freshly painful each time, to remember that that door was closed for good.

Adjusting slowly to the new situation, Miranda began to look about her with different eyes. Had she really not foreseen that in a matter of weeks after their arrival she would be alone here? Certainly she hadn't given much thought to how her own existence would be.

And how was it? The answer to that, unexpectedly, was that it was marvellous. She was living in a beautiful, neglected house which needed her, and on which she could expend the skills acquired in the Edinburgh years; the beautiful house was situated in one of the most beautiful glens in Scotland; she had Muff's warm and cheerful friendship, already leading to other contacts; and she was free to spend her days as she chose. She sometimes felt as though she had walked towards this enviable combination with eyes and mind tightly closed. Opening them to what was there, she was filled with delight.

Her principal worries about living at Kilgarth had evaporated without ever coming to a head. Pattie had not, it was true, liked all the changes, and she had definitely not liked the way Alexy treated her, but after one or two tantrums, a mug or pan lid hurled across the kitchen with a 'That's me, I've had enough, I'm out of here', Pattie had each time settled down again. On the day Alexy left she had appeared on the front steps, clearly more for her own satisfaction than from any desire to offer good wishes, to watch her drive away, and since that moment had slipped back into her usual easy-going tolerance. She still thought Miranda daft to want to clean rooms that no one went into, but consoled herself with the belief that she'd tire of that game soon enough.

Her general standard of work had not improved and nor had her cooking, but Miranda, treading carefully, was working on both. She did most of the cooking herself, and at the same time, aware that with convenience food always available she had got into bad habits, she learned a lot from watching Muff. Muff, a natural giver who enjoyed lavishing good food on people, had never so much as seen a Marks and Spencer quiche or a ready-made lasagne. She grew her own fruit and vegetables, had sources of game up and down the glens, and Miranda often went with her to collect a haunch of roe here or half a pig there. Muff loved food herself, and never stinted on cream, butter or wonderful sauces. She was serenely unconcerned about her weight or her figure, and Miranda couldn't imagine her thin, yet never thought of her as fat. She was so nicely in proportion, wore clothes and colours that were right for her, and always looked so smiling and content.

Gregory had responded with unexpected greed to the more appealing food on offer, though he made no comment, and the improved diet had its effect on his health. Perhaps the stimulus of company had made a difference too. Whatever the cause, he was not so content as before to hunch over a fire all day without occupation.

Cautiously, having consulted Charlie Fleming, Miranda introduced the subject of massage therapy. Though Gregory huffed and scoffed at the idea she returned to it a few days later, and found him ready at least to discuss it. Two weeks later he agreed to a session, 'Only as an experiment, and to put an end to this infernal nagging,' and though he expressed his opinion of the process afterwards in colourful terms which Miranda thought it lucky the therapist couldn't hear, vowing that he ached in every joint and couldn't move a muscle, she noticed that he didn't object when she proposed a second appointment.

Someone more eager for change and open to persuasion was Binnie. She said every time she saw Miranda how glad she was that they had all come to live at Kilgarth. Adam and Tim had come across the cottage early on in their explorations, on a day when both Olivia and Binnie were out in the garden and, having inherited Will's natural courtesy, though Tim could be shy when he was on his own, they had introduced themselves. Olivia had stumped off, but Binnie had chattered happily, and had always enjoyed seeing them. Alexy had gone under duress, once, and it had been a disaster, Olivia turning an alarming purple at her rudeness, Binnie twittering with rebuff and alarm.

Miranda had continued to call, not too often and never staying too long, and gradually it had become accepted practice. She had not, however, missed the gleam in Binnie's eye at her original offer to bring anything they needed from Muirend, and now that her own list had dwindled from its daunting length when she first arrived and she had more time to spare, she wondered if Binnie would like to go shopping with her.

'You don't need anything,' Olivia told Binnie repressively, when Miranda made the suggestion.

'Well, even if I don't, I can look,' Binnie said quickly, thrilled at the prospect of such a treat, but looking anxious too, as though fearing she might not be allowed to go.

'Of course you can,' Miranda said. 'We can just enjoy ourselves. We'll go for coffee somewhere, and perhaps browse round the second-hand bookshop. I haven't had time to check it out yet.'

'That's a waste of time if you like,' Olivia snorted, getting up and walking away. 'Binnie never got to the end of a book in her life. Pea brain.'

Nursery taunt, thirties vintage? Was Olivia by any chance jealous at the idea of Binnie enjoying herself?

'Do you normally wait for Olivia to take you to Muirend?' Miranda asked Binnie as they set off. 'You don't drive?'

'Oh, yes, dear. Well, I used to. One did in those days, you know. But of course I haven't driven for years.'

Why of course, Miranda wondered. 'You don't find it restricting, living here and not being able to go off on your own, to town, or to see friends?'

'On my own?' Binnie sounded amazed. 'Oh no, Olivia wouldn't like that at all. And besides, the car is hers. She wouldn't let me touch it.'

Miranda didn't pursue the subject, but observing Binnie's pleasure in such simple things as sitting in a hotel garden by the river for coffee and scones, or shyly examining the clothes, as though they could have nothing to do with her, in a new dress shop on the square, she made up her mind that it was time Olivia's stranglehold on her sister's life was loosened.

All these things she talked over with Muff, and to her too she could voice the deeper worries which dragged at her. She could tell Muff that she had no address for Alexy other than that of the university department, that letters sent there went unanswered, and that there had been no communication of any sort from Alexy since she left.

'I know I'm a fool to mind,' she said restlessly, 'but it seems such a jump from being always together to this complete silence. I can't get used to it.'

'You're not a fool, you're a mother,' Muff said gently, adding to cheer her up, 'unless that equates to the same thing.' She couldn't bear the way Alexy treated Miranda, but knew a partisan attack on her would be neither helpful nor welcome.

'Quite probably,' Miranda agreed ruefully. 'I seem to have such unreal expectations,' she went on after a moment, almost to herself. They were occupied in cleaning some wood blewits they had found in a belt of old birches above the

314

gorge, and she paused with one of the handsome fungi in her hands, oblivious to the beauty of its dead-leaf-brown cap and smooth lilac stem. 'Daughter at college, daughter writes home. That's what happens. But this is Alexy. Do you know, I've never so much as seen a letter written by her.'

'Not even thank you letters?'

'Alexy?'

'Does she never write to her father?'

'No need to as long as the money keeps coming, is there? Anyway, she resents him too much to have any contact with him. She did talk about going to live with him at one point, but only to get at me. It was never an option. But her bitterness towards him — I'm only just beginning to realise how I must have implanted that in her by my own attitude.'

'She'd probably think that way in any case. Absent father and all that.'

'You don't sound too convinced, Muff,' Miranda said with a grin. 'But did I seriously think,' she pursued, leaving the subject of Ian as too difficult, and reverting to her more immediate worry, 'that she'd be phoning home to ask me to send things she'd forgotten or found she needed? Am I mad? Alexy doesn't forget things, and if she needs something she buys it. Or did I imagine she'd phone to chat? Even I can't be that naive.'

Muff, her pretty face full of compassion, twirled a mushroom in her fingers and abstractedly sniffed its delicate fruity scent. It seemed unimaginable to her that a child could deal its mother such hurt, and she wondered if Alexy could ever when she was small have even faintly resembled boisterous, outgoing Fleur or contented Henry, at present zooming her wheelie chair from one kitchen unit to another, corralling an indignant Smith under the table where he knew from bitterly acquired experience it couldn't go.

'I'd got as far as realising with my brain that she'd more or less grown up and left home,' Miranda went on, speaking with more effort now, 'but I hadn't *felt* it. I hadn't truly thought how it would be. She's gone, Muff, and sometimes I wonder if I'll ever see her again.'

'Of course you will!' Muff abandoned the blewits and turned to hug Miranda to her cushiony bosom, ready tears in her eyes. 'She'll be home for Christmas, you know she will. Where else would she go?'

'Alexy? Anywhere that suited her,' Miranda said, dredging up an ironic humour.

'But won't she want to maintain the contact with her grandfather?' Muff, who knew of Gregory's long-term plans, craftily enquired.

'That's true.'

'Well, there you go.' Muff dived to stop Henry dragging down Miranda's bag, which she had thought safely out of reach, and tossed a few scattered toys onto the tray of her chair to divert her attention. 'And anyway, aren't Adam and Tim due home soon?'

'Yes, they have a leave-out weekend next week.' Miranda's face lit up and Muff, seeing it, smiled.

'You're pretty fond of those boys of yours, aren't you?'

'My prop and stay,' Miranda admitted, smiling too, and looking happier.

'That reminds me,' Muff remarked, sweeping the debris from the chopping board into the bin with the back of her knife. 'Colin said to tell you that he's booked a tee-time for early Sunday morning, the only time he could get. Wait a sec, I wrote it down. Ouch, Henry, don't, you can't go over my foot, it simply doesn't work . . .'

Miranda, driving home, knew she should be fairer towards Colin. He had been both welcoming to her and kind to the boys, giving them introductions to one or two shoots when he found they were keen to beat, and more than once taking them to play golf at Pitlochry. She was more thankful than she could say even to Muff for them to have this male contact, for she sometimes worried about her inability to deal with the problems of the stressful teens, which she knew they would never be able to talk about to her. Not that she imagined they would spend their time on the golf course pouring out their hearts on such matters to Colin Carmichael, and not that she thought Colin the ideal role model either, but adult male company must be good for them for a change.

Colin was a hospitable, sociable and good-tempered man, and Miranda knew it was unfair to cling to her first negative response to him. He was not the type who attracted her, certainly, being slim and dapper, even his casual clothes always carefully chosen and neat, but that wasn't

317

the basis of her lack of ease with him. The truth was, she thought that he abused outrageously Muff's loving generosity. It set her teeth on edge to see the way Muff's life revolved round him, and how he let her wait on him. After the years of, whether consciously or not, imbibing Danielle's views, which had conveniently reinforced her own anger towards Ian, it was hard to observe such ready subservience in action. As far as she could see, the only chore Colin ever undertook in his own house was handing out drinks. Otherwise he was cossetted, pampered and spoiled at every turn.

He had a particularly irritating trick, after Muff had slaved away (Miranda's choice of verb) to produce wonderful food for a dinner party, and he had come in from the office to do no more than have a leisurely drink, shower and dress and come down to chat to the guests, of saying as she finally sat down at the table pink-cheeked and breathless, 'Oh, perhaps some French dressing, darling' — or Parmesan, or chives or whatever — 'what do you think? Would that be nice?'

Miranda, surveying the beautifully laid table and the perfect food, would long for Muff to tell him if he wanted anything else to get it for himself, and would bite her tongue as Muff bobbed up saying, 'Oh, I should have thought of that, silly me,' and, apparently unfazed, began mixing a dressing or grating cheese.

On other occasions Miranda had heard him, as he sat watching television or reading the paper, ask Muff, struggling with a howling baby,

318

trying to answer a question from Freddie about supper and at the same time admire a piece of Fleur's artwork which was shedding glitter on the carpet, to pass him something just out of his reach. And Muff would comply without complaint or without, Miranda knew, thinking complaint was called for.

'You do run around after him,' she had been unable to refrain from commenting after one particularly turbulent teatime. Thomas and Jack were home from school, plus two friends, one of whom had announced, on finding on the table the current favourites of chocolate muesli bars, peanut brittle and walnut cake, that he was allergic to nuts. Muff had been trying to find an acceptable alternative, while Henry, who was teething, had refused to be comforted by Freddie, and Fleur, over-excited by the presence of four boys and driven to showing off, had knocked over her mug and sent apple juice everywhere. As Muff, with Henry in her arms still whimpering, at last came to join them, Colin had said, 'How about some fresh tea? This lot isn't very hot by now.'

Muff looked surprised at Miranda's comment. 'But I love looking after him. Why shouldn't I? I want to. He's the one who has to go out and do a boring job while I have the luxury of being home all day doing nothing.'

'Nothing?' Miranda queried, but she knew she would get nowhere.

'Well, only things I enjoy. I love my house and being with the children and looking after the animals and lazing in the sun when it's a fine day

319

and wearing what I like and having meals when I like. It's bliss to be at home, and it's so nice when Colin gets in. I always look forward to it. And when he's exhausted and has had a hard day I *want* to bring him a drink and get him to relax. Didn't you ever feel that about Ian?'

About to answer with scorn, as though Danielle's indoctrination had effectively done its work, Miranda was suddenly seized by a vision of what she had missed. Never to have been moved to that kind of giving, warm and spontaneous and total.

'No,' was all she could manage, her voice stifled.

Muff gave her a quick look, understanding Miranda's sudden change of mood with her instinctive sympathy. She slid her soft hand through Miranda's arm and drew it close against her side.

'You loved him, didn't you?' she asked gently.

A tiny pause. 'Yes,' said Miranda, still in that muffled voice. 'I did.'

# 25

Alexy came home for a week at Christmas. What she did with the rest of the vac — did they still call it that, Miranda wondered, with a bleak sense of the gulf that lay between her student days and her daughter's — was not divulged. Miranda was only thankful that she had appeared at all and that, in spite of looking paler and thinner than ever, she seemed to be in reasonable health. She was no more amenable, however, and spent her time in her room, with even louder music pounding out its maddening beat into the small hours, a constant source of friction.

Miranda told Pattie not to attempt to clean her room. They could sort it out later.

'Me go in there?' Pattie demanded with heavy sarcasm. 'I'd sooner keep ma head on ma shoulders, if it's all the same to you.'

Miranda, without much hope, did her best to make Christmas dinner an occasion to break down barriers. Her efforts met with mixed success. Gregory, to her surprise and pleasure, though she was careful to show neither, had allowed lunch with her to become lunch with the boys as well when they were home. More mobile than he had been for a long time, he now moved freely round the house, and appeared in the dining-room every day, though still preferring to have dinner alone.

Though he never admitted it, Miranda guessed that he welcomed having something new to think about, and as the boys were always ready to talk on subjects once close to his heart Miranda's fears that he would withdraw into surliness again were soon forgotten. Until she began to plan Christmas.

'Invite those two here? Over my dead body, which may of course be the result you wish to bring about. I'm not having them in the house, and that's the end of it.'

His proposed guests were equally unenthusiastic, or at least Olivia was.

'I can think of nothing I should dislike more,' she announced thunderously. 'My brother is not only spoiled, cantankerous and selfish, but he has no more conversation than a Brussels sprout. I wouldn't waste an hour of my valuable time in his company.'

Binnie, however, looked wistful.

'How about you, Aunt Binnie?'

'Well, Christmas used to be rather fun when — '

'Fun? It was ghastly,' Olivia boomed.

'Perhaps there was a little squabbling sometimes,' Binnie conceded, then after a glance at her sister's ominous expression went on more firmly, 'no, no, of course we couldn't dream of coming, Miranda dear. It's out of the question, though it's very kind of you to ask us.' But she did add in an apologetic whisper as she went to the door to see Miranda off, 'Gregory hasn't always been very kind to us, you know.'

Miranda wondered whether, if questioned,

Binnie would have been able to say by this time quite where the unkindness had lain.

Having failed in this mission, Miranda was adamant on another point. Pattie must join them.

'That moronic creature? Good God, she's not even clean. Do you seriously think that I . . . ?'

'She has no family nearby and nowhere else to go. She can't sit in the kitchen on her own, especially as she's not even taking the day off. I won't have it. We all sit down together. That's the way it's going to be.'

Miranda sounded firm, but hardly expected to carry her point, not least because 'all' included Alexy. But whether under that strange Christmas compulsion to conform which crops up in the most obdurate, or perhaps from greed, this ill-assorted group did convene at the appointed hour around the big Kilgarth dining table, and a semblance of goodwill was achieved. Or open battle was avoided, Miranda thought would perhaps be more accurate, since Alexy barely spoke throughout.

At least Pattie, though somewhat overcome, and wearing a floral cotton dress (wasn't she frozen?) which strained ominously round her but successfully held together for the course of the meal, was on her best behaviour. While Adam and Tim, keen to practise their carving, comparing Miranda's turkey favourably to the sad mockery served at school, downing as much wine as they could get away with and happily flown on the port Gregory grudgingly produced, kept the mood upbeat.

Miranda, torn between joy at having Alexy home again which had nothing to do with reason, and the more honest admission that having her in the house was hell, did her best to make an opportunity to talk to her during those brief days. Finding a moment wasn't easy, since Alexy rarely got up before lunch and Miranda herself was out more than usual, mainly ferrying the boys, whose social life had developed a lot more rapidly than hers, but also doing things like going to see Fleur Carmichael in the school nativity play, sitting through an elaborate lunch at the Semples, former neighbours in Muirend, and attending a stuffy drinks party at Dalquhat, where to her disappointment she knew hardly anyone.

She finally mustered the courage to invade Alexy's lair one afternoon when Gregory was napping and the boys were at Balgowan, helping to supervise clay-pigeon shooting for the Carmichael boys and their friends. As this would be followed by one of Muff's stupendous teas they had put up the merest show of reluctance. Overhearing them, Miranda had learned Thomas and Jack's new nickname for Muff.

'Mips?' It rang a faint bell.

The boys had watched her expectantly.

'Think computers,' Tim had said helpfully.

But Alexy, ready spoiler of the fun, had cut in contemptuously, 'She'll never get it. Million instructions per second,' and strolled away, bored.

'Not bad,' Miranda exclaimed, but she knew

the shine had gone off the joke.

Presumably she would find Alexy hunched over the computer now, she thought, knocking more loudly. What images fed her brain, images outside Miranda's own knowledge and experience? What contacts did she make? And what contacts in ordinary life, come to that? Oppressed by the hopelessness of finding any meeting point, still receiving no reply and perhaps willing to be deterred, Miranda was about to turn away when the door opened.

'What do you want?' The usual unadorned question.

'I should like to talk to you.' Miranda went for equal directness.

Alexy didn't ask, 'What about?' Instead she openly debated whether to accede, watching her mother with narrowed eyes. Then with a lift of her shoulder she turned back into the room, switched off her CD player and crossed to the computer, looked at what it showed for a moment, and returned the screen to the start menu. Miranda felt her cheeks burn at what seemed meant to convey deliberate concealment, though telling herself that what had been on the screen had probably been quite innocuous.

Alexy waited, without any prompting question, without the slightest look of enquiry.

Miranda wanted to suggest sitting down, but knew that would be met with a cool, 'Why?' and refrained.

'We've had so little chance to talk since you came back,' she began, and found with annoyance that her voice was already conciliatory. 'I feel rather out of touch with you, that's all.'

Alexy waited.

Miranda hurried on. 'It would be good to know how you're finding life at college. If it's all working out well, if you're happy there . . . ' In spite of herself her voice trailed away. What a fatuous word to have used.

Alexy let the silence stretch just long enough for Miranda to open her mouth to try again, then said with cold crispness, 'What is it you want to know? I'm not on drugs, I'm not pregnant, I'm not HIV positive, anorexic or bulimic. Let me see, what else might be worrying someone of your generation and outlook? Oh yes, I don't consort with the criminal classes. I can't think of much more that might have occurred to you. I eat, I wash, I work, my bowels move. Is that good enough?'

'Alexy, why do you have to be so — so *harsh*?' Miranda cried, stung to protest by this callously rattled-off list. 'Don't you understand, I only want to talk to you a little, to understand if I can how you feel about things, to know that everything's all right with you.'

Alexy allowed a couple more moments to pass. 'That everything's all right with me.' In her expressionless voice the words sounded ridiculous, as Miranda knew she had intended. 'I wonder what you can possibly mean by that.' Alexy pursed her lips and considered the carpet. Then her head came up and her eyes bored into Miranda's. 'Ah, you're concerned about my

326

emotional life — about *lurv*.' Now she let real disdain appear in her voice, but Miranda, instead of feeling intimidated, found herself wondering if Alexy had finally revealed a chink in her armour. Was the word so alien to her that she could only pronounce it mockingly? 'You want to know whether I have boyfriends.' Alexy put the term in inverted commas. 'Or a boyfriend. Someone suitable. No, can't help you there, I'm afraid, though I can definitely tell you I'm heterosexual. Oh, and not a virgin.'

'Alexy, I don't mean to — '

Alexy cut her short. 'You are a very sad person,' she said, without any particular emphasis, and let her eyes go back to the computer screen. That was all. She was waiting to be allowed to return to what mattered.

Would it ever occur to her, Miranda wondered, crouched a few seconds later on the stairs, that I have found it impossible to make my legs carry me any further; that I can only huddle here in the chilly air, wrapping my arms around myself, waiting for the pain to subside. But in her heart she knew that no thoughts of her would have survived the welcome closing of the door.

$\star \quad \star \quad \star$

By New Year Alexy had gone, and there was no mistaking the changed mood of the house. Even Gregory commented, if somewhat infelicitously from a mother's point of view, 'That damned girl of yours, she hardly lends much sparkle, does

327

she? What's the matter with her?'

Miranda chose to take the words as fellow-feeling rather than criticism. Gregory, she guessed, was chagrined not to have reached some better understanding with his granddaughter by this time. But she didn't attempt to answer the question.

She did her best to forget her sadness at Alexy's disappearance by laying plans for Hogmanay, though increasingly dubious about them. Pattie, declaring she was long past caring about 'yon daft caper' — was there a hint of wistfulness there for past glories? — agreed to look after Gregory, leaving Miranda free to go with the boys to the party at Balgowan.

But Miranda was disconcerted to find herself, once there, unable to shake off a persistent sense of being alone, which was idiotic when they'd been drawn in so warmly. She was glad to have an excuse to leave as soon as they'd seen the New Year in. She had told the boys what she'd planned, but made it clear to them that if they preferred to stay it was their choice. She would fetch them in an hour or two, or someone would bring them home. She was very touched when at the last moment they raced out to come with her.

Pattie, post-Christmas affability still in place, had been busy in their absence. For the first time in many years the lights were on at Kilgarth, fires high in hall and drawing-room, and apart from a good supply of alcohol and a small regiment of mince pies waiting to be warmed in the Rayburn, the traditional offerings of ginger wine and black bun were also laid out ready. Though Pattie, having done such a good job, appeared to have vanished. Not prepared to see her efforts wasted?

'I don't know if anyone will come, remember,' Miranda warned the boys, who were looking stunned at the sight of the hall, warm, bright, decked with holly and ivy, the tall tree in the curve of the stairs lit from top to toe. 'We could end up looking pretty silly.'

'So you've said at least twenty times,' Adam reminded her patiently, still gazing. 'Stop worrying, we shan't mind. This looks fantastic, though.'

'Cool,' Tim agreed. 'And anyway, we'll have a good lot to eat if nobody does come.'

Miranda wanted to hug them for being so positive, so easy, so loyal — for being who they were — but she managed to resist. They'd already been very forbearing about New Year kisses tonight. But suddenly she felt excited. Kilgarth, with its windows uncurtained and lights on everywhere, had looked splendid as they came up the drive. Welcoming enough, surely, to tempt a few revellers? She had just time to reflect, with a return of that hovering sense of being alone, how much Ian would have enjoyed seeing the house like this, when the great surprise of the evening swept everything else from her mind.

A movement above caught her eye, and there coming down the stairs, a faded velvet doublet sagging on his stooped shoulders, straggles of grey hair carefully brushed across his narrow skull, came Gregory, mouth clamped tight and eyes watchful, Pattie at his heels.

'Oh, Gregory! How lovely!' Miranda started forward spontaneously, immensely moved to see him, and knew by the way he accepted her arm, and by the slight tremor in his, that he had feared his presence would not be welcome. She imagined with quick sympathy how long the evening must have seemed as he waited for them to come back, and how often he must have been tempted to change his mind. 'Happy New Year,' she said softly. 'I'm so pleased you've come down. Nothing could be nicer.'

'Didn't fancy getting into my kilt,' he said, taking refuge from emotion in tetchiness, as she led him to a chair by the fire. He gestured fretfully at his ancient dinner-jacket trousers with braid down the sides. 'Looks damned ridiculous, all wrong. Couldn't think of anything else to put on. Too cold for bare knees at my age. This hall's always been a draughty hole.' He looked round with a jerk of his chin, as though defying the heat raying from the enormous fire to prove him wrong.

'Never mind your kilt,' Pattie put in, 'some carry-on I had finding that lot.' But she sounded complacent about the success of her handiwork, and coming to wish Miranda a happy new year unexpectedly gave her a whiskery kiss. The boys, looking alarmed, hastily turned their attention to the food. After this surge of cordiality, however, an uncertain pause fell.

'Well,' said Miranda. 'This could be it. Just us.'

'Then why not raise our glasses,' Gregory

330

proposed with creaky heartiness, 'and make the best of it?'

But the astonishing sight of Kilgarth, high on its hillside, lit like a cruise ship, was too intriguing to resist, and barely had a family toast been drunk than a car pulled up outside, and Charlie Fleming and his family, preferring glen first-footing to the Muirend version, came in trying not to look too thunderstruck.

They had only just left when Derek came wambling up with a couple of cronies from Muirend, though to Miranda's relief they only stayed for a dram apiece, unnerved by Gregory's gin-trap smile.

Several members of the Hay family arrived next, in a large noisy contingent which included a piper, and Miranda found herself wondering, as an impromptu eightsome swung round, with room to spare in the wide hall, how long it must be since anyone had danced in this house.

Though she'd been pressed to dance and would have loved to, after watching for a few moments she slipped away unnoticed. Going along the kitchen passage, not without a shiver, she pulled on boots and jacket, took a torch, let herself out of the back door and headed for the shrubbery path. What if they too had made preparations; what if they had waited hopefully and no one had come? It didn't bear thinking about. But at the cottage all was dark and silent. Good enough. She wasn't going to risk Olivia's wrath by waking her at this hour. What a thought. Conscience clear, Miranda raced back up the path towards the lights and music.

Having assumed that Muff would be busy with her own party — and Muff had let her think so — she was delighted to find her, with a good many of the Balgowan guests, spilling out of cars as she reached the drive.

'You can't think how fabulous the house looks from across the glen,' Muff told her, as they went in to find the dancers still in full flow. 'No wonder this lot turned up.'

Miranda, pausing for a moment to look at the scene objectively, noticing gratefully that a Hay cousin whose name she ought to know had drawn up a chair and was chatting to Gregory, seeing Adam busy at the drinks table and Tim hesitate as Pattie thrust a plate of mince pies into his hands, then summon his courage and start taking it round, found herself swallowing an unexpected lump in her throat.

As a move was made to leave, she found Muff beside her. 'You're coming, aren't you? Adam and Tim too, of course. You've done your bit. Time to party.'

'Oh, Muff, I really ought to get Gregory safely to bed,' Miranda began, then saw the eager look on the boys' faces fade. They wouldn't make a fuss if they couldn't go, she knew, they were always pragmatic about such things, but it seemed a shame for them to miss out.

'What are ye havering aboot?' Pattie, overhearing, took a hand. 'I'll see the auld — I'll see Mr Ross into his bed, never fear.'

Scarlet and perspiring, closely resembling a jelly taken out of the fridge too soon, Pattie didn't inspire confidence. But who cares,

Miranda thought with sudden recklessness. Gregory wouldn't come to any harm. A bit of cheerful ribaldry might liven him up for once.

'Why not?' Suddenly she was as eager as she'd ever been twenty years ago not to be left out, not to miss a second of whatever was afoot. 'Of course we'll come.'

'Wow.' The delighted grins of the boys lifted her spirits another notch.

As the hours unreeled, and she went without question wherever she was taken, there was a heady feeling of having stepped back into her youth. The mistakes and wrong turnings of the years no longer existed. Though the changes she found, superimposed on so much that was exactly as she remembered it in these well-known houses, gradually wove into a strange unreality where past and present were hard to disentangle.

Alltmore, for so long in Penny Forsyth's family, was the least changed. Miranda could have sworn, finding herself in the library talking to Robin Thorne from Baldarroch, now in his mid-twenties and already making a successful career as a wildlife photographer, that not an item on the desk or a needlework cushion on the sofa had been moved. Yet now in the scene were David and Barney Forsyth, between Alexy and the boys in age, the latter a chum of Adam's since beating together in the summer.

At Riach it was weird to find Joanna, whom she'd known as one of the Munros of Allt Farr, in early days only irregular visitors to the glen, now James's wife, with Laura, the daughter of her first marriage and two years younger than Tim, staying up for her first Hogmanay.

Going on to Allt Farr — she had no idea what time it was by then — the changes were so major, and she had drunk so much glühwein en route at a house belonging to some old admiral she dimly recalled dining at Cardoch House, that the whole thing took on an air of fantasy. The forbidding castle, where summer and winter evil draughts had coiled along corridors and up the winding stairs of stone, had been burned down and, she dimly grasped, the Munros were this very evening celebrating its partial rebuilding, which had created a house infinitely more manageable and comfortable than its predecessor had been. It was disorientating, too, to find intolerant Max humanised by a slight, young, gentle and smiling wife. By contrast it was reassuring to find that his mother, nowadays, it seemed, universally known as Grannie, while slightly less terrifying than Miranda had found her as a child, was as sharp-tongued as ever, and as eccentrically and colourfully dressed.

Some details of those chimerical hours remained clear however — that it had been wonderful to dance again; that among many excellent dancers Muff had had the lightest foot of all; and that it had been Tim, not Adam, who had plunged into the reels with zest, apparently equally dazzled by Laura and by Sally Danaher's stepdaughter Kirsty, over with a big crowd from Grianan and Drumveyn in the neighbouring glen.

Dawn was coming up as Miranda and the

boys were delivered back to Kilgarth. Then, as she was feeling with weary satisfaction truly home at last, sadness caught at her, the sadness which had lain in wait all evening. It had been the effect, doubtless, of music, euphoria and too much wine but, in each house filled with memories, she had expected Ian to be there. It had not been literal expectation; that she could have dealt with. It had been far more instinctive and insidious. She would turn her head, feeling he was at her side; would glimpse him across a room; when a reel struck up which they had always danced together she would look for him coming to find her as he always used to do. And each time it had been a fresh, sharp disillusionment to find he wasn't there.

# 26

This lively start to the new year marked a turning point for Miranda. Welcomed back to childhood scenes, finding so many contacts still in place, she felt some obscure barrier had been removed. She knew her own reluctance over coming to Kilgarth had had as much to do with creating it as her doubts over whether she would be able to cope with the intractable Rosses. She also knew she had needed those first quiet months to get her bearings. Now she felt more settled and secure. Decisions were behind her; she could begin to enjoy life again. It was clear that old friendships were still there to be tapped into at will, and every day she was more aware of her good fortune to be living in this lovely part of the world again.

Though, as always, she missed the boys when they went back to school, she took the chance after they'd gone to visit her mother and, perhaps because she was in a more positive frame of mind herself, found it easier this time to talk out some of her anxiety and guilt over Alexy. She came back with a real sense of contact re-established and of understanding back in place which was very comforting.

She was surprised and pleased to find that Gregory had missed her. He didn't exactly say so, but he was noticeably less irascible than before, and that had to be worth something.

It was Aunt Binnie, however, who unexpectedly turned out to be her chief source of entertainment and satisfaction during some dreary winter weeks when the hard frosts, dramatic blizzards and blocked roads of the past seemed to have been permanently replaced by lowering skies and lashing rain.

It was on a routine trip to Muirend that Binnie startled her by announcing that she'd like to drive.

Miranda blenched. 'Binnie, I'm not sure that — '

'I won't know till I try,' Binnie cut in, obviously prepared for argument, the soft skin of her cheeks pink with resolve. 'Olivia refuses to let me touch the car. Anyway, I'd be so terrified I'd be sure to do something awful,' hardly reassuring, 'but I thought with you, while the roads are quiet and there's no ice or snow or anything . . . Just to see?' she wheedled.

'Oh, Binnie.' It was hard to say no. Life on the whole had given Binnie a raw deal; it seemed little enough to ask. Miranda assessed the options. The main road was wider but even at this time of year would have traffic on it, while the hilly 'back' road, with one blind corner after another and so narrow that big vehicles had to squeeze by, was virtually deserted. If Binnie tried her hand here it would be possible to tell in a couple of minutes what skills, if any, she had retained.

In a couple of minutes Miranda was smiling. After initial nervous fumbling, and complaints about silly symbols that meant nothing, Binnie had pulled out and was away. Cars had always been part of her life, and confidence returned with astonishing speed, reflexes responding automatically, every dip and twist of the road stored in her memory.

'Binnie, you're amazing!' Miranda was full of admiration. 'I had no idea you could do that.'

'Nor had I,' Binnie admitted a little breathlessly, having misjudged the new exit onto the main road and been relieved to find nothing coming. 'You'd better take over,' she said, as they reached Sillerton and she could pull into the drive entrance. 'I think I need to recover a little.'

'Are you all right?' Miranda came to help her. 'You did magnificently.' It was true, but she was glad not to have to pilot Binnie through Muirend just the same.

'I'm fine, just a bit fluttery inside, you know.' She looked very pleased with herself, however, and, laughing, Miranda gave her a hug before tucking her safely back into the passenger seat.

'Any time,' she said. 'I mean it.'

It was a dizzy step into freedom, a major breakaway from Olivia's implacable stranglehold. Binnie had no great ambitions to jaunt far and wide, to Miranda's relief, content to confine her expeditions to Kirkton or Muirend, but with new independence came a new courage. She cast off Olivia's strictures, Olivia's views, and Olivia's taste.

'She's so funny about the shopping,' Miranda reported to Muff with amusement, but with affection too. 'It seems they've had the same list for years, mince, chops, and bacon sliced the way

Olivia likes it from Laing's, 'proper' bread from the bakery, and fruit and vegetables from that greengrocer on the square whose stuff looks sadder every week as he waits for the supermarket to kill him off. As a special treat they'd get their shoes heeled at the bicycle shop. Now Binnie wanders round Tesco's in a dream, thrilled by what she calls 'new food' like taramasalata and pitta bread.'

Not long afterwards Miranda was able to report, with even greater pleasure, 'She's had her hair cut, and not only that, she's had it lightened.'

'Heavens, how does it look?' Muff asked. 'Not that that matters, really, it's the enterprise that counts.'

'I know, she was so excited. It's taken years off her.' Miranda didn't add that, although straight from the hands of the hairdresser Binnie's hair had looked well-shaped and bouncy, by next morning it had been sticking out in sad little tufts. Binnie had been so serenely unaware of disaster, clearly still seeing what she had seen with such shy delight in the mirror the day before, that, even to Muff, Miranda wasn't ready to give her away. 'And you should see her clothes,' she said instead. 'She's discovered that shop down by the wharf, and she's buying all sorts of weird things, floaty scarves, tie-dyed tunics and the most gorgeous plum-coloured suede boots. You can tell she's been starved for colour.'

'What does Olivia have to say about it?' Muff didn't attempt to hide an unworthy *schadenfreude*. Friendly overtures in encounters with Olivia had invariably been curtly rejected. She was all for this reckless revolt of Binnie's.

'Um.' Miranda didn't seem as keen to recount dramas as Muff had hoped. 'She's seriously unimpressed, as you can imagine, but — I don't know — it's a bit sad, actually. Of course she tries to put Binnie down at every turn, and I could wring her neck when she does, but in a way I think she feels a bit stricken, as though she knows she's lost control and isn't sure how it happened.'

The truth was Miranda was worried about Olivia. And worried about Binnie too, in spite of the fun she was having, when she thought of how they lived. Going fairly regularly to call, whether invited or not, because she was determined to keep an eye on them, she had been shocked to discover how they existed during the winter. In its sunless hollow among the dripping trees, the cottage drew the damp like a sponge. Dark patches spread up the walls, windows swelled and jammed, and on really wet days wallpaper bulged from the walls, reluctantly sticking itself back on marginally drier ones.

Olivia and Binnie barely heated the place, relying for warmth on the sitting-room fire, only grudgingly switching on the bathroom towel rail when they thought the pipes might freeze. Otherwise it stayed off, and mildew patterned walls and ceiling, their bath towels never dried out properly and the soap went slimy. On the basis that when they were preparing a meal the cooker warmed them, they didn't heat the kitchen at all, and during the day, unless rain was actually driving in, had the door standing open exactly as it did in summer. Though Miranda had never seen their bedrooms, it was reasonable to assume that conditions there would be arctic.

The only thing she ever heard Olivia complain about, however, was mildew on her loofah. 'Always the same, have to buy a new one every year. Ridiculous expense.'

At a couple of pounds a time Miranda supposed it was cheaper than heating the bathroom. But, joking apart, it concerned her to see Olivia, who suffered from the same stiffness in the joints as her brother, wince at every movement, and to see Binnie's face pinched with cold. She would find the pair of them huddled as close to the fire as they could get their chairs, both wearing layers of woollies topped with, in Olivia's case, a Husky waistcoat at least thirty years old, and in Binnie's some colourful but frivolous new addition not designed for warmth.

It was hard to know whether to interfere or not. 'If it's what they choose,' she said doubtfully to Muff. 'They've always lived like that. They're used to it. I haven't any excuse for barging in.'

'But at their age cold and damp must be so bad for them.' Muff, a firm believer in comfort and cosiness, shivered at the thought.

'The trouble is, I don't know if they do it from choice or if it's all they can afford. I do know they have an unlimited supply of logs from the estate, yet they never seem to have a decent fire.'

It was impossible to guess how much they had to live on. Did they have savings, capital, pensions, insurance? It was equally impossible to ask them, and opening such a subject with Gregory was unthinkable, in spite of his more mellow mood. Though a free hand to run Kilgarth had been part of the deal in bringing Alexy here, Miranda knew that any attempt to probe Ross financial affairs would not be countenanced for a second.

It was a relief when spring came early, and both aunts seemed in better health. Alexy appeared briefly at Easter, collected a few things from her room, made her grandfather angry by avoiding him as much as possible, mortified Tim by mocking him about his silent, helpless infatuation with Laura Drummond, and bitterly offended Pattie by leaving her bedroom door locked when she took off again, telling no one she was going.

'Pattie, don't worry. We'll leave the room as it is. That's the way she wants it.'

'She does it to spite me.' Pattie's jowls quivered with affront. 'What would I want with her things anyway?'

But Miranda, who had always scrupulously respected the children's privacy, knew Pattie had not been the target, and she minded this locked door more than she believed even Alexy could have intended. In point of fact, every bedroom key at Kilgarth, where they existed, probably fitted every bedroom door, but she knew nothing but the direst emergency would make her go into that room.

She was glad to be able to concentrate on the boys, who suddenly seemed to be growing up at a startling rate. Tim, one of whose deepest worries had been that he would never be as tall as Adam, had shot up and overtaken him, and they both topped Miranda by inches. And this holiday, returning from a visit to Will's parents, they enquired diffidently if there was any chance of having rooms of their own. Adam also asked, for the first time, if he could invite a friend home for a few days before term began, as his parents had to return abroad early. He then threw in the casual rider that the friend's sister had nowhere to go either.

Gregory grumbled about the 'invasion', but supposed he couldn't stop them doing as they pleased. He laid down all kinds of rules beforehand, but in the event, apart from objecting if noise levels rose too high, and spending more time than had recently been his habit in the estate office, Miranda came to the conclusion that he almost liked having the house busy.

Luckily both visitors were happy with what Kilgarth had to offer, so entertaining them was easy, and it was a pleasure for Miranda to see the four of them enjoying exactly the things she used to enjoy at that age. And Ian used to enjoy. More and more often it seemed wrong that she was here, settled and happy at Kilgarth, while he remained in exile. Wrong too that it was Will's boys who had so readily become absorbed into this scene, while Alexy obdurately shut herself off from it.

Driving the four to Muirend, to play golf at Pitlochry, or to houses up and down the glen where a new-generation network of friendships was in place, she at last appreciated how uncomplainingly Georgina had done the same for her. She said as much in her next letter, then found herself wondering, with a chill of uncertainty, whether this could really be an ongoing pattern. Would Adam and Tim be able to put down roots, or, ultimately, would they bring their own families here?

She made herself look ahead for once, something she usually preferred not to do. What would happen when Alexy inherited Kilgarth? If her present behaviour was anything to go by, she would instantly turn everyone out. For herself, Miranda didn't think she would much mind. She could buy somewhere small and convenient in the glen and, for as long as they needed or wanted it, make it home for the boys. But should Alexy be given the freedom to act in such a way? Also, the prospect of being uprooted on a whim of Alexy's made her abruptly conscious of being alone, something she rarely dwelled upon. Perhaps, contradictory as it might seem, the renewed contacts with friends had brought it home to her too forcibly. Everyone was grounded in some family group, or had a partner.

That, she knew, was what lay behind this new, unwelcome self-awareness. She was seeing herself suddenly as a woman alone, and that had never worried her till now. After Ian left she'd been too busy being angry, and too occupied with Alexy, to think of it. Then Will had appeared in her life and there had been the even tenor of their years together. Struggling to cope with his loss, she had immersed herself in looking after the boys as well as Alexy, and in the demands of her job. All that was obvious, but she could see, looking back more honestly, that she hadn't had the courage to think about herself.

Surprisingly again, it was Binnie who made her more conscious of her solitary status now.

One summer morning she appeared at the big house, something unprecedented in Miranda's experience. It was soon after Alexy's birthday, which had passed without a word from her, and Miranda was still upset by it. She had been sleeping badly, and on this particular morning had come down late and was making coffee in the kitchen when Binnie's face appeared at the window. Pattie was out in the workshop haranguing Derek about a dripping tap he was supposed to have fixed, so Miranda was alone.

'Binnie, whatever's happened?' she asked, going hastily out, for Binnie looked quite distraught.

'The auld one's dropped off her perch. Good luck to her,' Pattie said with relish, as she and Derek, safely out of the firing line, watched from across the yard.

'Not before time,' he responded with a heartless cackle, not averse to having Pattie's attention diverted from his own shortcomings.

Binnie's face was sagging in shock, her hair wild, her eyes wide with distress, tears glistening in the folds of flesh beneath them. She clutched an envelope to the bib of her pink dungarees, and she was trembling.

'The post's come,' she began, struggling to find some coherent way to begin. 'Postie was early today. You won't realise because he leaves your letters in the hall, at least he used to, you may have changed the way . . . '

She was obviously speaking at random and Miranda's anxiety grew.

'Binnie, come in and sit down,' she urged.

'No, no, don't ask me to.' Even in this emergency Binnie was certain she mustn't cross the threshold, in spite of the fact that for the moment she couldn't quite remember why.

'Is Olivia all right?' Miranda asked.

'Olivia?' Binnie blinked bemusedly. 'Olivia?' She appeared to be groping to work out what her sister had to do with anything.

'Is she all right?'

Binnie stared at Miranda, then pushed that away as too difficult to deal with. 'Look, this came. After all this time. He's sent me a letter.'

After more than fifty years Sholto McDermott, the young officer over whom Binnie had so vainly fantasised, had resurrected himself. Now a widower, his sons grown up and married, he had moved back to Scotland and was living near Selkirk. Planning a little holiday in the north, and wishing to revisit old scenes, he had wondered . . .

'Darling Binnie.' As Miranda folded her in her arms, doing her best to calm her tremulous shaking, she formed the iron resolution not to let anything, if it was in her power to prevent it, hurt Binnie. Binnie the innocent and vulnerable; Miranda felt protective love for her rush up.

346

# 27

Miranda found Sholto both self-satisfied and dull. He was a slight man of medium height, his fair hair now white (did Binnie notice this?), and he was spruce in an over-careful way, with a tendency to permanent creases in his trousers and hair too recently combed. He wore his Air Force tie on every occasion and his blazer fitted too neatly at the waist.

He had, however, prospered. As an interior designer, Binnie obediently related, but Miranda thought when she learned a little more that painter and decorator might have been closer to the mark. However, whatever the job description, his business had been successful and he had opened branches in Exmouth and Sidmouth as well as Budleigh Salterton. His sons had both gone into the business with him, hoping perhaps that he would retire sooner than he had, but after his wife died there had been a general family review of their situation. His elder son had announced that his heart was really in carpets, while the younger, more dubiously in Sholto's opinion, admitted to a hidden yearning for the church. His ministry was of the jolly, vernacular variety, and Sholto found it altogether too touchy-feely and new-fangled for him. You could find yourself swaying and clapping with some pretty odd people if you weren't careful. Still, the church was the church, each to his own and all that, and Kevin could have done a lot worse.

The business had been sold, and Sholto, ever both frugal and shrewd, had made some sound investments to add to those he already had in place. Now, well into his seventies, and seeing interest rates yield less and less, he had decided the time had come to do some spending. He had made a list of the things lottery winners seemed to spend their millions on, then crossed most of the items out as hysterical extravagance. Holidays and travel had remained however, along with 'a decent car'. With a Porsche in the garage he had turned his attention to the cruise brochures. But now had come a snag. The image of being on holiday alone was not only a bit pathetic — and he had no intention of looking pathetic — it was worrying. No sense in making yourself a target; all kinds of women were ready to go after a chap with a bit of style and a bit of cash. So out came his address book, and he made a second list.

Binnie would never know how far down it she had come. It didn't occur to her that there had ever been anyone in Sholto's life but Meryl and herself. Her happiness that he had made contact again was so naive and left her so completely without defences that Miranda ached for her — and decided to keep an eye on the complacent and too affable Sholto.

He seemed, at the outset anyway, well-intentioned. In spite of somewhat misleading time-mellowed memories of Kilgarth during the war, where he had come as Gregory's fellow officer, and put out at first to find himself visiting a poky and uncomfortable cottage instead of the posh house he remembered, he was not deterred, and accepted Binnie's explanation of the family quarrel. In fact, when he came to think it over, he was rather glad not to have to see her brother. Though he had found Kilgarth a cushy number for leave in those wartime days, and a good bit grander than anything he was used to, he had privately thought Gregory Ross an arrogant so-and-so, and had put up with his patronising manner and filthy temper for the sake of the shooting, and a glimpse of a way of life which would never in normal times have been open to him.

Olivia of course poured scorn on him after every visit (he booked into the Kirkton Arms and called with punctilious correctness at appointed times to take Binnie out to lunch or dinner, or for a 'little run' in the car), usually in round old-fashioned terms like pipsqueak, whipper-snapper, frightful little man and TG.

Miranda had to think about that one. Temporary gentleman? 'I'm not sure anyone says TG these days,' she remarked, 'or would even know what it means.'

'Then they should read more,' Olivia said tartly.

It was obvious her nose was badly out of joint, and as the months passed and Sholto's visits became an established thing — for what man with his thirsty ego could resist Binnie's open admiration and willing compliance with his wishes? — Miranda began to feel more and more sorry for Olivia. Brusque and aggressive she might be, but there didn't ever seem to have been anyone on hand when she was growing up either to squash her or to encourage her to be nicer, or to have felt sympathy for her as she marched heavy-footed into a bleak and combative old age.

'I quite miss the double-act sometimes,' Miranda admitted to Muff. 'Binnie used to begin every other sentence with, 'Do you remember how we always . . . ?' or, 'You know how . . . ?' and Olivia would let her witter on till she'd quite finished, then say 'No,' and stump off muttering, 'Pure twaddle,' to herself. It never failed to flatten poor Binnie, but she never learned. Now Binnie doesn't need her endorsement or approval any more, and Olivia's quite lost.'

'You're not telling me Binnie's going to waltz off and marry her old lover's ghost?' Muff demanded. 'She must be seventy at least.'

'Just about, I think, but don't you think she looks much more spry and youthful these days? Thank goodness Sholto didn't turn up last year, he'd probably have disappeared again rather smartly. At least now Binnie is looking her best, with the new clothes and colours and make-up and all the rest of it. And she's stopped being so frightened of everything, which is more important.'

'Yes, thanks to you,' Muff said affectionately. 'Wasn't it lucky you came along when you did?'

'Maybe. But I still don't think Sholto will be impressed enough to marry Binnie.' Miranda had the impression that his life was so well-ordered that he didn't require the services of a wife, and probably, braving the hospitality on offer in the cottage, he wasn't convinced that in Binnie's case the services would improve on the satisfactory standards of his present house-keeper. What he did need was a companion for his travels, and the image of himself sitting eternally at a table for one encouraged him to make allowances. He need never worry about Binnie's accent and manners, and that was reassuring. Her clothes were a bit odd sometimes but he could influence her there. She was grateful to him, and she would never have any designs on his money because (and this he didn't much like but had to accept) the sort of money he had put together didn't mean a thing to her. But the main thing was, he could deliver her home at the end of each jaunt, resume his pleasant round in Selkirk, his whist, his golf, his Sunday pre-lunch drinks at his favourite hostelry, and forget all about her.

The jaunts, however, were frequent, and now that he had a satisfactory companion — there had been some disasters he preferred to forget — they could be more ambitious. A few days in Devon and Cornwall, in the nature of a trial run but not introducing Binnie to his family, were followed by a wine-tasting tour of the French vineyards, and by August he and Binnie were off on a Land of the Midnight Sun cruise.

It was not the only change this summer. Adam was in Greece with his girlfriend's family, and Tim for the first time found himself alone. Miranda was slightly concerned about this, having seen the two boys as a unit for so long, but she said nothing, waiting to see how Tim would handle it. She was impressed with the way he moved smoothly into a new pattern of his own. He was delighted to be taken on at Riach as ponyman for the grouse shooting (James hadn't quite had the energy to get round to mechanising yet) and, in spite of the long hours on the hill, was happy to cycle up and down morning and evening when lifts weren't available.

Sometimes he stayed overnight at Riach, for his attachment to Laura held firm, and Joanna Mackenzie was a hospitable mother who enjoyed having young people about, and thought it good for Laura to have an occasional break from the turbulent company of her younger stepsisters, James's twin girls. There was one tricky patch when Laura, more mature and cool-headed than Tim, though younger, told him not to be an idiot, she wasn't into relationships. Miranda, full of sympathy, wanting to warn him as gently as she could not to wear his heart on his sleeve but terrified of intruding, wished with an ache of sadness for him that Will had been there to help him.

Apart from this setback, which he dealt with in his own way, Tim had his father's quiet capacity to enjoy life, and a new interest in the history of the glen, with its many traces of iron-age civilisation, diverted his mind to some extent. Without Adam's over-shadowing presence he was emerging as his own person, and reminded Miranda more and more of Will, to her great pleasure.

Sometimes they would go down to the river on a quiet evening, or to the loch where the midges weren't quite so troublesome, to get a few trout for breakfast, and they drew closer in these peaceful hours, when they rarely spoke but were content in each other's company.

How different from Alexy's relentless disdain of all contact. She appeared without warning, some weeks after term had finished, gaunt in shapeless garments of much-washed black, and the first thing she did was to attack Pattie about the state of her room and demand that she sort it out at once.

Miranda, receiving the full blast of Pattie's wrath, simply said, 'Right.' As she whirled upstairs it did occur to her that having a fight would probably be enough to send Alexy straight out to her car and away again, but in spite of the spontaneous pleasure and relief she had felt to see her come scowling in, Miranda knew she'd rather this than have her behave so outrageously to Pattie.

For once she tore into Alexy without hesitation and, though Alexy certainly wasn't lost for scathing words, Miranda knew, as she took a few moments in her room to calm down afterwards, that her scornful daughter had been considerably startled to find herself under attack. She also realised, with a lift of satisfaction, that she had felt unusually sure of herself; unafraid of the consequences, in fact.

And about time too, she thought grimly, holding her wrists under the cold tap (the water was always icy at Kilgarth no matter what the season or the weather) and letting her heart rate slow. Now she must go down and help Pattie with dinner and do some feather smoothing.

After this stormy arrival Alexy settled down, as far as Miranda could tell, to work concentratedly on whatever assignments she had to complete before next term. She was as crushing as ever to Tim, but he too seemed to have found new ways to deal with her. Busy with his own pursuits, he let the stabs and sneers wash over him, and nothing could have impressed on Miranda more forcefully the gulf between the involved, contented lives the boys had established for themselves here, and Alexy's bitter, self-inflicted isolation.

In one respect only did Alexy show herself more amenable than before. She made some attempt this time to mend fences with Gregory, though Miranda couldn't help wondering, hating herself for the thought, whether Alexy had noticed that after a temporary improvement his health was deteriorating again. There was nothing wrong that Charlie Fleming could pinpoint; simply he was gradually failing in strength and had less and less appetite, in spite of all Miranda's efforts to tempt him with his favourite dishes.

She was interested to note that, although Gregory received Alexy's inept advances with a sardonic and astute evaluation of their worth, he was pleased by them nevertheless, and Miranda guessed, as she had suspected before, that for him Alexy represented all he had of Ian. Having driven his son away he would, illogical and

354

unfair as it might be, tolerate a good deal from her. These days he almost seemed to have given up fighting for fighting's sake, and it was a new source of satisfaction for Miranda to see how well he was beginning to get on with Adam and Tim.

It was a summer of more contacts and invitations for Miranda herself, and through Tim she was often drawn into the friendly scene of Riach and Allt Farr. At the latter particularly, where the cottages on the estate were used for holiday letting, there were always throngs of congenial people, half of whom seemed to be family members, and Miranda very much enjoyed this widening of her social horizons, and began to turn over in her mind agreeable plans for returning some hospitality when autumn came.

★   ★   ★

In the autumn Binnie and Sholto went to the West Indies for three months.

'Can you imagine that happening this time last year?' Muff demanded when Miranda told her about it. 'Binnie was such a pale, nervous, harassed scrap of a thing. I do think she's amazing. You've certainly opened the lid of her box. But what about poor old Olivia? I have to agree with you that it can't be much fun for her.'

'She insists that she's glad to get a bit of peace, as she puts it, but actually it's quite sad to see her. Without Binnie to bully she really has no purpose in life. I'm sure she's not looking after herself properly but I don't know what to do to help her, she's so stubborn.'

But on a bleak morning in early December, when the chilly mist shutting in Kilgarth condensed into dank, bone-aching cold as she went down the path to the cottage, Miranda found that the time for action had come. She saw as she opened the garden gate the hunched tweed shape of Olivia, down on one knee on the strip of mossy grass that ran down the side of the cottage, and oddly motionless.

When she called a greeting Olivia made a curious restricted movement with her head, as though she had started to look over her shoulder but found she couldn't. Or was she merely annoyed at her cherished peace being invaded? Moving more quickly, instinct warning that all was not well, Miranda went across to her frowning.

'Olivia, what are you doing?'

'Checking my mole traps. What do you think I'm doing?' Olivia retorted rudely, but still didn't turn or get up.

Now beside her, Miranda saw that she had the trap, one end set, in her hands, and was trying to press down the spring with her broad thumbs to catch under the second hook. Her hands were shaking, her shoulders hunched, her face grimly set. But what was most appalling, tears were squeezing out of her eyes and her lips were trembling.

'Olivia, whatever is it?' Miranda knelt beside her, feeling the icy cold of the spongy grass soak instantly through to her knees. 'Let me do that for you.'

'I can do it. Strong hands. I can always manage it. Binnie can't. Never saw such a feeble creature as Binnie, perfectly useless.'

Her voice slipped out of control as she spoke, and she began to sob in a harsh, desperate, shamed way which made Miranda's throat ache, and the trap, defeating her, sprang open.

'Olivia, let me take that. Yes, all right, I'll set it if that's what you want, but first let me help you up. This grass is soaking.'

'But that's the whole point, you fool, I can't damn well get up,' Olivia exclaimed furiously, but Miranda knew the anger was not directed at her. It was anger against the terrible power of old age, of failing strength, of loneliness and defeat.

Olivia hadn't intended to admit to what she had been doing, but the evidence was all there. The ladder was still in place, the loft hatch open, and a picture fallen from the landing wall, its glass broken. Olivia had been checking her mouse traps — was a head count of dead creatures her first treat of the day? — and had slipped coming down the ladder, falling heavily and taking the picture with her. She had lain where she had fallen for several minutes, she didn't know how long, getting steadily colder, then had finally dragged herself down the stairs and into the kitchen. She had tried to ignore the pain, though this she didn't tell Miranda, her mind bouncing off thoughts of what it would mean not to be able to look after herself, too terrified to grasp at rational answers.

Confusedly determined not to give in, she had hobbled outside intending to bring in the logs, though needing both hands to drag herself along the house wall, and then had noticed that the turf laid over her mole trap was disturbed. Managing to get down on one knee she had found herself locked in that position, and in the kind of pain that had told her all hope of struggling on would be beyond her. As Miranda, trying to get a firm hold on her unwieldy body, and beginning to think she would have to leave her there and get help, at last managed to get her to her feet, Olivia seemed almost more incensed that the trap had been sprung and the mole had got away than about anything else.

★   ★   ★

'You never need see her or speak to her, but she's moving into the house.'

'It's none of your business and it's not your house. You can't make decisions like that.' Gregory's stick slashed at the leg of the table in front of him; Miranda knew he would have liked it to be her ankles.

'I just have,' she said calmly.

'Well, she'll never come. Get someone in to look after her. She can afford it. Or better still, get Binnie back, it's time she did something to earn her keep.'

'Pattie's getting a room ready and Derek's coming to help me and I'm going round to bring Olivia back in the car. Now, this morning. That cottage isn't fit to live in, and she isn't going to spend another winter there.'

'If you think I brought you here to infest my house with every Tom, Dick and Harry . . . '

'Olivia, your sister, Gregory,' Miranda reminded him from the door.

Olivia argued as fiercely as Gregory at the idea of being taken to the big house, but once Pattie and Miranda had installed her in bed there, she became oddly — and worryingly — acquiescent. It was as though she had accepted that the fight was over and with that acceptance her whole personality seemed to alter and diminish.

Miranda was relieved when her argumentative spirit revived after a little cosseting. Charlie Fleming had found no broken bones, only severe bruising and a strained thigh muscle, and recommended a few days in bed. He had been concerned for some time about a persistent cough Olivia had been unable to shake off, and expressed his relief that she was out of the cottage in terms that made Miranda feel guilty at not having insisted on the move before. Particularly as, after a couple of highly charged confrontations which resulted in Gregory demanding lunch in the library every day, a demand which Miranda told Pattie to ignore, and after a bout of dragging up old accusations which proved to be strangely empty and meaningless even to the two aggressive old battlers, they settled down to a rumbling truce.

Adam and Tim, warned by Miranda on the way home for Christmas of what was in store for them, surprised her by finding the pair excellent value.

'None of it means anything,' Adam said comfortably, when Miranda apologised for the quarrelsome atmosphere. 'Seems to me they're enjoying themselves.'

'I like hearing about what it was like here when they were young,' Tim added. 'And some of the things Aunt Olivia says are really neat.'

How would Alexy react? The question gave Miranda more than the usual disquiet. The house still belonged to Gregory, and he had accepted the situation, seemed indeed, as Adam said, to relish it, but in Alexy's mind the house was virtually hers. She would certainly have something to say about this invasion. But there was silence from Alexy this Christmas, and anxiety gnawed at Miranda throughout the holiday. It was unreasonable, she knew, to be more worried about silence over a festival which Alexy trenchantly scorned than at any other time, and she was used by now to hearing nothing from her for weeks on end, but that didn't help the ache of loss, and the renewed agony of wondering where she had gone so wrong.

The silence stretched through the spring term, and the next news Miranda received was a call one Friday evening, from an almost incoherent friend of Alexy's who lived in Edinburgh. Alexy had been taken to hospital from this friend's flat a couple of hours ago, having taken what appeared to be a lethal quantity of paracetamol.

# 28

'They got her to the hospital in time. They were worried at first, because of the amount she'd taken, that there'd be irreversible damage — ' how often Miranda had thought of Will's wife Diana during the awful hours of waiting ' — but they say she'll be all right.'

Ian took her arm above the elbow in a firm grip and looked searchingly into her eyes. She saw that in spite of his air of healthy fitness his own eyes were strained and tired, and it was surprising but suddenly comforting to know he'd slept as little as she had. She had grown so used to accepting that he had left the problems of Alexy exclusively to her. It was a first tiny sensation of some of the load she'd carried alone for so long being lifted from her.

'Thank God for that,' Ian said, and the depth of his relief was unmistakable. 'It must have been hell for you, waiting to hear.'

For me? Miranda, her mind locked on Alexy, was scarcely capable of absorbing that. 'She's out of hospital, anyway, so they must be sure there'll be no after effects.'

'So where is she? You've taken her back to Kilgarth?' Ian obviously needed to adjust to this altered picture, and Miranda could guess at the thoughts which must have filled his mind during the interminable flight.

'She wouldn't go there.' Miranda's voice

shook. Remembering the violence of Alexy's objections, their battle on that point seemed abruptly one too many to bear. After the urgency and drama, the hours of crippling fear, the renewed bombardment of all the questions she had ever asked herself about where she had failed with this obdurately intractable child, and how she could have let things reach this point, Miranda had been devastated to find that still, more resolutely than ever, Alexy had resisted both her presence and her care.

'She's so angry, so bitter and unforgiving. I wasn't able to . . . she wouldn't . . . '

There in the crowded airport concourse, with strangers around them and the humdrum business of a flight arrival still going on, Miranda found her voice failing, her lips trembling, her knees beginning to shake. Helpless anger that she had not even been able to persuade Alexy to do this one thing, to come home, sought the first available target.

'She has far too much money, that's the trouble. You've always sent her too much money.' Resentment with Ian, so honed and familiar that it was almost soothing to clutch at it, whirled up into irrational attack. 'It's made her so completely independent. Why should she come home? She can go wherever she likes.'

She failed to read the blank shock which made Ian first open his mouth to protest at this, then clamp it shut again, his look of disbelief replaced by a searing hurt which in its turn he took care to hide.

'OK,' he said quietly, 'let's take all that as read

362

for the moment, shall we? I don't think there's much to be gained by going down that route.'

'No, I know. I'm sorry.' Miranda grappled with an almost panicky sense of disorientation as a long-held image was displaced by reality, just as a remembered face survives for a moment as it has existed in the memory for years, then is gone for ever as the new face, changed by time, is accepted by the eye. It made her feel guilty on quite a new level, to realise how simplistic and convenient she had allowed her view of Ian to become.

'Look, we need to go somewhere and talk,' he said, 'but first, why don't we have coffee or something here?' He'd drunk enough coffee to last him a lifetime in the past twenty-four hours, but he thought Miranda looked as though she would benefit both from sitting down and getting something hot inside her.

'Coffee? But Alexy — ' Miranda hadn't adjusted yet to the immediate emergency being over. Ian had come because it had seemed terrifyingly likely that Alexy would succeed in what she had set out to do, and the essential thing had been that he should get here as soon as he possibly could.

'Another ten minutes can't make any difference now,' Ian said, keeping his voice matter-of-fact. For how many hours had he believed they would, frustrated almost beyond endurance at being able to do nothing but sweat the time out. Now it appeared to him there was a more urgent need at hand than getting to Alexy. 'Come on.'

With his strong clasp on her arm feeling

utterly natural, hardly knowing where she was or what she wanted, still feebly trying to summon the shreds of an anger so shot through with other emotions that she could scarcely remember what it had ever been about, Miranda let him lead her to a table, and waited numbly while he fetched coffee and sandwiches for them both.

'When did you last eat?' he asked, noting again the dark circles under her eyes and the look of strain in her face, as he rapidly transferred the contents of his tray to the table. She was thinner, the gloss and look of vivid enjoyment in life which he always associated with her stripped away — by the events of the past two days or by the difficult years? — but her looks were the looks that could still draw him, would always draw him.

Miranda made a small negative movement of her head, unable even to start to work out an answer. When Ian put a plate with a sandwich on it in front of her she stared at it as though she didn't know what it was.

'It was good of you to come and meet me,' he said after a moment, not pressing her to eat. She had never met him before. On all those bleak visits when he had tried so hard to maintain the link with her and with Alexy there had been no question of such a thing, and he had minded every time, and then been angry with himself for minding. Her coming to the airport today had seemed, far too optimistically as he now realised, a signal that they might at last have arrived at a greater tolerance, even that in facing this crisis over Alexy together they could move on to an acceptance of the failures of the past. But that flashing attack about supplying Alexy with too much money, though he could guess at the anguish and exhaustion which lay behind it, had made him see how fatuous his hopes had been.

'So where is Alexy?' he tried again, glad to see that Miranda had drunk some of her coffee at least.

Her head came up and she looked at him with a desperation that moved him. 'I didn't even know!' she exclaimed, evidently locked into some different train of thought. The words came out harshly, too loudly, and she checked, visibly taking a grip on herself before repeating, 'I didn't know,' in a toneless, defeated voice which pierced him more sharply than her outburst.

'Didn't know what?' he asked gently.

'She's had this flat, or the use of it, all along. When she didn't come home during her vacs I always assumed she was in her digs in Durham. I don't know why I thought that,' she added miserably, as if to herself, looking unseeingly across the busy restaurant. 'A flat in Edinburgh. It belongs to someone she knew at school, who only uses it in term-time. Alexy was there. That's where she did it. The friend had left — her family have moved away from Edinburgh and she was going home for Easter — but she forgot her Filofax so she went back. That was all it was. If she hadn't gone back — '

'It's all right,' Ian said quickly, leaning towards her, longing to wrap her in his arms and comfort her but able to offer nothing more than protective closeness. 'She did go back. Alexy's fine.'

'But now Alexy's back in the flat. It's where she wants to be, she says. She refuses to leave.'

'Well, if that's what she chooses to do.' But he didn't like the idea, and he realised he'd got used to thinking of Kilgarth as Alexy's home, overcoming his initial reservations since it was now accomplished fact, and glad at least to know that continuity of family ownership would still exist.

Miranda stared at him, her eyes dark and hollow in her tired face. 'But don't you see, she's furious that she was found in time. You can't imagine how angry she was. It was a million to one chance that she was found. Her friend was going home for three weeks. She meant to do it. It wasn't the old cry-for-help stuff, it was most carefully planned. And now if she's left alone there, what is there to prevent her from trying again, with nothing to stop it working the next time?'

Ian watched her as the words poured out, trying to gauge how blunt he could be. Part of him felt as if he knew her through and through. To be sitting across a table from her once more, oblivious to everything around them, seemed the most normal thing in the world. At the same time he was deeply conscious that they were strangers, with years of hostility between them, and no link other than the biological fact of having produced a child.

But he was the child's father; that gave him the right to speak on this point at least.

'Miranda,' he began carefully, and to his surprise felt a physical response merely at saying her name, 'no one can prevent that if she's set on doing it. She's away at university all term and you can't monitor everything she does there. Even if she were at Kilgarth — ' it was strange to be using that name too, some separate part of his brain noted, and he wondered how long, until today, it had been since he had spoken it aloud ' — you couldn't prevent it happening. You know that. All that can be done is to try to find out what was driving her, and if possible address whatever brought her to this point.'

Miranda nodded, her lips tight. Then, with a stark misery in her voice that would stay in his mind for a long time to come, she said, accusations forgotten, 'But don't you see, it must have been because of me that she wanted to do such a thing, because of me that she's so blindly angry to find she's still alive.'

'Oh, sweetheart.' He ached for her, and there seemed nothing strange at that moment in using such a term. He doubted if Miranda had noticed it, however, for, having voiced the terrible conviction which had been racking her, the shaking threatened to overcome her again, and in an effort to subdue it she was sitting with her shoulders hunched up to her ears and her fingers pressed to her mouth, as though afraid its trembling would betray her into tears.

Anxiety for her, compassion, and something else, an astonishment to hear her make such an admission which he knew must be put aside for the moment, made Ian feel that any second now

367

he'd be shaking as well.

Miranda tightened her lips, made sure her voice was under control, and said, 'I'm afraid she doesn't want to see you. I'm sorry.'

'Yes, well, I'd expected that.' Ian had had plenty of time during the flight to recall with unwelcome clarity Alexy's rejection of him at their last encounter.

'She said if I took you back there she'd walk out and we'd never find her again.'

Ian, his face haggard, didn't attempt this time to hide how much the threat hurt. Then with some trouble he put it aside. It only rammed home what he already knew. 'In that case I think you and I should find somewhere a little quieter and a little more congenial than this to do our talking.'

'I've dragged you back for nothing, haven't I?' Miranda said guiltily, as they went out. It hadn't occurred to her till now. Even when she'd known Alexy was no longer in danger she had still seen Ian's arrival as the next obvious and vital step.

'You couldn't know that.'

'Was I right to let you know?' She stopped short, turning to him in frowning doubt.

'Miranda, of course you were. She's my daughter, for God's sake. Of course I'd always want to know if — anything happened to her.' If you needed me, he had almost said. Since the moment Miranda had told him what the situation was, he knew his chief anxiety had been for her. 'Come on, let's not get into all that here,' he urged. 'Where's the car? This wind's arctic.'

'Yes, it must be a bit of a shock to you,'

Miranda said sympathetically, walking faster, her mind ranging over possible places where they could be quiet and uninterrupted. She hadn't thought that far ahead and felt herself out of touch with the city, as though she'd been away for years. Also, the first choices that came to mind were of places where she and Ian had met during his visits after they'd parted, and every one seemed to be associated with harrowing memories.

In the end they went nowhere. As if the ordinary act of getting into the car had returned them to an everyday level of emotion, they began to talk spontaneously, though for the moment they left the fraught subject of Alexy alone.

'How has it worked out, this business of living at Kilgarth?' Ian asked, grateful to be out of the east coast wind. He'd forgotten how penetrating it could be; he needed at least one more layer of clothes.

There was suddenly so much to tell him and, though Miranda didn't consciously assess this, Ian was the only person in the world to whom the changes and events of the last year would mean anything. Estranged as he had been from his father for half his lifetime, he was still a Ross, and Miranda didn't need to question his interest. Her agonised worries over Alexy receded briefly as she talked, savouring the unfamiliar comfort of being able to share all kinds of trivia with someone known for always, whose starting point was exactly the same as hers.

'Don't tell me nothing's ever been done to

369

that cottage? It was pretty well uninhabitable twenty years ago,' Ian would break in to exclaim, or 'the same old Rayburn? Still supposed to heat the entire house?' or, 'Aunt Binnie with a lover appearing out of the woodwork after all these years, you have to be joking,' and the sheer ease of not having to edit or expand on anything was a pleasure in itself. He listened without interruption, however, as she told him of Gregory's increasing immobility and Olivia's fall, then said simply, 'Thank God you got her back into the house, and Binnie too. Well done you.'

Three simple words, but they brought home to Miranda the bleak fact that since Will had died, and she had been left responsible for so many people, there had been no one to offer praise. Her eyes stung, and she was thankful when Ian wanted to hear more about Adam and Tim, a subject even more rewarding than Binnie's happiness with Sholto.

'It sounds as though you've been lucky in your stepsons,' Ian commented, smiling in sympathy at the open affection in her voice, but unable to avoid a wry pang to think how very differently she spoke of Alexy. 'I look forward to getting to know them.'

Miranda turned her head sharply, the reason for his being here rushing back.

'But are you thinking of — ? Do you mean — ?'

He didn't answer at once, and she saw by the way his expression set in grim lines she hadn't seen before that his thoughts too were focused once more on the reality they faced.

'Look, whether Alexy wants to see me or not, I intend to talk to her,' he said. 'That's definite. What I don't intend is to let her give you any more grief. Here's what we'll do. You drop me off at the flat and leave me to deal with her. Then you can head back to Kilgarth.'

Was that it? Miranda felt as though a path leading away into some vague distance had been chopped from under her outstretched foot. She had imagined they were about to discuss — well, what? Thrown, she had to make a strenuous effort to readjust. What had she thought they had to talk about? Ian hadn't come to see her. He might have wanted to catch up on news of the family — or perhaps he'd just been giving her a chance to calm down a bit; her cheeks burned at the thought — but he had no connection with them any more. His purpose in coming had been to see Alexy, and now he wanted to be taken to her. Of course. Though, doing her best to ignore her jolted sense of anticlimax at the prospect of driving away, so soon, without anything more said between them, Miranda had the gravest doubts that Alexy would let him see her, or that he would achieve much if she did.

'Yes, I should get back,' she agreed hastily, hoping her dismay hadn't been too obvious. 'The boys are still at home, and Olivia will probably be scrapping with Gregory as usual . . .'

She hardly knew what she was saying. Her whole being had been concentrated on Ian's arrival, as though, magically, impossibly, the mere fact of his being here would solve everything. She could hardly take in the fact that in half an hour or so they would part again. How had she managed to whip up even the ghost of that old anger against him?

I need you, she pleaded silently.

But why? To do what? Alexy was safe for the present, and, as Ian had said, he could no more prevent her from making another similar attempt than Miranda could. But for one fleeting moment, as he had asked about the boys, she had thought he meant to come to Kilgarth. How ridiculous of her. The words had been nothing but a meaningless formality. Nothing had changed.

'It was good of you to come,' she said stiffly.

'Hey.' He waited till she looked at him. 'Don't be silly,' he said gently. 'Right?'

'And you still want to see Alexy?'

'That's what I've come for.'

'But I mean, now that she's all right? Now that she's — that it's over?'

'I'd like to try to talk to her,' was all he said. He might never learn what had driven his daughter to this extreme act, which had so profoundly shocked him. He might not be able to help her or get near her in any way, but whatever the outcome of a meeting for him personally, there were a couple of points he wanted to get across about the effect her actions had on her mother.

'I'll take you there,' Miranda said. She felt numb, shaken again but for entirely different reasons. She fumbled for the ignition, her head bent as though she had to look to see where the key went.

'Move over here,' Ian said. 'I'll drive.'

The simple act of doing as she was told without argument was a blessed resignation of responsibility. And anyway, she thought confusedly as Ian got out, tiredness catching up with her, it would have seemed all wrong to have him beside her in the passenger seat. That wasn't how it used to be.

They didn't talk as Ian drove towards the city. Miranda lay back in her seat, thankful for his nearness, for his physical presence, and thankful that, during this short interval at least, nothing was required of her. Ian had needed only the briefest of directions; it seemed comforting out of all proportion that he should head so confidently for the unknown flat.

'You're sure you're OK to drive home?' he asked, glancing at her with a concern she didn't see, as at last he found a place to pull in.

'I'm fine. And I ought to get back.' The small respite had revived her, and her positive tone half convinced him, though what he longed to do more than anything was persuade her to stay the night somewhere, check in there himself, and be on hand to keep an eye on her. He knew he had no right to suggest any such thing. Anyway, she'd always been the resilient type; she'd be all right. But he felt very blank indeed as he watched the car turn the corner and vanish.

Miranda was halfway across the Forth bridge before she attempted to reduce her thoughts to any kind of order. Till then she had concentrated on the traffic, on driving. Now she had time to be assailed by all the things which had not been

373

said. The brief time she and Ian had spent together in the airport carpark had fled away so fast. How could she have wasted those precious minutes on nothings about the house, the aunts, Binnie's clothes, for God's sake! She had asked nothing about Ian's life, and suddenly that mattered terribly. What hurried arrangements had he had to make, in order to get on the first available flight at her summons?

She hadn't even tried to say the one thing that now burned to be said, that her anger was without substance, based on no more than the lack of courage to admit her own shortcomings. She drove on automatically, hollow with the knowledge that she'd missed the only chance to say so that she was likely to be given.

It seemed all wrong to be driving away from Alexy, without having got to the root of what had made her do what she'd done. Miranda shivered, remembering the brisk approach of the hospital staff. They'd seen this a hundred times before. They had offered advice on who to contact for counselling and support. They had neither judged nor excused. They had simply done their job, and returned her daughter to her.

And now Ian had taken charge of that daughter. Miranda clung to that, reminding herself it was why she had needed him. But she couldn't shake off her bleak sense of anticlimax. What she had expected? She didn't know.

Well, for now, she told herself drearily, what she had to do was to get home.

# 29

It wasn't easy to focus her mind on the domestic scene when she arrived back at Kilgarth, or to answer questions adequately, making due allowance for the needs of the questioners, with their different sensibilities and different perceptions of what had happened. No one really knew what to ask, once the single crucial fact, that Alexy would be all right, had been established. They were awkward and tongue-tied, their minds baulking at a tragedy so incomprehensible and unimaginable coming so close, and they hardly knew in what terms loving sympathy for Miranda herself could acceptably be expressed.

For the first time Miranda felt conscious of how unwieldy the combined load of this ill-assorted group could be, though she knew they were all doing their best. The brief respite of being looked after herself had pointed up all too sharply the contrast with her normal situation.

Olivia, once it was clear that the danger was over, took refuge in the 'unforgivable piece of showing-off' approach, though she had the sense, at least in Miranda's hearing, to refrain from being quite as outspoken as usual, and her more stringent comments were reserved for Binnie.

Gregory said surprisingly little, and Miranda read in his grim silence a final acceptance of the truth, which had been staring him in the face for some time but which he had refused to admit. He hadn't succeeded in substituting a relationship with his granddaughter for the one he was beginning to acknowledge, if only to himself, he had destroyed with his son. He had been forced to recognise that Alexy didn't go in for relationships at any level, and was the last person to offer him the kind of unqualified affection he sought.

Binnie was fluttered and upset, her mind rejecting images too distressing to dwell on. She would successfully bury them, Miranda knew, soon convincing herself that nothing serious had happened. For now, she concentrated on the questions of where Alexy was and who would look after her till she was 'well enough to travel'.

Binnie had returned from the Bahamas in January to discover to her amazement that she'd moved house. She had found it hard to believe that Olivia could have agreed willingly to such an about-face, and at first was afraid every day that she'd be summarily ordered back to the cottage. But after a few nights in her old room (by her own choice), with its ancient hissing radiator, its faded flowery curtains which she'd made herself, and the nursery bathroom next door which no one else used, she had secretly resolved that she would never move again no matter what Olivia said.

She was also thrilled by what Miranda had achieved in the house. 'It all looks so polished, so *light*. As if there's more room somehow, though you don't seem to have changed anything. I don't know how you've done it.'

She remained serenely unmoved by Gregory's disgust to have his sisters inflicted on him again when he thought he'd got rid of them for good, and took his running warfare with Olivia for granted. Binnie had acquired a new confidence in herself during the past few months. She was valued, made much of, carried off to dazzling places she had never in her life expected to see. She was high on sun and blue oceans, on exotic food and leg-waxing, on frivolous clothes and make-overs and the youth she had never had. Soon Sholto (who no longer resented or envied her background since now it reflected favourably on him), would whirl her away again. Why should she quarrel with anyone? She enjoyed having Miranda on hand all the time, and the company of the boys when they were home, and countered her brother's more spiteful gibes by resorting to his nursery nickname of Grumpy Greggy, which seemed to satisfy any need she felt for retaliation.

★　★　★

Tired as Miranda was when she reached Kilgarth, and scarcely ready for its demands, she did make the effort to talk to the boys without delay. Alexy was near their age, and the fact that death had brushed so close to her couldn't fail to have a deep impact on them. Though both their parents had died comparatively young, they had belonged to the adult generation. Now Adam and Tim were faced by a quite different reality, and Miranda knew their minds must be turning

377

over many new thoughts. How must it feel to decide on such a step? What sort of awfulness in your life would make you want to do it? To stop living. Not to be there any more.

They didn't say much, their faces grave, both looking suddenly more grown up, but they made it clear that they were grateful Miranda had made the time to talk to them, and she was glad she hadn't given in to the temptation of postponing it until tomorrow.

'But what's she so unhappy *about*?' Tim burst out after a silence, his face bony with concern. As Will's had sometimes looked, Miranda was reminded, and felt she could hardly bear another layer of emotion to be added to the turmoil of feelings she was already dealing with.

'Tim, I honestly don't know,' she said gently. 'She's always been unhappy, ever since she was a baby, but she's never been willing to talk about it. I'm not sure that she can. Or maybe I'm not the person she would want to talk to.'

'Alexy doesn't talk to anyone,' Adam said, and Miranda caught the quick protectiveness on her behalf and was touched by it. 'But she's angry too, isn't she? I mean, about — well, everything. Angry at the world. Like Aunt Olivia, only not about things like people saying BBC Tew and not using a butter knife. It's more about how people are. How the world works. The human race. Herself, even. I don't know . . . '

He trailed into embarrassed silence, looking relieved when Miranda said, 'That's it exactly. I think Alexy finds it hard to accept anything around her without a fight, or to find pleasure in the small things most of us enjoy. I don't know quite what she wants, though, or if she knows herself. Perhaps she'll never find it.'

Miranda in her turn couldn't go on, and regretted the hopelessness she had allowed to creep into her voice. She had wanted to help the boys, not depress them even more.

'Then, what will happen?' Tim asked after a pause, as though he didn't want to ask but couldn't help it.

Miranda's lips tightened. 'Tim, I don't know that either. I can only try to help her, or to persuade her to talk to people more competent to help her than I am.'

Three years ago, when she'd found Alexy was bunking off school, and seeing her antagonism towards everyone and everything around her growing day by day, she had thought of seeking counselling of some sort. But, whether she skipped lessons or not, Alexy's marks had been more than adequate, and there had seemed no problem specific enough to justify such a suggestion. Or had she been too cowardly to make it, knowing how Alexy would react?

They had said as much as could be said for now, she decided, a great weariness suddenly overtaking her, and she guessed that the boys felt the same. But as Miranda got to her feet, nodding to them in turn with a tight little smile, not risking words of outright affection, knowing the treacherous effect they would have, Adam came to his feet too, to give her an unexpected hug. She had time to realise, as she concentrated on not crying in front of them, that for the first time its quality was adult and comforting, no longer the casual, vigorous, half-joking embrace of an adolescent.

Thank God she had the boys, she thought for the thousandth time, as she went downstairs jostled by a whole new set of emotions.

All through the evening she found she was listening for the phone, in a way she hadn't done since she was a teenager. When she had been listening for the phone to ring from this very house. What a strange thought. But Ian would surely let her know the outcome of his meeting with Alexy. Or would he? She began to feel less confident as time ticked by. He might assume Alexy would tell her herself. Or, if he'd met with little success, he might feel there was nothing worth reporting. Yet she couldn't imagine Ian being deterred if he was bent on achieving a dialogue of some kind. So she swung between doubt and conviction and, when the phone rang at last, flew to answer it with nervous eagerness.

It was Muff, loving and kind. Though it was a relief to talk to her without having to choose her words, as talking to everyone at Kilgarth seemed to require at present, Miranda couldn't pretend to herself that she wasn't bitterly disappointed.

As it became unreasonable to hope Ian might still call, she saw how absurd she'd been to believe he'd feel the need to get in touch. Why should he? Any shared involvement was far in the past. He was probably on a flight home already — she was shaken by the emptiness this reasonable thought opened before her — or, if not, in London awaiting an onward flight tomorrow.

But by the next morning Ian was at Kilgarth, and for Miranda past and present seemed to rush into collision.

Now that the family was so large they had breakfast in the dining-room, and to hear a car outside and see Ian getting out of it was at once so ordinary and so extraordinary that for a second Miranda felt as though she'd been turned to stone. She had the toast-rack, which she had just refilled, in her hand and after a second made a movement to put it down blindly, anywhere, not taking her eyes off the window, as though she had seen a mirage which might in the next moment waver and vanish. Someone took the toast from her; she wasn't aware who.

The east wind was as cold today as it had been yesterday, but the morning was bright, and sunlight fell on the gravel where Ian had parked his hired car. To see him head for the front door with his fit athlete's step, to see the sun on his dark hair and brown skin, produced so violent a dislocation of time and circumstances, and her own place in them, that Miranda hardly knew how to cope with it.

It was so normal to see him here, in what had been his home, that it seemed some weird hallucination that she, who had no real connection with him any more, should be living in it with his father and aunts — and with Will's sons. Why had she not seen that before; why had she ever imagined it was right to come? Then as she grappled with this unnerving disorientation,

381

more immediate questions rushed in. Had Ian contacted his father, or come unannounced? And what mood had he come in? How would Gregory react? Then, shaming her because it hadn't been the first thing she thought of, had something happened to Alexy? Something so awful that Ian hadn't been able to tell her over the phone?

With a choking exclamation of pure dread, Miranda whirled for the door. These thoughts had raced through her mind in an instant; behind her the boys were still wondering who'd come, and Olivia and Binnie were turning to each other in disbelief. Alarm was written on Binnie's face, while Olivia's revealed a sardonic anticipation of dramas in prospect.

Miranda pulled open the inner door, her icy hands fumbling. 'Ian! Is Alexy — '?'

'She's fine. Honestly, I promise you, she's OK. Sorry, love, I didn't mean to panic you. Only I didn't want to phone.' And give Gregory the chance to tell him to stay away. 'Are you all right?'

'Of course.' Another colossal effort at self-control, and they hadn't even finished breakfast yet. The feeble attempt at humour, easier to summon because Ian was there, even though it was Ian who had dealt the shock, helped. 'But it's so odd. I mean, seeing you here. I don't mean you shouldn't have come,' she added hastily. It's his home, for heaven's sake . . .

'Don't worry about any of that,' Ian cut in, taking her arm for a moment in quick reassurance. He gave her one smile, then turned, his face setting grimly, ready for whatever reception he was about to find, as Olivia and then the others followed Miranda into the hall.

But it was Binnie who got in first. 'Ian, darling boy! How lovely to see you after all this time. But it's barely nine. Have you had breakfast? You must have set off terribly early . . . '

The spontaneous words, sounding as though she thought he'd come straight from Australia, and absurd as they might be after an interval of twenty years, were unquestionably warm, and Ian's grin flashed in a way that, for more than one person present, stripped those years away as he stepped forward to kiss her.

'Um. So what can you possibly have to say for yourself?' Olivia demanded. She wasn't going to be so easily appeased. But she offered a screwed-up cheek as he went to kiss her in her turn. 'Think you can turn up when it suits you, do you, and be welcomed with open arms?'

'Oh, Aunt Livvy,' he said, following the kiss with a vigorous hug, 'why not leave all that to Dad? He'll do it even better than you.'

'Come and meet my boys,' Miranda said. Adam and Tim were hovering by the dining-room door, heads down and shoulders up, their new adult selves deserting them in their uncertainty as to whether they were part of this reunion or not.

'Good to meet you.' Ian came swiftly to shake hands with them, and they relaxed in obvious relief at the straightforward sincerity in his voice.

'Upstairs?' Ian asked Miranda, across the

small turmoil of the aunts as they began to fuss about coffee, breakfast, calling Pattie. 'Same room?'

Miranda nodded. 'But might it be better to — ?'

'Silly question,' Ian went on cheerfully, not listening, deliberately she thought. 'As if anything would have changed.' As he shook off the aunts and headed for the stairs he mouthed back at her, with a grin that really made it seem as if he'd gone out of the house yesterday, 'Don't worry.'

'Oh, goodness,' said Aunt Binnie, her jaw dropping as she stared after him.

'Humph. Well, he'll definitely need coffee now,' was Olivia's comment, and Miranda caught the gleam in her eye. 'Strong coffee at that. Pattie!'

★　★　★

'I should have done it long ago.' Ian, his face grim, flicked a stone across the gleaming pool where, in the past, they had so often fished for brown trout. Down here by the river, with the trees at their backs, though their tight-furled buds didn't offer much shelter yet, they were out of the wind, and the sun felt warmer. Though the sky was heaped with great pure masses of cumulus, and with this wind the sun would soon be gone, for the moment it drew vivid colour from the early spring landscape. Ian had found himself more moved than he could have imagined possible, as they'd come down the hill, to see once more the clean-cut patterns of spring ploughing in the stone-walled fields, to hear the voices of oystercatchers and peewits, and to watch a pair of mallard rise noisily, leaving bright trails of drops on the glittering water. The sounds of home, and behind them a quality of silence he had almost forgotten, a clarity of light too, and a tingle and crispness in the air.

Miranda didn't speak, knowing he was searching for words. She still felt disorientated herself, then and now merging and flowing like the patterns of dappled light on the water a couple of yards away.

'It took something like this, something major, to make me come. Something potentially tragic. It shouldn't have needed that.' Ian checked in the act of taking a stone to skim from his cupped palm, and looked unseeingly at the steep rise of the hill across the glen road. 'No, not potentially. It is tragic. The tragedy doesn't lie in whether she pulled it off or not, but in the fact that she felt impelled to do such a thing at all.'

'Did she talk to you? Were you able to discover any reason for what she did?' It struck Miranda that even now they weren't using the word. Suicide. Had any of them said it? So stark, so brutal.

'We did talk, a bit, in the end.' Ian had rarely in his life had to exert such moral force to achieve his purpose, or felt so drained afterwards. 'She doesn't like people, she says. She doesn't like living. When she looks ahead to years of the same she doesn't see the point.'

That couldn't be all. 'But she's so intelligent,

she does so well,' Miranda said helplessly, realising as she spoke how irrelevant this protest was. 'I mean, if she didn't succeed at anything, I'd understand better.'

'That appears to be part of the problem. She despises the world for allowing her to succeed without having to try. She can bank on success — in the world's terms. The sort of success, as she pointed out with scorn, that I rate. She doesn't want it. She's asked herself what it's about and failed to come up with answers.'

'But she's worked hard,' Miranda repeated, as though that could be made to mean something. 'Why did she bother to work? To get as far as she has?'

'I suppose because she has an excellent brain and an inherent dislike of inefficiency.'

'But she seemed to want Kilgarth so much. Isn't she looking forward to owning it? She was so determined that we should all come here, so that she could inherit.'

'Kilgarth? She loathes the place,' Ian said briefly, and a silence fell between them at the finality of that.

'In more personal terms then,' Miranda pursued presently. 'Doesn't she hope to meet someone she could love? Have children and love them too?'

It was only afterwards that she was struck by the way she had taken it for granted that Ian, after such a brief time with Alexy, should have the answer to these large questions.

'Miranda, she *really* doesn't like people.' Ian spoke gently, turning to look into her face. 'It's something hard to understand, I know. But it seems to be a lack in her, almost a form of disablement.'

I did that, Miranda thought, tears choking her. I wasn't able to give her what she needed. I didn't see. I should have insisted she had help. It was up to me to see that she was properly looked after. I was the adult, I was responsible.

'She didn't stand a chance,' she said violently, coming to her feet on the small patch of shingle between big, water-smoothed rocks. 'It isn't her fault.' But though she was on the very brink of admitting where the fault lay, she couldn't do it, and resorted to desperate, clumsy denial. 'She was so young when you left . . . '

She caught one glimpse of the hurt in Ian's eyes — and something else, disillusionment, she thought — before he got his feelings under control. It was clear that he had no intention of getting into an argument over this, no matter what accusations she threw at him, and it made her even more ashamed of her lack of courage.

'Well, between us we seem to have produced a pretty unhappy human being,' was all he said, his voice flat. 'The poor girl seems to have inherited the worst I could offer her, in genetic terms. She's the perfect Ross, in the mould of Olivia and my father, to name but two.'

The ironic admission gave Miranda time to pull herself together, and though she couldn't quite bring herself to thank him for refusing to let her start a fight, as she wanted to do, she clutched gratefully at the opening. She remembered Will saying much the same, though in rather different terms, and the thought of him steadied her.

'You were going to tell me how you got on with Gregory,' she said. 'What did he say?'

Ian gave her a long, considering look. He wondered if she had any idea how much her relentless apportioning of blame over Alexy hurt him.

'Sit down,' he said, reaching a hand to steady her when the loose stones shifted under her feet as she obeyed, grateful to him for not letting a row flare up.

He zinged a couple of pebbles over the water with a wrist movement she'd never been able to match. Then he said, 'I told him I didn't much care what he thought, I'd come back because I wanted to.' Catching her appreciative grin he thought how different it made her look. The smiling girl he'd loved. His heart lurched with a sharp apprehension of loss.

'And he said . . . ?' Miranda prompted.

Ian dragged himself back to the present. 'Not a lot. You've mellowed him in a remarkable way,' he teased. 'But my word,' he went on, his voice serious again, 'how he's changed. He looks so small. Shrunken. Defeated even, if that is a word that can be used about a Ross.'

'I suppose it's been a gradual process and I haven't really been aware of how much he's altered,' Miranda said, trying to see Gregory with his eyes. Had she failed here too? 'He's not been actually ill. But he does seem to have given up fighting. He barely murmured when I suggested Olivia and Binnie moving back in.'

'Yes, you've looked after that potty old duo pretty well too. And Will's boys. And Kilgarth.'

Miranda, pleased as she was to hear this, as many times as he cared to say it, took her chance to ask something which had been worrying her since he came.

'Doesn't it seem weird to you, that I'm living here, I mean? The place has nothing to do with me and — '

'*What?* It has everything to do with you,' he exclaimed. 'You're Alexy's mother, for God's sake. I must admit that when Dad announced he was leaving it to her I decided he was up to his old tricks, power games, playing one person off against another. I also thought it would be bad for Alexy to be manipulated by him, and to have so much thrown her way when she was so young. I still do. But that's happened, it's water under the bridge. And when I see what you've achieved I just feel so bloody grateful that you were prepared to come. To do my job really, and to put so much into it. Which is why,' he went on rapidly, not letting her interrupt, 'I want to ask you, not my father, if it would be OK for me to hang on here for a day or two?'

'For a day or two?' Miranda repeated, but the words were mere empty parroting, her thoughts racing round a dozen implications.

'Look, if you hate the thought forget it. That's why I wanted to ask you first.'

'No, no, of course you must stay.' She hardly knew which to seize on of all the responses his words had produced. 'This is your home and — '

'Hardly,' he reminded her, but he was smiling.

'However, it is yours. The decision's up to you.'

Miranda had a feeling, which she didn't think she really wanted to examine, of something half comprehended but obscurely dreaded having come close then receded again. She skimmed a very successful pebble across the pool.

# 30

Ian's presence changed the whole atmosphere of the house, in a way hard to define but impossible to ignore. For Miranda there was a sense that someone more competent than herself was now in charge. Her care for Kilgarth had been on the level of relining the curtains and getting the windows cleaned; Ian would check the state of the roof and get the windows renewed. Not that he gave any signs of wishing to change anything; far from it, he seemed very relaxed and was full of praise for all she had done. But the feeling remained of everything now being in safe hands, and for Miranda it was such a luxury that she saw no point in arguing with it.

She began to see, half rueful and half amused, that she was simply enjoying having a man around. How outraged Danielle would be at that, and how natural and lovely Muff would think it. Miranda began to realise how deeply, since coming back here, Muff's serene acceptance of the balance she and Colin preferred had influenced her. Not that she would like it herself, of course not, but it certainly suited Muff, and Miranda found herself these days readier to understand her contentment.

As the days passed and Ian made no move to go, she became conscious of other subtle shifts in the house. Tim and Adam adjusted to his presence without missing a step, as though accepting the filling of a gap they'd been subconsciously aware of all along. The aunts were openly pleased to have him back, Binnie gushingly affectionate, Olivia gruffer but allowing herself to be teased occasionally into barks of laughter, a sound that sent the boys into hysterical giggles.

The biggest change was in Gregory. The crisis over Alexy had been a shock to him, and he seemed to have learned at last that family affection was too precious to be carelessly tossed aside. In a way that Miranda found unexpectedly moving, he acquiesced in his son's return with a stiff dignity which couldn't entirely conceal a tremulous thankfulness.

One of Ian's reasons for braving a second dismissal from Kilgarth, as he explained to Miranda, had been to make sure that his father's, and his aunts', financial arrangements were in good order. He said nothing about his deeper concern for Miranda, whose future here, especially since he'd talked to Alexy, hardly seemed secure. He could see Alexy inheriting and without compunction heaving her mother and the two boys out, and it had been reassuring to establish that Miranda had more than adequate means to support the three of them. As to Kilgarth itself, exile had never lessened his feeling for it, and he had wanted to be certain that it wasn't falling into neglect and disrepair.

'The thing is,' he told Miranda, embarrassed for once, 'I've made an indecent amount of money in the years I've been away. I bought into the Hunter Valley winery at the right moment, the charter airline does well, I've got an interest in a movie studio. I've been lucky with everything, in fact. I don't want to butt in or anything, but I'd like to put funds in place to make sure the house and estate can be kept in good order. I don't know what you've done to Dad, but you've got him in such an amenable frame of mind he might even agree. What do you think?'

He grinned at her, relishing not only the taming of Gregory, but his own pleasure at the idea of being able to look after her again, however indirectly.

'But aren't there things you ought to be doing at home?' Miranda asked, obliquely saying, isn't someone, wife or partner, wondering what's taking you so long to sort out in Scotland? She had avoided the subject till now and Ian had made no reference to his personal life.

'I have some pretty competent people in place,' he said. 'They're well able to take care of everything.'

'I meant at home,' Miranda said awkwardly.

'Ah, at home.' Ian repeated the words without expression. His thoughts went to the luxurious penthouse in Kirribilli, where he spent very little time; to the hideaway on Orpheus Island, shared by a handful of rich, spoiled people like himself; to his North Sydney office, the golf club, the Yacht Squadron and the boat he kept moored at its marina. These things constituted home.

'I'm on my own,' he said brusquely, getting up and going to the window of the small sitting-room where, finding they had it to themselves for once, they had begun to talk. It was a habit Miranda remembered, indicating a dislike of what was being said and a wish to be free of it.

She hesitated. The obvious questions seemed too banal, anything hinting at sympathy inappropriate.

Ian turned, an ironic and for once even bitter look on his face. 'Sad, yes? Ageing playboy and all that.'

Miranda flushed at his tone. 'But there was someone, wasn't there? Heidi?' What convention made her pretend to search for the name? How could she ever forget it?

'Ah, Heidi.' Ian prowled back, his face sombre, and Miranda was conscious, as so often, of how his presence could fill a room. 'Well, that didn't last long. I was never at home. Something you'd understand, maybe?'

Her flush deepened. She longed to clutch at the chance to say she knew she'd given him every reason to escape from the flat, but the moment didn't seem right. They were talking about his life, not their past.

'I'm sorry it didn't work out,' she said diffidently, and Ian's eyes fixed on hers with a sudden intentness.

'Yes, well,' he said after a tiny pause. 'Perhaps I'm like my father, not cut out for relationships. And I've inflicted the same deficiency on poor Alexy, it appears.'

'What are we going to do about her?' How good it was to be able to discuss the problem. Miranda felt a welcome lift of relief.

Ian came to sit down again, as though he too felt this was more important than their personal differences, past or present. But go over the ground as they might, there was little constructive they could find to say. Alexy, twenty in a couple of months' time, was so fiercely her own person that if she resisted the idea of seeking help there wasn't a great deal they could do beyond assuring her of their support and love.

'And I do love her.' The yearning note in Miranda's voice brought a lump to Ian's throat. 'She's so quick and clever. She's got so much to offer. If only I could have . . . ' But she couldn't go on.

'I know you love her,' Ian said gently. 'That's never been in doubt. And if you want her to come home before term starts, I shall see to it that she does.'

Miranda turned to these words many times during the next few days, not questioning that he could make it happen. It seemed nothing short of miraculous to her, now that she'd had time to think it over, that Ian had been able in a single meeting to extract so much from Alexy, or understand so much of what lay behind her bitter intransigence. If only the contact could be maintained, and that start built upon. He could help Alexy as no one else could. But what would she do now? Would she want to go back to Durham to continue her course? There were no cut and dried answers where she was concerned.

Ian also knew there were no answers, but his care, as it had always been, was as much for Miranda as for Alexy. Day after day he extended his visit, making plans with Gregory for the financial underpinning of Kilgarth and the security of the aunts. But he hadn't come even close to his real objective when, seeing no other course open to him, he began to organise his return to Sydney.

With this in hand, he let himself indulge his own wishes at last. On a day of softer air than they had had since he arrived, when almost overnight a wash of spring green softened the landscape, when after a tingling start to the day it was like summer by the time breakfast was over, he suggested a picnic lunch up at the loch.

Miranda, finding herself increasingly tense as his departure approached, had tried more than once to make an opening to say some of the things she so desperately wanted to say, knowing that once he'd gone the chance would be lost for ever. Even so, she was thrown into a flurry of doubt and reluctance by this simple proposal. The boys were off about their own affairs. She and Ian would be alone, with no household demands to resort to as an escape route if things became difficult; and alone in a setting laden with associations, not all of which she was sure she could handle in her present emotional state.

But how churlish to say no. It was a marvellous day; you couldn't expect the poor man to picnic on his own. And surely they knew each other well enough to spend a couple of hours together without constraint. The last thing Ian would want to do was to get heavy. He only wanted to revisit a spot he'd always loved, before he went back.

Miranda was relieved to find that after all, as they took the well-known track, there was no tension between them. It was easy to fill eye and mind with the beauty of the morning, though Ian's eye and mind had room to spare for noting the deficiencies of Derek's keepering, and he expressed himself freely on the subject.

Once at the boathouse, however, a new mood overtook them. Getting out of the battered Land Rover which Derek used, crossing the few yards of turf to the old wooden building, with its air of having grown out of the ground, so completely was it part of the scene, they were both silent, and Miranda found her eyes stinging as a hundred memories of happiness and laughter, of being young and being in love, flooded back. Ian wouldn't be feeling anything of the sort, she warned herself, almost in panic that nostalgia could have such power. Men didn't think that way. They had more sense.

But as they reached the verandah Ian turned to her, and she read in his eyes feelings as heightened and vulnerable as her own. He reached a hand to her and, still not speaking, they stepped onto the weathered boards and went to the railing to look out over the loch, the rushes encroaching upon it brilliant green in the sunlight, the glen reaching away behind it into the soft distances of the hills.

Feelings, need, past sadness and loss, present response to this beauty and to Ian's presence, with that sense of rightness which his physical nearness never failed to bring, found expression in one simple, instinctive gesture. Miranda

397

turned her head and rested her forehead lightly against him.

Instantly his arms were round her, turning her to face him, folding her close to him. He stooped his head over hers, and an absurd delight filled him that she still fitted there so neatly. Bloody fool, did he think either of them would have changed height? But it was no time for sensible thoughts. Ian felt as though his journey to this moment had not been miles and miles but years and years.

They talked in a great flood of words, dipping into those years almost at random for things that it had seemed wrong not to share at the time, much of it merest trivia by now, some of it life-altering decisions. It didn't matter, they were greedy for it all. When Miranda spoke of Will, though her eyes and voice softened at his name, Ian was able to release in a single moment of acceptance the jealousy that had always made him ashamed, even after he had learned of Will's death. And he could talk at last of how badly he had let Heidi down, entering into the relationship knowing that it could never work.

They could laugh over Gregory's machinations, the laughter turning to compassion when they thought of the isolated and embittered existence he had wished on himself. Miranda could admit how much she had minded Georgina turning her back on Scotland, and how it had seemed almost a betrayal.

Close, intent upon each other, caught up once more in that feeling of completeness which being together always used to bring, it was possible for

Miranda to say at last, 'I made Alexy what she is, you know.' The guilt at the core of everything. 'I didn't want her when I was carrying her and I didn't want her when she was born. I expected a child of ours to be happy and loving and outgoing and when she wasn't any of those things I couldn't like her. I know it's appalling, but it's true. And that twisted something in her, as though she always knew it.'

Ian said nothing, knowing Miranda needed to unburden herself of this at last. He sat holding her in the circle of his arm on the rough bench, their backs against the sun-faded planks, sitting where they had sat so often in the past, and he listened quietly as the guilt slowly uncoiled and freed itself, guilt over her failures, as she saw them, and over other things it moved him to know she still minded.

'You know, once, when I'd insisted on racing after I was pregnant, though you didn't want me to, I fell and — ' it was still hard to say ' — as I was falling I prayed I'd lose the baby. I imagined, for those split seconds, what it would be like to be back at the centre of things again. I wanted to be fit again, slim, myself — and happy with you.'

'I always believed we could have gone on being happy,' Ian said, his voice not quite under control.

'I know. But I made life impossible. I should have said so at the time, only I never quite could, but I thought you were wonderful to be so positive about the baby, once you knew I'd let it happen out of sheer carelessness. You never once reproached me.'

399

Too moved to speak, Ian turned his head to kiss her hair. 'I've waited a lot of years for that. You can't think what it means to hear you say it,' he said after a moment. 'I've always hated to remember how I reacted at first, when you told me you thought you were pregnant. How crass I was that day, without a thought for how you must have been feeling.'

For them both, that scene in the bright shabby room in Charteris Wynd returned with searing vividness.

'It's odd, isn't it,' Miranda said, as a peace they could still hardly trust in overtook the long habit of hostility, 'that you've come back now, to Kilgarth I mean, to make sure your father's affairs are in order.'

This seemed an unwelcome change of tone to Ian. And he hadn't come for that, though it didn't seem the moment to say so.

'And it was because of money, and your refusing to go into the business,' Miranda paused, 'that you left. I was really proud of you, you know, when you stood up to Gregory over that.'

Ian laughed. 'You were furious! Don't let's get too carried away.'

'I was angry because we seemed suddenly to be up against all kinds of problems and I knew most of them were my fault. But I liked you for being independent, especially at such a price. Not many people would have done what you did.'

'Yes, and I really paid for it, didn't I?' he teased her. 'Just look at me now.'

'Oh well, you are Gregory's son. You were bound to come out smelling of roses.' But Miranda was still following her original line. 'This question of money.'

Ian wondered what was coming, and his soul shrivelled to think it might be some fresh attack.

'I know I've thrown at you lots of times that you spoiled Alexy by giving her too much,' Miranda said, frowning, 'but the truth is I was looking for any excuse to explain the way she behaved. In fact I was always grateful to you. Your generosity meant a lot to me, and it's awful to think I was too busy being angry to thank you.'

'Yes, well, you had some justification,' Ian was able in his turn to say. 'I did walk out after all, leaving you alone with a baby who was as difficult to cope with as any child could well have been. It's not my favourite memory, believe me.'

Miranda turned to him, smiling but with sudden tears in her eyes, and reached to touch his cheek. 'How simple it seems to say these things today,' she said. 'I can't bear to think how I went on fighting you, every time you appeared. I minded, you know, after Alexy was ill, when she was so awful to you that you stopped coming. And I've never told you how good it was to have you there, and how grateful I was.'

'Miranda.' When he spoke in that tone she was reminded that this was the adult, mature Ian beside her, not the young man whose image was so clear in these surroundings. 'It wasn't Alexy's rejection that drove me away. She's my daughter, I could have gone on coming to see her. It was your rejection, your antagonism that never seemed to lessen. I couldn't take being attacked over and over again for past failings. God knows I was as conscious of them as you were, but I couldn't change them. I had to walk away and try to make a new life for myself of I'd have gone mad. Well, that didn't work out, as you now know. The truth is, there's never been anyone but you. Nobody else, ever, could arouse the same response, nobody else ever felt part of me. Being young together, knowing each other all our lives . . . ' His voice faltered. 'Well, when there's love too, it adds up to a pretty powerful combination.'

'I know.' Miranda found she was trembling.

Ian felt it. 'You're cold. Let's walk a bit.'

Though it was a relief to make a move, having reached a point so difficult to deal with, as they went on up the track Miranda was aware of a strange emptiness at the withdrawal of touch, and wondered forlornly how the feeling could be so strong after so short a time.

But there was still the comfort of being able to turn back to shared memories, as well as things it had never been possible to talk about before. Ian told her how hard he had found it to come back to the flat, in the years when he'd been visiting Alexy, but how much he had missed the contact when it ended. And Miranda could admit at last that she had stayed on there far too long, partly out of cowardice but principally out of a need for closeness with Alexy which had really been a different need. Acknowledging this to Ian, she shivered to recall the loneliness of that time.

When she came to her conviction of never having given Alexy what she called 'a proper life', it was comforting to have him dispute the point with energy, reminding her how she'd made her life subservient to Alexy's in every respect — where they lived, her job, her social life, everything.

'So all in all we've been a pair of pretty fair idiots, would you say?' he summed up as, suddenly finding they were ravenous, they turned back towards the boathouse.

'I think on the whole I would.' Miranda spoke cheerfully to match his tone, but felt quick apprehension stir. What now? All very well to bare the soul and free her conscience of so many things which had nagged at it for far too long, but soon she'd be alone at Kilgarth again, and life would roll on, busy, agreeable and not without its rewards, and the joy of this brief time with Ian, like the past returning, would be nothing more than a nostalgic memory.

'You still don't know why I came back, do you?' Ian said, watching her as she began to unpack the basket he'd fetched from the Land Rover.

Her head came round. 'Alexy — '

'Well yes, of course I came because of Alexy.' Still watching her, he didn't miss the careful smoothing of her expression into ordinary polite interest as she turned back to the basket. 'I'd always come if anything happened to her, you know that. But don't you realise how much it meant to me that I could also see you? That's always been the most important thing, all I've ever wanted. Nothing else ever mattered a damn beside that.'

Miranda leaned back against the boathouse wall as though she needed support, her eyes meeting his, her face stiff with shock, arrested in the act of offering him a ham roll. Ian took it from her without taking his eyes off her face, disposed of it and took her hand.

'You know, there's a line of poetry I often think about, something you used to like. Christ, poetry, me!' he broke off to say in a more normal voice, grinning but oddly shy in a way rare for him. 'No idea where it comes from, but it sort of sums up how I've always felt. About you, about us. Something like, 'For I have promises to keep, And miles to go before I sleep . . . ' That's what's stuck in my mind. Promises to keep. I've longed for the chance to come back and fulfil the things we once vowed to each other. They matter to me. I feel as though the years apart have been nothing more than waiting time.'

Miranda gazed at him, still unable to say anything, and he went on, speaking with more difficulty, 'I thought — the reason I came to Kilgarth — well, I thought perhaps I could settle it with Dad, but only if you agreed, that I'd come over from time to time, make sure everything was all right, look after you even if only in practical ways. I thought that would be the nearest I could get to what I really want. But today, here with you now, talking about the things that went wrong, I began to feel — God, this is hard — ' He broke off, angry with himself, afraid he'd said too much.

'But you live in Australia,' Miranda said stupidly, conscious that her heart was bumping unevenly and glad to have his hand to hold onto.

'Miranda, please,' he begged, trying to make a joke of it. 'Do you really feel that's the main consideration here? You don't think for the moment that could be a side issue?'

'I think that wherever you live I can't live without you,' she said, 'and that's probably because even at such a moment you can make me laugh.'

'Back to laughter,' he said, with a sort of private astonishment that that could be, and she leaned towards him, her face full of loving amusement.

'You know, taking into account your genetic inheritance, you are a surprisingly nice person.'

And if the words brought the flicker of a reminder of what that inheritance had meant in Alexy's case, as they talked on in the spring sunshine, the quietness of the empty moor around them, time opening before them, there was also the hope that, with Ian back in their lives, welding the family into one again, they would at last be able, together, to give her an assurance of permanence and security which would heal and help her.

We do hope that you have enjoyed reading this large print book.

Did you know that all of our titles are available for purchase?

We publish a wide range of high quality large print books including:
**Romances, Mysteries, Classics**
**General Fiction**
**Non Fiction and Westerns**

Special interest titles available in large print are:
**The Little Oxford Dictionary**
**Music Book**
**Song Book**
**Hymn Book**
**Service Book**

Also available from us courtesy of Oxford University Press:
**Young Readers' Dictionary**
**(large print edition)**
**Young Readers' Thesaurus**
**(large print edition)**

For further information or a free brochure, please contact us at:
**Ulverscroft Large Print Books Ltd.,**
**The Green, Bradgate Road, Anstey,**
**Leicester, LE7 7FU, England.**
**Tel:** (00 44) 0116 236 4325
**Fax:** (00 44) 0116 234 0205

*Other titles published by*
*The House of Ulverscroft:*

## A QUESTION OF TRUST

### Alexandra Raife

Philippa, back in the Highland landscape where she grew up, once more among established friends, feels she is finally putting behind her the traumas of losing her family home and the failure of her marriage. But into remote Glen Maraich a stranger comes, to lie low while the dangerous operation in which he is involved is temporarily put on hold. Tough-fibred and self-sufficient as he is, Jon's many good qualities have been eroded by the dubious choices he has recently made. Philippa, however, makes an immediate impression on him. They are an unlikely combination. Both have painful memories they are not yet ready to share. Can they have a future together?

# THE WAY HOME

## Alexandra Raife

It is six years since the three sisters have all been together. The reason for their reunion at Calder Lodge is the death of their stepmother, Zara — an event that provokes several unwelcome discoveries. The three settle into their usual sibling pattern: Vanessa, the eldest, a domestic perfectionist in the classic maternal role; Jamie, back from her high-powered job in America, the rebel of the family; and Phil, the youngest, accepted as the low achiever, always ready to adore and admire the other two. But the familiar roles conceal inner turmoil. Each sister has a secret that she isn't yet ready to share, a problem she has to solve . . .

# THE WEDDING GIFT

## Alexandra Raife

Cass falls instantly in love with Corrie Cottage, perched on a grassy ledge of hillside on the borders of the Riach estate in Scotland. And when Guy suggests that they take it on as a wedding present to each other, she leaps at the chance. But as she becomes increasingly involved with the lives of her neighbours — Gina struggling with domestic chaos and a recalcitrant teenage daughter; socially competitive Beverley and her enigmatic husband, Rick — Cass finds her loyalties shifting inexorably from London, and Guy, to Glen Maraich — and her new friends.

# SUN ON SNOW

## Alexandra Raife

No one really wants Kate at Allt Farr, the rambling house in Scotland that sometimes seems more of an albatross than a family inheritance to the Munros. But they are used to dealing with the consequences of Jeremy's fecklessness, and Kate — a cast-off girlfriend — is one of those consequences. A fragile 'townie', Kate is unfamiliar with the way of life in a house like Allt Farr, and her ignorance of country ways exasperates Max Munro, the head of the household. But when disaster strikes, Kate finds she has earned herself a place at the heart of the family.